BITHYNIA

PHRYGIA

LYCIA   PAMPHYLIA   Tarsus

● Cnidus          CILICIA

● Patara                    ● Seleucia
                            ● Antioch

● Rhodes

A

                  CYPRUS
                  ● Paphos          SYRIA

THE GREAT SEA
(MEDITERRANEAN SEA)
                                    ● Damascus
                         Tyre ●    ● Caesarea Philippi
                    Ptolemais ●    ● Capernaum
                                   ● Tiberias
                    Caesarea ●     ● Nazareth
                       Joppa ●     ● Sychar
                       Lydda ●     ● Jericho
                    Jerusalem ●

                    ● Alexandria

EGYPT                                   ARABIA

# THE CROWN TREE

# THE CROWN TREE

# LeGette Blythe

John Knox Press
RICHMOND, VIRGINIA

Library of Congress Catalog Card Number: 57-6101

*Also by*

LeGETTE BLYTHE

MARSHAL NEY: A DUAL LIFE
ALEXANDRIANA
SHOUT FREEDOM!
BOLD GALILEAN
WILLIAM HENRY BELK: MERCHANT OF THE SOUTH
A TEAR FOR JUDAS
MIRACLE IN THE HILLS (With Mary Martin Sloop, M.D.)
VOICE IN THE WILDERNESS
JAMES W. DAVIS: NORTH CAROLINA SURGEON

*Third printing*

For Gloria, Julia, and Peggy

# THE CROWN TREE 1

Pontius Pilate, his broad back to the doorway, stood before a high window of Herod's Palace that looked northward beyond the city wall toward the forbidding stony slope of the Hill of the Skull.

"Excellency, you sent for me?"

The Procurator turned quickly to face the tall soldier.

"Yes, Centurion Longinus. Come in." The heavy scowl on his round face melted into a wan smile, and he half turned to point through the open window. "That one on the middle cross over there—is he dead?"

"He's dead, sir, I can assure you. And the two insurrectionists also."

"I wanted to be sure. It's good that they're dead already. Soon it will be sunset, and the beginning of the Jewish Sabbath. And these insufferable Jews, as you may know, insist that leaving a man hanging on a cross on their holy day is a sacrilege."

Frowning, he glanced through the window again, then quickly faced about, and Longinus fancied the fleeting expression on the Procurator's usually bland face had been compounded out of fascination and fear. "They're taking him down now. A rich merchant from Arimathaea was here to ask permission to put the Galilean's body in his own tomb. After he left I had the notion it might be a ruse to get the man down before he was dead, and revive him. Should that happen, Centurion, it would infuriate the High Priest and his supporters and lead no doubt to further turmoil. That's why I sent you orders to make sure that the man was dead before sunset, and to report to me as soon as he was. You're quite certain there could be no mistake?"

"You need have no further concern, Excellency. The man's dead."

"But he died quickly, Longinus. You had his legs broken?"

"We broke the legs of the other two, sir, but when we came to him I saw that he was already dead."

"But, Centurion, he could have been only unconscious from the pain. And now, should Joseph and his friends revive the man —" A dark scowl furrowed the Procurator's forehead and sudden fright pulled his full lips into thin lines. "By all the gods, Longinus—"

"Don't be alarmed, Excellency. No one will revive him. I made certain he was dead. I drove the point of my spear upward through his side into his heart."

"I was worried, Centurion." The Procurator visibly relaxed. He motioned to an ornately carved marble bench. "Sit down." Then he sank wearily into his bronze chair, braced himself on its flaring arms. "Longinus, I'm determined to avoid further trouble with these contentious Jews until I can get Sejanus to transfer me to some other post. Palestine sickens me. It is impossible to get along with these people. In fact, they can't get along with one another. The trial of the Galilean this morning showed it. Some declared he was the Jews' king, their long-awaited Messiah; but most of them shouted that he be crucified. How can any Roman governor ever please even a substantial faction among them?" He shrugged his shoulders, leaned back in his chair. "I want to get away, Longinus. I'm tired."

"They are an independent-minded people, Excellency. They're proud; they think themselves better than other nations. That makes them difficult to govern, of course."

"Nobody knows it better than I." As Pilate clutched the arms of the chair and leaned forward, the centurion, studying his face, had the feeling that the pockets beneath the Procurator's pale blue eyes had sagged and the lines at the corners of his eyes had deepened. "That brings me to the other reason I sent for you, Centurion. This may be the last opportunity I'll have to talk with you for a long time, since you're leaving tomorrow, I understand, on your return to Rome for another assignment."

He paused and the centurion nodded. "Yes, sir, I plan to leave Jerusalem tomorrow for Joppa."

"Longinus, I want you to do me a great service."

"If it is in my power, sir, I will."

"I think you can. It's this." Out of long habit he lowered his voice. "I want you to speak to Senator Varro for me. Your father has great weight with the Prefect. I'd like very much for him to suggest to Sejanus that I be relieved of the Procuratorship here and be given a post at Rome or in some province in another part of the world."

"I'll speak to my father, sir. He may be able to sway the Prefect."

"Thank you, Centurion." Pilate arose, and with nervous fingers combed his closely cropped graying hair. Then he walked over to the window, pointed. "He's down." He smiled grimly. "As long as he was hanging there, I couldn't seem to get him off my mind. But now that he's dead, I can think about more important matters." He strode back to his chair and sat down; he leaned on the polished heavy table, his arms outstretched before him, his hands clasped. "Tell me, Longinus, what did you think of that man?"

"He was very brave, Excellency, the bravest I've ever seen. In his torture he even prayed to his god for his enemies."

Pilate got to his feet again, half circled the chair, stood behind it, his elbows braced on its high back.

"I was the chief of his enemies, Centurion." He appeared to be talking more to himself than to Longinus. "I sent him to the cross."

"But I killed him, Excellency."

"You had no choice. You're a Roman soldier; you were obeying orders. But I was his judge. I"—the Procurator's round face twisted as though a sudden sharp pain had wrenched his heavy frame—"I could have freed him. But I sent him to the cross." He came around in front of the table, sat back against it. "My wife had a disturbing dream last night. She warned me to have nothing to do with that Jew. I ignored her message; I was anxious to please Annas and Caiaphas and the other influential Jews. I thought that the crucifixion of this man might so please them that they would cease their prattling to Sejanus. On the other hand, Centurion, I saw no crime in what the Jew had done. It appeared to me that it was entirely a religious quarrel, certainly no offense deserving death. That's why I sought to wash my hands of the matter." His scowl was heavy. "But the Temple leaders will continue to protest to Sejanus, and the Jew's followers say I crucified a god. You've heard they think he's a god?"

Longinus nodded. "Yes, that he was the son of their god, I believe."

"What do you think about it, Longinus?" Pilate's countenance was darkly troubled.

"I put little stock in the gods, Excellency. But I remarked as the Jew was dying that he must have been the son of a god, as his followers said."

"Why did you say that?"

"He was a man of such courage—a different sort of man from those I've dealt with before, whether Jew or Roman."

"I made a mistake in condemning him. I should have heeded Claudia's warning." He shrugged his shoulders, gestured nervously. "But the man's dead now." He stood out from the table. "Do what you can for me with the Prefect, Longinus. I'll be grateful." His grim features relaxed. "Your ship likely will have sailed from Joppa before I leave for Caesarea, and it may not put in there anyway, so I'll hardly see you for a long time. Farewell, Centurion. A safe journey home."

## THE CROWN TREE 2

The calmest actor in the dreadful drama of this frightful day, Longinus reflected as he walked along the narrow cobblestoned way that led eastward from the Palace of the Herods toward Fortress Antonia, had been the man who died on the center cross. Never before had he seen a man like that Galilean.

Throughout the ordeal of the trial—and the centurion doubted not that the hearing before Pilate had been a mockery of vaunted Roman justice—and throughout the jeers and the cruel scourging and the six hours of agony endured on the cross, the tall young Jew had not once quailed before his tormentors. Nor had he betrayed evidence of anger. His only concern, it had seemed to Longinus as he watched, sickened in the pit of his stomach though strangely enthralled, was that his god would forgive those who even then were torturing him to his death.

During the trial the Galilean had been serene while Pilate had revealed clearly his agitation. The prisoner's demeanor had been that of judge rather than judged. He had been composed, unafraid; the Procurator had been nervous, vacillating, plainly fearful. And for expediency's sake, to please those influential Jews who might make trouble for him, a Roman governor had sent an innocent man to the cross.

And I killed him, Longinus reflected. But I drove the spear into his side to make certain that his suffering was ended. I did it out of compassion. I get no pleasure in crucifying a man, any man. . . . Perhaps before the Jew died he understood. Once when I was looking up into his sweating bloody face his eyes met mine and he smiled. By the gods, yes; he smiled at the man who was killing him. Maybe he a Jew understood that I a Roman— Strange, strange, that Jew.

Longinus, his eyes on the rough cobbles, his mind painfully reviewing the awesome drama of those hours on the Hill of the Skull, did not realize that he had reached the corner of the stone house where another narrow way joined the one on which he was hastening toward Antonia. Then a swift shadow grasped at his feet, and he looked up quickly. But already he had collided with the soldier coming hurriedly along the other street.

"Pardon me, sir! I wasn't looking where I was going; my mind was on something else. I hope I didn't damage—Cornelius, by all the gods!"

"Longinus!"

"By Jupiter, Cornelius, I thought you were still in Rome!"

The other young man, also in the informal dress of a Roman centurion, clapped his hand on his friend's shoulder, then stood back grinning.

"By the immortals, Longinus, I wasn't expecting to see you in Jerusalem. Thought you'd be at Caesarea with the Procurator."

"I have been stationed there with him, Cornelius. But I came over here with Pilate for the Passover."

"Of course. I should have known that. But I missed it this year. I've just got here, in fact—hardly three hours ago. I'm being transferred here from Capernaum, Longinus."

"You are? By Jupiter, Cornelius, I'm being moved too. Going back to Rome for a new assignment."

"Well, by the immortals! When you join the Roman army you never know where you'll be next, eh? But maybe you'll be sent back to Caesarea. I was in Rome only three months ago and expecting to be sent off to Gaul or Germania or maybe Britannia, but they returned me to Capernaum."

"No, I don't think I'll be sent back to Palestine. At any rate, I hope I'm sent to some other province, or kept at home."

"Then you've had enough of old Pilate?"

"Yes, Centurion, too much."

"I understand he's a misfit, doesn't know how to get along with the Jews." He grinned. "But say, Longinus, where were you going when we ran into each other so unceremoniously? To Antonia, by any chance?"

Longinus nodded. "Yes, I've just left the Procurator. He's lodged at the Palace of the Herods."

"Good. I was going to Antonia too. Let's be on the way; we can talk as we go along. When are you leaving Jerusalem?"

"Tomorrow. Going across to Joppa, where I'm hoping to get a vessel some time next week sailing a straight course for Rome. I'm anxious to get home. By the way, Cornelius, how were our families?"

"All very well. I saw Senator Varro and your mother the day before I sailed. They seemed in the best of health and spirits. And my father and mother were also."

"Good. And how was your sister? Is she married yet?"

"Lalage wasn't married when I left, but she professed to be desperately in love with that moon-faced Publius—"

"Publius?"

"An idler whose father is one of the ministers in the employ of Sejanus. I doubt if you ever knew him, Longinus. They're probably married now. But it won't last long; they're both too spoiled, especially Lalage. It'll take a man to keep her in domestic harness—somebody like you, Centurion." He paused, grinning. "But maybe you're already married."

"No—no wife for me. Married life is not for a soldier on duty in a province like Palestine; it's not fair to the woman."

"Oh, I don't know." Cornelius grinned. "We seem to be getting along all right—thus far."

Longinus stopped in his tracks, astonished. "You married? Pyrrha?"

"Yes. We were married just after I got to Rome. And in a few weeks I had my orders sending me back to Capernaum. Before too many more months, Longinus, there'll be a little recruit."

"Wonderful!" Longinus slapped his friend on the back. "You and Pyrrha. I'm glad, Cornelius."

They continued toward the square of the Praetorium, which sat over against the frowning high battlemented Fortress of Antonia, headquarters of Rome's military in Jerusalem, and talked of what had happened to them since they had last seen each other. As they neared the end of the way and could see the tower, Longinus pointed.

"There's Antonia." But suddenly his expression betrayed puzzlement. "Cornelius, how do you happen to be just now going to the fortress? If you've been in Jerusalem three hours—"

"I've already been up there and stowed my gear. Got to Antonia just before the storm struck. When it was over I walked down to the Temple, and from there down Mount Moriah and back by a friend's house on Mount Zion."

"Hadn't you had enough exercise already?"

"I was looking for some acquaintances from Capernaum—

Jews. When I didn't see them at the Temple, I went to the house
they customarily visit when they're in Jerusalem. But the door to
the courtyard was barred and nobody answered my knocking."
He saw that Longinus didn't understand. "The men I was looking for, plain Galilean fisherfolk, are followers of a young rabbi
from Nazareth whom I've been interested in ever since he cured
my young Greek servant of a severe palsy. Some time ago this
rabbi and his followers left Galilee to come up to the Passover
Feast, and rumors have been circulating that the Nazarene might
run afoul of the Temple authorities, who have become very
jealous of his amazing power over the common people."

"How was it this man healed your servant? Is he a physician?"

"No, he's a spiritual leader of remarkable, unexplainable abilities to heal the sick and maimed. He cured the boy without
seeing him, even while a considerable distance from him."

Quickly he revealed the details, but his friend obviously remained unconvinced; his smile indicated an amused skepticism.

"Do you think this rabbi is some kind of god, Cornelius?"

"I hardly know what I think about him, Longinus. I put little
faith in our Roman gods, just as you do. But this man has some
strange source of power that I can't explain. His followers—Jews
in the main, of course—call him the son of their Jewish Jehovah.
Some claim that he is the Jewish Messiah and are determined to
enthrone him as the Jews' king. The Temple leaders, on the other
hand, seem determined to make him out a revolutionary against
Rome—which he isn't—and to cause him to be crucified."

They had come out into the square before the Praetorium.
Longinus stopped.

"Wait, Cornelius." His expression had sobered. "This Galilean,
was he a tall, sturdy fellow with a twin-spiked beard and reddish
brown hair curling to his shoulders? And was he called Jesus
of Nazareth?"

"Yes. Can it be that you have seen him here in Jerusalem?"

"He is dead. He died on the cross today on the Hill of the
Skull—just before the storm struck."

The centurion from Capernaum did not exclaim, though

Longinus had expected him to swear by all the great and little gods of Rome. Instead, he resumed walking toward Antonia, and when he spoke it was in calm tones. "It was a monstrous thing Rome did, Longinus. This good man has done no man ill, has done so many men good. But Rome did not know him. Crucified!" He shook his head sadly. "The horrible death of insurrectionists and highwaymen, of slaves and foul murderers." Suddenly he paused, turned to stare at his friend. "You know, Centurion, it's a strange thing, an unbelievably mysterious thing, but the rabbi said he would come to Jerusalem and be put to death. Simon told me about it."

"Simon?"

"A fisherman from Galilee who has often supplied my table, one of the rabbi's friends. He was the principal one I was looking for when I went down to the Temple. Simon said that Jesus told his followers that he would come to the Passover Feast and be offered up as a sacrifice for the sins of the people. But Simon said they didn't understand just what the rabbi meant; it was a great mystery to them."

"What did he mean, Cornelius?"

"I don't know myself. But the Jews attach great importance to the offering of sacrifices to their Jehovah." He looked off toward the white marble walls and porticoes of the Temple, glistening in the narrowing band of sunshine above the shadows lengthening from Jerusalem's western wall and the city's closely pressed squat stone houses. "Often you can see smoke arising from the burnt offerings." Then he leaned closer to his friend.

"But he said something else, Longinus, and it may be that he has undertaken to carry it out."

"What did he say?"

"Simon told me that only a few days before they left Galilee to come up for the Passover, the Nazarene declared to his followers that he would come here and be killed, but after three days in the tomb he would arise. But the rabbi's followers couldn't believe that he meant actually that he would be killed; they were confident he would take on the role of their traditional Messiah and declare himself the Jews' king." Suddenly his eyes narrowed. "How long was he on the cross, Longinus?"

"Six hours."

"Few die that quickly. And the Nazarene was a man of powerful physique."

"But he had been scourged almost to death, Cornelius. I marveled that he survived on the cross that long."

"Maybe, though, he was only in a heavy coma. Perhaps that would explain—"

"He is dead. He was dead before the execution squad left the Hill of the Skull; I can vouch for that."

"But how could you know, Longinus?" He was insistent.

"Because I killed him."

"*You* killed him! By all the gods, Longinus—"

"I was in command of the crucifixion detail. And at the end, to make sure he was dead and would suffer no longer, I drove my spear up under his rib into his heart."

The countenance of the centurion from Capernaum blanched. "Longinus"—his voice was low and edged with tragedy—"you didn't know what you were doing!"

"Those were his words as he hung there. He prayed to his god to forgive us. He said we didn't know what we were doing."

Cornelius made no reply. In silence they walked alongside the garden of the Praetorium. A low stone wall separated it from the Pavement before the Praetorium, where this morning Pontius Pilate had sat in judgment on Jesus of Nazareth. Over beyond Mariamne Tower, erected by Herod the Great to the memory of the wife he had murdered but never ceased to love, the sun was fast dropping toward the Great Sea and the shadows were pushing far out into the square. To their right, beyond the wall, the garden now in early April was already fragrant with a multitude of flowers arranged in orderly pattern among the evergreens.

They had neared the gate in the wall when suddenly Longinus stopped, stooped down. At his feet lay a withering shoot of rhamnus thorn that had been twisted carelessly into a rough circlet. He picked it up.

"By the gods, Cornelius," he said, fingering it gingerly, "this must be the crown they made for the Jew this morning when they were mocking him. It must have fallen from his head when he bent down to take up the crossbeam as we started for the Hill of the Skull. Look here, on these thorns"—he bent closer to examine the circlet—"dried blood." As he held it toward Cornelius the twist was released; the straightening limb lashed out and a thorn caught the ball of his right thumb. The spurting blood reddened the thorn sprig.

"By Jupiter, these thorns are sharp!"

But he did not fling the limb away. Instead, he leaned across the low wall and idly pushed the torn end into the soft earth of the garden. Then he turned and with Cornelius beside him strode diagonally across the resplendent mosaic of the Pavement to the fortress. Still silent, they crossed under the wide arch of the great portal.

## THE CROWN TREE 3

Early the next morning, without having seen Cornelius again, Longinus set out for Joppa. As he rode through the gate that opened on the road to the port city, he breathed deeply of the balmy spring air.

It was even fresher outside the walls, he was convinced; it seemed more bracing, invigorating. Perhaps it was all in his feelings, for the air inside the city was clean and fresh; yesterday's storm had washed away the dust and the smells and left Jerusalem's walls and turrets glistening in the morning's bright sunshine. But outside on the Joppa road Jerusalem and Pontius Pilate were now behind him, and soon all Palestine would be. A new assignment awaited him and promised more diverting experiences. And, like the Procurator, he would be relieved to get away from the Jews and their incessant bickering.

Where the road climbed a rise to drop down sharply on the other side he turned in his saddle and looked back. It could well be his last view of Jerusalem. Nor would he care.

In twisting spirals the smoke was lifting above the smoldering piles of refuse in the Vale of Hinnom below Jerusalem's south wall, for never were foul Hinnom's flames completely extinguished. His eyes swept the noisome valley and along the walls above squalid Ophel to Mount Moriah and another wispish gray curl arising above the gleaming white Temple, where the priests were offering the morning sacrifices to Israel's Jehovah. This great marble pile, the seat of Israel's one god, was, he knew, the very heart and core of Jewry.

But then his eyes fastened on another spot known also to every son of Israel, a rounded bare knob as abhorred by the good Jew as the Mount of the Temple was revered. On the scarred and ugly summit three crosses stood starkly outlined. Quickly Longinus faced about, rode down the slope toward Joppa.

Almost two weeks later the Alexandrian grain ship *Pharos* came into port there and when it had finished loading, Centurion Longinus Aemilius Varro went aboard. The vessel, he had learned, would touch at Paphos on the island of Cyprus and then sail directly for Rome. With good wind they would reach Paphos on the third day.

The winds continued favorable; the *Pharos* moved steadily northwestward. They were hardly an hour outside the harbor of Paphos when Longinus, crossing the deck to starboard for a better view of the island's southern shore, noticed a girl leaning against the rail and looking out across the placid water. He strode over to her.

"Are you leaving ship at Paphos," he ventured, smiling, "or will you—I hope—continue with us to Rome?"

She turned to face him. He saw that she was a Jew, young—though, like most eastern women in early adolescence, with a figure fully developed—and pretty, with black hair framing dark eyes that were appraising him candidly but with neither boldness nor timidity.

"My mother and I are stopping at Paphos." Her voice was pleasant, and she was smiling. "Mother came from Cyprus. We have many relatives and friends on the island."

"And you live at Joppa?"

"No, Jerusalem."

"Jerusalem? I was on duty there hardly three weeks ago."

"You were? For the Passover?" Her eyes showed growing interest. "Were you stationed at Fortress Antonia, or were you one of the soldiers brought from Caesarea by Pontius Pilate to help keep us Jews in subjection during the Feast?"

"I was one of those Pilate took with him from Caesarea." Longinus laughed. "But not to keep you in subjection. Our duty was to help maintain order." He bowed. "I'm Centurion Longinus, commander of a century in the Second Italian Cohort; I'm on my way to Rome for transfer to a new duty."

"I'm Damaris, granddaughter of Annas, former High Priest, and niece of Caiaphas."

"You are? I saw them the day before I left Jerusalem."

"Where? At the Temple?"

"No, at the Praetorium. It was during the trial of a man before Procurator Pilate."

He saw a cloud darken her countenance. "Why were they trying the man?"

"He was charged by the Jewish authorities with some serious offense against the Jewish law—blasphemy, I believe it was, some violation of the Jewish system of religion. A detail from my century had the prisoner in custody."

"Are you talking about Jesus of Galilee, the wonderful teacher, the holy one whom they crucified on the Hill of the Skull?"

"Yes, that was the one. But you seem to be agitated about it. Why? Your grandfather and the High Priest Caiaphas, along with the other Temple leaders, demanded that he be crucified."

"I know that; they were determined to have him killed." Her black eyes were sorrowful. "But not all Jews of influence were against Jesus. Joseph of Arimathaea and the Rabbi Nicodemus stood with him, and in many a house on Mount Zion—even in the house of the High Priest himself—he had secret followers. My mother and I—" She paused, and her expression betrayed a mounting tension. "Were you among those at the Hill of the Skull when they crucified him?"

"Yes, I was in charge. But I had no choice. As a soldier of Rome I had to obey the orders of the Procurator."

"You *had to kill* the Son of God!" She drew away from him along the rail, scorn and horror darkening her pained countenance. "I must go back to my mother." She turned to leave. Then she whirled about to face him. "You've been away from Jerusalem almost three weeks, you say. Then you don't know! No, you haven't heard!" Her laugh was tense, mirthless. "You crucified him, but you couldn't hold him in the tomb! He arose on the third day, the day after the Sabbath, as he had promised he would! He came to visit his disciples while they were at the house of one of Mother's friends on Mount Zion. They saw him and talked with him and felt of the wounds in his hands and side." Her black eyes blazed. "You killed him, but you couldn't keep him in the tomb. He conquered death, even as very soon now he will conquer your evil Rome!"

Her chin high, she turned and walked swiftly across the deck.

## THE CROWN TREE  4

Longinus slumped on a coil of rope in the stern and watched the angry white water boiling up in the trough cut by the *Pharos*. The vessel was moving easily now, running with all sails aloft like a great white gull skimming the surface in search of an unwary small fish. Off the starboard the dancing shadows of the sails pointed toward the not far away coast of Italy. But they pointed likewise over and beyond the spine of the narrow peninsula to a province he had left many days behind but could not forget, and as clearly as he saw the green Italian hills he envisioned also the leering Hill of the Skull and three crosses up-raised.

In another hour the sun would drop into the Great Sea and when it rose again the *Pharos* likely would be outside the harbor of Ostia. Then by midday the vessel should be able to push up the sluggish yellow Tiber and drop anchor at the wharf near the ancient Sublicius Bridge. And in another few minutes he would be entering the mansion of Senator Marcus Aemilius Varro on Esqueline Hill.

"By the immortals, what did that girl mean?"

Quickly he glanced about, but no one was near. He wondered how many times before he had spoken the question aloud. And why in the middle of his thinking about anything else should this question invariably emerge into the forefront of his consciousness? He hadn't seen her since the few minutes they were together on the starboard deck. An hour later she and her mother had disembarked at Paphos.

But what had she meant? Where had she heard such a pre-posterous story? Yet hadn't Cornelius been told that the man had said he would be crucified but in three days come alive?

His father's mansion on Esqueline and his return home forgot, Longinus sat on the coil of rope and watched the churning water and the greening vineyards of Italy. But he was looking beyond them and up into the sorrowful eyes of a tall young man nailed with iron spikes to the center cross. He could not shut out the haunting vision of the suffering Jew. It had followed him, even across the Great Sea. But the man in the vision, if vision it was, showed no anger, sought no vengeance. He seemed only to bear a heavy weight of sorrow. Could it be that really he had come forth from the tomb?

"I don't know whether he has come to life or not, but I do know that he was dead when I left him on the cross to report to Pilate."

He peered around hurriedly, for once more he had spoken aloud. But no one had heard.

Longinus stood up, turned his back on the churning waters,

walked quickly across the deck. Inside he would find lively company, dispel this strange mood.

He was on deck again the next morning as the *Pharos* neared Ostia. The wind had borne it steadily northward. But once the vessel entered the harbor and began to ascend the Tiber, it was forced to labor against the strong current of the muddy river. Nor could the *Pharos* go ahead of the heavy traffic moving slowly toward the capital. Longinus had been standing at the starboard forerail, but he began to pace the deck impatiently as the ship came up behind a line of plodding corn barges and a heavier scow transporting huge building stones. They seemed hardly to be besting the stream's flow.

But shortly after the noon hour the *Pharos* came into Rome. On the left bank and almost straight ahead, reaching down to the water's edge, he could see the luxuriant flowers and trees of the gardens Caesar had given the people, and beyond them the steep rise of Janiculum Hill, Rome's Jewish quarter. Quickly he looked the other way.

Now the vessel was rounding the bend in the channel that turned sharply right to go past the Emporium sprawling a thousand feet along the eastern bank and noisily alive with the day's commerce. Slaves scurried along the wharves and in and out of the warehouses. Nubians and Ethiopians, their black bodies naked but for bright-colored loincloths and shining as though they had been oiled, bent their backs to bales and boxes of merchandise. Blond men of Germania, with corn-colored hair falling to their shoulders and great muscles bulging to their tasks, wrestled with heavy crates and hogsheads. Swarthy shorter men from Gaul and Dalmatia and Macedonia and Thracia, captives of Rome's thundering legions in many a distant conquest, struggled in the midday sun. And now and then an overseer's long whip uncoiled like an angry serpent.

Beyond the Emporium the Aventine Hill rose above the Tiber's yellow waters, and farther on the Palatine and Capitoline Hills pushed upward, their slopes crowded with temples and palaces. Then straight over the ship's bow and beyond the forest of marble statuary and porticoed white temples of the Roman Forum, Longinus saw again the other fabled hills of ancient Rome, and his spirits lifted.

To the left and farthest away, Pincian Hill flaunted its mansions and gardens, alive with glowing color. Next, and directly beyond the Forum, was Quirinal; one of the magnificent villas climbing its slopes was the home of Senator Flaccus, father of Cornelius. Straight past the Forum's center and across the great way that ran out to Castra Praetoria at the city's northeastern wall rose Viminal Hill, and beside it but covering a much larger expanse was the Esqueline. The *Pharos* was veering left now with the turning of the river, and as it cleared the open end of the Circus Maximus horseshoe he had a quick glimpse of his father's villa almost at the summit of the mansion-studded slope. And straight across from Circus Maximus, its lower region hidden by the towering stands of the great stadium, he could see the houses massed closely together on the western side of Caelian Hill.

Longinus was one of the first passengers to go ashore. When he had given instructions for the delivery of his baggage, he walked quickly from the wharf past the malodorous stalls of the Cattle Market with its temples to Fortune and the Goddess of the Dawn. Without pausing he continued eastward until he reached the magnificent Basilica Julia. Along the crowded, statue-lined street between the basilica and the Temple of Saturn at the foot of the Capitoline he elbowed his way into the Forum at its western end. At the Millenarium Aureum, the resplendent milestone put there by Emperor Augustus to mark the beginning and crossing point of the immense consular highways system, he stopped. Around him on all sides from the flat of the Forum up the slopes arose a forest of marbled magnificence.

A sudden great lift and swell of pride exalted him. He stood at the heart and pulsing center of mighty Rome, mistress of the world. From this gilded bronze column, roads and connecting sea lanes reached out miles upon thousands of miles to bind together the far-flung provinces of the Roman Empire—Hispania, Germania, Gaul, Britannia, Macedonia, Asia, Syria, Palestine, Africa.

Along these roads and seaways Rome held commerce with every race and region, enforced her iron authority, administered justice impartially in accordance with Roman law. Roman justice . . .

A fleeting shadow clouded his countenance.

"No. That's past. The Great Sea has been crossed. This is Rome. I'm home now." But the words had not been said.

Quickly he went diagonally across the Forum Romanum, turned left at the Basilica Aemelia, and walking briskly northeastward, came out in front of the Forum Julium. Turning eastward again at the Temple of Minerva, he took the broad way that ascended the long slope of Esqueline Hill.

## THE CROWN TREE 5

His father was not at home when Longinus reached the house. His mother, who greeted him with warmest affection, explained that Senator Varro had gone down to Capri with Prefect Sejanus, who wished to consult with Emperor Tiberius on some important matter concerned with administration of certain provinces. They had been three days away from Rome already, she reported; she was expecting them back perhaps on the morrow.

Late in the afternoon, after he had bathed and dressed, the centurion visited Senator Flaccus and his wife on Quirinal Hill to carry them the news of Cornelius. He did not see Lalage. She had recently married Publius, they revealed, and had gone with him to Misenum for a short season's stay with a friend who some weeks before had opened his summer villa there.

On his return to his father's house Longinus had the evening meal with his mother, and soon afterward, tired from the long voyage, he went to bed. On the soft couch in his marbled chamber he stretched his long legs and settled comfortably for relaxing slumber.

But he was not to have it. In strange and troubled dreaming he was once again in the midst of the stir and fluster of Jerusalem during the Passover season. On weary, dragging feet he tramped the narrow and tortuous ways of noisome Ophel from Dung Gate to the slope of Mount Moriah and the great colonnaded white Temple; he crossed the bridge spanning the Valley of the Cheesemongers, climbed the slow rise of Zion and the great houses of Israel's affluent, and plodded past the sprawling Palace of the Herods to come out after a while on the Pavement before the Praetorium, where Roman soldiers were mocking and scourging with metal-tipped leather whips a bedraggled, bleeding Galilean above whose blood-streaked face a twist of thorn was circled.

A quick and burning pity for the tormented Jew flamed through him. But he stood silent, made no move to rescue the man, who now, of a sudden, was looking down upon him from a cross planted atop the Hill of the Skull beyond the city's wall. The young Jew's eyes were heavy with sorrow and pleading. Then a shudder, that seemed to grow out of his feet spiked to the upright, shook his gaunt frame.

"It is finished," the Jew suddenly said, his strength gone, and closed his eyes.

Longinus discovered his spear in his right hand. He clutched it with both hands, raised it upward until its sharp point touched against the chest and beneath the lowest rib of the dying Jew. A quick deft thrust would end the poor fellow's suffering. Now—

"No! No! No-o-o! I can't kill the son of a god! No, by the immortals! No! No-o——"

"Longinus! Longinus, my boy! Longinus!"

The cross and its burden were gone, vanished. He opened his eyes. His mother was shaking him, her hand firm on his shoulder. He recognized her by the thin light of the small bed lamp she had brought, but even more clearly by the feel and movement of her hand, for many a time in his childhood years she had wakened him as he screamed in the frenzy of a frightful nightmare.

He sat up, rubbed his eyes. "I was dreaming, Mother. I was back in Palestine. I—I—" He shook his head to clear it.

"Yes, son, I know. I heard you moaning and tossing. I came in to awaken you, and just as I reached the bed you began screaming."

"It was a nightmare, Mother. But I'm all right now. I'll go back to sleep and be all right."

She stroked his hair, and with the end of her fingers gently massaged his temples.

"You were tired from the long voyage, Longinus. And it may be difficult for you to rid your mind of unpleasant experiences in the course of your duty abroad. But you're home now—in your own home, son. Put the past behind you." She had sat down on the edge of the bed. Now she arose, tucked the bed covers beneath his shoulders. "Good night, and good rest."

She went out quickly with her little lamp, and the bedchamber was dark. Longinus settled down under the light covering, turned on his side.

## THE CROWN TREE  6

Senator Varro returned late the next day. He revealed that Prefect Sejanus had been summoned to Capri to report on the situation in the region of Thessalonica in Macedonia, for Tiberius had received information that the whole area was seething with incipient revolt against Rome as a result of the recent action of the Roman administrator there.

This official, perhaps on orders of Sejanus, the Senator suggested, had materially increased the tax levies, and widespread murmurings and actual opposition had followed, so that in many instances he had been compelled to dispatch Roman troops to enforce the collection of the added heavy taxes. At the home of one of the richest merchants in all Macedonia an altercation had taken place, and one of the soldiers had been killed by a servant. The enraged soldiers had then slain the merchant and one of his sons who had interposed.

This man's wife had died years before. Only a son and daughter remained, and they were seized at once and sent away to be sold as slaves on the block in Rome. The slain man's vast properties, which included lands, merchant ships, and manufacturing plants in several countries, were confiscated.

It had been widely suspected in the Senate, his father added, that the wily and grafting Sejanus had profited greatly in the confiscation of these properties. And whispers had reached the ears of the Emperor.

"But I thought that Sejanus in everything but name was the Emperor," Longinus observed.

"He is powerful, there's no denying it. And for a long time, particularly since Tiberius withdrew to Capri four years ago, Sejanus has been doing virtually as he wished, and growing vastly rich in the process. But"—he leaned nearer his son and lowered his voice, though no servant was in the peristylium where they were relaxing—"a day may come, and perhaps shortly, when his word in Rome is no longer law. Never even whisper this, Longinus, but there are those in the Senate and elsewhere who believe that Tiberius now suspects that when his son Drusus was poisoned several years ago, Sejanus was at the bottom of that; they believe, and possibly the Emperor does also, that Sejanus has his eyes on the throne."

"Has the Emperor ever indicated who will be his heir to the throne?"

"I don't think he has; I believe, however, that he prefers his grandson Tiberius, son of Drusus; I'd say the next Emperor will be either young Tiberius or Caligula."

"The gods preserve us if it's Caligula."

"Yes, I agree. And speaking of Caligula, in your traveling about Palestine have you ever met up with his crony, Agrippa?"

"No, Father, but I understand Agrippa's at Tiberias in Galilee. I think Herod Antipas and Herodias set him up there in some sort of magistracy that provides him a living."

"He is doubtless scheming some way to get his hands on enough money to return to Rome."

Longinus laughed. "Yes, sir, no doubt."

"Well, perhaps you'll see him when you get back to Palestine."

"When I get back to Palestine? May the gods forbid." Longinus stared at his father. "I don't want to go back there—ever. Father, why did you say that?"

"Don't be alarmed, Longinus." The Senator was smiling. "I don't know that you're going back. I don't know where you're going next. In fact, you might be assigned to stay here in Rome. But why"—his expression suddenly was serious—"do you have an aversion to returning to Palestine?"

"It's the Jews. Like Pontius Pilate, I've had enough of their chattering and bickering. By the way, the Procurator asked me just before I left to request you to intercede for him with Sejanus. He wants a transfer to some other province."

The Senator shook his head. Sejanus, he was confident, would not be willing to transfer Pilate. The Prefect was little concerned with the fact that the Procurator had embittered the Jews against Rome. While he saw to it that ample tribute money poured into the government coffers—and the pockets of Sejanus —he would in all probability remain at Caesarea. Let the Jews howl and beat their breasts over Pilate's flaunting the Roman ensigns in the Jews' holy places and perchance lifting the while some of the Temple's vessels of silver and gold.

"So long as Pilate keeps the revenue flowing into Rome," the Senator gave as his opinion, "Pilate will remain in Caesarea. After all, isn't that the function of a Procurator? Isn't that what the word means?" He selected a fig from the wooden bowl on the ebony table beside them, pulled out the stem and flung it into the fountain at the center of the peristylium, split open the fruit and bit into the luscious pink inside. "But when you see Sejanus tomorrow, Longinus, you can pass on to him Pilate's request." He chewed reflectively. "Son, why are you so reluctant to return to Palestine should Sejanus have in mind sending you on some other mission or assignment in that province?" His eyes were searching, intent. Longinus could not evade.

"It's because of the Jews in general, Father, but also in par-

ticular because of an incident that occurred in Jerusalem the day
before I left there."

In detail he related the story of the mock trial, the merciless
scourging, and the crucifixion of the Galilean Jew, and of his
own part in the sordid drama outside the city's wall. He told of
his meeting with Cornelius late in the afternoon, shortly after
the man's death, and of their discussion concerning the belief of
certain Jews that this crucified man was the Messiah of Israel,
the son of the Jews' Jehovah. Nor did he withhold the fact that
in his dreams night after night the sad, pleading eyes of the
Galilean had looked into his.

"Pontius Pilate is a man of great stubbornness but little courage," Senator Varro declared, when Longinus had finished the
recital. "Doubtless the Galilean was convicted unjustly and was
most shamefully dealt with. Crucifixion is a horrible manner of
execution anyway, Longinus, and often even the most hardened
soldiers attempt to evade serving on a crucifixion detail. Having
to crucify that man was a frightful assignment for you, my boy,
and it made a terrifying impression on your mind. That's the
reason for the bad dreams. But you'll get over that; time will dull
the experience and the remembrance of it."

"I hope you are right, Father. Perhaps if I stay away from
Palestine the remembrance will fade. But if I go back, everything,
I fear, will be revived. I haven't told you the strangest part of the
story, however."

Then he related his conversation with the girl on board the
*Pharos* outside the harbor of Paphos, and to it he added the report as Cornelius had related it that the Galilean had said he
would be crucified but would arise on the third day after his en-
tombment.

"But surely, Longinus, you can't for a moment believe any
such foolishness. We're living in modern times, when the superstitions and witcheries of the olden days have all but disappeared
among enlightened peoples. You know I never did put any re-
liance even in our Roman gods. They have their place, doubtless.
They give a certain comfort and bring a certain discipline, too"

—he smiled—"to the unlearned and superstitious. But certainly, my boy, you can't be very serious about so-called spirits sailing around in the air or prowling beneath the earth. I fear"—suddenly he was grave—"that you may have absorbed, however unintentionally, some of the oriental mysticism that seems to be in the very blood of the eastern peoples."

# THE CROWN TREE 7

Ordinarily a centurion, commander of but a hundred soldiers, would not be summoned into the presence of powerful Lucius Aelius Sejanus, prefect of the Praetorian Guard.

But Longinus was the son of Senator Varro, and Marcus Aemilius Varro was no ordinary senator. Besides being possessed of great wealth, Senator Varro long had been influential in highest places—even with Tiberius himself, it was generally believed.

More important in the wily Prefect's planning, however, was the fact that the Senator had lent large sums to the profligate Prince Herod Agrippa and in other ways had favored both Agrippa and his sister Herodias, wife now of Herod Antipas, tetrarch of Galilee. Rumors had even circulated in Rome for a time that Senator Varro had helped Herodias cut the matrimonial ties with Herod Philip to knot new ones with his half-brother Antipas. And now the Herods were living at Tiberias, the glittering new capital of Galilee on the western shore of the little sea. To assure further the success of the venture he was planning in Palestine, Sejanus reasoned rightly that it would be well to have in charge someone who possessed the friendship of the House of Herod.

So the Prefect sent for Centurion Longinus. Now they were closeted in the sumptuous apartment of Sejanus.

"I want you to return to Palestine, Centurion," he said, after they had chatted a moment. "But not to Caesarea. Up the coast from there, near Ptolemais, in the vicinity of the Belus River, above Mount Carmel."

There, he went on to reveal, were the glass manufactories and textile plants of a wealthy Macedonian who had been slain in his home by Roman soldiers after a dispute that arose out of their attempt to collect certain taxes. The man's properties had been seized by the government—Sejanus smiled meaningfully as he related it—and his son and daughter sold into slavery.

"In order to obtain maximum returns from this property, Centurion, we must continue to administer it. That means that the glassworks and the looms must be operated efficiently. I understand that the finest products are made there, goods that bring handsome prices." He leaned nearer, smiled craftily. "Centurion, I'm sending you to take charge of the Roman constabulary at nearby Ptolemais. But obviously that's an assignment hardly requiring a man of your talents. What I want you actually to do is to see that these properties are profitably managed." He paused, studied the centurion's face a moment, resumed speaking. "This manufacturing, in the glass furnaces particularly, uses up slaves rapidly. But I'll see that an ample supply of fresh slaves is always available. And, I might add, anything else you may require."

He sat back, smiling, his sharp small eyes intently appraising Longinus.

"Centurion, one other thing. The—let us say—potentials for your adding to your personal fortune are tremendous, virtually what you choose to make them. You understand?"

Longinus nodded. "Yes, Excellency." But nausea was clutching at his stomach. "When must I leave Rome?"

"As quickly as you can arrange it. I want no time lost."

The centurion arose to go, thought of Pontius Pilate's request. Quickly he presented it.

Sejanus smiled blandly.

"I'll consider it. Pilate's a bumbling ass and a coward besides. He needlessly and witlessly offends the Jews. He should be transferred. But of all the procurators in the Empire none is better

than Pilate at keeping the revenue coming into our treasury."
He licked his lips, grinned.

## THE CROWN TREE 8

On the afternoon of the day Longinus rode out of Jerusalem
toward Joppa on the journey that would take him to Rome,
Centurion Cornelius was relaxing in his quarters on the third
level of the towering Fortress Antonia.

An orderly entered with a message from the commander. It
was an order to set up a guard at the tomb of the Galilean crucified the day before.

"Very well." The centurion nodded. "The order will be carried out."

The soldier turned to go, when Cornelius spoke again. "Tell
me, do you know why the commander wants a guard there?"

"Sir, the orders came from the Procurator. I only know that
there are reports going about Jerusalem that friends of the crucified Jew might attempt to steal the body." He saluted, departed.

Cornelius selected a detail of soldiers and an hour before sunset, which would end the Jewish Sabbath, set out westward with
them along a narrow way walled by stone buildings here and
there connected by archways above the twisting, now almost
darkened street.

They went out through the Damascus Gate and turning left at
the foot of the ugly rise of the Skull entered a small garden.
Across from them they saw a group of men pressing about the
mouth of a large tomb cut into the granite of the hillside. They
went over to the men.

"Is this the tomb of the Galilean crucified yesterday?" Cornelius asked.

"It is. And you must be the soldiers sent by the Procurator to
guard it."

"We are," Cornelius answered the man, a Jewish priest whom he presumed to be one of the Temple attendants. "But why put a guard over a dead man?"

"This blasphemer"—the priest thrust out a fat thumb in the direction of the tomb's mouth—"is dead, that's true. And he'll remain dead. But he promised his misguided followers that after three days in the tomb he would rise up again and walk forth alive. Now we fear they may try to steal the body and proclaim it among the people that he did arise. Tomorrow's the third day." He spat ostentatiously. "We want the tomb sealed and the body kept in there until everyone is agreed it is rotten."

Cornelius, scowling, pointed to the tremendous, roughly circular granite slab that had been rolled into place to close the tomb. "It would take several men to roll that stone back from the mouth. But nevertheless we'll seal it, and you can remain and see it done, if you'll be the better satisfied."

Quickly the soldiers made a stiff mortar of clay and pushed it into the spaces between the tomb's mouth and the stone closing it. When they had finished Cornelius took off his large signet ring and pressed it deep into the clay.

"Now the tomb is sealed," he said to the Jews, as he replaced the ring on his finger and brushed away the particles of clay adhering to it. "If anyone moves the stone, the seal will be broken. But I think you need have no fear."

The priest nodded. "It is well that you did that, Centurion." He turned to his companions. "Now let us be gone. This is no fit work for the holy Sabbath."

Then with their robes hitched high above their sandals, the Jews went quickly from the garden. Already the shadows of the trees and shrubs were long across the grass.

Cornelius stationed the soldiers about the mouth of the tomb so that no one could approach it without being discovered, and sat with them until darkness had fallen and the Sabbath of the Jews was ended. Then he stood up, spoke to one of the men.

"Decius, I'm going back to Antonia to arrange for a relief detail. I'm leaving you in charge. Don't let anybody get to the tomb. But be slow with your swords. Some of the rabbi's friends, grieving for him, may come here to weep and pray to their god. Respect their grief, but don't let anyone tamper with the stone." He started away, turned to speak again. "I'll be back with your relief about sunrise."

At the fortress he made arrangements quickly for the relieving detail, and went to his quarters and soon to bed, where a long while he lay sleepless pondering the strange and tragic fate of the young rabbi from Nazareth. In the blackness of his unlighted chamber he could see clearly the face of the Nazarene as it was the afternoon he had talked with him outside the gates of Capernaum.

With remarkable clarity the events of that distant day unrolled before him. His servant boy, to whom he had become greatly attached, had developed a burning fever and was moaning and tossing in delirium. And when the frenzied efforts of the physicians apparently had given the youth no relief, he had gone in search of the rabbi of whom the fisherman Simon so often had spoken. He had encountered the man as he was coming back into the city from a small mountain on the slope of which he had been speaking to a great throng, for already this Jesus was drawing multitudes to him as he preached up and down the lake region of Galilee.

Cornelius recalled his plea to the rabbi that he heal the boy, and the rabbi's response that he would gladly go at once to the sufferer's bedside and restore him. And then lying there in the darkness the centurion remembered the sudden swift upsurge of faith in this smiling young Jew which he himself had experienced as he had stood talking, and his own words, strange indeed for a Roman, in answer to the rabbi's promise:

"Rabbi, I'm not worthy that you should enter my house. But if you will only say the word, then my little servant boy will be healed. I recognize authority, Rabbi, for I am a man of authority, with soldiers and servants under my command, and when I speak they obey."

"Of a truth," the Galilean had said to him then, "in all Israel

I have not found so great a faith. Go, my brother, and as you have believed, so be it done unto you."

Strangely exhilarated, he had returned quickly to his house. There he had found the boy calm, fever gone, restored.

Now this magnetic young man, this rabbi of mystic authority and strange powers, lay dead at the hands of Rome, sealed away behind a great stone in a borrowed hillside tomb.

So thinking of Jesus of Nazareth and the monstrous injustice that had brought him to this tomb, Cornelius drifted into a restless sleep of jumbled dreams peopled by Simon of Capernaum and his fisherman friends the Zebedee brothers, and Pontius Pilate and Lalage and a host of others. In the midst of them he saw again and again the rabbi of Nazareth and Centurion Longinus, who carried in his hand a long spear moist and reddened at its tip.

Cornelius awakened early, assembled the relief detail, and when they had breakfasted started with them toward the garden at the foot of the Hill of the Skull.

But hardly had they crossed the square before the fortress and entered the narrow way leading to Damascus Gate when one of the soldiers of the guard detail at the tomb came on a run around the bend in the cobbled passage.

"Centurion, the crucified Galilean"—the soldier was breathing hard—"has escaped from the tomb! Decius sent me—"

"Escaped! By all the gods, how could a dead man escape! Did you all go to sleep and permit his friends to steal the body?"

"No, Centurion! Nobody fell asleep, and not a man came near the tomb, but the stone was rolled back and the body no longer is in the tomb. I can't explain it, sir, but—"

"What did happen? Speak up, soldier!"

"We were all at our stations, and awake. We'd been calling out to each other to make sure that none slept. As the dawn was about to break we felt the earth trembling, and looking toward the tomb, we saw the stone rolling back from the mouth. The stone, Centurion, seemed to have a light about it. It was strange—" He shook his head. "We were paralyzed with fear,

I must confess. One of the men said he saw an apparition sitting on the stone. I didn't; I was too afraid to look. But I do know there was nobody there but us!" His eyes were wide, frightened.

"Let's go, men! On the double!" He motioned with his head to the still panting soldier. "Go back with us."

Just beyond the Damascus Gate Cornelius almost collided with a big barrel-chested bewhiskered Jew coming on the run toward the city, his brown homespun robe held high on his bulging knotty legs and his coarse heavy sandals thick with dust from the cobblestones.

"Simon! By all the gods, man, what—"

"Centurion Cornelius!" The big man interrupted the centurion's questioning. "The Master has arisen, Centurion! He has left the tomb and returned to life—as he said he would!" His eyes, wide with wonder, blazed from beneath his tangle of untrimmed eyebrows, and his great hairy chest heaved. "It's the third day, and he's alive again!"

"But how do you know this, Simon?" Cornelius had halted the detail. "Why do you say he's alive now?"

"The tomb's empty. I saw it myself; I've just been there. An angel of the Lord rolled back the stone, and the Master walked forth." The big man was beginning to get his breath again. "He told us he would arise on the third day. Didn't I tell you so?"

"Yes, but how do you know he's *alive?*"

"The angels told the women, Centurion." Simon paused, for Cornelius was staring incredulously. "It was this way. We were on our way to the tomb—the younger of the Zebedees and I. Just before we reached the garden Mary of Magdala came running up to us, excited and out of breath. She told us the Master was not in the tomb and she was coming to report it. We all started running for the tomb, but John got there first. He stopped at the mouth but I went on in. It was just as she had said. The Master was gone. The linen winding sheet was on the floor beside the bier, but the napkin that had been rolled about his head and face was still in its original folds at the head of the bier."

Cornelius made no comment, and Simon, his eyes flaming, went on: "Meanwhile Mary of Magdala had come up and when I came out of the tomb she was standing there weeping and peering inside. You see, the woman thought somebody had stolen the body away."

"The women?"

"Yes, Centurion. They had gone to the tomb to anoint the body with spices, because it hadn't been properly laid out for burial, since it was nigh the Sabbath when the Master was taken down from the cross."

Cornelius nodded, and Simon proceeded:

"When I came from the tomb, the women ventured inside. In a moment they came running out again, wildly excited. I was talking with two of the soldiers who had been on guard there. The women ran up to me and ben Zebedee, their eyes on fire, and said they had seen two angels inside the tomb and that the angels had revealed that the Master was not dead and his body stolen away but that he had risen from the dead." Simon's countenance suddenly was solemn beneath the forest of reddish brown whiskers, and then it began to flame again and with his right fist he smote the palm of his left hand. "Don't you see, Centurion? Though when he was telling us we were unable to comprehend his words, that's what he said he would do!"

Cornelius spoke to the soldiers. "Let's get on to the tomb, men!" He turned again to the fisherman. "Where were you going, Simon?"

"To the house of Mary of Cyprus on Mount Zion. I must bear the tidings to the others of the Master's band. I think I'll find them there."

Stories, rumors, wildly fanciful reports were racing through Jerusalem like flames sweeping a Judaean field of ripened grain. The stories varied, but the core of each was the startling assertion that the rabbi of Nazareth, that strange young Galilean of commanding presence and compelling words who on the day before the Sabbath had been crucified by the Romans, had now returned to life.

Long before the sun had set on the cavernous, twisted alleyways of ill-smelling Ophel, Jerusalem's squalid region in which was caught up in one unsavory clustering the great burden of the city's destitute and despised and sickly and abandoned souls, the thrilling tidings were flying everywhere on many an excited tongue.

Abijah the water carrier had first brought the news into Ophel. Running and leaping down the slope of Mount Moriah, his half-emptied goatskins slapping at his big-knuckled knees, he had screamed to every knot of Ophel dwellers along his way:

"He is indeed the Messiah! He has arisen from the dead! The crucified Galilean is alive again! The rabbi of Nazareth has walked forth from the rich man's tomb!"

In the square before Dung Gate he dropped his sloshing burden on the dust-thick cobbles and flailed out with skinny, blackened arms as he shouted his joy. Quickly a crowd of the curious ones gathered about him—idlers lounging in the spring sunshine, beggars, shopkeepers venturing away from their wares but with watchful eyes alert for grabbing thieves, metalworkers grimy from their bellows, tanyard laborers smelling of freshly killed hides, their strigils still grasped in blood-flecked, greasy hands.

"I tell you he's alive! The rabbi's risen from the tomb!" He swallowed a great gulp of air, exhaled it. "He's conquered death!"

"But how do you know this, Abijah?" one of the tanyard workers demanded. "Why thus arouse our hopes?"

"Yes, why lift us from our despair only to let us fall into a lower pit after we have learned that you speak words the truth of which you cannot establish?" another asked. The fellow, gaunt and shriveled, leaned on a twisted stick. "Why raise up within us a false hope, Abijah?"

"But I speak the truth!" Abijah, his breath recovered, waggled his finger in the man's face. "He healed your withered leg, Jahaz. You couldn't raise yourself off your mat until that day he restored you. I thought you called yourself one of his followers."

"I did, Abijah. I had faith in him. Like many others, I thought he was the promised Messiah of Israel." His wizened countenance clouded. "But would the glorious Messiah die on an accursed cross at the hands of Israel's enemies?"

"But he's alive *now!* He triumphed over Rome and death!"

"You continue to say it, Abijah, but how do you know? Have you seen him alive, since he was laid in the tomb?" The tanyard laborer was insistent. "Have you heard him speak?"

"No, I have not seen him, but—"

"Then cease your proclaiming that he's alive, and leave us to our grieving. Don't try to raise false hopes, Abijah. Aren't we already greatly cast down?"

"But up at the Temple I have just now seen Simon of Galilee and the younger of the Zebedees, and they gave me the tidings."

"That they had seen Jesus—alive?"

"No, but certain women, Galileans too, told them that an angel revealed—"

"Say no more, Abijah." The man from the tanyard shook his head sadly. "I knew you were but raising us up to cast us lower into the pit."

"But Simon and John said—"

"Simon. Faugh!" He thrust out his grime-covered hand in violent gesture, and his scowl was heavy. "Didn't the fisherman run when the guards laid hands on the rabbi in Gethsemane, and in the courtyard of Annas the next morning didn't he deny that he even knew him?" He lowered his tone. "Simon has lost his reason. Fright and remorse have unhinged his mind. Get you gone, Abijah, and have no more of this senseless talk."

But he did not still Abijah's tongue. Hoisting across his shoulder the carrying strap of the goatskin vessel, the water carrier went off along the way that led downward toward the Pool of Siloam, shouting with every slap of his sandals on the rough cobbles that the rabbi of Nazareth had risen from the dead.

Soon along the narrow darkened alleys and in crowded and foulsome hovels the awesome words of the water carrier were being echoed by countless lowly ones who once again were daring to hope.

The words reached likewise up the rise of Mount Zion and into the homes of the affluent and the privileged, some few of whom had counted themselves followers of the young rabbi of warming smile and comforting strong words who but a week before had come into Jerusalem to finish his mission.

Simon himself, straight from his chance meeting with Centurion Cornelius near Damascus Gate, had brought the dramatic tidings to one of these great houses on Zion, the home of Mary of Cyprus, a wealthy widow who early in his ministry had become a devoted follower of the Galilean preacher and at whose home his disciples often assembled during their visits to Jerusalem. It was in a large upper room of her house that Jesus and the twelve had gathered for the Passover meal and from there had gone across the city to the Garden of Gethsemane, where he had been arrested the night before his crucifixion.

The fisherman had found several of the Master's now disconsolate little band. From their panic of the garden experience and the subsequent execution of the leader whom they had confidently expected to see crowned Israel's mighty new David, they had slipped back into the city to grieve together at the shattering of their beautiful great dream. James ben Zebedee, brother of John, and Nathanael and Philip were there, and while Simon was revealing his startling news Matthew entered the courtyard. Matthew had left a lucrative position of tax collector in Galilee to join the Master's band.

"But you did not see him, Simon," Matthew said, when the excited fisherman paused in his recital. "And isn't Mary of Magdala given to seeing visions?" A smile trembled on his bearded face, wearied and drawn with anxiety and fear and bitter grief. "She loved the Master with a great devotion, she looked forward with such zeal to seeing him crowned Messiah and King of the new Israel, and then after all was lost and she saw him dead on the cross, she must have longed with such fervor to see him alive again that her burdened mind gave way, Simon, and she did see him restored to life—in her imagining."

Gravely James nodded his head, looked from one man to another.

"It must have been that way, Simon, though God knows I wish I could believe it was as you have related it." His countenance showed his inward turmoil, pain. "If only you yourself had seen him, my brother. If only he had shown himself to us. O God in Israel!"

James sank down on the marble bench in Mary's courtyard, braced his sweating wide forehead on the heel of his cupped palm, looked with unseeing dulled eyes at the flagstones beneath his weary feet.

Soon John ben Zebedee came, and when they had arranged with the other disciples to meet there at Mary's house for the supper meal, he and Simon set forth for the Temple in hope that they might come upon others of the Master's scattered band. There they had seen Abijah the water carrier and given him the tidings.

## THE CROWN TREE 10

But before another sun had lifted out of the desert beyond the Dead Sea, the small group of irresolute, frightened, hopelessly dejected Galileans suddenly had been transformed into men of fire and indomitable courage.

The change had taken place at the house of Mary.

What had happened there in the upper room after the evening meal quickly became the subject of a new sweep of even more incredible stories that differed in small details but were developed around one astounding assertion.

But even before the new tidings could spread downward from Zion across the Valley of the Cheesemongers to be borne with amazing speed through the maze and stench of Ophel and up Moriah to the Temple area, the story was being told in that same house by Mary herself. Early that morning she had sent her servant Amaziah with an urgent message to her friend Hannah, wife of one of the sons of Annas and sister-in-law of the wife of Caiaphas.

"Tell her to come quickly and fetch Damaris with her, but to say nothing to anyone else in the house. Nor tell her anything yourself, Amaziah, except that I have good tidings for her; I want the pleasure of observing her countenance when I reveal them."

Amaziah, like his mistress a follower of the Nazarene, had returned now with the two women. He brought them to Mary, who received them in a chamber on a level above the street, and closed the door behind them so that the talk of the three would not be overheard.

"Hannah," she said, her face alight with a great eagerness, "Jesus has arisen! He's alive again!"

"Yes, Mary, I heard the report yesterday." She was smiling, but Mary fancied she read in her friend's countenance a trace of disappointment. "We heard the story that the tomb had been found empty, and that Mary of Magdala, who had gone there with certain other Galilean women, had seen him and spoken with him. But the poor woman has been through such a fright and season of distress—"

"Hannah, Damaris," Mary interrupted, unable longer to withhold her report, "Jesus was here—in this house—last night!"

"O God in Israel! Here—Jesus—you saw him?"

"No, but all the twelve except Thomas, who wasn't here, and

of course, poor Judas. You knew that after the crucifixion he hanged himself—"

"Yes. And I heard my husband talking with Caiaphas about it. Caiaphas was pleased with the way in which they had tricked Judas into betraying his Master." Then Hannah's eyes were aflame again. "But, Mary, you say he was here and they saw him —Jesus was here!"

"He was here, of a truth. He talked with them, and they felt of the wounds in his hands and his side. And, oh, Hannah, he was hungry, and he even ate a piece of broiled fish!"

Then as calmly as she could she related what had happened the night before. The ten Galileans, assembled together for the first time since the frightful experience in Gethsemane, had eaten the evening meal in silence. When they had finished, still sorrowful and greatly depressed despite the report brought by Mary of Magdala and Simon and John ben Zebedee, they had gone up the outside stone stairway to the rooftop's upper room, and barred the door behind them.

"What I learned concerning the things that happened after they had shut themselves in the chamber was told me afterward by the Galileans themselves, who appeared on fire with excitement and a consuming zest," Mary hastened to explain. "I know they couldn't have been telling anything but the truth."

After they had been in the chamber a short while, she went on, Cleopas and another man came to the house and asked for them. Amaziah led them up the stairway and after they had knocked for admission, the door was opened and they went in.

"They told the men that as they had been walking that afternoon on the road to Emmaus they had been joined by a stranger who walked with them into the village, and then they besought him to remain with them for the evening meal.

" 'Soon it will be getting dark,' they said to him. 'Stop therefore with us at the inn.'

"He agreed and they sat down to an early supper. As they had walked along they had told him of the crucifixion of their beloved Master and he in turn had shown them how the Scriptures taught that the Christ would be offered up in that manner. Now as they prepared to eat they felt that they had known this stranger, and as he asked the blessing and broke the bread, they suddenly recognized him." Mary's eyes were ablaze. "Hannah, the stranger was Jesus himself!"

"That's what Cleopas told them?"

"Yes, the very words. Simon and several of the others told it to me." Her countenance glowed. "But there is more, much more, to relate, Hannah. What I have told is but a small part of the report.

"While they were talking among themselves and questioning the two, and wondering how such a thing could have been, suddenly Jesus was there in the chamber with them!

" 'Peace be to you, my brothers!' he said to them.

"They were frightened almost out of their wits, for they thought they were seeing an apparition. But he talked with them and gently chided them for their lack of faith in him and their refusal to believe the reports that he had arisen.

" 'Why are you afraid?' he asked them. 'I'm no ghost. Feel my hands. Put your fingers in the holes where the spikes were driven. See the holes in my feet.' He pulled back his robe. 'Behold the wound from the centurion's spear. A ghost has no body.'

"But they still seemed fearful and unconvinced that it was Jesus. Then he said a simple thing.

" 'I'm hungry,' he told them. 'Have you anything here to eat?'

"They brought some honeycomb and a piece of broiled fish left from their supper, and he ate it right there before them. That convinced them, Hannah. They knew he was no apparition conjured up out of their great distress and fervent hoping. Suddenly they were overwhelmed with a great joy. Today they're new men, Hannah; they're on fire to conquer the world for the Master."

The startling report that the crucified Nazarene had come from the tomb on the day after the Passover Sabbath quickly reached the alert ears of High Priest Caiaphas and old Annas, his crafty father-in-law, the former High Priest. And before they could devise a scheme for refuting the dangerous story, other tidings even more amazing reached the Temple. This Jesus, it was being proclaimed throughout Jerusalem, had reappeared bodily to the members of his band of Galileans. Now with even greater fervor these fanatics were declaring that he had established his claim to be the Messiah of God.

"This story must be refuted, and quickly," Annas declared. "Else shortly it will spread throughout all Israel." He pondered, his fat jeweled hand stroking the luxuriant growth of his heavily oiled beard. Then his little eyes danced and he pursed his thick red lips. "We must twist it into a humorous account, with the Romans the butt of our laughing. And I think I know how to accomplish it."

So emissaries of the High Priest were sent to talk with several of the guards who had been at the tomb, and they carried a pouch laden with golden coins. Later a story began to be circulated that the guards had fallen asleep at their posts and while they slept certain friends of the crucified Galilean rolled back the stone and stole away with the dead body. And some among the Jews, supporters of the Temple hierarchy, believed it. But throughout Ophel and in several great houses on Mount Zion countless others shook their heads and called the purported confession a fabrication of the Temple leadership.

From one of these houses several days later Hannah and her daughter Damaris came to Mary's home to say farewell before departing the next day for Joppa, where they planned to take a ship sailing for Cyprus. On the island they would visit relatives and friends of the two families, for Hannah, like Mary, was a native of Cyprus.

When they had chatted a few moments and Mary had given her friend messages to bear to certain beloved ones there, the daughter of the House of Annas, her countenance alight, her voice eager, could restrain no longer her question:

"Mary, have you had any other reports concerning the Lord Jesus?"

Now Mary's eyes flamed and her tone quickened.

"Yes, he has met again with them, this time with all eleven, and now even Thomas knows he has arisen in the flesh. They are going down to Galilee, where he told them he would meet them shortly. Simon himself related to me what transpired. He said that as they talked together during his first appearance to them the Holy Spirit settled upon them and they became as new men. Jesus told them he was bestowing upon them the power to live spiritually and was commissioning them to represent him on earth.

" 'Those who receive your message,' he said to them, 'shall be set at liberty from their sins, but those who receive it not shall continue under the burden of their guilt.'

"I hardly understood the meaning of these words that Simon reported, but this I do know, Hannah, that whereas a week ago those Galileans were wretched and fearful and like wax in the summer's sun, they are now suddenly become men of fire and stone."

At Joppa Hannah and her daughter had the good fortune to find the Alexandrian grain ship *Pharos* loading and almost ready to sail for Cyprus. They had landed at Paphos and were visiting in the home of a cousin there when reports began to be brought to Jerusalem that the young Nazarene crucified on Skull Hill at the end of the Passover season had met repeatedly with his Galilean disciples in the region of Capernaum and on one occasion had even shown them where to cast their nets in order to catch a great haul of fish. At another time, it was told, he appeared to a multitude of some five hundred persons.

And then of a sudden, Simon, the Zebedee brothers, and others of the eleven were seen in the courts of the Temple and at the Synagogue of the Libertines; and over Jerusalem among the followers of the Nazarene sped the story that Jesus had returned.

Abijah the water carrier was one of the first to hear it. "He is the deliverer indeed!" he shouted along the alleys and into the dark dives of Ophel. "Shortly he will declare himself the new David, call down ten legions of angels, and drive from the land the Roman despot!"

But no trumpets sounded and no angels descended from the calm skies above Jerusalem, and on an afternoon in mid-May the eleven came again to the home of Mary of Cyprus.

"He has gone," Simon said to Mary as the others started up the stone stairway to the upper room.

"Back to Galilee, Simon?"

The grizzled fisherman of Capernaum shook his head.

"No, he has returned to the Father."

"I don't understand." A shadow crossed her puzzled countenance. "He isn't dead?"

"No. He has ascended. But have no fear, Mary. He will return. He promised us."

Still she could not comprehend.

"I don't understand either, my sister," he said gently. "I only know what he said to us, and what I saw. Of late we have been much with him, and he has sought diligently to teach us how we are to proclaim to all the world, beginning here in Jerusalem, that through him men can be saved to new lives and freedom from the domination of sin.

" 'You are witnesses of what has happened,' he told us; 'therefore go you out into the world and tell the good news to everybody. And I will be with you at all times, even unto the end of the world.'

"When he had finished his instructions and had commissioned us as his agents to spread forth his good news, he led us out once again through Dung Gate and beyond Gethsemane over the crest of the Mount of Olives. There he stopped, and raising his hands, gave us his blessing; and as we stood looking, awed and speech-less, he arose into the air and moved upward into the heavens until he was lost from our sight. Now we have returned here, where he was so often with us"—he pointed toward the rooftop chamber—"to spend a season in prayer to God."

His eyes aglow beneath the tangle of his splayed eyebrows, Simon of Capernaum turned away and mounted the stairs to join the ten.

## THE CROWN TREE 12

But of this latest report concerning the mysterious Galilean whom he had crucified, Longinus in Rome naturally had heard nothing. Nevertheless, he had been unable to dismiss from his thoughts the courageous and forgiving tall young man who on an unforgettable sultry afternoon at Jerusalem had died—was it at the thrust of his spear?—that most agonizing of deaths.

Now crafty and unscrupulous Sejanus without knowing it had brought the crucified man once more into the forefront of the centurion's wondering. Crossing busy Rome from the Prefect's palace to his father's home, Longinus threaded the narrow, heavily traveled streets and began the ascent of the Esquiline. Noticing no one he passed, paying little heed to any of the famil-iar memorials and statues along the way, the centurion in retro-spection was seeing only the sinister Hill of the Skull and a man impaled on a cross.

He had left him dead as he descended the slope that day to report to Pontius Pilate. "By all the gods, I know he was dead!" Yet Cornelius had reported that the Galilean had told his fol-lowers he would arise from death, and on the ship the girl had declared that he had carried out his vow. But how can a man raise himself out of death? They had said he was a god. And can a god be also a man? But are not gods only the fanciful imaginings of men? And I know he was a man, and I *know* he died.

Whether that Jesus was god or man or both, Longinus realized, the Prefect was bent on returning him to the wretched little province in which Jesus had lived his short years and died a horrible death. In returning to Palestine, would he find himself confronted by a resurrected dead man, perhaps now vengeful even though while dying he was forgiving? But after all, how, by the gods, can a dead man come to life?

Senator Varro was resting in the peristylium when his son returned from the palace of Prefect Sejanus.

He saw immediately that Longinus was dispirited, sensed a mood perhaps of apprehension.

"You didn't get along well with the Prefect?" he asked.

"He was pleasant enough," Longinus answered. "But, well, Father—" He shrugged. "I'm not going back to Palestine. I'll resign from the army." Calmly then he related what had been said in his audience with the Prefect.

When he was finished, his father eyed him a long moment before he spoke.

"Sejanus wouldn't accept your resignation, son," he said. "On the contrary, he would be furious with you, and he might even attempt reprisals against me, thinking perhaps that I had counseled it. The Emperor, too, might be angered. No, Longinus, the thing to do is to go out to Palestine and make the best of the opportunities this new assignment will provide. After all, it could be the means of your making quickly a sizable fortune. And as I said the other day, after a short stay in that province you might be transferred to Rome again, and always there's a chance that Tiberius will replace Sejanus."

Longinus accepted his father's counsel, though with misgivings, and three days later he obtained passage aboard a merchant vessel leaving the Sublicius Bridge wharf in two days. But he looked forward with no enthusiasm to the long voyage eastward.

Before embarking, he decided, he would visit Senator Flaccus and inquire if he might carry a message from him to Cornelius.

So this afternoon he crossed from the Esqueline over to Quirinal Hill.

A servant admitted him into the atrium, politely indicated a chair, and went to summon his master. But before Longinus could sit down, a girl came out from behind a large flowering shrub in the peristylium and advanced toward him.

"Longinus, I'm so glad to see you!"

"Lalage! By Jupiter, I hardly knew you! You've—you've—"

"Grown up!" She laughed gaily. "You've been away in Palestine a long time, Longinus."

"Yes, I suppose so," he said, his eyes intent, appraising. "It's not that you weren't beautiful when I left, Lalage, but now you're so—so—"

"Developed, maybe?"

He laughed, caught her hands in his, pulled her close.

"Yes, developed into a stunningly beautiful creature, Lalage." He pushed her away at arm's length, studied her. Slowly he shook his head, frowned, shrugged. "And married. By all the gods, Lalage, I stayed too long in Palestine." Then he smiled. "How's Publius, the fortunate fellow? Senator Flaccus told me the other day you two were visiting a friend at Misenum. Is Publius also back in Rome?"

"No, I left him there two days ago and came home." She tossed her chin up in a pretended pout. "We had a quarrel. We've had them before, but this one was bad, Longinus, terrible. Publius is so demanding." Then she smiled. "But Father said Senator Varro told him only this morning that you are being sent back to Palestine and you aren't happy about it."

"That's true, Lalage. I came to see if your father had a message to send Cornelius. I'll likely see him before I've been back there long."

"Father's gone out—down to the Forum, I believe. Philo's probably searching for him now; he didn't know he had just left. Let's go sit in the peristylium before the fountain, Longinus. Father should be here shortly."

At that moment the servant returned, bowed. "The master has

left the house, sir, and no one seems to know where he went. But soon he will return for dinner. Perhaps, sir, you will stay—"

"Yes, Longinus," Lalage interrupted Philo, "stay with us for dinner. Then afterwards we can talk and you can tell me all about Palestine and your experiences there."

"No, I thank you, Lalage, but I must go home and get my packing done." He grinned. "Some of my pouches, in fact, haven't been unpacked since the journey home. Perhaps, though, I'll see you again before I sail day after tomorrow."

"Longinus," she said, edging nearer, "I'm unhappy too that you're leaving Rome. I'd thought that maybe—" But she broke off, smiling coyly. "Please come back to see me before you sail."

He didn't. But that night he dreamed again. Not this time of the Galilean, smiling down upon him sadly from the cross, but of the girl, tall and slender, her dark hair piled high, her lips red and pert, standing enticingly before him in a white silken stola bound at the narrow waist by a securely laced golden girdle.

## THE CROWN TREE 13

With Centurion Longinus aboard, the Egyptian merchant ship *Ptolemy* slid away from the wharf and nosed out into the current of the muddy Tiber. By nightfall the vessel had cleared the harbor of Ostia and was edging slowly southward along the coast of Italy. Two days later it put in at Puteoli, where it was tied up another day for unloading and taking on merchandise and a few passengers.

Longinus was already beginning to tire of the sea when more than a week later the *Ptolemy* entered the harbor of Syracuse on the eastern shore of Sicily after having paused for a day at Rhegium in the narrow strait between the island and the Italian peninsula. But from Puteoli the movement of the vessel had been almost due southward and when it sailed from Syracuse directly eastward the voyage had hardly begun.

Poor winds slowed the long crossing of the Ionian Sea, and when the *Ptolemy* at length came in sight of the southern tip of one of the promontories of Peloponnesus the centurion would have been willing to go ashore anywhere, even in Palestine, still almost a thousand miles eastward. But the island-studded Aegean Sea had yet to be crossed and stops were to be made at Cnidus and Rhodes and at Patara on the southern coast of Lycia.

Longinus had made no friends and few acquaintances aboard the *Ptolemy*. He was the only Roman army officer on the vessel, he discovered shortly after leaving Rome, and none came aboard from stations in any of the provinces whose port cities the ship had visited. Many of the passengers were Egyptians, business men and a few students, returning to Alexandria from Rome. Some were Jewish tradesmen on their way to Palestine, and boasting of their clever business dealings abroad. Others were olive-skinned, black-haired Syrians with chattering tongues and dancing black eyes, some from Antioch and the coastal regions, others from the desert country beyond Damascus. And on the *Ptolemy*, as aboard every ship sailing those waters, were Greeks—merchants, artists, students.

But though in a personal way the centurion had little association with the other passengers, in the long weeks they had been together on the *Ptolemy* he had come to know their faces, and he was quick to spot a new passenger once the man had come aboard. Sometimes he had stood at the rail and watched as relatives and friends from the pier had screamed and waved affectionate, frantic farewells. Earlier today he had seen two young Jews enter the ship just before it sailed out of Paphos.

Now the *Ptolemy* was sailing easily before a fair wind south of the island. Longinus sat in the stern and watched the water boiling white and frenzied in the vessel's wake. Suddenly he thought of the girl he had seen standing at the rail of the *Pharos* that day as the ship neared Paphos. She was on her way to visit relatives on Cyprus. He wondered if she had returned, perhaps long before now, to her home in Jerusalem. And he recalled with what horror and revulsion the girl had hurried away when she

discovered that he had been in charge of the Nazarene's crucifixion.

A long shadow stabbed at his feet and he looked up. The two
Jews who had boarded the *Ptolemy* at Paphos had paused almost
at his side.

"Peace be unto you!" the taller one said, and the short one,
nodding, gave a similar greeting.

"Unto you be peace!" Longinus responded, smiling.

"We were going to the rail at the stern and didn't see you
until we had almost stepped on you, and—" Abruptly he paused,
and his face lighted warmly. "But you a Roman return the
greeting of Israel as an Israelite would!"

"I'm well acquainted with the manners of the Jews." Longinus
laughed. "I've lived a long time among them." He stood up.
"I am Longinus Aemilius Varro, centurion in the Second Italian
Cohort."

"I am called Joseph Barnabas. I come from Cyprus," the taller
said, bowing, "and this my new friend is Saul of Tarsus."

The youth from Tarsus, though small of frame, was strongly
built, apparently, with sturdy shoulders and a good chest. But
his short robe revealed well-muscled legs noticeably bowed, perhaps from soft bones in his early years. One eyelid drooped, and
the centurion wondered if the eye were sightless or nearly so;
but the other eye seemed to have taken unto itself the strength
of both, for it was sharp and flashing as though from an inner
fire. His heavy eyebrows, black and profuse and almost meeting
above his large nose, emphasized the sparseness of hair receding
from the high dome of his forehead.

Saul bowed and smiled, and the smile so transformed him that
instantly Longinus sensed a magnetism and a power in the young
man that gave him new stature and presence.

"Centurion, did you serve at Caesarea?" he asked.

"Yes." Longinus evidenced his surprise at the question. "But
how did you happen to name Caesarea?"

"I knew that one of the maniples of the Second Italian Cohort
under Pontius Pilate was stationed there."

Barnabas laughed. "My new friend is well informed about the Romans. He's a Roman citizen, in fact."

"But I thought you were Jewish."

"I am, and proud of it," Saul answered. "My father is of the tribe of Benjamin and a Pharisee of the Pharisees. But being a citizen of the free city of Tarsus, I am likewise a citizen of Rome."

Longinus turned to Barnabas.

"You call him your new friend. But you seem to know much about him."

"We've known each other less than a week. But in that time we have talked much. We met at the wharf at Paphos. He was coming ashore from the ship that had brought him from Seleucia after he had come there from Tarsus. I was there to see to obtaining passage to Joppa. I discovered that he, too, was on his way to Jerusalem to study under Rabban Gamaliel. So I took him home with me to await the arrival of the *Ptolemy*. And now"—he gestured with expressive hands—"we're soon to be fellow pupils of the great teacher."

Longinus stepped over to the rail, leaned against it, quizzically regarded the taller Barnabas.

"My asking this question may be foolish," he said, "but as I was returning to Rome some time ago I happened on a very beautiful Jewish young woman who was standing on the deck as we approached the harbor of Paphos, where she and her mother went ashore. I can't recall her name at the moment, but she said she was the granddaughter of the High Priest Annas. I wonder if by any chance you might have met her or heard—"

But already Barnabas was beaming.

"Damaris and her mother Hannah," he interrupted. "Several weeks ago they sailed from Cyprus to return to Jerusalem. Yes, I saw them often. They were good friends of my cousin Mary who lives at Jerusalem. I expect to visit them as soon as I get there. Damaris and I—" Abruptly he paused. "Then you're the centurion she told me about, the one who—" He stopped, his face suddenly serious.

Longinus nodded. "But it was a duty I did not relish."

Saul's good eye was questioning Barnabas. The taller youth nodded.

"Crucifixion is savage, barbarous," Saul declared. "I would not defend Rome." He was looking at Longinus. "But if any crime deserves such a death, it's that of a man making himself equal with God."

For a moment no one spoke. Then Longinus turned to Barnabas. "Did the girl tell you that the Nazarene arose from death and walked out of the tomb?"

"Yes. And her mother did too. They said the man's followers met with him at Mary's house, and that the stories of his resurrection were sweeping Jerusalem."

"Lies! Lies! Blasphemy!" Saul's wide-open eye was blazing, and the lid of the half-closed one twitched. "Curse them, God in Israel!"

Saul turned and spat over the rail into the sea.

## THE CROWN TREE 14

A freshening wind in the night sped the *Ptolemy* toward Palestine at the eastern rim of the Great Sea, and late the next afternoon as Longinus stood at the starboard forward rail the lowering sun at his back lighted the rounded barren crown of Mount Carmel lifting straight ahead out of the sea.

Just to the left of Carmel would be the harbor of Ptolemais, he knew, and on beyond it on the side of a hill the village of Nazareth and beyond Nazareth the little Sea of Galilee.

His hands clutching the rail, his eyes staring at the sun-dappled mountain edging up from the water, Longinus caught himself trying to discover on its summit three crosses.

"No, by all the gods!" With open palm he smote the rail. "That is finished—and forgot!" Turning his back to the coastline rising ahead, he strode from the deck.

The next morning the vessel entered the breakwater of the harbor and in another hour he stood with his baggage on the wharf of Ptolemais. He hadn't seen the tall Jew Joseph Barnabas and his strange-looking small companion since they had talked two days ago on the deck. He was wondering if he would ever chance on them again, when he saw them coming toward him along the wharf.

Seeing him, they stopped.

"Centurion, you must have reasoned as we did. We thought it would be a good plan to give our legs a stretch on land." Then Barnabas saw the piled baggage. "You are leaving the ship here? We thought you were returning to Caesarea."

"No, I have a new assignment—to command the troops here at Ptolemais."

"Under Pilate?"

Saul blinked his drooping eyelid. "You'll be under the command of Proconsul Petronius, who's stationed at Antioch, won't you, Centurion?"

"Yes." Longinus smiled. "You do know much about the Romans."

They stood and talked with him until the porters were ready to move his baggage.

"I must be going," he said, smiling. "A pleasant voyage." He was turning to direct one of the porters. "I was about to forget," he said quickly, as he faced about. "I have a good friend at Jerusalem. He's the Centurion Cornelius. He was formerly stationed at Capernaum, where he was very friendly with the Jews, even contributed money to their synagogue. You may chance on him. Should you do so, please tell him I have been sent back to Palestine and hope to see him before many weeks."

"He's stationed there with the army, Centurion?"

"Yes, at the Fortress Antonia."

"We'll go to see him, and bear your message. I recall that Hannah spoke of the Centurion Cornelius, who was known to her through some of the followers of the Nazarene."

Saul scowled, but said nothing.

Longinus bowed. "Thank you. And a good voyage the re-
mainder of the way. Farewell."

"Farewell, and the God of Israel protect you."

Now the smaller man bowed.

"Farewell, Centurion."

## THE CROWN TREE 15

Before she and her daughter had rested from their long voyage
home, Hannah called in her servant Hadrach.

"Tell us how it has been going with the followers of the
Nazarene while we've been away, Hadrach. Do they still insist
that he has arisen, or have Simon and the Zebedees and the others
lost heart and gone back to their Galilee fishing?"

"No, Mistress, they haven't lost heart. On the contrary, they've
become men of great boldness. They declare with even more assurance that Jesus is Israel's Messiah and the one through whom
Israel's salvation will be achieved. They preach it at the Temple,
in the Synagogue of the Libertines—wherever they find people
who will listen."

At the Feast of the Pentecost, Hadrach went on to reveal, under
the power of Simon's preaching a great multitude—some insisted
as many as three thousand people—had professed their faith in
the risen Jesus and joined the rapidly increasing fellowship of
the Nazarene's followers. In that throng had been people from
the lands rimming the eastern shores of the Great Sea—Parthians,
Mesopotamians, natives of Phrygia and Pamphylia and Egypt
and Cyrene, Greeks, even Romans. Upon these people of many
tongues and customs the Holy Spirit that day had descended,
Hannah's servant declared.

The next day Hannah was given a similar report by her friend
Mary of Cyprus. The apostles, twelve again now that Matthias
had been named in the place of Judas of Kiriot, came often to

the house on Mount Zion, where with Jesus they had eaten the last meal before his death. Here in her house, Mary told Hannah, they said he seemed close to them; in the upper chamber they felt they could almost see him and touch him, and hear his warmly comforting words.

But also to her house, Mary revealed, came many others. The hungry and the naked, the distressed and the afflicted, swarmed up the slope from Ophel, for the growing fellowship still had its greatest strength in the regions of Jerusalem where the poorer people lived.

In the days of his short ministry, for the harried and driven and often hopeless dwellers in Ophel the teachings of Jesus, emphasizing as they did the all-encompassing love of God the Father and the brotherhood of all men His children, had been cheering and greatly consoling. Many of them had listened to these magnetic words as Jesus himself had spoken them; now that he had ascended they were listening with a new eagerness to the compelling words of Simon and others of the Twelve and such new leaders as young Stephen the goldsmith, who lately had been named one of seven deacons to see to the temporal needs of the growing fellowship.

"But they come also to eat, Hannah," Mary observed, "for at every sunset food is put on the tables in the courtyard, and none leaves with stomach not satisfied. There are even some among the more affluent in the fellowship who have sold their property and given the money to the deacons that it may be used to buy food and clothing for the destitute. These see no need for putting by a little money, because they look daily for the Master's return. I fear that some will come to want."

Her countenance suddenly serious, she looked out over the descending rooftops toward the spiraling, drifting smoke from the fires of Hinnom beyond Jerusalem's south wall. Then quickly she smiled again, faced her friend on the terrace beside her.

"But not all the followers of Jesus are from the poor and downtrodden out there"—she swept out her arm in the direction of Ophel—"or the fisherfolk of Galilee. You remember, of course, that Rabbi Nicodemus and Joseph of Arimathaea were his friends, and since his resurrection and departure from us there have been others among the city's rich and powerful and highly esteemed who have entered our fellowship, quite a number of them, of course, secretly."

But while the new fellowship of Jesus of Nazareth was growing and spreading even beyond Judaea and Galilee, Hannah was soon to learn that under the wily scheming of her father-in-law Annas its enemies were laying plans to destroy forever what they held to be a blaspheming, heretical sect. Nor was anyone in Jerusalem better placed than Hannah to keep informed of these plottings of the Temple leadership, since often she and her daughter were in the homes of Annas and Caiaphas, who apparently had never suspected that they were members of the crucified Nazarene's mad band.

So in the months that followed their return from Cyprus, Hannah and Damaris began to hear mentioned the name of a strange, intense young man they had met one day on the island in the company of Joseph Barnabas, cousin of Mary. This youth, a native of Tarsus, had come with Barnabas to Jerusalem and enrolled as a pupil of the brilliant and benign Rabban Gamaliel, Israel's wisest and most esteemed teacher of the law. One afternoon at the house of her father-in-law Hannah had overheard him talking with Caiaphas. They were discussing Saul; she had caught the name.

"We must use him to advantage," she heard old Annas declare. "He's a young man of boundless energy, and he is passionately devoted to upholding scrupulously the law of Israel. We should find for him some important task in combatting this heretical sect, which if we don't soon destroy may even drive us from the Temple."

"Yes, Saul's a fanatic," Caiaphas agreed. "And he is fearless. He is likewise a student of the law. We should use him."

Later at Mary's house she had spoken of Saul to Barnabas, who was making his home there.

"I love him like a brother," Barnabas told her. "Saul loves

Israel and Israel's God with a great passion. He walks with an utter fearlessness what he believes with all his soul is the right path." Slowly he shook his head. "But I have been unable to get his consent even to listen to my presentation of Jesus as the Messiah of Israel. He only rages, and his anger boils within him." Barnabas' countenance was sad. "He no longer comes to this house. We sit no more together before the bench of Rabban Gamaliel. I am greatly distressed for Saul, but he has a will of iron."

Then one day as he looked along the stone seats before Gamaliel, Barnabas saw that Saul had not come to hear the discourse of the master. Nor was he there the next day, or the next. Several days later Barnabas summoned up courage to speak to the rabban about his friend's continued absence from the lectures. Could Saul be ill?

"No, my son, Saul is not sick in the body. I have inquired. His views are no longer in accord with my reasoning." The gentle old man stroked with thin, gnarled fingers the white screen of his long whiskers. "The pupil has dismissed his rabbi. Saul has a remarkably brilliant mind: his brain is the storehouse of a great wealth of knowledge, and it reasons with an amazing clarity. But it is a coldly reasoning instrument upon which God has not yet laid His warming finger. Let us pray that He does so, and speedily."

Saul did not return to the lectures of Rabban Gamaliel. Nor did he visit Barnabas at Mary's house. The man of Tarsus had disappeared. But from time to time word came that he had been seen disputing angrily with certain ones of the fellowship of the Nazarene who had been emboldened to speak out in the courts of the Temple or other places where the devout of Israel were accustomed to assemble.

Barnabas learned also from Damaris, in whom his interest had been growing steadily since the day he met her on Cyprus, that Saul had been closeted on several occasions with Annas and Caiaphas.

But several weeks later he got a glimpse of Saul. He and Simon had gone that afternoon to the Synagogue of the Libertines, for they had learned that Stephen, the first of the deacons, was to expound his belief that the crucified and risen Jesus of Nazareth was indeed the Messiah of Israel sent by Israel's God in fulfillment of the ancient prophecies.

From where they had taken their place near the entrance Barnabas early spotted the short, slender man of Tarsus, who leaned out from the right wall near the rear of the synagogue in a menacing crouch as though any moment he might spring into the aisle and go leaping with flailing arms toward Stephen, who in black prayer mantle was addressing earnestly the thoughtful congregation. But because of the press of worshipers, Barnabas could not approach Saul, and soon he had lost sight of him.

And before the week was ended Barnabas had set out with Simon and the two Zebedees on a journey down into Galilee.

## THE CROWN TREE 16

Centurion Longinus quickly discovered that Ptolemais, though on the coast of Galilee, was, like most port cities of Palestine and Phoenicia, more Greek than Jewish. But within its walls were many other peoples, men of different races, colors, and religions. Desert dwellers of Syria, Egyptians, workers lately from the copper mines of Cyprus, tradesmen from Antioch, freemen and slaves, rich men and vagrants, sailors in port from long voyages, a motley multitude had been sucked into the ancient port city to throng its narrow streets and elbow their ways into its grimy waterfront inns and brothels.

Ptolemais reminded Longinus of Caesarea. He was thankful it was more like that coast city than like Jerusalem. Its wharves and market places were alive from early morning until past sunset with the incessant chatter of its cosmopolitan population, but the Greek language in its many dialects was heard more often than the Aramaic of the Galilean countryside or the teeming tenements of Jerusalem's Ophel.

From the moment of his coming ashore from the *Ptolemy* he had been busily engaged. No one had met him that day at the wharf; he presumed that the orders from Sejanus placing him in command of the garrison there had not been received. So he had engaged three Syrian porters to carry his baggage up from the harbor to the square stone fort, and had gone ahead of them.

The minute he entered the high-walled courtyard of the fort Longinus saw that much work awaited his taking over the command, for immediately it was evident to him that the physical properties had deteriorated and that discipline and morale had slackened. The walls were yellowed and soiled and in need of whitewashing; the doors to the frowning, squat building and the heavy shutters on the windows had gone too long without a fresh coat of paint; the grass in the plots at each side of the main entrance appeared not to have been cut in weeks, and the shrubbery was untrimmed.

Orders had been received at the fort from Prefect Sejanus, Longinus learned on arriving, but they had transferred the commander at once to another post and he had left in charge a soldier who had been unable or not eager to administer properly the duties of his new assignment. So for the first week the centurion was busily engaged in restoring the garrison to the appearance and proficiency of the usual Roman provincial outpost.

Then he had gone down the coast a few miles to the sandfields at the mouth of the Belus River to inspect the glassworks confiscated from the estate of the slain Chionides.

He had found the manufacturing plant in operation, but operating inefficiently and producing glass of inferior quality. When he had asked one of the overseers, a red-necked leathery leering fellow, what had caused the evident deterioration in the plant's work, the man had replied with a growl that there was no longer anyone to direct it.

"Where is the man who formerly operated it?" the centurion asked.

"That's what we'd like to ask you, soldier. That's what we'd like to know ourselves. We've had many reports, but which can we believe? He's gone; that's all we know. And he's been gone a long time. Nor will these works ever be run to advantage, I'm thinking, until he comes back."

"Who was he? What's his name?"

"His name is Galenus. His father was a Greek named Chionides, a rich man who lived in Thessalonica. Galenus went home to visit his father—that was months ago, soldier—and he hasn't come back. And the works have suffered much for his having been away so long."

The centurion did not reveal what he knew. Instead he pursued his questioning. "But why haven't you been able to keep the glassworks operating efficiently during his absence?"

The overseer's lips curled with sarcasm.

"Because none of us has the brains of Galenus, soldier. In the first place, we can't turn out good glass the way Galenus could, and when it's not good we can't sell it as well and for as good prices, and when we can't get the money we can't buy enough food for the slaves, and when they get weak from empty bellies they soon die and there's none coming to replace them." He shrugged. "Can't you understand that, soldier?"

Longinus might have been angered at the fellow's insolence, but he laughed instead.

"You've made it very clear, overseer. What's your name, and where do you come from?"

"Rufus. From Bithynia." He looked the centurion in the eyes. "What's yours?"

Longinus was startled at the fellow's brashness, but he answered calmly. "Longinus. From Rome. I'm a centurion. You must be a friend of this Galenus."

"I'm his slave. But he treated me like a friend." He swept his arm in an arc that embraced the glassworks. "He treated all of us right. That's why the business prospered, soldier."

"And that's why you, even though you're his slave, have been trying to keep the plant producing while he's away?"

The overseer nodded. "That's the reason."

"Rufus"—the centurion's expression was serious but his eyes had warmed—"I've been sent here by the Prefect Sejanus, the man who acts for the Emperor Tiberius, to operate the properties of the merchant Chionides. Your master Galenus may return some day, or he may not; I don't know. But while I'm running this plant I'll expect you to obey me as you did Galenus. The Prefect will demand good production." He paused, looked the overseer in the eyes. "If you aren't telling me the truth, I'll shortly discover it."

"What I have told you is the truth, soldier."

"Good. Then these are my orders to you. You say the slaves are weak and hungry. Stop the plant at once; keep on duty only enough men to see that the furnace fires don't go out; release the others from their tasks, and allow them to remain at rest all day tomorrow. You'll go with me back to Ptolemais and we'll purchase ample food and medicines, and when we return you'll see that they are all well fed and their disorders treated. Tomorrow those who are too old or otherwise not able to work longer you will free, and send them on their way if they wish to go. Soon we will have fit slaves to replace them, and then we can begin making good glass."

The overseer for a short moment studied the centurion. Then he spoke.

"You can trust me, soldier; you won't be disappointed. Already you're beginning to remind me of my master."

## THE CROWN TREE 17

The next few weeks were feverishly busy ones for Longinus. Each of the three major assignments he had been given by Prefect Sejanus could well have consumed his full time, for administration of the fort had grown lax and both the glassworks at the River Belus and the textile and dyeing plants up the coast toward Tyre had almost ceased to operate.

Two days after his visit to the glass manufactory he had made a quick survey of conditions at the textile mill. He found that operations there were being directed very inefficiently by two men who apparently had served well under the supervision of the son of Chionides, the same Galenus of whom the slave overseer Rufus had spoken with such respect and esteem. But he was pleased to discover that the slaves were generally in much better condition than those employed at the glassworks, mainly because the work in the textile and dyeing sheds was far less rigorous than laboring beside the roaring furnaces of the glassblowers.

Hardly ten days later a vessel loaded with slaves sent by Sejanus had sailed into the harbor of Tyre. The Prefect with promptness was fulfilling his promise to provide adequate workers to sweat out their lives in the confiscated plants; with equal promptness, Longinus was quite certain, he would demand efficient and highly profitable operation of these enterprises. So he saw to it immediately that the slaves were unloaded, examined and given medical treatment if needed, classified, and assigned to their new tasks, most of them to the glassworks.

But each day before leaving the fort to visit the plants the centurion had posted the day's schedule for the garrison and had given his subordinate officers strict and detailed instructions for enforcing it. This morning he was completing his orders for the day when his orderly entered and saluted.

"A visitor to see you, Centurion."

"I wonder—" Instinctively he frowned, for he was anxious to leave in a few minutes for the textile plant. But he arose and followed the orderly to the door.

"Cornelius!" He embraced his friend warmly. "Man, I'm glad to see you." He stood back, beaming. "But how do you happen to be in Ptolemais? I thought you were stuck with the Jews in Jerusalem." He led Cornelius into the room, pointed to a chair. "Sit down, and tell me the news."

"I came to see you, Longinus. That's the only business I've

got here. I was at Capernaum and decided I'd run over to Ptolemais and see how things were going with you."

"I'm glad you did. I've been wondering how you were doing. But, say, what's happening at Capernaum?"

"Nothing of consequence, Longinus." Cornelius grinned. "It's little more than a leave. I inveigled the commander at Antonia into sending me down there to brief my successor on a few more or less routine problems; that's all."

"But how'd you know I was here, Centurion?"

"You're an important man; you're one of the favorites of the Prefect. We have to make it our business to keep up with you, Centurion." Cornelius was grinning. "We have our spies, you know, our informers." But quickly he dropped the banter. "Longinus, don't you remember meeting two young Jews who came aboard your ship at Paphos as you were coming out from Rome?"

"Oh, yes, I understand now. I remember I told them you were at Antonia and to give you my greetings."

"They did. And also a week ago I had a letter from Lalage; she said you'd been sent back to Palestine to have charge of the garrison here."

Longinus shrugged. "Thanks to Sejanus, the old reprobate." Quickly he revealed the Prefect's scheme for turning to his own advantage the tragedy that had overtaken the Greek merchant and his family. "Now I'm commander of this fort, but my principal duty is to operate for Sejanus the Greek's properties confiscated by our government, impartial administrator of justice for the world. Ha!"

He sat back in his chair, his countenance sobering, for his outburst suddenly had called to mind something else.

"Cornelius, on the ship going over one day on the deck I saw a young Jewish girl from Jerusalem; she told me that the day after I left there the Galilean we crucified came to life and walked out of the tomb. She told me he came to her mother's house and met with several of his band. You've been in Jerusalem most of the time since then. Tell me, how did she ever contrive such a story?"

Cornelius looked the centurion full in the eyes.

"She didn't contrive it, Longinus; he did come to life."

"By all the gods!" Longinus leaned forward, his eyes ablaze. "Cornelius, you mean *you* believe that fantastic story? *Why?*"

Cornelius' expression was thoughtful, his reply deliberate.

"It is fantastic, Longinus, the most utterly fantastic experience I've ever had. But I can't *disbelieve* it."

"Experience? What do you mean, Cornelius?"

"I almost saw him myself. I got to the tomb shortly after he left it. I talked with the guards I'd left there the night before— I'd been put in command of the guard detail—and they swore the Nazarene left the tomb himself, that nobody disturbed it."

Then in calm, dispassionate manner he related in detail what had occurred that morning after the Jewish Sabbath, his subsequent conversations with Simon, the Capernaum fisherman, and the Zebedee brothers, whom he had also known well during the period he was in command of the Roman garrison in that city.

"But those fishermen were his friends, members of his band; they were so distressed at his death that they must have grabbed at his promise to arise and in their mental stress fancied they'd actually seen him."

Cornelius shook his head. "I don't think so. Those fishermen are pretty rugged fellows, not likely to be having wild fancies, I'd say." He leaned forward. "But it's not so much what they've told me and other people, too," he said; "it's how they've been acting, Longinus. They're different people, man. They were frightened and defeated men when the Nazarene went to the cross. But now! Centurion, those fellows are on fire. They feel that they can whip the world! It's amazing how they've changed. Would they have got that way from imagining something?" He sat back, his eyes on his friend's face. "And there's more to it," he added, leaning forward again. "The Nazarene has been seen down here in Galilee *since* the crucifixion. On this trip, no later than yesterday, I've talked with people—plain, unimaginative folks, Longinus—who told me they saw him!"

"But, by all the great and little gods, Cornelius"—Longinus'

bronzed forehead was ridged with small furrows—"you say people told you they had seen the Galilean alive, but I tell you I
saw him *dead*. I thrust my spear point into his heart, and I saw
his blood pour out. Can a man rise up and walk from his tomb
with a hole in his heart?"

"No." Cornelius pondered the question. "But if the man were
also a god—" He paused. "You told me yourself, Longinus, that
after he died that day you said he must have been the son of a
god."

"Yes, I did." But his eyes were sharp and demanding. "If this
Galilean did come to life after he was dead, then how do you
explain it? And do you really believe that he did?"

"I certainly can't explain it. But, yes, Longinus, I *have to*
believe it."

Cornelius remained with him for lunch, but left early in the
afternoon for Tiberias. From there he would journey straight
south alongside the shore of the little sea and the twisting Jordan
valley road to Jericho and then Jerusalem.

That night despite his fatigue Longinus lay sleepless. In the
blackness of his quarters in the ugly square fort he clenched his
eyes shut against them, but like scenes from a Grecian play the
events and actors of that Passover day in Jerusalem passed
starkly before him. He knew he was afraid to go to sleep; he knew
what sleep would bring.

"By Jupiter and dark Pluto, Cornelius has brought him back."

When finally he did fall asleep, the vision came. But this time
the Galilean was not impaled on the cross. He stood before the
mouth of an open tomb. But his deepset sad eyes still were looking unblinking into his own.

The man's hands were extended forward slightly, the palms
toward him, and in the center of each palm the centurion saw
a ragged hole edged about with the reddish-purple of tortured
flesh. His homespun robe was pulled wide to reveal his arched
hairy chest, and just beneath his heart a great wound gaped.
From this wound, Longinus saw with a growing nausea, blood
and water gushed in a thickening stream.

The water and blood came up to cover the soles of the Galilean's coarse sandals, and then the sandals; and his ankles were wet and red, and the sticky redness moved up his brown, muscled legs. But still the man stood alive and erect and commanding, and his eyes compelled.

As he watched, held fixed by the eyes drilling into him, Longinus felt his cheeks and his forehead warm and moist; he lifted a hand to them and as he was lowering his hand he saw it; the hand was dripping red with the blood of the Galilean, wet and foul with the blood of the wound.

"No! No! By all the gods, I took no pleasure in it!"

Screaming, he sat up, the vision fading. He moved a hand across his pillow. It was drenched with his perspiration. He opened and closed his hands, hot and moist; he felt of his cheeks and forehead; they were streaming.

A light was bobbing toward him; he had awakened the orderly asleep in the small room beyond his.

"Centurion, are you ill?" He was holding the lamp high and he blinked his eyes as he sought to see. "You were screaming, sir. I was afraid—"

"Nothing's wrong." Longinus was rubbing his eyes. "Sometimes I have nightmares. But it's over; I'm all right. You can go back to sleep."

"It must have been a bad one, sir. You're white as a sheet. You look like you'd seen a ghost."

## THE CROWN TREE 18

In the clear light and crisp air of early morning as he rode along the coast toward the dyeing and weaving plants Longinus pondered the dream that had so terrified him. For it was nothing more than a dream, he kept assuring himself, a vivid and startling regrouping of ideas and images remaining in the subconscious mind from the conversation with Cornelius that in his troubled sleep had pushed up into the forefront of his thinking.

He sought to reconstruct the pattern of the dream and elaborate it with details out of the pieces of their talk the morning before. Nor was it difficult to do. Cornelius had spoken at length of the empty tomb, the sealing stone rolled back from its mouth, of the amazing report to him of the frightened guardsmen, and the strange stories of Simon and the Zebedees. It had all centered about a tomb no longer occupied. And he himself in questioning the rising from the dead of a man he had seen die had reminded Cornelius of the great gash in the Galilean's side from which the impounded blood and water had poured. The dream then was but a natural piecing together of the images their discussion had evoked in his hardly conscious thinking and a propulsion upward of these images to form a sharply delineated, striking new picture.

He rode on northward through the warming sunshine, relieved that his objective analysis, his clear reasoning, had resolved his frightful experience of last night into the only thing it could have been, a dream. Off left the waves of the Great Sea rolled in to beat against the rocks of the shore that would smooth into long stretches of sandy beaches as he neared the site of the textile works. Behind over his left shoulder Mount Carmel at the tip of a circling promontory appeared to be rising high out of the sea, and on his right and close at hand, it seemed in the morning's clear crispness, Jebel Jermuk, the highest point in Galilee, thrust its rounded bald peak above the range of ancient boulder-lined bare mountains.

A solid world, Longinus observed, compounded out of tangible, material, demonstrable things, an earth of the known and the seen and the real. At night, perhaps, when the world is put away for a time in darkness, man may be forgiven for hearing voices when no man speaks, for seeing unembodied spirits, for dreaming fanciful dreams. But in the daytime under the searching fierce brightness of the sun what literate, sane man would dare believe that a dead man had arisen on his bier and walked

upright from his tomb, what modern-day man of the world—
Cornelius does.

He remembered his friend's words. The story of the Nazarene's
resurrection was fantastic, the most utterly fantastic experience
he'd ever had, Cornelius had admitted, "but I can't disbelieve it."
That's what he'd said. And a moment later he'd been more defi-
nite: "I can't explain it, but I have to believe it."

Yet Cornelius had not seen the risen Jew. He had not touched
him, heard him speak, even laid eyes on him. But he'd freely confessed that he had to believe the man had triumphed over death.
Why?

Men in whom he had complete confidence had told him they
had seen the Galilean alive after the crucifixion. That was one
reason. Cornelius had faith in these men, he believed in them.
He was willing to accept their testimony, to make it his belief.
Faith. What is faith? Isn't it but the leaping from one solid, firm
footing of certainty across a deep canyon of doubt to a safe and
secure position on another rock-anchored stronghold? Must not
faith outleap reasoning? "I can't explain it," Cornelius had said,
"but I *have to* believe it."

Faith crosses from the tangible, the seen, the known, above the
abyss of doubt to the intangible, the invisible, but still the known,
the immaterial but still the certain. For are not the intangible
things, the invisible, the inaudible, the things of no substance, in
reality the only solid, enduring, unchanging, imperishable, abiding things?

The words of the old Greek tutor of his childhood came back
to Longinus. The man had been a slave, purchased on the block
in Rome by his father; but in all his life Longinus had never
known a less enslaved man. He lived in the world of the spirit,
and the enslavement of the body, relaxed as it was in the household of Senator Varro, for him had little meaning.

"Don't you see, my son," the old man would often say in his
gentle, persuasive way, "that the only real things, the only things
that cannot be destroyed, are those things that you cannot touch,
or see, or feel—as you feel this stylus in your hand—or hear with

your ears? Can you see or taste or roll between your fingers truth, Longinus? Can you weigh on the scales of the fish market goodness, my boy? Can you take a bite out of beauty and chew it and swallow it and feel it warm in your stomach? And yet what is more nourishing, more filling, more satisfying than beauty? What can ever destroy truth? Can all the decrees of Rome's Emperor change the sum of two and two to five or three? And what of beauty? These Corinthian columns, this marble mansion, will one day be dust and rubble, for it is built of material things, but who can mar one whit the pure beauty of the things of the spirit?"

Invariably the old teacher had ended his discourse with an amplification of his thoughts concerning that quality of his trinity which embraced the other two, Longinus remembered as he rode toward his day's tasks.

"Can you go to the market, my boy, and purchase with one denarius or ten thousand golden talents a measure of goodness and place it in an ephah basket or pour it into a wineskin? Yet what is more real, what is more enduring, what is possessed of more strength and power than goodness? Does it not embrace all virtues, does it not comprehend all authority?"

From that level often he would expound his views of theology.

"Despise not the gods, Longinus," the old man would say in his gentle quiet voice. "The good gods are symbols of the various attributes of goodness; the evil ones are the antitheses of these virtues. Uphold the good gods, oppose the evil ones." And then the good old tutor would smile, his tired eyes merry and sharp again. "Of course, I worship no gods, my son. As Rome and Greece conceive them, or fancy they do, they have for me no validity, no reality, and therefore no permanence and strength." And then quickly his tone would change to seriousness. "But mistake not, Longinus, I am a worshiper of that spirit which brings together into one all the attributes—and more even—of all our good gods. He is the eternal, the omniscient, the omnipotent One, the force and the being that encompasses and binds into one harmonious whole our trinity of truth, beauty, and goodness."

Then, the centurion recalled, the old teacher's eyes would soften and his voice would slow almost to a murmur. "Remember this, my son, if you forget all else: The real things, the imperishable, abiding things, are not the things you see and feel and walk upon and hold in your hand. Those things will perish. One day even Rome will be only a page in a book, one day the strength of her armies will be dust under the feet of strange men. Even the beauty of Greece will pass away and the Parthenon on the Acropolis will be but tumbled stones. But ten thousand centuries after this earth has vanished the things of the spirit will endure in all their strength. Never forget, Longinus, that this all-inclusive force—this eternal almighty power that rules the earth and all time—is goodness, which I call God, my son. Know then that to do good is Godlike, to *be* good, Longinus, is to be God, to take upon yourself His nature."

. . . God is good, good is God. To be good is to take upon oneself the nature of God.

Suddenly the idea struck upon his thinking like the blow of a fist between the eyes. Gone, driven from his consciousness, were the waves and the rocks, the yellow spread of the sand, the distant blue bulge of Jebel Jermuk.

Had this Galilean, this poor young carpenter from lowly Nazareth, having been utterly and completely good, taken on the nature and authority of this all-inclusive god of whom his tutor had so often talked? Had he of a truth, being God and spirit, been able to put off his mortal body on the cross, as one would shed his toga, and then the third day after take it up again, only to lay it aside once more to enter the invisible but enduring and invincible life of the spirit?

That would explain this strange young man of Galilee, that would make comprehensible the amazing talk of Centurion Cornelius.

"But if that is true, then I really killed God!"

The implication brought new fears, a quickening tension.

"But if of his own accord he put off his mortal life and entered into the world of the spirit, then he cannot hold me or Pontius

Pilate or his Jewish enemies responsible for his death," he protested aloud, "for how could any mortal kill God unless God were willing to die, unless God had ordained it?"

That would account for the fact that in none of his dreams had the Galilean seemed angry. He had revealed only sorrow, perhaps sorrow that he remained misunderstood.

"Then these were not dreams; they were not buried ideas and images welling up into the foreground of the mind as I slept. The Galilean has been coming to me, trying to communicate with me and prove to me that he was no ordinary man. Now that I understand, and admit his divinity, he will no longer pursue me, and I will have peace."

He rode along and the crisp air blowing from the Great Sea cooled him, and he was pleased that his clear thinking at last had resolved this difficulty that since that memorable Passover day at Jerusalem had been troubling him. . . . Face every problem squarely, apply to it sound reasoning, and generally you will perceive that it has either diminished greatly or entirely vanished. How true had been the words of the old tutor. . . . He was glad that he had confronted this enigma, thought it through to solution. No longer now his nights' rest would be—

"No! No! I cannot rationalize this thing!" Involuntarily he had tugged at the reins so that his horse had stopped, and he spurred the animal forward. "If he was God, if he *is* God, I killed God! I cannot excuse myself because I was ordered to do it; that I was obeying Pilate does not justify me. I killed the Galilean and the Galilean was God; were he not God he could never have walked from the tomb of the merchant. But how do I know he arose? How? How? How indeed can I ever *know?*"

Suddenly the palms of his hands were moist and perspiration burst from his forehead, and the breeze from off the water no longer cooled him, and he rode under the deadening burden of his own condemnation.

. . . How can I ever know the truth about this Jesus? How can I ever rid myself of the burden of my guilt—if he is a divine being?

. . . Cornelius is near to knowing it. He must be. And those Galilean fishermen have no doubt that their master was divine. They have utter faith in him, Cornelius said. Faith. Yes, again faith. The bridge from the known to the known, spanning the black chasm of doubt.

. . . But the Galileans were his followers. They loved him, and he loved them. He even loved his tormentors, even me. But they had faith. Could it be that their faith in him led them to a knowledge of him, if indeed he is a divinity, if he partakes of the nature of the one-God of my old teacher, if he is *the* one-God? Can it be, by all the gods known and unknown, that this Jesus is seeking to nourish in me a faith in him? . . .

His thoughts were in a ferment and his mind had become of a sudden a battleground of contending ideas and emotions; perspiration ran down his forehead to strain through his eyelashes, it dripped from his chin, and he felt it cold and wet beneath his shoulder blades.

"But I am a Roman soldier," he said after a while as though in argument with himself. "I have never believed in the lares and penates of our Roman households; I have laughed at the whole pantheon of the gods as inventions of superstitious men. But even they had stature, for what Roman in any of the distant provinces would have worshiped a poor Galilean carpenter youth?" His troubled eyes swept the sands of the beach and the waters of the Great Sea and turned to look upward to the naked towering of Jebel Jermuk. He rubbed his fingers across the drying palm of his free hand. "I am a practical man. I must believe what I can see and feel and experience. Is faith any more than superstition, despite the old Greek of my childhood? Are not the Galilean's followers but misguided illiterates of fanciful minds? I killed a man on the Hill of the Skull; I crucified a good man and an innocent man, it is true, but nevertheless he was a *man*." Longinus spurred his jogging animal. "I must break myself of the spell of these dreams."

When he reached the plant he plunged into the day's heavy schedule. He stood beside the purple-splashed slaves as they extracted the yellowish-white marrow from the little Murex shell-fish, which shortly would change to green and then to purple to provide the finest dyes for the most expensive textiles. He watched the ground pulp of the Buccinum bubbling in great leaden vats as other slaves skimmed off the shells and dross. In the weaving sheds he gave rapt attention to the manufacturing of the gorgeous materials. He was determined to understand thoroughly each step in the process; if he was to operate these enterprises, he would do it to the satisfaction of Sejanus and of himself.

In the hard work of the daylight hours he would earn sleep free of nightmarish dreams, or as his old teacher doubtless would have preferred to understand and express it, free of nocturnal visitations from out of the eternal world of the spirit.

He would rid himself of the crucified carpenter.

## THE CROWN TREE 19

Longinus was standing with Rufus in the shade of one of the sheds at the glassworks. Suddenly he pointed out to sea.

"That trireme's putting in to our wharf, I believe. Maybe she's stopping to take on the glassware. Is everything properly crated, Rufus?"

"Yes, Centurion, boxed and ready to ship. And pretty fair quality, too, this shipment."

The graceful vessel was turning to port to cut straight across the swells, its three banks of oars lifting and dropping in easy rhythm as the big square sail began slowly to sink along the great mast. They watched it coming in, saw the oars pause upraised on the port side as those on the starboard lifted and fell to align the ship with the pier and ease it into docking position.

"They're about to tie up. We'd better get down there, Rufus. It may be that they'll want some of the slaves here to help with the loading."

But before they stepped onto the wharf from the gravel beach the overseer Rufus, his eyes on the ship's deck, exclaimed:

"They're getting ready to unload slaves, too—for us, Centurion, don't you suppose?"

Longinus nodded, for slaves, their manacles rattling as they shuffled across the deck to disembark on the wharf under gruff orders of several knavish-looking guards, had begun to emerge from the ship's dark hold almost before the vessel had stopped moving. One of these guards, a soiled fellow who seemed to have fared worse on the voyage than many of his heavily bound charges, came running across the wharf.

"Centurion," he said, "we've got a load of slaves for the glassworks. Do you know who's in charge up there?"

"I am," the centurion answered. "If you see to putting them ashore we'll get them up to the mills. What shape are they in?"

"Fairly good condition, sir. A few sick but not many. We had a fast voyage out from Rome."

"Were they sent by the Prefect Sejanus?"

"Yes, sir. He had them purchased on the block there and loaded at once. And we've had good winds." He gestured toward the slaves, who were now coming down from the trireme in a long line, each fellow shackled to the one in front of him. "A little rest and they should be able to go to work. We'll get them up there for you. Have you a place to put them?"

"Yes, there are barracks for them. We'll provide medicines for any that are ill, and——"

"Master! O Master!" Rufus, in a frenzy of excitement, was pointing toward one of the slaves near the end of the line. "By the great Zeus, O Master!" He broke away, raced across the boards of the wharf, almost fell on his face before a broadshouldered, stocky fellow with a bandage bound across his forehead. The man lifted an arm pinioned at the wrist to place the hand gently on the overseer's shoulder, but Longinus did not hear what he said.

"Who's that fellow?" he asked the guard. "Do you know his name?"

"He's a Greek, a patrician fellow, I hear, and very rich before his enslavement. I think his name's Galenus."

"Unbind him immediately!"

"But, sir, he's a slave now. He might try to escape."

"He's my slave! Free him at once, and when you've done so, tell the overseer over there with him to fetch him to me!"

Already the guard was running back toward the end of the line of shuffling slaves. Longinus watched him pull a knife from his belt, saw back and forth with it on the leather thongs about the slave's wrist until they parted. In another moment the freed slave and the overseer Rufus stood before him.

"Centurion, you ordered him released from his bonds?" The overseer could hardly repress his great excitement. "Do you know who this man is?"

Longinus nodded, smiling. "The guard told me, but I would have known anyway, watching you." He looked into the slave's eyes. "Are you not Galenus, whose father owned this plant, which you operated?"

"Yes, I'm Galenus." He rubbed his wrists where the thongs had bound them. "I operated this plant and the dyeing and weaving establishments this side of Tyre."

"Rufus has told me about you." He turned then to address his overseer.

"See to these"—he waved toward the line of manacled men— "as you did the others, Rufus. If any are ill, give them medicines and treatment. And let them all rest until they are fully refreshed. And another thing: ease their bonds so that none suffers."

"Yes, Centurion." Already Rufus was motioning to the slaves' guards. Longinus turned now to the Greek.

"Let's go up to the office at the glassworks," he said. "There are several important things I wish to discuss with you, Galenus."

That night in the centurion's sleep the Galilean returned to stand towering before him. But this time there were no wounds, no drying blood. He stood erect, square-shouldered, commanding. His bronzed forehead was smooth, serene, his cheeks red with the sun and his coursing rich blood, his twin-spiked beard trimmed, anointed, his homespun brown robe immaculate. He held out his hands in friendly, inviting gesture, and Longinus, looking deep into his compelling eyes, saw that now they were no longer sad but warmly approving.

This time the centurion did not wake up screaming.

Three days later a vessel from Rome came into the port of Ptolemais. It brought Longinus two letters. The first he read was from his father. It revealed startling news. The Prefect Sejanus was dead, strangled by order of the Senate after he had been accused by the Emperor of plotting to overthrow him. Sejanus, Senator Varro wrote, had formed this conspiracy after having been angered because Tiberius had recommended that Prince Gaius, known to all Romans as Caligula, wastrel son of the great General Germanicus and his wife Agrippina, be named heir to the throne. Caligula's old grandmother Antonia had sent Tiberius a secret warning telling of the Prefect's plotting.

A veritable reign of terror had followed the slaying of Sejanus, his father reported, but now Rome was quiet again, a new prefect had been named by the Emperor, and he had retired into his usual calm at Capri. "As soon as I deemed the moment propitious," the letter continued, "I went to see the Emperor, told him how you had been sent off to Palestine by Sejanus, and petitioned him to order you returned to Rome for some more interesting assignment here or in this region of the Empire."

The Emperor had granted the Senator's request. He was ordering him to return to Rome for a new assignment, perhaps to Gaul or Germania, or maybe to fill a post in the capital.

"So you will shortly receive the official order of transfer," his father added. "I'm writing you that you may be ready to sail for Rome on the first vessel leaving Ptolemais on a voyage westward, for I know how eager you are to get out of Palestine."

The second letter was the official communication. It directed him to sail as quickly as he could arrange for the continued operation of the plants. He refolded the letter. That would be no problem. Old Sejanus, perhaps but a few days before they choked out his life, had sent him Galenus.

Eight days later the *Venetia,* one of the fastest triremes in the Empire's naval service, bound from Alexandria to Rome, sailed into the harbor of Ptolemais. Longinus presented to the commander his orders from the Emperor. When the *Venetia* sailed out, the centurion was aboard.

## THE CROWN TREE 20

From his visit with Longinus at Ptolemais, Centurion Cornelius had come eastward to Tiberias and then straight southward along the twisting road of the Jordan valley to Jerusalem.

Simon and Joseph Barnabas had returned also from Galilee, though the Zebedee brothers had remained behind in the region of Capernaum to aid their father for a season with the fishing. Now in the heat of the early afternoon the first of the apostles with Barnabas and Mary of Cyprus was seated in the shade of an ancient olive that stood near the fountain in Mary's courtyard.

She had been chiding the big grizzled Galilean because he had not come to lodge at her house with her young cousin immediately upon their arrival in Jerusalem.

"Don't you know that the first of our Lord's apostles is always welcome to abide under my roof and eat from my table? Don't you know that I am honored to serve you, Simon?"

"I do indeed, Mary," he answered, his eyes bright in the forest of whiskers and tangled confusion of eyebrows, "and I do thank you. But I wished to spend a time in talk with the brother of the Lord concerning the progress of our fellowship, and so I lodged with James in Ophel. But"—his eyes lifted to sweep the windows above the stone steps that went up along the wall—"I love every stone and shrub here, especially that upper chamber, though there's always a sadness, too, in returning."

"I understand, Simon." Mary spoke softly. "But you are welcome here, and our house is honored by your presence. And now tell me, how do things go in Galilee? What of the fellowship there?"

"It's growing." His grizzled face was serious. "But in Galilee, Mary, opposition is increasing, just as it is here in Jerusalem. The Sanhedrin knows that many souls are being added to the Master's brotherhood, and they've got their agents down in Galilee, too, fomenting trouble, trying to stir up the people against us."

"But what of the people, Simon?" Mary's concern was evident. "What are they saying, what course do they take?"

"Many are stiff-necked and refuse to believe that the Messiah has already appeared. Others are openly hostile; they protest loudly that we blaspheme the Holy Name and betray the faith and destroy the law. The fellowship is growing, but its enemies are diligent." His brown eyes were intent. "James tells me that's the way it is in Jerusalem too."

"That is true," Mary agreed. "We've added many, but hostility is growing likewise. The Temple leaders are determined to destroy the fellowship. But Stephen and others in our group are laboring just as zealously to strengthen it. There aren't many days when he isn't standing up in the Synagogue of the Libertines or one of the courts of the Temple proclaiming that the Messiah has come."

"Stephen is a bold one; he isn't afraid of them."

"Yes, Stephen's on fire for the Messiah. He's so bold that already the Temple leaders are murmuring against him, I hear from Hannah. He is so consumed with love of the Lord's cause that he gives little time any more to his goldsmith's shop. He is seen more often at the Synagogue of the Libertines than in the Street of the Workers in Metal."

"But is the first of the deacons likewise zealous in caring for the widows and orphans and administering to the hungry and naked amongst us? That was the principal task we gave him."

"Yes, I can testify to that," Mary assured the big Galilean. "Stephen permits none to go hungry or naked or without place to lodge. The complaints that once were raised to high heaven by the Greek-speaking women, who charged that we were not sharing our goods and money in fairness, have all but ceased since the appointment of the seven deacons."

Joseph Barnabas, who had been listening intently to the conversation of his cousin and Simon, chanced to be looking toward the heavy gate in the high wall that protected Mary's courtyard from the noisy cobblestoned way. He remembered that he himself had neglected to replace the bar when he had returned less than an hour ago from Obed the tanner's shop down in Ophel where he had taken sandals to be repaired.

In that same instant the gate was flung violently open and Mary's servant Amaziah, his face red and sweat-streaked, his twisted robe bulged out at his waist above his rope girdle, came racing toward them.

"They are dragging Stephen to the stoning ground!" Amaziah was breathing hard. "Hurry, Joseph, in the name of the God of Israel, go to his help before they kill him!" He recognized the big Galilean. "And you, Simon, can't you command the ears of the mob?"

"Stephen! No!" Simon was incredulous. "Amaziah, this can't be! Who incited them? How were they so bold?"

"The Jews who deny our Messiah. It's their work. Stephen was teaching in the Synagogue of the Libertines. I'd stopped there for a moment of prayer—" The servant was struggling for breath. "They disputed him, angered at his words, and quickly seized him and dragged him before the council of the Sanhedrin, and testified falsely that he blasphemed against the Temple and the law"—he paused again, his breath still coming hard—"and answering them, he flung brave words in their teeth and called them stiff-necked and uncircumcised in heart, and betrayers and murderers of the Just One. Whereupon, they were so inflamed against him that they seized him—" He broke off, breathing heavily. "Hurry, men, if you'd help him, before it's too late!"

They had risen quickly to their feet.

"But which way did they go, Amaziah?" Joseph's eyes were blazing.

"They were pulling him down the slope of Moriah toward

Dung Gate when I last saw them. Saul of Tarsus in the lead was
haranguing—"

"Saul of Tarsus! God in Israel, my friend Saul—"

"Yes, your friend, Joseph. Many were screaming against
Stephen and tearing their clothes, but it was Saul who was in-
flaming them."

"God help me! I've got to get to Saul; I've got to overtake
them!"

Barnabas hitched up his robe, ran for the gateway, disappeared
through it.

## THE CROWN TREE 21

Down Mount Zion toward steaming Ophel Joseph raced. He
ran along narrow cobbled ways, once across a flat roof and down
an outside stairway to gain a lower level, through alleys crowded
with workers busy in front of their shops, half-naked children
playing, plodding donkeys almost hidden under merchandise
piled high, mangy dogs nosing in rotting garbage.

At the square in front of Dung Gate he accosted a thin stoop-
shouldered fellow with a great hawk-beaked nose squatting in
the doorway of a cobbler's shop.

"Did you see a throng pass here dragging a man to the stoning
ground?" he asked.

"Yes, and if you want to heave a stone at the fellow while he's
still alive"—he paused, and without getting to his feet studied
the heavily breathing Barnabas—"or else have in mind going to
his aid, you'd best not be delaying to ask questions." He nodded
in the direction of the gate. "They went through there. Nor can
you harm him or help him now, I've a notion."

But already Joseph Barnabas was running again. Beyond Dung
Gate he took the Bethany road, crossed the brook Kidron, raced
up the slope toward the Garden of Gethsemane.

Then off to the right he heard the noise. It was a beastly, horrid sound, like the distant snarling of fighting, hunger-driven dogs, punctuated now and then by a shrill, maddened shriek of some hate-possessed hireling of the Temple priests. Without slowing his pace, he turned in the direction of the sound.

As he topped the rise and ran down the slope that led toward the Bethlehem road beyond the point where the Valley of the Cheesemongers merged with the Vale of Hinnom, Barnabas saw them. But he couldn't see Stephen.

"God in Israel!" he gasped, for it seemed that his pounding heart would burst from his chest. "I'm too late! He's already dead and buried under their stones!"

The stoning ground was a shallow ravine edged about by piles of rocks that the farmers through the years had carried laboriously from the fields. Barnabas ran straight toward the screaming, cursing men and youths rimming the declivity, toward the forest of arms upraised—long, thin, burnt arms, hairy white fat arms beaded with sweat, angry arms flinging stones.

"Hold! In the name of God," he shouted, "he's done nothing to deserve death!"

But nobody paid heed. Roughly he grabbed the arm of a tall bearded fellow about to hurl a heavy rock poised almost above his head, so that the missile fell past his shoulder to strike a few inches from his feet.

"What do you mean, brazen lout?" the angered man demanded. "You almost caused me to drop that stone on my head."

"You're stoning an innocent man. He's a loyal son of Israel, a true follower of the Lord Messiah, a good brother in—"

"Then you're one of them!" the fellow screamed. "Look, neighbor"—he grasped the shoulder of a stocky Sadducee beside him—"here's another of the blasphemers. He's upholding this enemy of the God of Israel and His Temple." He bent down to pick up the big stone. "This one deserves the same fate as that apostate in the pit!"

But Joseph Barnabas had darted away, was pushing through the howling, maniacal throng to the edge of the depression.

Stephen was on his hands and knees, and already his white body, stripped of clothing, was torn and bleeding. Now he raised his head and looked high into the heavens above Jerusalem's walls.

"Let me to him! Let me to him!" Joseph was trying to push between two stout men at the edge of the pit. But several hands grabbed him.

"Stay away from him, you fool!" a swarthy Jew commanded. "Can't you be content to stand here and hurl your stones? Venture down there and you'll get a stone against your own head!"

Joseph Barnabas protested no more, for suddenly his eyes were held fast. Stephen had raised his long forearm and was pointing. His eyes were wide open; an expression of ecstasy flooded his blood-streaked countenance.

"I see him!" he shouted. "I see the Lord Messiah coming on the clouds of heaven! He comes to meet me! He comes to—"

A stone as large as Stephen's head struck his right shoulder a glancing blow, knocking him flat on his face. But he seemed hardly conscious of it, for he was up again on his knees, his gory face ablaze with rapture, his arms outstretched. But now his expression changed, the rapture faded.

"O Master, forgive them." The tone was clear, pleading. "They don't understand what they are doing. Forgive them, Lord."

The very words of Jesus on the cross. Often had Barnabas heard Simon repeat the dying words of the Lord Messiah. God in Israel, how can he pray for these sons of hell, these fiends who torment and kill him? How, why, O God of Israel?"

Barnabas could not take his eyes from the enraptured, bloody face looking with ecstatic wide eyes into the heavens above the walls enclosing the ancient city. Stones now were raining on him, but still his eyes looked upward. A jagged rock struck his leg extended along the ground and Barnabas saw the flesh crushed and bleeding. But Stephen seemed oblivious of the stones bruising and gashing and breaking him, and he looked upward and beyond his tormentors. The sun was on his mangled bloody face and a glory wreathed it.

"O God in Israel, how can he? How can he?"

But now Stephen was speaking again, his bruised, bleeding arms outstretched.

"Lord Jesus, receive my spirit."

His voice was calm, clear; the words came up from the pit distinct and tranquil. A moment he continued to stare upward, beyond them, oblivious of them, entranced, and then his eyes lowered to his assailants rimming the declivity. But in the eyes Joseph Barnabas saw no trace of hate or anger, only sorrow and pleading.

"O Lord"—Stephen bowed his head—"hold not this sin against them. Forgive them, O my Lord Messiah, forgive—"

A huge rock struck the back of his bowed head, and Stephen pitched forward into the blood-splotched stones.

Barnabas, sickened with grief and hate, looked up quickly to discover if he could who had thrown the missile. Beyond Stephen, past the ring of assailants, he saw a young man standing beside a pile of stones on which many in the crowd had flung their mantles and robes. Evidently he was guarding the garments while the others were about the heinous task.

But this man was not watching the garments now. He was staring, his expression intent, his whole frame rigid, at the inert mangled white body of the first of the deacons, on which the relentless stones were falling. The sunlight, as now he bent forward, his eyes still on the dying man in the pit, was reflected from the rounded dome of his balding head.

"God in Israel!" Barnabas smothered his sudden scream; he had recognized the man. "Saul of Tarsus! O Saul! Saul!"

He jumped down into the pit to cross to the other side. He must get to Saul, reason with him, implore him, plead with him. Stephen now was beyond help; the motionless white body, bloody and crushed, already was half covered in stones, and still they were falling, though Barnabas paid no heed to them.

"The Romans! Fly, men! Soldiers from Antonia!"

The voice was screaming behind him. And other voices. Now the stoners were rushing toward Saul for their garments. Joseph

Barnabas clambered toward the rim of the pit's farther side.
"I must get to Saul. O God in Israel, help—"

But he said no more. A last flung stone meant for the inert
broken body of Stephen glanced off his skull, and Barnabas
crumpled among the rocks.

## THE CROWN TREE 22

"After him, Amaziah!" Mary screamed, as Joseph Barnabas
raced from the courtyard. "Try to overtake him and persuade
him not to attempt to dispute with the mob. He'll only be killed,
and he'll do Stephen no good!"

"I'll go with Amaziah," Simon said. "I fear too that no one
save God can help our brother. You, Mary, send quickly a servant
to fetch Hannah and her daughter to be here with you."

Outside the gate Simon explained: "Joseph is young and rash.
He may run afoul of that inflamed mob and be stoned too. And
it would go hard with Mary, who looks on her cousin as though
he were a son."

They went toward Ophel as fast as they could, and when they
reached the square in front of Dung Gate they heard the commotion. An instant later a detachment of Roman soldiers, racing
down Mount Moriah from the direction of Fortress Antonia,
dashed past them and disappeared beyond the gate. By the time
they could go through the gateway and cross the brook Kidron
they encountered men and youths coming on the run toward
Ophel. Simon accosted one of them, a man he remembered having seen loitering in the shade of the porches flanking the Court
of the Gentiles at the Temple.

"What of the goldsmith Stephen?" he asked.

"He won't trouble the High Priest any longer. He's dead and
buried beneath a pile of stones," the fellow answered, hardly
pausing.

They stopped another man and inquired of Joseph Barnabas, but they could learn nothing of him. Concerned for the youth, fearfully distressed at the fate of Stephen, they started back toward Mary's house.

The three women were waiting in the courtyard.

"I'm not greatly surprised that it happened," Mary said. "I've been afraid it would. Stephen has been preaching with such fervor and boldness, and all the while the anger of the Temple priests was mounting against him, as Hannah well knows."

Her friend nodded.

"Yes, they have been plotting against Stephen; they've been determined to close his mouth."

"And now our enemies will increase their efforts against us, won't they, Simon?" Mary asked, her face grave.

"But they shan't prevail," Simon declared. "Didn't the Lord himself tell us so just before he left us?"

"Yes, often you've repeated his words, Simon. We lean on you. You are our consolation."

"The rock that supports us." Hannah nodded agreement.

"Rab Simon"—Damaris' eyes showed her concern—"do you suppose anything has happened to Joseph?"

"I don't think so, daughter," he sought to reassure her. "He'll likely be here any moment."

Hardly had he said it when there was a heavy belaboring on the gate and Amaziah ran to open it. Joseph Barnabas, his head bandaged, entered the courtyard. Beside him was the Centurion Cornelius, and several Roman soldiers were following them.

Damaris ran to Barnabas.

"Are you sorely hurt, Joseph? And were you trying to defend Stephen?"

His wry smile relieved her. But quickly his countenance was solemn. "Have you heard—about Stephen?"

Mary explained that Simon and Amaziah, who had sought to overtake him, had brought the tragic tidings.

"But how did you get hurt, Joseph?" she asked him.

He related what happened, how he had tried to get to Saul,

how he remembered nothing after that until he was revived by Centurion Cornelius and his men.

"Centurion, we are grateful," Simon told the Roman. "At Capernaum you were our friend and helper. In Jerusalem you continue that good work."

"I regret that we were too late to save the other man. That mob had no authority to deal with him. But they had killed him before we got there, Simon. I set a guard over the body, however, and I assure you no one will molest it. I presume you'll wish to give it proper burial soon."

"Yes, we will, Centurion, and we thank you," Simon told him. "We'll gather those from the fellowship and put away the body of our brother Stephen."

Damaris had been listening intently, and she seemed puzzled at the centurion's words and demeanor.

"Centurion, how does it happen," she ventured to inquire, "that you Romans were interested in trying to save the life of a member of our fellowship? Can any Roman have a kindly feeling for a Jew?"

"She doesn't know who you are, Centurion," Simon spoke up, before Cornelius could answer. "Damaris, the Centurion has long been a friend of the Jews and even of the Master. It was his servant boy whom Jesus healed at Capernaum. He contributed to the needs of the synagogue there."

Damaris was smiling now.

"Then you were stationed in Galilee and knew the Master while he was ministering in that region?"

"Yes, my post was at Capernaum. That's how I happened to know Simon here and others of the Nazarene's band."

"I had the feeling that all Romans were our enemies." She had become serious again. "When Mother and I were going to Cyprus I met on the ship one day a centurion who said he had been in charge of the soldiers who crucified Jesus, and when Joseph was coming from Cyprus in company with Saul they talked with this same man—"

"Yes, I know," Cornelius interrupted. "He sent them to see me.

And not long ago I saw him at Ptolemais, where he's now stationed. Longinus is one of my dearest friends." He spoke now to Simon. "And he is still greatly disturbed concerning the Nazarene and can't seen to get him out of mind. He's troubled by visions."

"He's likely a man of compassionate heart." Simon ran blunt fingers through the fan of his beard. "Centurion, maybe the Lord has laid his hand on your friend."

## THE CROWN TREE 23

Weeks had passed since Stephen's mourning friends had laid away in the tomb the broken body of the first of the deacons. But the enemies of the Nazarene's fellowship were not relenting.

The agitated passionate soul of Saul of Tarsus, the most determined of these enemies, was aflame with zeal for the preservation in its utter purity of the true worship of the God of Israel.

Little time Saul spent now at his loom or squatting with needle and thread and shears at his bench in the Street of the Tentmakers near Jerusalem's eastern wall in the region between Dung Gate and Mount Moriah. No longer was he seen on one of the low stone benches at the feet of Rabban Gamaliel. That revered old grandson of the great Hillel, Saul was now definitely convinced, had grown lax toward the enemies of Israel's God and His law, was discoursing too much on compassion and love and forgiveness and not enough on the necessity of Israel's adhering firmly to the requirements of the law laid down by Moses.

Rabban Gamaliel, Saul had been told of late, had even spoken with great severity against those who had taken part in the stoning of the apostate Stephen, had declared the act sinful, had even dared to suggest that it was akin to murder. So Saul had vowed he would go no more to hear the famous teacher. Nor in these recent days, he conceded, would Gamaliel have welcomed him.

But though the student from Tarsus sat no more at the feet of the master, he spent longer hours in prayer, lying prostrate on the hard stones of the Temple courts, calling upon the God of Israel to give him resolution, to strengthen his arms that he might flail with more severity those who were daring to blaspheme against God and His Temple and flout His laws. He prayed God to harden his heart against them, to shut his ears to the sound of the lash on the backs of those who had deserted God to worship the blasphemer of Galilee, the carpenter Jesus of Nazareth who had made so bold as to call himself the Messiah and yet had suffered and died, as other thousands had done before him, on the shameful cross of the Romans.

"Embolden my spirit against them, O God of Israel, that I may neither weaken nor relax in waging war upon those who follow the false Messiah, and deny to Thee the proper worship, and dishonor Thy Torah, and are lax in offering to Thee the sacrifices that are Thy due." Thus Saul prayed, his face pressed against the cold pavement. "Give strength to our arms that we may so punish these evil ones, O God, that we bring them to a true repentance, so that Thy commandments may be obeyed and Thy Temple and Thy Torah revered, so that Thy Name may be exalted by all Thy children Israel."

Often as the young man from Tarsus prostrated his ungainly small body in prayer he lay in a wide space apart from the other worshipers, for already the mention of his name had begun to bring fear and trembling upon countless ones in Jerusalem, especially among the Greek-speaking Jews, who naturally were more lax in their observance of the many strict laws of orthodox Jewry. As he walked along the narrow streets or came into the courts of the Temple, many shrank away or openly fled from him. The name Saul of Tarsus to unnumbered ones had become a stench and a loathing.

Nor did these people lack good reason to fear Saul. Scores already had felt on their backs the sting of lashes wielded by Temple guards assigned by the High Priest to do Saul's bidding. Under the heavy blows of metal-tipped thongs and the bludgeoning of staves ringed at their ends with copper, some had screamed, "I am willing!" and had promised to give strict obedience henceforth to the requirements of the ancient law. But the greater number had borne the torture tight-lipped and unyielding, some even in a state of rapture at being permitted to suffer for their Lord Messiah who had embraced shame and torture and death in their stead.

Saul had no authority to punish men and women because of their belief in Jesus as the Messiah. He was empowered only to give the lash to those who had been delinquent or perverse in observance of the laws of Israel. Some were whipped ostensibly because they had violated certain statutes, others because they had failed to offer sacrifices in the Temple as the law required. But virtually always the victims of Saul's fanatical zeal were Greek-speaking Jews, many of them from distant lands and ignorant of the subtleties of Jewish law and tradition. Most of them were residents of Ophel, poor and unlettered and hardly able to murmur proper prayers in the Temple. And it was soon evident also that those who felt the lashes of Saul's heavy-handed henchmen were of the fellowship of Jesus.

For the man of Tarsus had one driving passion. He was determined to rededicate Israel to the undefiled worship of Israel's God by stamping out utterly the iniquitous sect of the blaspheming followers of that false and dead Messiah, Jesus the crucified Galilean who had claimed himself one with the God of Israel.

This morning Saul with several of his guards—for he ventured forth infrequently now without them—had visited the Synagogue of the Libertines. They had entered the sanctuary singly and had mingled unobtrusively among the worshipers. Saul, his mantle high about his neck and shoulders, had remained just inside the doorway. So careful had they been that their presence hardly had been noticed until two of the guards, at the nod of a man among the throng of worshipers, had laid hold on a tall thin fellow and dragged him forth from the congregation. Immediately they had hustled him before one of the minor Jewish courts, where witnesses testified that he had been lax in fulfilling the law's requirements for the offering of sacrifices of repentance. The court promptly had condemned him to be lashed.

Now in a chamber behind the tribunal room Saul stood above this man, who lay stripped but for his loincloth. At either side of the prostrate fellow stood a Temple guard, whip in upraised hand. Already the man's back was a swelling mass of welts, and blood trickled around his ribs to drip on the stones of the floor.

"Are you ready to cry 'I am willing' and hereafter give yourself without stint to obeying the law and honoring the God of Israel?" Saul demanded.

But the beaten man made no reply. He lay still, his face against the floor. During the lashing not a sound, except an occasional smothered gasp, had escaped his lips.

"Answer me, stubborn son of hell! Don't you know that I have authority to lay on the lash until you cry 'I am willing'?"

But still the man said nothing. He lay face downward as if unmindful of the whips poised above his naked and torn flesh. One of the guards, his eyes on Saul, raised his arm higher to strike, but with a look Saul restrained him.

"Who are you?" the Temple's agent demanded, his face darkly scowling, his good eye ablaze with anger. "Why do you with such stubbornness ignore the God of Israel and those who minister in His name, why do you so willfully disregard His laws and so obstinately refuse to obey them?"

"You know who I am, Saul." The man twisted his tortured body slightly to look Saul in the face. "Weren't you seeking me? Didn't you contrive with traitorous Barak for him to point me out to your hirelings even while I was in the synagogue worshiping the God of Israel?"

"I don't know you. He only said he would point out one of the worst apostates in that synagogue."

"Then you don't recognize Amaziah, servant of Mary of Cyprus, to whose house you once came often with your friend Joseph Barnabas?"

"Of a truth I didn't know you, Amaziah." Saul's surprise was not feigned. He motioned to the two guards. "Go into the next

chamber with the others. When I have need of you, I'll call out."
The men withdrew. Saul reached down to take the beaten man's
hand. "Get to your feet, Amaziah. Sit there." He motioned toward
a bench against the wall. "It gives us no joy to punish those who
defy the commands of the Lord God of Israel," he said, almost
with a tone of apology, when Amaziah had sat down. "But God
has commanded me not to withhold the hand that grips the lash;
I am but the servant of the Most High." He paused, and then
his voice was calmer. "How is it with Barnabas, Amaziah? It
grieves me greatly that he persists in his sinning. I love him like
a brother." He held out his right arm. "I'd give this arm if by
so doing I could cause him to repent of his great sinning."

"Barnabas is committing no sin in loving and serving the Lord
Jesus the Messiah, who is God's Son, the one who died on the
cross as a sacrifice for the sins of men his brothers; Barnabas is
but serving—"

"Blasphemy! Curse the words of your lips!" Saul's face was
livid. "Did Joseph Barnabas teach you such heresy?"

"No, nor is it heresy. I listened to the words of the Master
himself, and also to Simon and Stephen and others. But Barnabas
believes as we do in the Lord Jesus Christ as the true Messiah of
God, the sacrificial lamb sent of God to remove from us our
guilt, whose sacrifice of himself makes unnecessary our offering
of lambs and doves on the Temple altar, whose—"

"Cursed be your words and the lips that speak them!" Saul
spat.

"Thus you speak today, Saul," Amaziah said calmly, as unper-
turbed he looked the man of Tarsus in the eyes, "but another
day is coming, and may the God of Israel grant that it is not
long delayed, when *you* will believe even as we of the fellowship
of Jesus believe."

"Thrice cursed be your blaspheming lips!" He leveled his forefinger at Amaziah and his bald forehead flushed with his anger.
"Don't you know that I could call my men back and have you
flailed until you repent of this frightful sinning?"

"I know you can have me lashed whenever you will it, Saul,

but I'll never repent of these words I've spoken. In professing my belief in Jesus as the Lord Messiah and my love for him I have not sinned against the Most High, as one day *you* will know and testify."

But Saul did not summon his men. Instead, his teeth clenched, his lips thinned to a pallor, he strode from the chamber.

That night as he lay on his mat sleep did not come easily. When he did fall asleep, dreams troubled him. He saw bleeding, lacerated backs, scores, hundreds, a multitude of tortured backs of men and women; he saw the loaded leather thongs ripping and slashing, and welts and stripes crossing and criss-crossing, and blood dripping and flowing to merge into a great and growing crimson stream, the blood of men and women yielding themselves even with ecstasy to the torture in testimony to their faith in a young man come forth from humble Nazareth in Galilee. He saw their lips, sealed and silent even when the thongs cut and tore the living flesh. And from out of the mass of bleeding backs and clenched lips a finger pointed to him and a voice spoke. It was calm and serene and there was authority in it. "Another day is coming, when *you* will believe even as we of the fellowship believe."

"No! Never! Never!" He knotted his fist and struck at the extended taunting finger. His fist struck the wall beside his mat and the sudden pain awakened him. "Dreaming again."

He had dreamed many nights of the hand of Stephen raised aloft in pleading to God for forgiveness, not of himself for his own sinning but of those who were stoning him; he had heard in his dreaming the calm voice of the goldsmith praying.

"But I did not murder Stephen." He had said it before, many times. Now he was saying it again. "He was stoned for blaspheming the God of our ancient land. He was justly dealt with. He deserved death."

He went to sleep again after long tossing, and once more the accusing finger pointed. "One day, O Saul of Tarsus, even you who murdered Stephen will be one of us in the fellowship of the carpenter!"

The next morning Saul awoke early and prayed fervently that God would banish from his dreams the voice and the pointing finger; at the Temple he fell on his face and besought strength of will to punish with greater severity the enemies of God and His Torah and the defilers of His Temple. Then he called together certain of the guards with their tall hats and white aprons and the tablets of authority hung on their chests, and they proceeded once more to the Synagogue of the Libertines.

In the weeks that followed Saul not once relented in his determination to erase from the congregation of Israel the new sect of the blasphemers. Men and women were set upon and dragged from their cramped and fetid hovels in Ophel and beaten until their backs ran red and the lead-tipped whips were dappled with crimson. They were pulled forth from the courts of the Temple and the synagogues of the Greek-speaking Jews; they were accosted in front of the gates of the city and on the roads that ran out from it. And invariably the hostile judges ordered them lashed.

Saul of Tarsus became a terror and a curse, and men seeing him slunk into alleys and the dark recesses of the ancient capital; women and children, recognizing him, ran away shrieking. But the man did not relent. Cries and tears and stripes and blood seemed but to strengthen his resolve, for in his heart he was convinced that he was serving well and in perfect devotion the one true God whom he worshiped with all the stubbornness of his keenly reasoning brain and unbending will.

As the scourge of Saul increased and persecutions grew more and more frightful against those of the Greek-speaking Jews of the fellowship of Jesus, many fled into hiding and abandoned the assembling of themselves together at the Synagogue of the Libertines or those other places where the foreign Jews customarily drew together. Members of the growing band began to hold secret meetings in the homes, often in some dark and dungeon-like chamber in Ophel built hard against the city wall or tunneled deep into its ancient stones. Sometimes Simon as the first of the Lord's apostles led services of worship; often he stood up and talked of the days when he and the others of the Twelve walked with Jesus up and down and across the tired and troubled face of Galilee and Samaria and Judaea, and of the teachings of the Lord and the resonance of his voice and the quick warmth of his smile. Other times James bar Zebedee or James the brother of the Lord led the service, and there were meetings at which the three, with Joseph Barnabas and Mary of Cyprus, along with Hannah and Damaris and others of the leadership in Jerusalem, were all present in some secret, hidden chamber. With them, unseen but felt and warmly comforting, was that Holy Spirit the Master had promised would be sent to sustain them.

But many others, fearful of Saul and the Temple guardsmen, fled from Jerusalem and returned to their home cities in the lands that bordered the Great Sea, so that soon other bands of the fellowship of the Nazarene began to take root and grow throughout all the region of the Dispersion.

Saul, hearing about this scattering of the seeds of the hated blasphemy and convinced that in Jerusalem he had broken the strength of the evil brotherhood, went to the High Priest and petitioned him for a letter of authority to pursue and apprehend and return to Jerusalem for trial and punishment those traitorous Jews who were now planting everywhere the new idolatry.

## THE CROWN TREE 24

Joseph Barnabas had not seen Saul of Tarsus for months. But he had received many reports of Saul's determined hostility, which had been confirmed the afternoon Amaziah, slashed and bleeding from the lashes of the Temple guardsmen, had returned from his encounter with the leader of the fellowship's enemies.

Damaris and her mother, however, since they were members of the household of old Annas, no longer the High Priest but still the shrewdest and most powerful of the Temple leadership, had been able to follow more closely the activities of Saul. Servants at the house of Annas and also those attached to the household of Caiaphas were secretly members of the fellowship, and they kept Hannah and her daughter informed of Saul's visits to their masters. Frequently Hannah revealed to Mary and sometimes to Barnabas the reports the servants had fetched.

So today when one of Hannah's servants came with a message from Damaris, Barnabas wondered if her request in some way were related to something Saul had done. The servant said that Damaris had sent him in haste to say that she wished to meet him within an hour at the shop of Obed the tanner. Barnabas had inquired the purpose of their meeting.

"I don't know, sir. She only said for you to meet her there, and that it was urgent." The fellow lowered his voice so that the other household servants might not overhear. "But I do know this, sir. Shalim, one of the High Priest's servants who is of our fellowship, came to her this morning and whispered information that must have been of much concern, because the moment he left she sent me to seek you out quickly."

Within the hour he was at the tanning yard. Piles of hides lay on the ground, so close together that he had to pick his way between the malodorous heaps. The whole place and the neighborhood about it were enveloped in a nauseous stench that arose from the hides, some from animals freshly killed at the slaughtering stalls below Dung Gate, others already giving off foul odors from the putrefaction of bits of flesh clinging to them. Several men were working with the loathsome hides, some scraping away the flesh and fat and others attempting to clean them with water already evil-smelling and thick with gore.

Barnabas went directly to Obed.

"Some time ago, you remember, you repaired some sandals for me. It was good leather you gave me then. Now I want to purchase leather suitable for a large pouch." He spoke loudly, so that the others, if they chose, might hear, and his eyes wandered over several stacks of finished leather.

"There's leather inside of a better quality than this." Obed motioned toward the door. "Your friend—she's inside," he said under his breath as they moved in that direction. "These men are of our fellowship, but aways one must be cautious, eh? Inside you'll be safe from prying ears, should there be any; nor does anyone here know she's the High Priest's niece, I'm convinced." He opened the door, admitted Barnabas. "You two can appear to be selecting the leather," he said when he was inside. Then he went out.

"I have grievous tidings, Joseph," the girl said, when Obed had closed the door behind him. "I had to let you know. Hadrach tried to find Rab Simon but couldn't, so you must see them as quickly as you can and consult on what should be done. Too much time has been lost already, I'm afraid. Saul of Tarsus may even now be—"

"Saul of Tarsus! God in Israel, Damaris, has he sought to molest you? Would he dare—"

"No, no," she interrupted, to reassure him. "He's planning a new attack on the fellowship. And maybe he's already begun carrying it out."

Quickly she related what they had learned from the servant Shalim. Two nights before, the High Priest had called to his palace certain members of the Sanhedrin. During the group's deliberations Shalim had served wine and fruit, and through a door purposely left ajar he had heard much of the talk. When Saul of Tarsus was admitted, Shalim had become doubly suspicious.

"The next morning Shalim found an excuse to come to our house to report what he had heard, but my mother and I were away, and this morning he came again. Then we sent Hadrach to find you. Shalim hadn't been able to hear all that was said at the High Priest's palace, but he did hear enough to know that Saul was being commissioned by my uncle to go to Damascus—"

"Why Damascus? To persecute our people there?"

"Yes. Divers ones of the fellowship that fled from Jerusalem went there, you know. Shalim said he heard Saul propose that he be sent to Damascus, where our congregation is growing fast, to arrest our leaders and bring them to Jerusalem to stand trial. He reminded them that the High Priest's authority over the Jews extends beyond the borders of Israel; he can order their return to Jerusalem. Saul must have convinced them that the seeds of our sect are taking root and growing in that region."

"He's right," Barnabas agreed. "But he himself has done more than anyone else to scatter the seeds of faith in the Lord Messiah. His lead-tipped lashes have sent these seeds flying over the lands bordering the Great Sea. But when is he starting for Damascus? And did Shalim learn by what route he would travel?"

"All Shalim learned was that Saul would start as quickly as he could. He may be on his way now." Her countenance was grim. "Shouldn't something be done to warn our brethren at Damascus?"

"Damaris, I'm going to see Saul and persuade him not to go to Damascus! If he's already started, I'm going to overtake him and turn him back!"

"But what if he won't turn back? Saul is stubborn, you know, and he's convinced he's doing the will of God. What if he won't listen?"

"Then I'll kill him!" His countenance was dark. "I love him, but he is no longer my brother. He killed Stephen. He persecutes the fellowship of our Lord Messiah, he's—"

"No, Joseph, that's not the way!" The girl shook her head, and her dark eyes were frightened. "You must not go after Saul. You might get killed yourself. Nor would the Lord Messiah want you to kill him." Her sternness fled her face, her tone was pleading. "You mustn't, Joseph. I don't want you to."

"A woman's reason."

"But a good one nevertheless."

He promised he would not seek out Saul until he had talked with the first of the apostles. So they separated and he returned to the house of Mary.

Simon was there. Joseph told the big fisherman what he had learned from Damaris, and what he had told the girl.

"No, Joseph," Simon said. "You must not kill Saul—never!"

"Even in defense of the fellowship? But how can it flourish until we change Saul's course, and how can we change him short of killing him?"

The first of the apostles laid his big hand on the young man's arm. "Put out of your mind and heart all such rash and ungodly thoughts, Joseph. The Master's kingdom cannot advance through murder, however justified it may appear to be."

"God knows I would not wish to kill Saul, whom I have loved like a brother even though we are enemies. But isn't he an enemy of the Lord Jesus? Must we stand idle while the enemies of the Messiah seek to destroy those who follow him?"

Rugged Simon slowly shook his head.

"Saul has done us much evil of late, son, that is true. But it is not for us to say that he deserves to die. That is within God's province. It is for us to pray that Saul repent of the evil he does and turn toward the true light of our Lord Messiah."

"But, Rab Simon, I—"

Simon interrupted his protesting.

"I understand how you feel. Wasn't I impetuous, too, and rash? Who was more bold to speak out when he should have held his peace, to act when he should have remained still? In Gethsemane that night wasn't it I who struck off the ear of one of Caiaphas' servants?" Then he patted the young man's forearm. "Isn't it for the God of Israel to rebuke Saul? Should we act for God? No, God forbid, Joseph. It may be, it could be"—a grim smile spread over his face—"that God has plans for Saul. Didn't He have plans for an unworthy plain fisherman of Galilee?"

"Nevertheless, Rab Simon, shouldn't someone go to Damascus to warn our brothers that Saul is planning great mischief against them?"

"That might be good counsel, Joseph." He reflected. "Yes, Ananias and the others at Damascus should be warned that Saul is coming against them. And while the messenger rides for Damascus we in Jerusalem will pray that God turn aside Saul from the error of his present way by changing him into a friend and brother in the fellowship."

"Rab Simon"—Joseph's eyes did not falter—"I pray you let me carry the warning to our brothers in Damascus."

## THE CROWN TREE 25

Saul of Tarsus and the Temple guards assigned to accompany him took the precipitous boulder-bordered road that dropped downward from Jerusalem to Jericho.

From a cord about his neck was suspended the tablet of authority from the High Priest; in his heart was an intense, consuming flame of desire to destroy utterly those who refused proper obedience to the Lord God of Israel and His Torah. "I burn within me, O Lord of Heaven, for the true worship of the One God." The words arose unspoken from the depths of his soul. "Strengthen my hand to punish Thy enemies, that I may cleanse Israel of those who follow the false Messiah, who flout Thy commandments and dishonor Thy Temple and its priests."

Saul could feel in imagination the palm of his hand rounding upon the handle of the lash, he could hear the thongs swish through the air to descend upon the broad back of a recreant son of Israel prostrate before him, he could see the white skin gashed and the blood oozing and welts rising, and stripe crossing reddening stripe. "O God, harden my heart that I shall not pity, that I shall never stay my hand against them."

He held up the hand before his eyes, which sometimes now itched and burned, and he fancied a sudden darting pain in his fingers and along his arm. He studied the palm, opening and closing the hand, and examined the back of it, tanned with much sun, and the third joints of the fingers black with hairs. This is the hand that reached forth for the shed garments of those who stoned the apostate Stephen, that held the whip that added lashes to the back of Amaziah, servant of Mary of Cyprus, at whose house I was accustomed often to visit my once devoted friend

Joseph Barnabas. This hand has borne misery and pain to many. Can it be that these eyes smart because they have looked on sorrow and hurt of my own making, is this hand being punished because it has wielded the whip? Can it be that God in His inscrutable way is warning me to stay my hand against those who declare allegiance to that Galilean they proclaim the Messiah of God?

"Never! It is rather the Evil One who would tempt me into relaxing my hand against them!" He spoke the words aloud with such vehemence that the man nearest him turned around. Saul saw his puzzled expression. "The sun hasn't addled my brain," he said. "I was just thinking aloud."

No, he reasoned, there is no pain in the hand. It's my imagination. My eyes sting and smart, but they have troubled me for months. Feeling pain in the hand is but a machination of the Evil One to dissuade me from my course. He would defend those who blaspheme the Holy Name, who treat with contempt certain of His laws and fail to do proper honor to the House of His dwelling. "O God, remove every doubt from my heart, strengthen this hand against them, and give iron to my resolve to chastise those who would dishonor Thee and Thy servants on Mount Moriah!"

He set his heart and his feet to the road and steadily they went down toward Jericho. That night they made camp on the fertile plain north of the walled city. And before the sun had risen over Mount Nebo east of the headland that bordered the Dead Sea they folded their tents, packed them on their beasts, and started straight northward toward Galilee.

Up the steaming trough of the meandering River Jordan they journeyed day after day along the greening floor of the bottom lands, past jungles of tamarisk, its pink-white flowers stirring gently on thin feathery branches, waving reed grass three times the height of a man, slender even taller papyrus stems surmounted by tufted bunches of hairy streamers, flaming poplars, lotus trees, graceful willows bending above the twisting channel, mimosa, henna, capers, lavender.

Through the glories of this ancient land of Israel they pushed relentlessly up the narrow cleft cut by the descending river. But the eyes of Saul of Tarsus, even when they were free of the smarting, were not on the trees and flowers and waters of the Jordan, for he saw only the urgency of the mission that was speeding him to Damascus to fall with fury on the enemies of Israel's God.

He did not slacken his caravan's pace. Hardly stopping long enough at night to gain refreshment for the next day's journey, he drove his men and beasts toward the little Sea of Galilee. Having reached it, he swung left and traveled along its western shore as far as Tiberias, capital city of Herod Antipas the Tetrarch, where he took passage and crossed on a northeasterly course to land in Gaulanitis below Bethsaida, where the shoreline curves to go southward.

Nor did they pause long on the shores of ancient Bashan. Once again they moved northward, reaching within a day's steady journeying the region of the Waters of Merom. Above this tiny lake, drained by a narrow stream that emptied into the northern end of the Sea of Galilee, and almost at the gates of Caesarea Philippi they turned eastward toward the desolate and stony wastes of Hauran steaming beneath a pitiless sun.

Beyond the desert, level in a fertile plain of clear streams and luxuriant growth, was Damascus.

. . . A few more days and we shall have reached the walls of the old city and His enemies will be in my hands. Strengthen my will, O God, soften not my hand against them. My hand. This hand. . . .

He held up the right hand, flexed the fingers.

. . . It has been paining me, of a certainty. Perhaps the Evil One is determined to try me, to test me utterly. But more likely it comes from the strain of helping with the unloading and loading of the tents on the camels. . . .

He shook his hand, let it fall again to his side. The pain would pass shortly.

But travel through the sand and gravel and hot stones of Hauran's desert country was slow and torturing. They plodded along beneath a sun that seemed all the more merciless when looking back over their shoulders they could see in the heat-shimmering distance behind them the eternal snows mantling Mount Hermon.

Sometimes, too, the desert was wrapped about in a deadly calm and then suddenly all the winds of heaven would seem unloosed upon it, and Saul and his men and beasts were lashed and flayed by whirling sand and gravel that tore at their mantles and stung and bit into uncovered flesh. If by good fortune they were plodding at the time through stretches of upthrust boulders, rounded and smoothed by countless such storms, they would throw themselves prostrate behind these rocks and, wrapping their heads with their mantles, lie still until the storm had passed. And Saul, his face buried in the sand, would seek of God assurance that neither storm nor other enemies would be permitted to endanger his mission to Damascus.

. . . O God of the calm and the storm, protect me that I may do Thy will, that I may be Thy instrument of vengeance upon Thine enemies. Suffer me to go to Damascus and seize and return to Jerusalem those whose words and deeds are become a stench in the nostrils of the Lord God of Israel. . . .

In the intense light that followed the clearing away of the storm clouds, the burning bright light that enveloped them with the quick settling of the swirling dust, Saul read the answer to his prayer. The God of Abraham and Isaac and Jacob, the God of the Chosen, even his God, would guide his footsteps and his hand.

So wearily and steadily the small caravan of Saul of Tarsus pushed onward toward the ancient walled city in Syria's spreading plain. And after a time they neared the border of the desert and saw, far and low in the east, the walls and towers of Damascus.

. . . Soon now, O God, very soon. . . .

Perhaps even on the morrow he would present his tablet of authority to the priests at Damascus and command their aid in seeking out the blaspheming Jews of that city. He would first apprehend one Ananias, the principal leader of the sect of the Galilean and most wanton of the Damascus blasphemers, a man of whose evil teachings and acts the High Priest had heard much. He would bind Ananias and carry him with his followers to face the priestly tribunal in Jerusalem. The court likely would condemn him to the stoning ground, for is he not as guilty as was Stephen? And would not a way be found to outwit the Roman soldiers and do Ananias to his deserved death?

. . . This time, O God, this hand will not be content to receive the mantles of those who cast the stones. This hand too will hurl stone after stone until the body of the blasphemer is covered in stones and blood, until the Evil Spirit that tempted this hand is exorcised by righteous action in the cause of the God of the Chosen People. . . .

The trudging Saul stopped in his tracks. Twenty paces ahead and a little to the left an outcropping of small rocks broke the evenness of the desert's sandy floor. Toward its center several stones, some smoke-smudged and others brown-streaked with iron rust, formed a low circling mound.

Saul pointed. "The stones! The stones!"

"Like countless others in the desert, Rab Saul," the guard nearest him observed. "Some passing Syrian camel drivers paused here to cook their evening meal."

But the eyes of the man of Tarsus were fixed on the piled stones, for the others did not see what he was seeing. They did not see the white body, torn and bloody, on its knees in the center of the mound of rocks, grim and gore-splattered. They did not see the long forearm, gashed and dripping blood, lifted and pointing across the steaming sands. They saw not the wide eyes open and serene, the expression of ecstasy flooding the sweat-streaked and blood-stained face. Nor could they hear the triumphant ringing voice: "I see him! I see the Lord Messiah coming on wings to meet me!" Those beside Saul could not see the stones descending upon the broken and bleeding body as it fell on its knees under the avalanche of stones and then pushed upright to the knees once again and turned the bleeding countenance full on Saul. They saw not the rapture on that face, the glory blazing from it. Nor did they hear the clear, pleading words: "O Master, forgive them! Forgive them, Master, for they know not what they are doing."

They saw, however, that their leader's eyes were riveted on the small mound of begrimed and rust-smeared rocks. They saw him lift his right hand, as if to shield his eyes from some ghostly vision, and they saw the hand, trembling as with an ague, fall again to his side.

"God in Israel!" they heard Saul cry out. "Stephen!"

"Too much sun." The man beside the one who had spoken to Saul gravely tapped his forehead. "We must raise a tent quickly and provide him shade and rest, else he may shortly suffer a sunstroke."

But Saul heard.

"No," he said, shaking his head sharply as though to clear his vision, "it was but a passing illusion. I'm fit again. There is no time to be lost. Let us push on to Damascus."

. . . Protect me, O God, against the wiles of the Tempter. Keep me from the clutches of the Evil One who even here at the gates of Damascus would turn me aside from the defense of Thy cause. . . .

They had trudged hardly a mile farther when the storm struck them in full rage. The men dropped on their faces, their mantles wrapped about their heads, their feet drawn up into their robes. Camels and donkeys crouched low into the sand, nudged their heads under their ribs.

Then just as quickly as it had burst upon them, the storm was gone. As they arose and shook out the sand from their garments and prepared the beasts for resuming the journey, the clouds moved away, the swirling sand settled, and the sun blazed out, lighting the whole upturned bowl of the heavens in burning, merciless brilliance. To the men about Saul it seemed that the sky never before had been so clear and shining, the heat never more oppressive. It enfolded them like a blanket of finest thick wool. It fell upon them from the great clear height of the heavens, it arose about them from the burning sand.

"Rab Saul," said one, "should not we pause half an hour and

rest from the sun and heat? It would be small trouble to raise one tent for shade."

"No." Saul pointed. "The walls of Damascus rise high on the horizon. We are nearing the city. Let's push onward. We'll soon be there, and in the city we'll find refreshment."

So saying, he started trudging again, across the hot sands toward the city. But almost in the same instant the very doors of the sky seemed to swing wide and a great shaft of white light, blinding in its brilliance, centered on the little caravan struggling forward. The men fell to the earth and shut their eyes against the pain of the light.

Then Saul heard the voice. "Saul, Saul, why do you persecute me?"

The man of Tarsus lay prostrate, the men saw as they arose, but this time his face was not pressed into the sand. He was on his back and his wide fearful eyes seemed to be looking unseeing straight into the center of the dazzling light.

"Who are you, Lord?"

The men knew these to be the words of Saul. And they saw his lips move, and his whole frame was trembling. But they saw none other.

"I am Jesus whom you are persecuting." Clearly Saul heard the voice, strong but resonant, compelling but gentle.

Saul answered the voice. "Lord, what will you have me to do?" The tone was that of pride suddenly shattered.

"Arise and go into the city. There it will be told you what you are to do."

Saul twisted his sun-blackened body to bury his face in his palms against the hot sand. And now, it seemed to those watching wide-eyed and fearful, the light appeared to lose its greater brilliance and fade into the usual brightness of a midday sun on the heated desert.

. . . O God, forgive me! Forgive me, Master, forgive, forgive. . . .

He drew up his knees under his burnt body, lifted his face from the sand, struggled to his feet as hands reached out to help him.

"Rab Saul, I—we—what—"

Saul seemed not to hear. He opened his reddened eyes, raised his left hand before his face, moved it in a half circle in front of him.

"Let us go straightway into Damascus," he commanded.

The man supporting him saw that the old fierceness had gone from his strong eye and the tone of cold authority from his voice.

"But, Rab Saul—" He stopped, for the man of Tarsus had turned slowly to look in the direction of the guard's voice.

"I am blind," Saul said. "I can see nothing." He paused. "But not so blind now as I was through the years until a moment ago when I looked into the eyes of Jesus of Nazareth the Messiah of God."

From eyes they perceived to be sightless they saw tears overflowing to run down his bronzed and sun-blackened cheeks.

"Take me by the hand," he said, as he held forth the left hand. "Lead me into Damascus."

The right hand, the fingers knotted, hung by his side.

## THE CROWN TREE 26

At a wretched khan two days' journey eastward from the Waters of Merom Joseph Barnabas and Amaziah, whom Mary had required to accompany her cousin, halted their camels. The khan, a cluster of low huts forming a rough square, sat on a gentle slope that ran down to a brackish pond in the midst of juniper and carob trees.

Inside the court the two men threaded their way between Syrian camel drivers squatting above small fires over which they were broiling meat. The strong cooking odors mixed sourly with those from the dried camels' dung that served as fuel and the pungent, sweaty stench of the drivers and the resting animals.

"This place fouls the desert air," Joseph observed, blowing through his rebelling nostrils. "It smells worse than Ophel."

Soon they found the proprietor, a begrimed Syrian with a heavy unkempt beard and darting small black eyes. "Has one Saul of Tarsus, a tentmaker from Jerusalem, availed himself of the hospitality of your pleasant khan within the last several days?" Joseph asked, after they had concluded their haggling over the charge for the night's lodging.

The fellow lifted his crumpled headdress, pushed soiled, stubby fingers beneath it as far as the goat's-hair rings that held it in place, scratched his scalp vigorously.

"I remember none by that name," he answered, wrinkling his forehead into a frown. "Did he have a large caravan and do you know whither he was traveling?"

"Likely he had several men with him and a number of camels and donkeys," Joseph Barnabas replied, "and he was on his way to Damascus."

"Was he a man of imposing looks and the appearance of wealth?"

"No. On the contrary, of unimposing appearance. A man younger than his looks, sturdy but of slight build, his head balding above the forehead, beginning to stoop a bit and slightly lame."

"But nevertheless quick to assert his authority, a nervous fellow never calm and seeming to have some great weight on his mind, something driving him—"

"He sounds like Saul. When was he here?"

"Saul? Saul, did you say?" The innkeeper wrinkled his brow, ignored the question. Suddenly his face brightened. "Now I'm sure I did hear that name spoken. They called him Saul—Rab Saul, one of them said—and they spoke with deference. There was something said too about being on a mission and the need of starting before the sun. They did start early, too. It was before day yesterday they set out—in the direction of Damascus."

"We must likewise get started before sunrise," Barnabas told him. "We are two days behind Saul, and we're anxious to overtake him."

"It could be that storms will slow them," the man said. "But

they would likewise delay you." He shook his head. "I doubt if
you can overtake them before they reach Damascus."

Nor did they, though they pushed their camels. And storms,
swirling across the hot face of the desert, had destroyed even the
footprints of Saul's plodding men and beasts.

"We're too late, Amaziah," the younger man said as they came
in sight of the walls of the city. "Already dire harm may have
come to our brethren in Damascus."

But they plodded forward through the sand and the heat. Nor
inside the walls did they pause for refreshment until they had
come upon someone who knew where Ananias lived. They found
the brother at his house.

"Praise the God of Israel and His Messiah, Rab Ananias,"
Joseph Barnabas exclaimed. "We were fearful that already you
had been molested. You are in grave peril. We came from Jerusalem to warn you."

Quickly he related the story of Saul and his evil plans, and how
they had sought either to overtake him and persuade him to de-
sist from his sinful scheme or to get to Damascus ahead of him
and warn those of the fellowship. Joseph even confessed that he
had thought of killing his former friend if the other courses
failed.

"But he came ahead of us, Rab Ananias," he concluded his
recital. "He and his hireling assassins may strike at any moment.
He is armed with a tablet of authority from the High Priest to
take any of the sect to Jerusalem for punishment, even you."

The old man smiled. "Have no fear, my brother. The Lord
God has slain that Saul of Tarsus. He is no more to be feared."

For an instant the countenance of Joseph Barnabas was solemn.

"He was my friend, Rab Ananias. I loved him like a brother.
We sat together at the feet of Gamaliel. But he became the fierce
enemy of my Messiah, and that made him my enemy." He ventured to smile. "And now, praise God, He has removed the greatest of our Lord Messiah's enemies. Our God protects His own."

"Yes, God protects His own!" The old man's expression was
as benign as the silvered locks of his hair and the thin beard

combed into a fan across his hollowed chest. "But now you brothers must wash and eat, and when you have been refreshed from the journey I will reveal to you how the Lord our God has slain His enemy, Saul of Tarsus."

An hour later he led them from his house.

"We are going to the house of one Judas who dwells in the Street Called Straight," Ananias revealed.

When they reached the dwelling of Judas, he spoke to the servant who answered their knock.

"Take us to him who is called Saul of Tarsus."

The man nodded his head in the direction of the stone stairs that went up alongside the house. "In the room above. The door is not barred."

They started climbing the stairs.

"A good place in which to conceal the body until it can be disposed of," Barnabas observed. "The ways of God are mysterious. He brought Saul all the way to Damascus to avenge here the slaying of Stephen." He shook his head sadly. "I had hoped he would become our brother in the fellowship."

"God's ways are ways of mystery," Ananias agreed, "and of a truth He has worked strangely to avenge Stephen."

They crossed the flat roof to the door of the room, evidently Judas' guest chamber. When Ananias opened the door, they felt the stir of cool air. The old man stood back for the two to go ahead.

In the half-light they saw the body of a man on a mat in the corner. But as they approached, it moved.

"But you said—" Barnabas stopped, astonished.

"I said the Lord God had slain Saul. That is true. The former Saul of Tarsus is no more." The old man smiled; his voice was gentle, calming. "He was slain three days ago as he neared Damascus. He was destroyed utterly in the only manner an enemy can be destroyed—by being transformed into a friend, henceforth a friend and brother in the fellowship of our Lord Jesus Christ. Is it not so, Brother Saul?"

"It is so indeed," the man on the mat answered. "The old Saul is dead, may the God of Israel be praised." He seemed tired by the exertion of speaking. But he twisted about to face the old man standing above him. "Ananias, who are these others?"

"How do you know that I am called Ananias?"

"In a vision I was told your name and that you would come and heal me." He raised himself on his elbow. "I am blind. I have seen nothing since I looked into the face of Jesus the Messiah and talked with him in the desert as I was approaching Damascus."

Barnabas, speechless, saw that Saul's eyes were bloodshot and swollen and the edges of the lids red and inflamed, and the lashes were matted together. His sightless eyes turned now on the old man. "Ananias, how did you know you were to come to me?"

"The Lord likewise appeared to me in a vision and told me to come into the Street Called Straight and inquire at the house of one Judas for a man named Saul of Tarsus. When I was about to argue with the Lord because I'd heard much evil of Saul, the Lord would not hear me but commanded me forthwith to come minister to you so that you might receive the renewal of your sight."

Still silent, Barnabas watched as Ananias took from the fold of his robe a white napkin and unfolding it, revealed a small cruse. On the corner of the napkin he poured a trickle of thick oil from the cruse, and bending over the inert Saul, began to apply it gently to the inflamed eyes.

"Brother Saul, as I have just revealed to you," he said, and the old man's words were gentle and comforting, "the Lord, even Jesus who appeared to you on your journey to Damascus, has commanded me to come to you that you might receive again your sight and be filled with the Holy Spirit."

"May God be praised, I know it."

"But he said another thing concerning you. The Lord declared that you who have been his great enemy would become unto him a chosen vessel, that you would bear his name to the Gentiles, and before kings, and that he would show unto you how great things you must suffer for the sake of his name."

Bending down again over Saul, his gaunt knees on the edge of the mat, Ananias wiped the inflamed eyes gently with the dry portion of the soft napkin, and then he got stiffly to his feet. Reaching down, he grasped Saul by the hand.

"Rise up, Brother Saul, and in the name of the Lord God of Israel and Jesus His Son our Lord, receive your sight!"

Saul struggled to his feet, stood blinking his eyes until they rested on the old man.

"I see! I see again, praise be to God and His Messiah our Lord Jesus!" Tears were streaming from his reddened eyes and rolling in unrestrained tiny rivulets down his cheeks.

"Go over to the window and pull back the curtains, brother," Ananias said to Amaziah, "so that Saul can see the better. Now, that is good, Amaziah," he added, when light flooded the room.

"Amaziah?" Saul was staring at the man near the window. "Forgive me, Amaziah," he said, his tone humbled and pleading, when he had recognized Mary's servant. "Forgive me, I pray you."

"Freely I forgive you, Saul. Not one lash do I hold against you. And likewise Joseph Barnabas here forgives you."

"Barnabas! Praise God! Barnabas, my brother!" He stepped forward to meet the smiling Joseph, and they fell into each other's arms. Then quickly they stood apart. "God forgive me, Joseph, forgive my grievous sinning. Never has there been a greater sinner, never, never!" His eyes now were on the floor and his shoulders shook. "But as God is just, so is He merciful. In these last days of my most grievous sinning I have never had you out of my mind, Joseph, nor have I ever been able to escape from the face of dying Stephen. I have never been able to put away from me Stephen's ecstatic countenance as he went to meet the Lord Messiah, whom he must have seen from the stoning pit." He turned to look toward the window. "O my Lord Jesus, I thank Thee for the face of Stephen that has led me inexorably to Thee!"

The man who had been Saul of Tarsus the scourge seemed now unmindful of the three men beside him. He was staring straight into the light. A new glory illumined his undistinguished face, more homely now that his eyes were red and tear-filled and his cheeks streaked with his weeping. But the glory was not of the light from the window.

Saul closed his eyes and his lips moved, though no sound came forth. Then quickly he dropped to his knees and slipped down to prostrate himself on the mat.

"Let us go." Ananias touched Barnabas on the shoulder. "He must now talk with the Lord."

At the door Joseph Barnabas turned to look back. Then without a word he followed the two from the chamber.

## THE CROWN TREE 27

For the first several months after the *Venezia* landed him in Rome Centurion Longinus Aemilius Varro was stationed at Castra Praetoria, the sprawling camp of the Praetorian Guard at the northeastern corner of the city's wall. Summoned the day after his arrival to the palace of the new prefect, he had been informed that he would remain in the capital on temporary assignment until plans had been completed for sending an army into Gaul on an important mission; then he would accompany that army northward.

Frequently during these months in Rome on evenings when he was off duty he visited the Quirinal Hill mansion of Senator Flaccus, and usually he found Lalage there, for she and Publius, though still married, were seeing less and less of each other. From her father Lalage had heard the story of the crucifixion of the Galilean by a detail commanded by Longinus and of the strange effect the man's death had had upon the centurion. In conversations with Senator Varro her father had learned of the nightmares Longinus had been having and of his aversion to returning to Palestine. And Cornelius had written them from Jerusalem the amazing report of the Galilean's having come forth alive from the tomb.

The girl had considered the man's crucifixion of no importance except in the way it had affected Longinus; she had dismissed the report of his resurrection as the fanciful imagining of certain superstitious Jews. But one night several weeks after his return from the duty at Ptolemais, when Longinus had seemed unusually meditative and unresponsive to her efforts at gaiety, she had thought of the crucified Galilean and chided him with having a morbid fear of the long-dead Jew. His face had flushed, his perturbation was evident, and a few minutes later he had left. She had not mentioned the crucified man after that, nor had he. And one day weeks later he had come to the house on Quirinal Hill to say farewell once more. Preparations were finished for the mission to Gaul; he was leaving the next morning.

For months Lalage heard nothing of him. Then one day her father told her that Senator Varro had informed him that he had received a message from his son. Longinus was expecting to complete his assignment in Gaul within the next several months. And he had inquired about her, had asked if she had divorced Publius.

But the centurion hadn't returned from Gaul as he had hoped he might. Instead, he had been sent into Germania. Nor did he know, he wrote Senator Varro, how long the new duty would keep him away from Rome.

Lalage wondered if he had learned that finally she had divorced her husband. She wondered if he would ever return to the capital. Strangely, she had been thinking this morning of Longinus as she sat idly in the solarium. Then Philo had rapped gently. A guest, he reported, awaited her in the peristylium.

Quickly she drew on her dressing robe, pulled tight the belt and knotted it; then she went into the peristylium.

"Longinus! By bountiful Mother Ceres! Where did you come from? When did you get here?"

He caught her in his arms, laughing, pulled her close.

"From a long way, Lalage, and I arrived only last night." He held her out from him, studied her. "By Jupiter, you aren't a day older—just more beautiful!"

They talked a long time. He was in jovial mood. He told her of his experiences in distant Gaul and Germania and of the strangely different people and customs of these remote provinces. Fleetingly the thought came to her that Longinus had forgot the crucified Jew. She hoped he had. She would be careful to say nothing that would remind him of the Galilean.

Finally he told her why he had come.

"Tomorrow night Caligula is giving a banquet honoring Agrippa, who is back in Rome and in the good graces of the Emperor once more. I'd hardly got home when he learned about it from the Prefect, and early this morning he sent a messenger bearing an invitation to the banquet and instructing me to bring you." He grinned. "It's orders from the Prince. Will you go?"

"Then you're asking me because you were ordered to do it?"

"No, Lalage." He laughed. "Because I want you to go with me. I was anxious to get home so I could see you. I thought of you all the time I was away in the provinces. Will you go—on my invitation?"

"Will I go?" Her laugh was high and merry and excited. "Longinus, for a long time I've been wondering if you would ever come back!"

## THE CROWN TREE 28

"Turn it off! Turn it off! By the gods, stupid one, will you boil me alive like a lobster in a kettle?"

Already Lalage's young slave woman, on her knees beside the ornate bathtub sunk into the marble floor of the sumptuous tepidarium, was turning the tap above the silver lion's-head through whose mouth the steaming water was pouring in a diminishing stream.

"Now, Aspasia, turn off the cold, too," the girl in the bathtub commanded, her tone calming. "That's good. Now start scrubbing me. And use plenty of soap."

Beside the thin silken pillow on which she knelt the slave woman had set a large silver tray filled with small dishes of delicate ware, jars, and vials, and an array of cosmetic instruments—creams, pastes, oils, perfumes, pumices, soaps, depilatories, small scissors, a bone strigil, razors, a file for the nails, brushes, sponges. Quickly she selected a sponge, soaped it well, and bending down, began to scrub gently the white stem of the girl's neck, taking care not to soap the black hair piled high on her head and held securely by a ribbon of flashing scarlet. When the woman had finished bathing the shapely shoulders and arms and, as the girl leaned forward, the straight white back that went down to a thin waist and gently rounded hips, she paused.

"Now my feet and legs," her mistress directed, as she lay back in the warm, heavily scented suds and lifted a foam-covered small foot. "And be careful, Aspasia. You know how it tickles."

The bath completed, Lalage sat up, waved an imperious hand.

"Take them away, Aspasia—out to the solarium. While you're doing my face and hair I can be getting some sun. Then go quickly and summon Ariadne and Chloe to manicure my nails. Bring my things, too—the ones you've laid out—to the dressing room. And a towel, stupid one, and my dressing gown of fabric Cornelius fetched me from Phoenicia."

She lay back in the water. "While you're doing that I'll relax a moment"—she winked a dark eye at the slave balancing the tray as she got to her feet—"and meditate wickedly on what could happen after the banquet this evening." But quickly her mood changed. "Hurry, awkward legs. By Bona Dea, this time I don't want to keep Longinus waiting."

The slave already was opening the door. "Yes, Mistress Lalage, I'll be prompt. If I can only find those two young scatterbrains—" The door closed behind her. Lalage heard her footsteps as she crossed the dressing room to enter the peristylium.

Aspasia had been gone but a moment when Lalage sat up, and in one quick motion stepped from the water. Shaking her arms and body free of the clinging drops, she scampered into the dressing room, leaving wet footprints on the marble squares. In the center of the small octagonal chamber, her wet body shivering from the sudden onrush of cool air, she smiled with evident delight as her tapering fingers gauged the curves of her hips and her eyes surveyed the length of her lithe frame; and a myriad of slender, glistening young women smiled back, for on the eight walls, centering the spaces between the carved marble pilasters, long rectangles of highly polished bronze reflected Lalage's figure until on all sides an infinity of white bodies stood trembling and smiling between unending lines of shining marble sentinels.

But just as quickly the smile was gone and she was screaming for her maid. "Aspasia, where are you, slow bones? Bring the towel; I'm freezing. Aspasia, what can you be doing?"

She heard the slave woman's sandals on the marble of the dressing room, and then the door opened and the girl, her arms filled with clothing, entered.

"One of these days," Lalage stormed, "I'll lose my patience and have you sold to a Jew in the Forum Piscatorium, and you'll bear for him a dozen brats smelling forever of fish and garlic!"

Carefully Aspasia laid out the clothing on the tiled bench. Then, a large yellow bath towel over her arm, she approached her shivering mistress. "The girls were just finishing serving Senator Flaccus his afternoon fruit and wine," she explained unhurriedly, "but they'll be here by the time you are ready to go into the solarium."

"Forgive me, Aspasia," the girl said, as the slave began vigorously to rub her shoulders and back. "I won't sell you to a Jew in the Forum Piscatorium; I'll merely have your mouth poured full of hot lead and have you thrown into the Tiber." She steadied herself with hand on the bent shoulder of the slave woman and lifted a foot to be toweled.

Aspasia, drying now the other foot, smiled. "Thank you, mistress, for such consideration."

Playfully Lalage tweaked the pink ear even with her waist. "How could I ever get along without you, Aspasia, even for one day?" She put her foot to the floor, stood erect, stretched. "I'm dry now. Rub me down, but quickly; don't dally over it."

From the tray the slave maid chose jars and vials, and with deft fingers rubbed ointments and sweet oils into the white skin glowing now from the vigorous toweling.

"That's enough for this time, Aspasia," Lalage said after a while. "Now a light dash of the Arabian"—she pointed to one of the vials—"and after that a touch of the Campania behind each ear. I believe the Centurion Longinus might have a weakness for the Campania." She winked saucily. "What do you think, Aspasia?"

"I should think rather that the Centurion Longinus would be attracted to my mistress. But that would be discrimination, not weakness."

"By the bountiful Ceres, Aspasia, you are a clever one—a diplomat, a poet, and a philosopher. Now fetch me the robe, little one."

Aspasia stepped over to the bench, picked up the crimson silken dressing robe. Then she bent down again, caught up lightly a bit of gossamer. "Perhaps my mistress would wish to put this on first?"

"Yes. Fetch it, and help me with it."

Again she supported herself, as she stood on one foot and then the other, with her hand on the bent back and shoulder of the maid as Aspasia helped her into the weightless film of sheer silk.

"Now the robe," she commanded. "Don't you think it's gorgeous, Aspasia? My brother is so thoughtful, and don't you love the rich color? Cornelius has excellent taste."

"It is lovely," Aspasia agreed.

"It's amazing what beautiful things come from Phoenicia. How do you suppose those Phoenicians are able to obtain such a lively, sparkling crimson?"

"The dye they use comes from two shellfish found on the Phoenician coast, called the Murex and the Buccinum Lapillus. Your robe was made of material double-dyed—first with the preparation obtained from the Murex, which gives a dull purple color, and then in a vat containing the extract from the Buccinum—"

She paused, for Lalage was regarding her open-mouthed.

"How in the world did you know this? Sometimes you astound me with the things you know. Who told you about this dye the Phoenicians use?"

"Once on a visit to Tyre I went out to the plants and watched the workers dyeing the fabric which had been made in the weaving sheds of my father's—" She stopped.

"But I thought your father was a merchant in Macedonia."

"He was," Aspasia said, after a moment. "But he owned properties in other lands also."

"Then you must have had many beautiful things, Aspasia. Did you ever have any clothes from fabric like this?"

"Yes. I remember a gown of this exact shade, and how it matched the stones in a necklace given me—" Abruptly she broke off, and turned her face away.

"By your father?" she asked gently.

"No, a friend."

"A man, Aspasia?"

"Yes."

"You loved him?"

"Yes." She faced Lalage, her countenance impassive. "Mistress, don't you want to go into the solarium now?"

"A Greek?" Lalage ignored her question.

"Yes, from Antioch in Syria."

"Were you to be married?"

"We were betrothed. He was on his way from Antioch to take me to his home when—" She paused, looked away.

"When the Roman soldiers came to your house?"

The slave girl nodded, her eyes beginning to fill.

"It's a hard world, Aspasia."

"For many, yes."

"And the only one we'll ever know, too, don't you think?"

"I don't know, Mistress. Sometimes I think and hope— It would be grossly unfair to many if this were the only life."

"But it is, Aspasia. It must be. So the only thing for us to do is to make the most of it. I agree with your Greek philosopher

Epicurus. This life is the only one we'll have; live it to the fullest; enjoy it. To do so one must have money and power, Aspasia, and money gives power. Isn't it so, little one?" She caught up the vial of perfume, held its slender mouth against the ball of her finger, pressed the finger to ears, neck, shoulders. "I suppose some of the blood of that Flaccus of a hundred years ago, old Quintus Horatius, must flow in my veins, though I don't particularly relish being related to a poet. But he had the right idea about life, Aspasia. Live it, by all the gods! Rich food, as we shall have tonight at Caligula's banquet; fine clothes"—she fingered the silken smoothness, caressing it to the curves of her supple figure— "and luxurious indolence, and for me, men, Aspasia, strong, handsome men, always men, like Centurion Longinus, by Bona Dea!" A shadow clouded her smile. "By Bona Dea, ha! There are no gods, my kitten. There are only men—men to tease, beguile, bewitch, enjoy! For a woman with fire in her veins, Aspasia, what is there to life but a man!"

Just as suddenly her exuberance was gone. "This man of yours, Aspasia. Is he a soldier, and strong and handsome?"

"Strong and handsome, but not a soldier, Mistress. He's a physician, and a philosopher, too."

"What is his name, Aspasia?"

"He is called Luke."

"A physician and a philosopher. What does he think of the gods of Assyria? Does he worship Astarte?"

"I don't think he believes in those gods, Mistress, nor the Greek gods, nor those of Rome."

"Then he's an Epicurean, an intelligent man, Aspasia."

The girl shook her head. "No, he's no Epicurean. He believes in a god and an afterlife. I suppose he believes very much like the Jews."

"Surely not like the Jews, Aspasia!"

"Mistress, don't you want to go into the solarium now and let me do your hair? The Centurion Longinus may be coming soon."

"Yes, we'll go now. Summon Chloe and Ariadne to do my nails."

In a few moments she was settled on a chair in the solarium, with one of the young slave girls at each hand and Aspasia busy with preparations to begin the hairdressing.

"Your betrothed doesn't believe in our gods or those of the Greeks, but believes like the Jews, you were saying." Though Lalage denied the existence of gods, she seemed eager to discuss them. "How did it happen that he, a Greek, was interested in the religion of the Jews?"

"It was not altogether the orthodox Jewish religion that interested him, Mistress; it was a new religion that has recently come out of Palestine. He heard of it from a group of adherents who came to Antioch from Jerusalem."

"A new religion! Poor superstitious people. As if there were not already too many of these delusions called religion."

Aspasia made no comment, but busied herself with her task. After a while Lalage spoke again.

"What does this new religion teach?"

"The orthodox Jews teach that there is but one god and he rules all the earth and the stars of the heavens. This new religion, if I understand what Luke told me, teaches that this god sent his son to live in the world to redeem it from its errors by being sacrificed to him."

"How silly! How could an intelligent man like you say your Luke is believe in such a fantastic story?"

"I don't know that he believes it. But he was assured by the men from Jerusalem that this man actually did come to earth, live like an ordinary man, and die as a sacrifice, and has now returned to live with the father god."

"Where did this happen, and when? And was this son burnt on an altar, like an ox?" Lalage's shrill laughing caused Aspasia's comb to slip from her hair. "That story's less plausible than some of those told about our Roman gods."

"It happened only in recent years, and in Jerusalem, Luke was told, as I understand it. The son of the god was nailed on a Roman cross, and after three days he arose—"

"By all the gods!" Suddenly Lalage's derisive tone was gone.

"Could that have been the man Longinus crucified? I've heard him and Cornelius speak of the fellow. Some sort of religious man, they said, a strange character whom they don't seem to be able to forget. Did Luke learn his name?"

"A Galilean carpenter called Jesus, if I'm not mistaken."

"That's the fellow!" Lalage pulled away her right hand from the nimble fingers of Chloe, regarded the newly manicured nails. "An utterly preposterous notion! A vagrant penniless Jew smelling of sweat and garlic and dying friendless on a Roman cross, and such a fellow being worshiped as a god. Ridiculous! Old Tiberius, who owns palaces and estates and uncounted vast wealth and is master of the world, is the nearest thing to a god I know about, and I'd say he's a poor imitation. I can't understand why crucifying a nobody like that Galilean should cause anyone to lose a minute's sleep. A god, bah! Every sensible person knows there are no gods. And if there were, you'd never hear of one coming out of that benighted, dreary Palestine." She sat up in her chair, so that the girl more easily could manage the hairdressing. "Hurry, Aspasia, Longinus is all the god I'm wanting tonight, and he'll be here any minute. And if we're late, that silly Caligula may have one of his tantrums!"

## THE CROWN TREE 29

Ariadne and Chloe had finished Lalage's hands. She had inspected and approved, and now the girls, each with a foot cradled between her knees, were busy shaping and buffing the nails.

Aspasia with deft fingers fastened the emerald clasp of the delicately fashioned gold chain that went around her head and supported at the back a bag of thinnest gold mesh into which her raven-black hair had been knotted at the neck. The sparkling clasp sat in the center of her forehead below loosely waved short curls, and the hair on top of her head, parted lightly in the middle, had been combed over the crown and woven into the rounded flaring knot.

"Now my mirror, Aspasia." The girl brought it, held it so Lalage could inspect the completed coiffure. "It looks wonderful, little one. You've excelled yourself." She pulled the mirror nearer. "But you'll have to do something about my eyebrows, and here's a drooping lash." She pointed. "Do you see it?" Aspasia nodded, reached for the tweezers. "Jerk it; it hurts less that way."

When the girl had removed the offending lash and thinned and smoothed the arched brows, Lalage sat upright again. "Now my face, Aspasia, and do hurry. Longinus may be here any minute."

Quickly the slave girl applied rouge to the cheeks and a whitening compound lightly to her forehead and temples. Then carefully she reddened Lalage's lips.

"Put on the blue lines rather heavily," Lalage instructed her next. "It's bright here in the solarium but in the banquet chamber the light will be subdued. But do hurry, small one."

"Yes, Mistress. It will take but a moment." She selected a pencil from the tray and with quick, practiced fingers traced the lines of the veins in each temple. When she had finished, she reached for the mirror, held it before Lalage. "Is there anything else now to be done, Mistress?"

The girl studied the face in the mirror. "No, I don't think so, Aspasia; you've done well." She stood up. "Now help me get my clothes on. You girls come too; we'll need you with the gown."

They went into the dressing room, and quickly she pulled off the robe, stood a moment surveying herself in the mirrors.

"I'll need a little extra height for Longinus," she observed, more to herself than the slaves. "He's a tall one, even with his abominably close-cropped hair. Fetch me the gold openwork shoes, Aspasia; you know, the ones with the emeralds and rubies." She held her feet for the two girls to slip the shoes on, and they fastened the jeweled clasps. Then she stood evenly, regarded herself again in the mirrors. "These high heels will help. Now quickly, Aspasia, help me on with my things."

From the bench Aspasia lifted up a gossamer thin white under-skirt, held it out in a flaring circle. "Come, you girls, help with this."

"Yes," Lalage added, "and don't let it touch me when you put it over my head; I don't want my hair or face spoiled."

Carefully the three lowered the garment to the girl's thin waist, pulled it out smooth, fastened the tiny clasp. Then they stood away.

"I know what you're thinking, Aspasia," Lalage said, smiling. "You're thinking it's shamefully transparent, aren't you?"

"Perhaps with one other underskirt, Mistress, and then the gown—"

"Another won't be necessary. The stola will be enough. The lights won't be bright, and I want to be—enticing, little one." She spun about on one foot, watching in the mirrors her revolving figure, to which the fitted skirt clung revealingly, and then she stopped. "It was with such a garment of China silk woven on the island of Cos, I've heard, that Cleopatra enticed Julius Caesar and Mark Antony." She ran her palms caressingly along her hips. "But hurry, Aspasia; help me on with the gown."

It was of shimmering white silk, heavier in texture and less transparent than the skirt. With great care they slipped it over Lalage's coiffured head and adjusted it to her figure. "Be careful, girls," Aspasia cautioned. "You might pull a thread."

"Yes, it's a shame what my father paid for this stola," Lalage observed. "It actually cost him more than its weight in gold, not counting the gems. In fact, it cost him as much as you did, Aspasia, though I'm certain your Luke would have paid much more for you."

The stola was floor-length, so that only the tips of the girl's jewel-encrusted shoes showed; from the shoulders it was fash-ioned in a wide V that dropped down to the line of the waist to reveal the greater portion of Lalage's milk-white back; while the front above the waist was formed of two very low-cut sections that crossed each other to end in narrowed small loops supported at the throat by a thin golden chain circling the neck and held by a round onyx clasp. Another chain, woven in a mesh of fine gold threads fastened at the front by a clasp embedded in a tremendous imitation emerald, emphasized the slenderness of her waist.

Aspasia was fastening this resplendent belt when from the peristylium someone rapped gently on the dressing room door. Chloe ran to respond. Through the crack in the door Lalage saw the servant.

"Yes, Philo. Is the Centurion Longinus here for me?"

"He is, Mistress Lalage." Philo bowed. "With the sedan chair and the torchbearers. He awaits you in the atrium."

"I'm ready, Philo. Tell him I'll be out in a minute." Quickly she appraised herself in the mirror. "Look, Aspasia, am I all right? Will I do?"

"You are beautiful, Mistress. The Centurion is certain to be charmed."

"I hope so. Now quick, Aspasia, get me my palla—the Tyrian wool one; it's in my room, I believe. Bring it to me in the peristylium." She went out the door and Aspasia followed. In a moment she came back with the cloak, a soft light wrap in dark crimson. Quickly she draped it about Lalage's bare shoulders.

"Thank you, little one. You needn't wait up for my return. I'll be very late—I hope." She tweaked the girl's ear, went with eager short steps into the atrium.

He heard her coming, stood up.

"Lalage, you look lovely!" He was studying her with obvious admiration. "Your palla's of double-dyed Tyrian wool." He caught the edge of the cloak with one hand, held it out and rubbed it with the fingers of the other. "And the very finest texture."

"But how did you know, Longinus? Whoever heard of a man, and a soldier at that, knowing about textures, and dyes, and women's clothes?"

"It just happens that that was my business while I was stationed at Ptolemais—knowing everything I could about such things, and making them." He caught the other side of the coat, held it wide. "By all the gods, Lalage, and what a gorgeous gown! If I don't take great care to keep you out of Caligula's reach tonight, he's likely to take you away from me."

"That silly, buffooning effeminate! By the great and little gods and goddesses, Longinus, I wouldn't—I'd never—"

Centurion Longinus wagged a forefinger in front of her pert nose.

"But they say he has a way with women. And one of these days the old man will be dying and then either the grandson Tiberius or the grandnephew Caligula will be Emperor, and I'd wager it would be Caligula. But let's go, Lalage; we'll be late if we don't hurry, and that could throw him into one of his spells of raging."

Rapidly they walked through the atrium. Outside, he helped her into the sedan chair, a large double one with two sets of bearers at the handles. Ahead and behind the sedan waited slaves holding aloft great flaring torches. Longinus raised his hand.

"To the Imperial Palace."

Then he stepped inside, sat down facing Lalage, drew the curtains.

## THE CROWN TREE 30

One of the strangest friendships in all the Empire was that of Prince Gaius Caesar Germanicus of the reigning Julio-Claudian dynasty and Prince Herod Agrippa of Israel.

Gaius, whom all Rome called Caligula, was not yet twenty-five; Agrippa was nearing forty-seven. The Roman's highly acclaimed father, General Germanicus Caesar, son of the old Emperor's brother Drusus and grandson of Mark Antony, had died when the boy was only seven. Born while his mother Agrippina was accompanying his father on a campaign in the north, Gaius had been brought up in army camps and as a child had worn army uniforms, including small boots made especially for him. From

the Latin word for boot, *caliga,* he had got the nickname Caligula, or Little Boot. All his life he had been a pampered and dissolute wastrel.

Agrippa, too, had been orphaned early. The father, Prince
Aristobulus, and his brother, Prince Alexander, had been slain
by their father, the wicked but able Herod the Great. Agrippa
had been reared at the imperial court and in temperament, taste,
and training was more Roman than Israelite.

Both Caligula and Agrippa had spent recklessly and riotously
fortunes to whose accumulation neither had contributed. Though
there was a marked disparity in their ages, in their appetites and
indulgences they were much alike. Many hours they had spent
together—idling in the palaces at Rome and Capri, competing in
the chariot races at the Circus Maximus, visiting the theatres and
gladiatorial games, frequenting the brothels. And now Caligula's
banquet to which Longinus and Lalage were threading their way
in tortuous procession through crowded streets was celebrating
the return of his crony to Rome.

The Herodian prince had arrived recently in the capital from
Alexandria; his wife Cypros and their three children had remained behind. The family had come to the Egyptian capital
after a difficult period in Galilee as the unwelcome guests of
Tetrarch Herod Antipas, Agrippa's uncle and husband of his
sister Herodias.

Agrippa was nearer the age of Drusus, the son of Tiberius and
named for the Emperor's brother, grandfather of Caligula. They
had grown up together from childhood and had been inseparable
friends until the mysterious death fourteen years before of the
Emperor's son. The story had persisted that Drusus was poisoned
through the plotting of Sejanus, but the mourning Tiberius had
refused for a long time to believe the Prefect guilty.

After the death of Drusus, Tiberius had announced that he
wished no longer to see the friends of his son because they would
remind him of the departed heir. And to make the situation
worse for Agrippa, the Herodian prince had made debts that he
was unable to pay. Stern old Tiberius, who believed firmly in

upholding the rigid virtues of ancient Rome, forbade Agrippa to come into the imperial presence until he had paid the debts. So Agrippa reluctantly had sailed away to Judaea.

There he had become destitute and was considering killing himself. But Cypros restrained him and implored aid of Herodias. So Agrippa was made a magistrate of the city of Tiberias.

Soon he was again in debt and disrepute and went to live with Flaccus, president of Syria, where his welcome was short-lived, and he moved to Ptolemais on the coast, where Centurion Longinus had seen him several times before he slipped away in the night aboard a vessel that landed him at Alexandria. There the alabarch was prevailed on to lend him two hundred thousand drachmas. Then he sailed for Rome.

Arrived in Puteoli, Agrippa wrote Tiberius and asked if he might visit him at Capri. The Emperor received him graciously, but hardly had he been installed there when news came that Agrippa had fled Palestine to escape payment of large debts. The old Emperor ordered him away until the debts were settled.

Undaunted, Agrippa went to Antonia, sister-in-law of Tiberius, who had been a devoted friend of Agrippa's dead mother, and pleaded with her to lend him three hundred thousand drachmas. She did, he paid off the money owed and went back to Capri, where he was again welcomed. And now tonight he was being honored by Caligula in Rome.

Racially the Herodians were not Jews, but Idumeans from the mountainous narrow region extending from the southern end of the Dead Sea to the Gulf of Aquabah, the ancient land known as Edom. Their religion, however, what religion they had, was the faith of Israel, and to this faith Herod Agrippa gave strict and manifest allegiance, particularly when in Israel. But tonight Herod Agrippa sat beside Caligula in Rome's Imperial Palace.

Already he was in gay mood when Longinus and Lalage entered the great banqueting chamber and were shown to a table from which they had an unobstructed view of the Roman prince and his guest. Agrippa was talking animatedly with Caligula and from time to time he would lean over and whisper in the ear of a lavishly gowned young woman whose rippling laughter made her elaborately coiffured blonde curls dance.

"Agrippa is in his prime tonight," Longinus whispered to Lalage. "Perhaps he's arranged another loan."

Lalage laughed, but laid her hand on his arm.

"Yes, but not so loud. Stories get back, you know." She was studying the girl beside Agrippa. "That isn't Cypros sitting with him. I wonder who she is?"

"The young wife of some old Senator, no doubt. She looks most—promising." He grinned, winked.

"Yes, and she looks artificial, too. It's apparent that some poor woman from Germania lost her hair to supply that woman's blonde wig."

"I thought it was real, Lalage." He laughed slyly, pinched her arm lightly. "But I'd hardly noticed her. I like black hair, you know."

"You saw her before you did Agrippa or the gracious host. You needn't tell me that blondes don't catch your eye, whether the hair is real or from some other head." But nevertheless his words pleased her.

Slaves were pouring wine in the tall goblets before them and others were serving their red-glazed Arretium plates. Lalage sipped her wine.

"Delicious," she declared. "And I'm hungry. I'm going to eat. You can look at the blonde with Agrippa, if you prefer."

Soon the conversation in the chamber had dwindled to a low hum as the guests joined the host in concentrating their attention upon the lavish food. But after a while Prince Gaius twisted slowly around on his tapestried couch and rose to unsteady feet. A hulking, hairy youth with a narrow small head, already balding, set between huge ears and surmounting a spare frame sagging at the middle from the weight of a stomach fast rounding from heavy dissipation, he stood a moment as the great chamber became completely still. Then he lifted the golden goblet.

"A toast, my friends, to our beloved Prince Agrippa of Israel, who has returned to us from a long stay in his country." The guests lifted their wine goblets. "To Agrippa. May the gods grant him good health, good fortune, good friends, and"—he grinned crookedly and giggled, and the arm holding the silver cup sagged —"good frivolity!" He drank, and the diners drank with him.

But he did not sit down. Instead, when he had set down his goblet he clapped his hands together, and a secretary advanced quickly from his station just behind Caligula's couch; he handed the prince a rolled parchment.

Unrolling it carefully, Caligula held it at arm's length, smiled inanely. "Now, my friends, I have for you a special treat. In honor of Prince Agrippa I have composed a poem, which I shall read to you."

"By the gods," Longinus said in an undertone to Lalage, "I've been afraid of that."

Lalage laughed, but with restraint. Then she bent over, whispered in his ear. "Be careful, Longinus. He'd forgive your insulting his grandmother more quickly than your questioning his ability as a poet."

The poem honoring Agrippa had virtue in that it was short, and when the guests had vociferously applauded its recital, they settled down to the enjoyment of the prodigal feast. There was lavish entertainment, too. Caligula had even arranged for the production, in the square enclosed by the banquet tables, of a scene from a play in which he would have the leading role. He withdrew now on weaving feet to an adjacent small chamber, where he was helped into his costume. Returning, he gave a performance whose fervor served to compensate for its inadequacy in talent. At one point Caligula gestured with such vehemence that he was overbalanced and fell on his face. But servants ran to set him again on unsteady feet and he resumed his performing. Some minutes later the servants rushed him from the chamber, happily in time, when his overburdened stomach, aroused perhaps by his histrionic efforts, threatened to rebel. But the undaunted thespian returned to finish the performance, and the guests, by now hardly in condition to be critical, roared a thunderous approval.

Of course there was dancing. Slave girls from the mountainous regions of Greece, others from Spain, a troop of Numidian women who wriggled and twisted their glistening black bodies in amazing contortions, did dances native to their homelands. In the midst of one of these dances the women guests sat up with squeals of drunken laughter when at a signal from Caligula a servant pulled a silken cord that from containers concealed among the ceiling decorations released upon the diners thin showers of perfume.

But even this aroused them but briefly. Soon men and women were slumping inertly on their silken couches or reclining with their heads almost in their plates. Caligula's head rested on his long hairy arms crossed on the table. Agrippa, more alert than his host, reclined on his elbow. Already the soberer guests, realizing that Caligula's entertaining was finished, had begun to leave.

Longinus swept his hand in embracing gesture. "Rome's patricians," he said, his tone almost a sneer. "For this we enslave the world and haul its treasures here."

Lalage sensed the recurrence of his brooding mood of the days that followed his return from the tour of duty in Palestine that had ended with the Passover crucifixion of the Galilean Jew, for as the banqueting had progressed he had grown more introspective.

"Let's go home," she suggested, laying her head on his shoulder. "Caligula won't awaken before midday tomorrow. He won't know when we left." She squeezed his arm gently. "Besides, I want to have you to myself. The household will be in bed. I even told Aspasia she need not wait up. We can sit in the peristylium and talk as late as you'll stay."

But when they entered the mansion on Quirinal Hill Philo was awaiting them. His solemn countenance indicated concern.

"Mistress Lalage," he announced quickly, "a soldier from Capri awaits Centurion Longinus in the atrium."

"From Capri! By the gods, Philo, you mean from the Emperor?"

"I understand so, sir."

In the atrium the soldier stood up, saluted; he handed the centurion a rolled parchment. "Centurion Longinus, I come from Emperor Tiberius who has been in conference at Capri with the Prefect. I was commanded to bear you this message."

Longinus thanked him, unrolled the parchment.

Slowly his countenance colored. "By all the gods! By all the great and little gods and goddesses!" He rolled up the parchment, tossed it on the ivory-inlaid citrus wood table. "It will require no answer, soldier. You may return to your post, and thank you."

The soldier saluted, without a word withdrew.

Longinus, apparently oblivious of Lalage's great concern, for a while said nothing. When he did speak, it was more to himself than to the girl. "The inept, ostentatious, bumbling fool!"

"You surely don't mean the Emperor, Longinus?"

"No." His face was dark with his scowling; he seemed hardly to realize Lalage was beside him. Then he looked up. "No. Pontius Pilate. He's had more trouble—serious trouble. Now it's with the Samaritans. The Emperor's sending a cohort of seasoned, picked soldiers to Palestine."

"But you, Longinus? The message—was it from the Emperor?"

"The Emperor signed it; the Prefect probably dictated it. It's an order giving me command of this cohort, with Cornelius second in command. They're moving Cornelius from Jerusalem over to Caesarea and sending me back to Palestine with headquarters at Caesarea too. That bumbling Pontius Pilate is always playing havoc." He paused, and when he spoke again his tone was lower, as though he were talking to himself. "Ever since that day in Jerusalem—" He laughed, but it was mirthless, and tinged with resignation, perhaps even with fear. He turned to the girl. "But it's not Pilate's imbecility that is sending me back to Palestine, Lalage. *He's* calling me. I've been expecting him to; I knew he would one day or another."

In his eyes now she saw an expression of bafflement, as of some small animal entrapped in a snare or of a gladiator enmeshed in his antagonist's net and helpless.

"He's been pursuing me ever since that day in Jerusalem," he went on, his tone deliberately calm. "He followed me to Rome and back to Ptolemais and to Rome again, and out to Gaul and Germania, and he came back with me to Rome. I have never been able to escape him. At Ptolemais I determined to put him out of my mind forever, and I tried, Lalage; I tried to leave a dead man in his tomb." His solemn eyes mirrored wonderment touched with pain. "He *was* dead—I know it—but he refuses to *stay* dead."

She caught his hands, held them in firm grasp, looked him in the eyes.

"Listen to me, Longinus. By all the gods, you must forget this foolish delusion. The Emperor Tiberius is ordering you back to Palestine—the Emperor Tiberius, I tell you!"

"Ha! You think so, little one? The Emperor signed my orders, that's true. But *he's* calling me back, the Galilean we crucified that day on the Hill of the Skull, that tall man on the middle cross."

## THE CROWN TREE 31

Three days before the departure from Ostia of the ship on which Centurion Longinus was to sail for the new tour of duty in Palestine, a Praetorian Guardsman knocked at the door of Senator Marcus Aemilius Varro's mansion on the Esqueline with a message for the centurion.

"Prefect Marco wishes to speak with you in his office at once, Centurion," the soldier reported. "It's urgent, he said."

Longinus called a servant to bring his toga, and they walked down the slope of the Esqueline and through Viminal Gate to Castra Praetoria, where the Prefect received him immediately.

"Tribune Longinus—" The Prefect smiled. "I'm addressing you properly," he interpolated, smiling, "because you have been promoted. I had planned to announce it before you sailed for Caesarea, and I'm doing it now." Then his countenance sobered. "But you aren't going to Palestine, Longinus—for the time being, at least. I'm sending a message to President Vitellius of Syria, who is likely now in Jerusalem or Caesarea, explaining why with the Emperor's approval I'm changing your assignment." He smiled wryly. "It was routine with Tiberius; he doesn't know what your new duty is to be. I know Vitellius wants you and needs you, and perhaps before long you can go out to Palestine."

He paused, and his grim countenance relaxed appreciably.

"I have every confidence in the ability of Vitellius to rectify the situation in Palestine that has resulted from Pontius Pilate's mismanagement, which has led Vitellius, you might not have heard yet, to depose the Procurator. When Pilate arrives from Caesarea the Emperor may do with him as he wishes; I don't care. He's caused us nothing but trouble throughout the ten years he's held the position. But so much for Pilate."

The Prefect for a moment studied Longinus intently, then he spoke.

"This assignment I have for you is of more consequence to Rome than would be your return to Palestine. But it's one that will require the exercise of diplomacy, and it must be accomplished, let us say, without the beating of drums."

Longinus nodded. "You'd want the situation handled in a way that would appear routine"—he smiled—"if it appeared at all?"

"Exactly, Tribune." He leaned forward, lowered his voice. "A number of very important people are concerned, one of them the Emperor. Tiberius, you know, is growing old and at times he's crochety and difficult to please." He smiled glumly. "Because of Sejanus, he probably looks with suspicion on the very office of Prefect. So if this matter isn't handled carefully, Tribune, it might involve us all in considerable difficulty—even danger. For that reason you must follow my instructions explicitly."

"I'll do my best to do so, Prefect Marco."

He nodded, looked Longinus in the eyes.

"Did you know that Agrippa has been arrested—by the Emperor's orders?"

"Indeed, no, Prefect! When? Why? I thought that Agrippa was a favorite of the Emperor."

"Generally so, yes. But now Tiberius is very angry with him. Yesterday out at his villa at Tusculum he ordered me to arrest the Jewish prince, and now Agrippa's in chains and even in danger of losing his head." He leaned back. "Tiberius had come in from Capri, and it happened shortly after he reached Tusculum. A fellow named Eutychus, one of Agrippa's freedmen, had been charged by him with stealing certain garments; he was bent on vengeance. Yesterday, after trying for months, he got the ear of Tiberius. He told the Emperor that once while he was in a chariot with Agrippa and Prince Gaius he heard the Jew say to Gaius that he hoped the Emperor would die soon so that Gaius might become Emperor."

"And the Emperor believed this freedman?"

"Yes. Tiberius, they say, had begun to notice that Agrippa was paying much attention to his great-nephew but virtually ignoring his grandson Tiberius. Recently, Tiberius learned, Gaius gave a banquet for Agrippa."

"I was there, sir."

"I know it." Marco smiled. "It might surprise you, Tribune, what I do know sometimes. Well, the Emperor, hearing the fellow's story and the other stories about Agrippa and Gaius, probably came to the conclusion that the two were actually planning his death. After his experience with Sejanus, no doubt Tiberius could believe almost anything. At any rate, he was furious and ordered that Agrippa be put in chains at once."

"And does my assignment have something to do with that fact?"

"Yes. But let me say another word before I explain. No sooner had I ordered Agrippa bound than the word got to Antonia. The Emperor's sister-in-law, you doubtless know, was a devoted friend of Agrippa's long-dead mother. Through the years she has befriended the wastrel—lent him much money, I've been told."

He paused, as if for confirmation.

"So I've always understood."

"Your father, I've also heard, has helped Agrippa. And Senator Varro and Antonia are friends, aren't they?"

"My father was a good friend of her son General Germanicus and he esteems her as a most noble lady."

"So does the Emperor, and so do all of us," Marco agreed. "Yet she and Tiberius are divided over Agrippa. You can appreciate my difficulty, Tribune, because you know well the various persons involved. For instance, there's Gaius." He hesitated. "Perhaps I shouldn't say this, but you understand, Longinus. The Emperor is old; he could die any time. If he dies, as the situation seems now, either his grandson or Gaius will succeed him. If it should be the young Tiberius our being severe with Agrippa would cause us no trouble; he'd probably have Agrippa's head soon after he took the throne." He leaned forward, gestured with outthrust hands.

"But should Gaius get the throne and we had been harsh with his crony Agrippa—" The Prefect drew the edge of his hand slowly across his throat, smiled wanly. "Well, Longinus, that's why I have called for you to come here. I want you to take charge of the guarding of Agrippa. See to it, without in any way offending the Emperor should word reach him concerning it, that Antonia's wishes are carried out, as far as possible."

"It's a difficult assignment, Prefect Marco. I'll be frank, sir, I don't relish it. But I'll discharge it to the best of my ability."

"Good." Marco leaned across the desk, out of long habit lowered his voice. "Tribune, see to it that at all times a soldier is chained to Agrippa. I think that whenever possible you should assign centurions to guard him. His guards should be men of agreeable disposition, and he should be allowed all reasonable privileges. But be sure he is kept where there'd be no chance of the Emperor's seeing him, and under no circumstances"—Marco pounded with the heel of his fist—"must he be allowed to escape."

When Marco dismissed him, Longinus went at once to visit the prisoner.

"I've been assigned by the Prefect to have charge of you, Prince Agrippa," he explained, when he was alone with the man now fettered at his wrists. "The Prefect wants to make your imprisonment just as endurable as we can arrange it."

He told Agrippa that he would have the privilege of being served his meals by his own freedmen, and that he would have much freedom of movement. But at all times he would be chained to a guard.

"It's a hard fate that has overtaken me, Longinus, but nevertheless I'm thankful to the God of Israel, whom I freely confess I've poorly served, that you've been given charge of me." His smile was glum. "I don't now see how it could, but if my fortune should change for the better, I'll not forget your kindness to me. The Emperor is an old man; he might die soon, and if Caligula succeeds to the throne, I'll have the opportunity to repay you. On the other hand, he might suddenly become enraged and have me beheaded—or crucified." He shrugged his shoulders. "I'm not a Roman citizen, you know." His face clouded. "I'm sure such an end for me wouldn't cause my esteemed uncle and brother-in-law, the Tetrarch Herod Antipas, any loss of sleep. Nor even his wife, my devoted sister Herodias."

Suddenly he smiled, and then he told Longinus that shortly after the Emperor had ordered him seized and bound he was standing in a group of prisoners when an old German, seeing his despair, sought to reassure him.

"'You won't continue long in these chains,' he prophesied, 'but will soon be delivered from them, and will be promoted to the highest dignity and power, and will be envied by all those who now pity your hard fortune.'"

"Maybe the old man did have the gift of prophecy. Maybe you'll yet be seated on your grandfather Herod's throne."

Agrippa shook his head.

"No such good fortune could come to me, Longinus. The God of Israel has turned His face away." He brightened. "If the man is really a seer and I should go back to Palestine as tetrarch or king, then I'll surely ask the Emperor—" He broke off, suddenly considering. "Caligula could well be Emperor, and if he is and I'm not dead before then, I'll ask him to send you with me to Israel as Roman adviser to King Herod Agrippa, eh? You have had considerable experience in Palestine, haven't you, Longinus?"

"Yes," he said, "I have." But he did not elaborate.

## THE CROWN TREE 32

Emperor Tiberius, ailing and aging fast in his great villa at Capri, never forgave the prince of the Herods. For weeks, chained to one Roman soldier after another under the careful watch of Tribune Longinus, Agrippa wondered what fate awaited him.

Then on a day in early spring word came to Castra Praetoria that Tiberius Claudius Nero Caesar, who had ascended the throne an already old man of fifty-five and had reigned twenty-two years, five months, and three days, was dead. He had been spending a short season at Misenum at the magnificent villa of the late Lucullus, the story went, when he fell into a fainting spell and appeared dead. But some moments later signs of his imminent revival threatened to end the rejoicing of those about his couch, and it was then that some resolute Roman seized the opportunity of serving well both the old man and the Empire by smothering Tiberius with a firmly held pillow.

Soon came letters from Gaius Caesar Germanicus. One to the Senate announced that he had succeeded to the throne left him by his late beloved great-uncle. A similar letter came to Governor Piso of Rome. Still another ordered the commander of the Praetorian Guard to remove Prince Herod Agrippa from the camp prison and return him to his own private house. The new Emperor had intended to free Agrippa immediately, but his wise old grandmother Antonia had warned him that the act might be considered an affront to the memory of the late Emperor.

Some days later Gaius himself came, bearing to Rome the body of dead Tiberius, for whom he prepared a spectacular funeral. When these rites had been concluded, he ordered that Agrippa, still in his bonds, be freed of his shackles, shaved, bathed, and given fresh clothing. He commanded further that the chains with which he had been bound be weighed with care. When all this should have been done, Agrippa was to be brought to the Imperial Palace.

The next day, when Agrippa stood before Gaius, the new Emperor's face, thin at the temples and hollow-eyed, seemed neither fearsome nor entirely ludicrous.

"Hail, friend Agrippa!" he exclaimed. "The fortunes of both of us have changed greatly since that day we rode together in the chariot, or even the night we sat beside each other at the banquet in the palace of old Tiberius, isn't it so?" He laughed with such a cackling vehemence that his small head bobbed on the slender stem of his turkeylike neck.

"Indeed, O my lord and Emperor, you have spoken truthfully," Agrippa agreed. "I am overcome with happiness that the words I spoke then, which for a season did me much mischief, have now been fulfilled in the elevation of my lord to the throne of mighty Rome, to the great glory and advantage of the Empire!"

The flattering words pleased Gaius. He acknowledged them with a bow, and his smile warmed the hollow eyes.

"I did not know that you were such an orator, Agrippa," he declared. "You would be a success in the Forum or on the stage." He bowed again, and then turned his head to give orders to a servant back of his elbow. "Go, fetch them."

Now the young Emperor was once more facing the Herodian prince.

"Agrippa, I have determined to give you a new and great responsibility, one that you can well execute, I am confident." Caligula's deepset eyes were gleaming with pleasurable anticipation. "The situation in your homeland, as you know, is not good. The Procurator Pontius Pilate has failed utterly in pacifying Judaea and lately has so aroused the enmity of the Jews that

President Vitellius of Syria has deposed him and ordered him
before the Emperor for trial. When he arrives here I shall banish
him or behead him; I care not a fig which sentence I pronounce."

The servant had returned, Gaius saw.

"Now, Agrippa, my dear friend," he continued, "it is my will
that you be king of the tetrarchy of Philip, and likewise of the
tetrarchy of Lysanias." He motioned to the servant, who had
been eyeing him in anticipation of the command, and the man
brought to him on a large silken pillow a resplendently jeweled
crown. "Kneel, Prince Agrippa, and accept this crown, and with
it the ancient rights of rule over your people."

Agrippa was on his knees before the Emperor. Gaius took the
crown, raised it aloft, and then lowered it squarely on the black
locks of the prince of the House of Herod.

"Rise, King Agrippa," he commanded.

As those about the chamber bowed low to the new king, Gaius
motioned to Agrippa to be seated on a large and ornately carved
chair that had been placed near his own. Then the Emperor
spoke again in low voice to the servant, who went swiftly from
the chamber. In a moment he was back, bearing in a dazzling
coil on another silken pillow a long golden chain.

Gaius picked up the chain and walking to the chair from
which King Agrippa had arisen as the Emperor had stood up,
placed it about the new ruler's neck.

"This chain which I present to you in token of my everlasting
friendship, O King Agrippa, this unending golden chain sym-
bolic of my undying affection, is of the exact weight of the iron
chain with which you were bound by command of the late
Emperor."

King Agrippa bowed discreetly, remembering the crown now
balanced precariously on his head.

"The value of this great chain of gold is immense and in itself constitutes a lordly treasure," he said in firm voice, "and yet
it is as but one lone denarius compared with the generosity and
nobility of my lord the Emperor."

The sunshine streaming through a great window of the high-ceilinged chamber ran along the golden chain about Agrippa's neck and flashed from the stones of the new monarch's resplendent diadem.

But in the quickness of the sunshine's flashing the thoughts of Tribune Longinus, who had brought Agrippa to the palace, fled from the golden crown and the beaming face beneath it, for the crown and its jewels had recalled for him another circlet and another face.

In the suddenness of the ray of dancing sunlight Tribune Longinus in imagination had journeyed across the Great Sea and through a gateway to the Pavement before Jerusalem's stern Praetorium and with utter fascination was looking upon a face and a crown he had never been able to put out of his thoughts.

This face he was seeing was not that of a smiling proud king but of a poor country carpenter dying, and this crown was not fashioned of gold and gems but of a branch of thorn hastily twisted.

## THE CROWN TREE 33

One of King Agrippa's first requests of Emperor Gaius was that Tribune Longinus be assigned to the king as his Roman aide and adviser. The request was granted by Gaius, who at the same time named the tribune to serve as Rome's liaison officer in the new court.

Not many days later King Agrippa was summoned to the Imperial Palace to sit with the Emperor in the trial of an important case concerned with affairs in Palestine.

When Agrippa and his new aide were received by uniformed servants at the Palace, they were escorted immediately to the great tribunal chamber, where the trial already had begun. Emperor Gaius sat on a thronelike chair behind the judgment bench, and as Agrippa and Longinus entered the Emperor motioned to the king to come sit beside him. As Agrippa took his place, Longinus slipped into a section occupied by aides of the Emperor.

A defendant stood grim and erect before Gaius. Longinus could not see the man's face, but from his dress and demeanor it was evident that the accused was a person of rank.

The Emperor had been addressing this man when Agrippa and Longinus entered the tribunal hall. Now he confronted him again, and the great chamber was grimly hushed:

"It is further charged that through your failure to be guided by the customs, habits, traditions, and religious feelings of the Jews you have been responsible in large measure for the deaths not only of countless subject peoples in Judaea and Samaria, but far worse, of many soldiers of our Empire"—he paused, and his scowl darkened—"even choice young men from our capital city itself, and by your failure to administer in proper manner the duties of the office of Procurator, it is also charged, you have given encouragement to sedition and strengthened the hopes of those who would free themselves of Rome's protection."

Gaius paused, coughed, and a slave came quickly with a golden goblet. As the Emperor was swallowing the water, the accused turned his head, so that Longinus had a quick glimpse of his face.

"By all the gods," he said to himself, "Pontius Pilate!"

Though the Roman governor had been a man in his early middle years when Longinus had last seen him on the afternoon of that unforgettable day in Jerusalem, now Pilate was an old man, the tribune was shocked to discover. His then round and florid face, wider because of the closely cropped iron-gray hair, was now drawn and lined, and his hair, thinned into a rim above his ears, was entirely white. His shoulders would be sagging, the Tribune felt, had he dared let them.

The Emperor handed the goblet back to the slave, faced the deposed ruler.

"Pontius Pilate, for the good of the Emperor and the Empire, President Vitellius of Syria has stripped you of your authority and sent you to Rome to stand trial before the Emperor on the charges I have enumerated. Have you anything to say in defense of yourself and your administration of affairs in Palestine?"

Longinus, watching absorbed, saw Pilate's shoulders drop momentarily, but he raised them, as though by great effort, and looked into the calmly smiling face of the young Emperor. At the same time he lifted his hands waist-high and rubbed them together nervously.

"Once more Pilate attempts to wash his hands," Longinus said inaudibly as there came to him vividly the remembrance of this man on the morning of that same day in Jerusalem as he called for a basin and ostentatiously sought before a howling multitude in the Pavement to wash his hands of the innocent blood he was about to shed.

But even more clearly, so clearly that he had the distinct feeling that living flesh stood before him, Longinus saw that other one—erect, calm, dignified in his bedraggled robe, entirely unafraid, tall. He grows taller, thought Longinus, and Pilate shrinks, shrivels.

But now the once arrogant, proud Pilate was speaking:

"I tried to serve well my Emperor, O my lord Gaius." His voice was trembling on the edge of breaking. "But always I have been opposed at every turn by the intractable, violent, stubbornly obstructive Jews, a race of all the peoples of the earth the most hostile to our Emperor and our Empire! I have sought by force of arms to subdue them, but they have bared their throats and their breasts to the swords of my soldiers and have invited them to thrust them through rather than give way one step. I have tried by persuasion and agreement with their demands to govern them. But it has all been to no avail; they remain the most ungovernable, obstinate, antagonistic race it has ever been my misfortune to encounter."

"The Jews as a race are determined people and violently opposed to the rule of Rome, although there be some among them most loyal and friendly to Rome and her Emperor." Gaius bowed toward King Agrippa, then turned again to address the deposed Procurator. "But this is no defense, Pontius Pilate, for no ruler of

a Roman province should lack the courage or ability to procure
the equitable and efficient conduct of Roman government in that
province, regardless of who the subject peoples may be." He
waggled a soft finger above the judgment bench. "You are an
experienced Roman soldier. You've been serving as Procurator
ten years. In that time you should have learned when to be ob-
durate and when to be lenient; but you have learned nothing;
you've been hard when you should have been soft, and weak
when you should have been unyielding. Your administration of
the Empire's affairs in Palestine, Pontius Pilate, has grown pro-
gressively worse rather than better."

Gaius faced Agrippa again. "Haven't I properly appraised his
governing in Palestine, O King Agrippa? Is there anything you
would add?"

"I've had little personal knowledge of the Procurator's conduct
of the government, O my lord the Emperor," Agrippa replied.
"But the reports I've had from many sides are entirely in accord
with what you have just said. He has gained for the Emperor and
the Empire the hostility of countless peoples when he could have
gained their friendship and help. He has blown hot when he
should have blown cold; when he should have been ice he was
fire."

"King Agrippa speaks wisely. Instead of a friend of your Emperor and Empire, Pontius Pilate, you have been an enemy; not
purposely, I agree, but actually, and out of inability and a cowardly heart."

Gaius paused, and a smile lightened his thin face, and when he
spoke again his words were calm, almost gentle: "Pontius Pilate,
what have you to say for yourself before I give judgment?"

The deposed governor turned shifting eyes to the right and
the left, but they met only impassive, stony staring. He faced the
Emperor, licked his bloodless lips.

"O Sire, have you ever sought to deal with the Jews? Can you
understand to what extent their stubborn wills, their divisions
even among themselves, their defiance—"

"Silence, Pilate!" The Emperor's sharp words cut him short.

"You've said all that before. That's no defense. It's but the babbling of a weakling." He leaned forward, pointed his finger at the white-faced, now trembling Pilate. "Hear me! I approve the action of President Vitellius in deposing you as Procurator. You've served ill your Emperor and your Empire, you've been both arrogant and cowardly, and under your administration Rome's reputation for measuring out full justice has been grievously befouled. I adjudge you guilty of the charges brought against you."

He paused again, and his smile was friendly, beguiling.

"Pontius Pilate, you well deserve the ax of my headsman or the arrows of my archers." His tone was gentle, calming. "But I won't decree death for you. Instead, I decree that you be stripped of office and all honors and rank, that your property be confiscated, and that you be banished at once"—he hesitated a moment —"to Vienna Allobrogum to remain there in perpetual banishment." It was not until that moment that his face flushed angrily, and his voice was sharp: "Guards, take him away!"

That evening Tribune Longinus climbed Quirinal Hill to visit Lalage. He related what had happened at the Imperial Palace.

"He probably got what he deserved—or less," Lalage commented.

"I agree," Longinus said. "He deserved much more. Pilate was a disgrace to Rome." When he made no further observation she saw that he was of a sudden in deep study.

"Then should you be concerned for his fate?"

Longinus faced the girl, his expression intent, his countenance unsmiling. "I was thinking that it was under old Tiberius that *he* was condemned, and Tiberius is dead, smothered under a pillow; that it was before Pilate that he was taken and then by him sent to Herod Antipas, who could have released him but didn't and mocked him instead, and it was Pilate who turned him over to me to be crucified. Now Pilate is deposed and sent off into perpetual banishment." He smiled ruefully. "There remain now only the Tetrarch Herod Antipas—and the Tribune Longinus."

In Damascus, Joseph Barnabas and Amaziah did not see Saul again after they left him on his mat in the upper chamber of the house of Judas in the Street Called Straight. When they had rested with Ananias a short while, they said farewell to the old man and turned again toward the desert.

"Have no fear of Saul," Ananias had assured them as they were departing, "for hasn't the God of Israel told me in the vision that the man of Tarsus would do mighty works in the name of Jesus? When next you hear of Saul, my brothers, you'll thank God that He spared him to labor in the Messiah's vineyard."

But as they journeyed southward from Damascus they talked much of the amazing turn Saul's mission into Syria had taken, and despite the assurance of old Ananias they wondered if the man of Tarsus had really undergone a change of heart. Was he now a sincere, devoted adherent of the Nazarene whose followers he had been persecuting so grievously only a few weeks before? Had he actually been struck blind, or was it but the fierce sun of the desert burning itself deep into his already weakened eyes? Was Saul truly a convert, a disciple now of the Lord Messiah, or was he cunningly devising some more devilish, more cleverly cruel scheme through which to entrap the Master's followers in Damascus?

Pondering the report they would make to Simon and the other leaders of the fellowship, they went down through the valley of the Jordan until they arrived in Jericho, from which they took the steep and robber-haunted road up to Jerusalem.

Meanwhile another traveler, a friend of Ananias, the Greek physician Luke, was nearing the end of a long journey likewise from Syria. Luke was about the same age as Barnabas and like the Cypriote was of a philosophical turn of mind. As a very young man he had become interested in the various religions of the world, and as he had been revolted by the licentious rites practiced by the worshipers of Antioch's Aphrodite he had been attracted to the solemn and inspiring ritual of the Jews in their worship of their one-God, Jehovah. One day in the synagogue at Damascus he had made the acquaintance of Ananias and it was from him that he had first heard of the Galilean carpenter who some of the Jews at Damascus believed was their long-awaited Messiah.

Luke had been intrigued by the strange story related by the old man about this young God-son who had been sent to earth by his God-father to redeem mankind through his sacrificial death on the hated cross of the cruel Roman conquerors. As he had sailed eastward from the harbor of Seleucia, seaport of Antioch, on a journey into Macedonia he had thought much of this new religion of the Jews, and when he reached the home of the merchant Chionides, whose daughter Aspasia was Luke's espoused, he related to the girl what Ananias had told him.

From Aspasia's home near Thessalonica he had gone on to Athens and when his business there was finished he had taken a ship that had returned him to Seleucia. That had been months ago, before Centurion Longinus had returned to Rome from his tour of duty in Germania.

Now Luke was going back to Thessalonica to claim Aspasia as his bride and carry her home with him to Antioch. As Barnabas and Amaziah neared Jerusalem on their return from Damascus, a thousand miles across the Great Sea at the head of the Aegean Luke stood before the gate of the merchant Chionides and knocked.

In a moment now he would be admitted, cross the great paved courtyard, and enter the house to be welcomed by his beloved. As he awaited a servant's opening the gate he could hardly maintain an outward calm. For weeks he had looked forward to the day he would stand before this gate.

The house of the Macedonian merchant sat on a slope that overlooked the Via Ignatia and the distant harbor of Thessalonica. On clear days Chionides sometimes could identify his own vessels as they came into the harbor or departed for Antioch or Tyre or Caesarea to the east or Rome to the west. He could watch travelers from many lands moving along the great highway that joined the western lands with the Orient; along this road too he could see from time to time his own caravans bringing in or bearing away merchandise of many types and much value. From his rooftop in the cool of late afternoons he could look down on highway and harbor and ponder the worth of his great possessions. Luke likewise often had wondered if his prospective father-in-law could reasonably appraise the value of his holdings.

The gate was opening. Luke stepped forward. The servant, seeing him, seemed startled and for a moment said nothing; then he spoke.

"You are Luke the physician?"

"Yes. And you are—Tyrtaeus? But why are you at the gate? Don't you serve in the house of Chionides?"

"Formerly I did, yes." The man seemed embarrassed, hesitant.

Luke was puzzled at his attitude. "Aren't you going to invite me in, Tyrtaeus?" he asked, laughing. "But first tell me, how's your mistress Aspasia?"

Plainly the servant was troubled. He seemed not to know what to say. "I can't answer your question, sir. Nor can I invite you inside." He hesitated a moment, his countenance grave. "Great evil has come upon this house."

"Aspasia? Where—what—" The physician's face had paled.

"She's not here. She was carried away."

"Carried away? What do you mean, Tyrtaeus?"

"The Romans came, sir. I don't altogether understand; it was something to do with the payment of the tribute money; this region hereabouts was lagging, I think. The soldiers came to my master's house and were demanding and unreasonable; an altercation arose and Chionides opposed them vigorously. The soldiers began to plunder the house and my master and the sons and servants resisted."

"And Aspasia?"

"Chionides was killed and one of his sons. The other son and the servants were chained and carried away to be sold as slaves, all the property was confiscated, and a new master now occupies the house; the paintings and statues, the silver and gold plate—"

"But what of Aspasia? Speak out, Tyrtaeus!"

"I was hesitant about saying, sir." The servant's eyes were on Luke's dust-covered sandals. "She too was carried away by the soldiers to be sold as a slave, I was told."

Luke, sickened, sought to learn what had become of his beloved, but Tyrtaeus knew no more. He himself had escaped only because on that fateful day he had been sent by Chionides on an extended mission to Apollonia. Returning two weeks later, he had found a new occupant in the merchant's house and himself the slave of the new owner. He had learned all he knew of the fate of Chionides and his family from other slaves in the community.

Disconsolate, Luke returned to the city, sought of many Thessalonians news of Chionides and his family. But few were able to give him helpful information; some even seemed afraid to be considered friends of the slain merchant. One man who conducted a cobbler's shop near the wharf did reveal, however, that the son of Chionides had been put aboard a ship bound for Rome. But he thought that the daughter, bound also, had been put on a vessel, formerly her father's, that was scheduled to touch at Seleucia before going on to Alexandria.

Luke bought passage on the first ship for Seleucia.

The vessel sailed steadily eastward, hardly pausing at the ports in the Aegean Sea and along the coasts of Lycia, Pamphylia, and Cilicia, though in his impatience he felt that it was making little progress. When it did reach Seleucia he went ashore and began asking shopkeepers and others near the wharves about those ships that had arrived recently with cargoes of slaves aboard. He haunted the market places and talked with many slave dealers. Finally one man recalled that he had seen slaves unloaded from a vessel that until recently had flown the flag of a Greek merchant at Thessalonica. The cargo included Greek slaves, men and women, and perhaps others from Germania and Gaul.

"Can you tell me what disposition was made of them?" Luke tried to be casual but he was afraid that in his anxiety he had revealed more than a monetary interest in the slaves.

"It would be difficult to say now. But if you're interested in purchasing some comely wenches or boys or even some men, I can tell you where—" Suddenly he paused. "Can it be that you are seeking any certain one, perhaps a woman beloved—" He stopped again.

"It could be that such a person is among those you saw being unloaded. Can you tell me where they were taken?"

"I fear for you if you seek one among the women," he answered. "They were sold on the block to a slave dealer who took them by camel train to Damascus, I was told, where he expected to gain a handsome profit by selling them to the brothels."

His face blanched, his lips a thin line, Luke thanked the man, turned away. Before the sun had set, he was journeying eastward toward the walled city in the desert.

## THE CROWN TREE 35

In the shadow of a great monolith that provided shade from the searing heat of the afternoon sun Saul of Tarsus lay stretched and resting on his thin mat. All morning he had trudged eastward across the plain from the direction of Damascus, which he had skirted, leaving it on his right hand to the northward as he had journeyed from the great desert on Syria's borders toward the promised coolness of snow-covered Mount Hermon.

Saul had decided to remain beside the great rock until the first light of morning, when he would arise and be on his way. It was pleasanter traveling before the sun had risen high to scorch the arid land through which he was trudging; too, the rock would be a protection against the night's chill winds.

He lay with his head on a small stone that served as a pillow and lifted his face to catch any stirring breeze. That was how it happened that out of his better eye he saw the man coming slowly toward him across the shimmering sands. When the stranger was still two hundred paces away, he suddenly crumpled and fell face downward upon the heated floor of the desert.

Instantly Saul was on his feet, and grabbing his water-gourd, he ran toward the fallen traveler. Reaching the man, he bent over and shaded his face from the sun, and poured a few drops from the gourd between the man's parched lips.

"Come, my brother," he said, when he saw that the man was conscious, "let me help you to the shadow of that great boulder, where you can have more water and rest from this stifling heat." He tugged to help the taller man to unsteady feet, lifted an arm about his own rounded shoulder, which he held with one hand while he thrust his other arm about the spent man's waist. Slowly they made their way to the safety of the rock, and he let the traveler gently down on the mat.

"Thank you, friend," the man said, looking up wearily. "You've saved my life. Another few minutes out there and I'd have stayed for the jackals and the vultures."

"It was little I did, brother. I'm thankful to God the Father and Jesus my Lord Messiah that I happened to be looking in your direction when you fell."

The man struggled to sit up. "You are from Antioch, then, and one of them?"

"I'm from Tarsus, and called Saul. And I'm a follower—and an apostle born out of time—of him who is called Jesus of Nazareth, the Messiah of the Jews and the saviour of all who call on his name." He took up the gourd again, pulled out the stopper, and bending over, gave the exhausted man several swallows. Then the stranger lay back on the mat.

"There are such as you in Antioch," he said. "I'm called Luke the physician. I am a Greek from Antioch and I am acquainted with some in that city, and likewise in Damascus, who share your religious beliefs. When I'm rested"—he closed his eyes wearily—

"I'd like to hear more concerning this Messiah of whom you speak."

Soon he was asleep. Saul, leaning against the smooth wall of the sheltering stone, napped lightly. But before the now cooling sun had dropped into the Great Sea beyond the extended backbone of the Lebanons he arose and opened his pouch, from which he took food for their supper—a loaf, cheese, olives, pressed dates, dried figs. Luke, arousing, pointed to his pouch. "Take from it likewise. I was prepared for desert travel"—he grinned weakly—"except for stamina."

"We'll eat tomorrow's breakfast from your pouch. Do you feel refreshed? Are you ready to eat?"

"Yes, I'm hungry. The shadow of this rock and the sleep have restored me." He stood up, stretched. "It wasn't just the walking in the desert sun that exhausted me. I've gone sleepless and in great distress the last many days and nights. I've just come from Damascus, where almost without ceasing to rest I have walked the streets and talked with countless slave dealers and others, and even visited the many brothels seeking my espoused, all to no avail. I was almost spent when I struck out this morning from Damascus to begin my return journey to Antioch."

When Saul had asked the blessing of the God of Israel on the food they were about to share, Luke began to recite the tragic story of Chionides and his family and his own efforts to find Aspasia. "So now I go to Antioch to search there as I have searched at Damascus. I don't know anything else to do."

"There's one other thing—the most important. You can ask the Most High to hold your beloved in His care and protection."

"But I'm a Greek. I've never put great store by our Grecian gods and though I've studied your religion I don't know how to approach your god."

"He is not alone the God of Israel, Luke my brother," Saul declared. "He's the God of every nation and all the world, the sun and moon and stars; He is the Omnipotent and the Omniscient."

Luke had picked up a fig, was lifting it to his mouth.

"I have given much study to the works of the philosophers and have considered carefully the many religions; nevertheless, in matters of religion I have little learning." On his countenance Saul read a new earnestness. "Would you pray to this god of yours—this one-god—for me and ask him to guard my beloved and lead me to her?"

"Indeed I will, and gladly," Saul answered.

In the thickening twilight and undisturbed vast silence of the desert they knelt on the sand and Saul besought God's protection of Luke's beloved and prayed that in His good time He would reunite them in peace and joy. "In the name of Jesus our Lord Messiah who sacrificed himself, O God, for our redemption, we make this our petition. Amen."

"Friend Saul," said Luke, as they sat back against the rock, their sandaled feet pulled up under their robes, for now the air was beginning to be edged with chill, "I feel better, as though I had been comforted in some strange way. Do you really believe that the god of Israel can hear and answer the prayer you have just offered him?"

"Indeed, Luke, I believe it with all my heart and mind."

"And this son of whom you spoke, this Messiah of the Jews who is the son of your god. Is there actually any such being, or is he a sort of beautiful figure of imagination, a symbol of what we call the perfect, a personification of truth, beauty, goodness, a—"

"He is all that, Luke; he is perfection as your Greek philosophers understand the term. But Jesus Christ the Messiah and Saviour is likewise a person. He was born in humble Nazareth, a village in Galilee, not so many years before I was born at Tarsus. He grew into manhood, and for a few short years went about Galilee and Judaea teaching the ways of God and ministering unto those who would accept his ministering. And then as a propitiation for man's sinning he gave himself as a sacrifice on a Roman cross at Jerusalem, and the third day after he had been put away in the tomb he arose. Now he has ascended to the Father to make continual intercession for us his brothers."

"Then you believe that he arose from the dead and ascended

to some region remote from the earth? But other religions hold the same views concerning certain of their gods. How, then, do you know that this carpenter of Galilee, of whom I have heard those in Antioch also speak, actually arose from the dead and continues to live? How do you *know* this, Saul?"

"It's a fair question and deserves a truthful answer. And I tell you that I know that Jesus the Messiah lives because since his death at Jerusalem he has talked with me."

"What!" Luke sat upright. "He has talked with *you?*"

"Before God, he has. Not many months ago it was, and but a few furlongs from this very spot."

Then as they sat on the now cold sand and watched the sparkling sharp stars blossom in the dark dome above, Saul recounted his story.

"It's past believing had I not heard it out of your own mouth," Luke declared, when Saul had finished. "In the twinkling of yonder great star you his enemy became his servant, his friend, his brother."

"Yes, and his worshiping slave."

"It's an amazing story. It should be written down, Saul, as you have related it to me. Some day you should write it."

"But I'm not a writer; I'm a tentmaker."

"So you've told me. Nevertheless the story of how you fought this Jesus, then came face to face with him and were transformed into his follower and now proclaim him where heretofore you had denounced him and punished his adherents—that story deserves to be recorded, Saul."

"Were it to be written by someone who can make words do his bidding, a philosopher, Luke—like you."

"Perhaps you jest, but some day, after I have found Aspasia and can give proper thought to it, I should like to record your story."

"You are kind, Luke. But if you wish to write a great story, one that needs to be written, my brother, and one that properly done will move the earth, then write the story of our Lord Messiah himself."

"But I never knew him, Saul. I haven't—"

"You *can* know him even as I know him. Never have I seen him in the flesh, yet I know him and am known by him. It can be the same with you. But there are many now living who knew him in the flesh, Luke—people in Galilee and Judaea, folks out in the countryside, in the villages and cities, along the shores of the sea. They talked with him, listened to him talk, they saw his marvelous works. They could tell you of his teaching, his journeyings, his ministering. If you could go through Galilee and Judaea, retracing his steps, and talk with those people, even his apostles, and the others—James the Lord's brother, and Lazarus whom he raised from the dead, and Mary and Martha, the sisters of Lazarus, and many another one—if you could visit with them and gather the threads of that story, and then put it down, Luke, you would have a narrative exceeding any that has ever been written."

A moment Saul was silent. Nor did Luke speak. Then in the shadows Luke caught the movements of Saul's hands in characteristic gesture.

"I'm traveling to Jerusalem to see Simon and the others," he resumed his speaking. "The Roman Empire is an immensity no man can cover in his searching. Don't despair for your beloved, for haven't we placed her in the hands of God? Then for the moment leave her with God, and journey southward with me. In Jerusalem you'll see many who knew the Lord. Perhaps when you've heard them talk you'll want to write down what you learn from them. It could be a beautiful story, Luke, the most beautiful story ever put to paper."

Arrived in Jerusalem, Barnabas and Amaziah went to the home of Mary of Cyprus, where they found Simon and certain other leaders of the fellowship to whom they told the amazing story of the conversion of Saul.

For days and weeks they kept eyes and ears sharp for his return. But they saw and heard nothing of the man from Tarsus. They inquired of him in talking with pilgrims journeying to Jerusalem from the regions of Syria, but no one knew anything more about the once blatant chief enemy of the fellowship. As season followed season and feast days came and were gone, the name Saul of Tarsus was heard no more in the synagogues of the Greek-speaking Jews or down in fetid Ophel or along the slope of Mount Moriah. Saul had become a man happily forgot.

In these days no man lifted his hand against the followers of the Lord Messiah. In the great white Temple and in the synagogues the adherents of Jesus worshiped alongside the orthodox Jews. So long as they observed with faithfulness the laws of Moses, so long as they followed the prescribed forms of worship, offered sacrifices and paid tithes, they were not molested.

The household of Mary of Cyprus continued to worship regularly at the Synagogue of the Libertines, where Stephen had preached with such eloquence and boldness and from which he had been dragged away to his death. Here many of the Jews of the Dispersion, Israelites visiting the capital city of Jewry from the lands bordering the Great Sea, came to worship the God of Israel, and often among them would be a follower of the Messiah. Pilgrims in Jerusalem for the feasts were likewise often among these worshipers, and strange faces were not uncommon.

For that reason Barnabas and Amaziah gave little attention one day to a stranger who stood in the shadows at the rear of the synagogue. Nor were they concerned when the man came over quietly and spoke to Barnabas, for often before pilgrims had come to them with questions.

"I'd like to speak a moment with you," the stranger said to Barnabas. "Will you go outside with me?"

"I will. I'll go gladly," Barnabas assured him.

In the better light they could see that the man was wearing a long and worn brown robe and a headdress, sweat-begrimed and frayed, which concealed much of his face. He was stooped somewhat and his arms and knotty legs and feet encased in broken sandals were burnt to the color of leather long exposed. One eye was closed to a slit and the other was reddened as if he had been weeping.

"You don't recognize me, Joseph Barnabas?" He smiled, and reaching up with his left hand, removed the headdress to reveal a rounded high dome bald and burnt.

"Saul! Saul my brother! God be praised, you've returned to us!"

The two men, laughing and weeping, fell into each other's arms.

"Joseph Barnabas! God be praised indeed, my brother Barnabas!"

He clung to the taller man, his right arm clutched about his waist. Then he released him and turned with squinting eyes to Amaziah. "And my brother Amaziah! Have you forgiven me the stripes I laid on you?"

"They were long ago forgiven, Brother Saul."

Saul stood back to survey the two.

"It is good to be back in Jerusalem," he declared, a warm smile creasing his leathered face. "It's been so long—in time but longer in experience—since I was within these walls. And what of Simon of Capernaum, and the other apostles of Jesus? When have you seen them, and how do they fare?"

"Simon is at my cousin's house; the Zebedees are in Galilee; James the Lord's brother is living here in Jerusalem. They all fare well, Saul, and the fellowship increases." He paused. "But what of you, my brother? How have you fared?"

"Better than I deserve, Joseph. I have spent much time in the desert, as you doubtless have surmised. There is much to tell you about, and to tell Simon likewise. I am anxious to see him; it is of the greatest importance to me that I talk with him."

"Then let us go now to Mary's house. You must lodge there, Saul; Mary would be unhappy if you didn't."

"On the way here I encountered a Greek physician who traveled with me. He is now at an inn where we obtained lodging. But I would be happy to go with you to Mary's and see Simon. I have many things to tell him, but even more important, I would learn from him." He tugged at his bedraggled robe. "Let us go there." A quick smile lightened his dark face. "That house means much to me now."

The first of the apostles was not at Mary's house when they arrived. Simon had gone down into Ophel to visit James, the Lord's brother. But by the time Saul had bathed and dressed in fresh garments from the common store, and the shadows of the house had lengthened to fill the courtyard, Simon came through the gateway. The big Galilean appeared spent from the day's labors, but when Barnabas brought Saul to him his energy was quickly renewed.

The members of the fellowship ate their supper together and then Simon led Saul out to the stone bench under the ancient olive near the fountain.

"We can sit here without being disturbed," he said, "and I am anxious to hear your story. It must be a thrilling one, judging by the report fetched by Barnabas and Amaziah. And doubtless much has happened to you since then."

"Little has actually happened to me since that day on the road to Damascus, for most of the time I have been away from men," Saul replied. "Some days after the Lord restored my sight, I departed from Damascus and went into the desert. There in prayer and fasting and much searching of my soul I sought to learn about the Master. I didn't have the privilege of knowing Jesus in the flesh as you and the other apostles had, though on the road to Damascus he appeared and talked with me." For a moment

Saul was silent as he looked straight ahead into the deepening twilight that was beginning to blanket Jerusalem's rooftops. "But I do count myself an apostle, and in the desert I learned of him."

"Out in solitary places, away from the haunts of men, one may commune with God and come upon great truths, Saul, as you have discovered for yourself. John the Baptist went into the wilderness, and even Jesus spent much time in solitude. He was a great one for tramping alone in the woods and fields and by the lakeside." Simon seemed to be talking as much to himself as to the man beside him. But then he spoke directly to Saul. "Have you come straight from the desert of Syria?"

"No, Simon. In the desert I preached about the Lord Jesus to certain tribesmen of Aretas, king of the Nabataeans, and thereby gained his enmity. He tried to capture me but I eluded him and got back to Damascus. Aretas then set up guards at the gates of Damascus to seize me when I should come out. Meanwhile enemies of the Lord Messiah within the city likewise tried to arrest me. So a member of the fellowship concealed me for a time and when the hour was propitious lowered me in a basket over the wall of the city. From there I crossed below Damascus to come out on the way that leads southward, and I continued on to Jerusalem to see you."

All the while grizzled Simon had been nodding his head gravely, his eyes staring out across the massed roofs of Ophel, his thoughts apparently far beyond Jerusalem's walls. Now he leaned forward, rested his big hand on Saul's knotted sun-blackened knee, twisted his head around to look into Saul's face. "Tell me, Saul, what did you learn in the desert?"

"I'll tell you gladly, Simon Peter. But first, I would like to hear of the Master from the first of his apostles. It must be that nobody knew him better. What was he like?"

Simon straightened, leaned his head back against the cool stone of the bench, considered. "There has never been a man like the Master," he began, measuring his words. "Some in ways have resembled him, but none has approached him. He is alone among the sons of men, Saul."

"Yes, I agree. But how did he look, what was his appearance?"

"He was a tall man, well set up, square-shouldered and erect, with long smooth muscles that were not bulging like mine. His hair was of the color of a chestnut fully ripe, and was parted in a seam in the middle of his head. It came down smooth to his ears but fell in a curling fashion to his shoulders. He had a high, smooth forehead, straight nose, and strong mouth that smiling revealed white, straight teeth evenly set; his beard was thick and of the same color as his hair, but not very long and ending in two well-trimmed spikes. He had dark gray eyes and his skin was of a ruddy color, heavily burnt by the sun, for most of his time he spent outdoors."

"But I have heard it said, Simon, that he never smiled, that—"

"That is not true," the fisherman hastened to interrupt. "I've heard that report too, repeated by those who didn't know him. Answer me this, Saul: Would a man who never smiled, who went about with a long face, attract to himself great throngs of men and women who followed his every word, would he draw to himself children, even small ones, who pushed and scrambled to clutch his hands and sit on his lap?"

"It is not reasonable that he would."

"Of course the Master smiled, Saul; and many a time I heard him laugh too. He had a gay, free laugh, the sort that made everybody who heard it want to laugh with him. The Master was no sour-face, Saul. Of course, he often revealed his sadness, too; sometimes it seemed that he would be overcome by it, for he carried on his shoulders a great burden of sorrow. He seemed hurt deeply by the distress and suffering of his brothers about him; he was always striving to lift their burdens from them. And he likewise carried the weight of the world's sorrows and shortcomings. But it is not true to say that Jesus never smiled, was always sad."

"You must miss him greatly, Simon?"

"Yes, as the days go by, Saul, I seem to miss the Lord all the more. When he was with us I didn't realize how privileged we were. Now that he's gone, I miss his soothing, calm words, the quick flash of his smile, the gentle strong touch of his hand on my arm." A moment he was meditative. "Never did a man have a friend like the Lord Jesus."

"But don't you feel that you still have him with you, Simon?"

"Oh, yes. Sometimes I can almost feel his hand on my shoulder."

"It is strange, but that's the way I felt in the desert; he was there beside me."

In the growing darkness Simon related experiences with the Master, recounted memorable stories Jesus had told in illustrating truths he was seeking to emphasize, relived that final tragic week in Jerusalem—the last meeting of the Twelve in Mary's upper chamber, the sham trials, the crucifixion, the triumph of the first Easter morning, his encountering his friend the Roman centurion Cornelius near the tomb, the thrilling days before the Lord's ascension.

"You have taught me much, Simon," Saul assured him. "It is what I wanted to hear—and especially from your lips."

Simon nodded solemnly. "I like to think back over those days; it does me good. But now, Saul, tell me what you learned during those lonesome days in the desert. Did you receive a command from the Lord?"

"I had a vision and received a command. Nor can I ignore that command."

"Tell me about it, Saul."

"On the desert sands and in the cities of Arabia I sought in prayer and study to learn the nature of the Messiah. The Master who came to me on the road to Damascus, I had quickly realized, was not the Messiah I had envisioned in my earlier study of the Scriptures and the interpretations of the rabbis. The one who came to me, Simon, was vastly different, worlds and stars above and beyond the Messiah I had been seeking in prayer and study."

"You hold then, Saul"—Simon's tone revealed a sudden concern—"that the Lord Jesus is not that Messiah for whom we Jews have been looking with great longing through the many years of our trials?"

"I hold that Jesus *is* that Messiah for whom we Jews have been looking with a great longing, Simon, but I hold likewise that he is far more. We have seen with narrowed eyes the Messiah who was to come; with our limited vision we have been measuring the Illimitable."

"I am just a plain unlearned fisherman, Saul. But I lived close to Jesus and for me he is the Messiah of the Chosen People. I loved him when he walked with us up and down Galilee, and when he sailed with us on Gennesaret in calm and in storm. I love him even more now." He lowered his head so that his rounded beard flared against his chest. "Saul, I don't understand your words. They only confuse me."

"I would not want to say or do anything to confuse you, Simon." Saul spoke gently. "In the essentials you would never be confused anyway. You, the first of the apostles, possess the truth. You are grounded in it; you cannot be shaken." He grasped the knee of the fisherman; his voice was earnest. "Hasn't the Lord himself called you 'the Rock,' my brother? What greater praise has ever been given any mortal? Confused by words? Not you, Simon. Never. When I walked the path of error I knew of you. Your name to me then, when you were my enemy, was a symbol of strength. You are strong, stable. You, Simon, are made firm in God. For God is love."

Simon stood up, faced the younger man.

"Saul, you are a Pharisee of the Pharisees. You have gleaned the wisdom of many books. You sat at the feet of Gamaliel. Your words leap up like tongues of flame, flash forth like the polished blade in the hand of the swordsman. But I am a man of slow wit, and stumbling words, a man—"

"Stumbling words? Flaming words, rather. Words of power and music and life! Didn't your brave words in one day bring three thousand souls to the feet of the Lord Jesus?"

Simon sat down again, was for a moment silent. Then he faced Saul.

"You are generous with your praise of me. But nevertheless, I'm a man of no great learning. Though I'm called the first of

the apostles and along with James the Lord's brother am reckoned leader of the fellowship, I am not learned in the laws of
Moses and the interpretations of our great rabbis."

"Answer me this, Simon. Did I travel from Syria to consult
with the learned rabbis? Was I led by the vision to seek of them
knowledge of our Messiah?"

"No, but it was because I knew Jesus as few others knew him
that you sought me out, wasn't it?"

"Precisely. And you've revealed many things I wanted to know
about Jesus. Your words, together with what he has told me of
himself, have completed him for me as he completes God for me."

"As he completes God?" Simon's tone betrayed dismay. "But
isn't this blasphemy, Saul? How can God be completed? Isn't He
complete in Himself?" He shook his grizzled head. "Your words
frighten me."

"God has always been altogether perfect and complete in Himself and to Himself," Saul answered, "but He has not been so to
man. To man, until He sent His Son the Messiah—our Lord
Jesus—God was imperfectly known. We had the law, it is true,
and the prophets. But we cannot reach God through the law,
nor do we understand well the words of the prophets. We had no
way of knowing what God was like, Simon, no picture of Him, no
reflected image, until He sent us His Son. Now through Jesus we
can behold the universal Father, the God of heaven and all the
world."

"The God of heaven and all the world? What do you mean,
Saul? Isn't the God we worship rather the God of Israel, the
Father of the Chosen Race? Can you say that He is likewise the
God of Rome and Athens and Corinth and Alexandria and those
others of the pagan world?" In the thickening shadows the fisherman was shaking his head. "Is He also their Father? On the contrary, won't He bend these pagans to His will, won't He shake
them as a reed is shaken in the wind, won't He destroy His
enemies and vindicate His own? And won't He do all this, Saul,
through His Messiah, our Lord Jesus?"

"In His good time I believe that He will do all this and more,

Simon. And He will do it through His own Son the Messiah, who is our Lord Jesus, the very radiance of God the Father, the Pathway over which all the earth can mount upward to God."

"But those who do mount upward to God through faith in the Messiah, Saul, mustn't they take upon themselves circumcision and the law before they are admitted to our fellowship in the Messiah?"

Saul shook his head.

"No, that was not the truth that came to me in those days in the wilderness of Syria's desert," the younger man declared solemnly. "That is precisely the view I had of God as I drew near to Damascus that day. I had been trying to limit God, to set a wall around Him, to claim Him for ourselves the Israelites alone. But God cannot be limited, Simon, nor can God's Son. Didn't Jesus teach that all men are sons of God and didn't he call all men his brothers?"

"Yes, Saul. But didn't the Master mean that they should first enter into the bond and household of Israel? Do you believe that an uncircumcised Gentile refusing to put himself under the law can yet be a son of God and a brother of our Lord Messiah?"

"I do believe it, Simon, with all my heart." Saul's tone was entirely frank. "I've no right to limit God or His Son the Messiah. I can't make God another King David, another great ruler and protector of Israel, nor can I limit Jesus His Son by thinking of him as such." He looked out across the descending slope now studded with the lights of many lamps. "This will be my mission, Simon. I shall proclaim that the Lord God our God is one, that He has sent His Son to afford us through him a glorious salvation. I shall proclaim that salvation is given us freely through His abounding grace, that we can never obtain salvation of ourselves through obedience to the law—which we can never completely and perfectly obey—but by faith alone, through acceptance of him whom I so long and bitterly scorned and sought to slay forever but now accept joyfully as my Lord and Saviour and loving brother." Saul stopped, seemingly spent by the ardor of his words, the surge of his emotions.

When Simon spoke again, his voice was calm and gentle.

"Saul, my young brother, I don't understand clearly your words. But I don't challenge them. I lived a long while with the Master and loved him with a great passion, though often I was weak and faithless. I still love him—more than I loved him then —and I know in my heart that I will forever love him and that he will forever love me." He reached out and patted the younger man's knee. "But this I also know, Saul. The Master came to you and revealed himself to you, and you were transformed; in the twinkling of an eye you were turned about and set on another course, made a different man. Now you love him and he loves you, as he has always loved you even though you raged against him and sought to destroy his followers. But though I don't comprehend some of the strange things you have uttered here tonight, Saul, I can't say that you speak in error. I don't dare, my brother, because hasn't the Master talked with you and told you many things?"

He was silent a moment, and then he leaned closer to Saul, lifted his big arm to place it across Saul's shoulder.

"It may be that some day my slow brain will comprehend the words you speak; it may be that I'll agree you speak the truth completely, who knows? What is to be is in God's hands. But this I do know, Saul my brother. I know that the God of Israel—the God, as you have said, of all the world and the stars of heaven— has now on His side a mind and a tongue that will work mightily in His name."

Simon's arm dropped about the younger man's shoulders, pulled him near in a quick embrace.

"May God will it so, my son and brother in the Lord Jesus." He stood up. "It is getting late. Let us go seek our rest. We have talked long, and tomorrow there will be much to do."

Nor did James understand any more clearly than Simon the strange words of Saul, who now professed to be a devoted follower of Jesus.

"Don't we all remember well, Saul, how you chastised us with many stripes, how you instigated the stoning of Stephen, how you swore you would obliterate utterly the sect of the Messiah? Now you tell us you are a follower of Jesus. You say that now you love him with the same passion with which you once hated him. Yet you traduce us his brothers of the Chosen, as you yourself are, and you traduce him, for was he not also a Jew and a blood descendant of David the great king?" James shook his head, so that little beads of sunlight danced in the oil with which his beard had been anointed. "Saul, I cannot understand your words."

"It grieves me that you do not understand me, Rab James," the man of Tarsus declared sorrowfully, "all the more because you are the brother of the Lord Messiah. Yet I cannot be true to him and speak otherwise, for these are the words that came to me from him, and I must say them."

"Then where would you speak them, Saul? Would you dare stand in the synagogue and speak these words?"

"I would so dare, and gladly."

"No! Once already you have sown tribulation among us, Saul of Tarsus. You must not once again molest our fellowship, which is now living in peace even with those who deny our Messiah."

"But I would be molesting no one, Rab James. I would only be telling the people what I learned from our Messiah during the long days and nights in the desert of Syria. I would only be telling them of the true belief in our Lord Messiah, how love and faith have transcended the law, how we climb upward to God not by perfectly obeying His commandments and striving in good works but rather through our love for Him and our faith in the Lord Jesus who affords us salvation through faith and not by works."

"You cannot preach such things in the synagogues of Jerusalem, Saul of Tarsus." Sorrow and wrath strove to master the Lord's brother. "Would you, too, be stoned as a blasphemer? I cannot allow you to stand before our people and make light of the law of God and set it down as something of little weight. I cannot permit you to traduce the chosen ones of Israel and make them equal before God with those uncircumcised and unwashed pagans beyond Israel's borders who neither know the provisions of the law nor care that they are ignorant."

"But, Rab James, I would not be traducing the law nor my brothers the Jews. To obey the law is good, to be of the Chosen People is most fortunate. But neither is essential to salvation. The uncircumcised Gentile who has faith in the Lord Messiah as the instrument of salvation afforded by the grace of God stands as close to the throne of the Lord of heaven and all the world as any blood son of King David."

The brother of the Lord swayed back and forth slowly in gesture of deep sorrow, and the motion stirred the long silken hairs of his thinning beard. "Would you once more destroy us of the fellowship?" The question seemed addressed more to himself than to Saul. "Would you divide Israel once again into two armed and bitterly contending camps?" He continued to rock to and fro. Then he stopped, and his eyes took sudden fire. "If you did, Saul, who in the synagogues would stand with you against the rest of us?"

In the days that followed Saul's visit to James in noisome Ophel Saul did try to tell the people of the new truth that had come to him in the long solitude. Oftentimes Luke was in the throng that milled about the Temple courts or the Greek-speaking synagogues where the followers of Jesus were more accustomed to congregate, for he felt that in such places there was always a chance of coming upon Aspasia or meeting someone who might give him information about her. Luke listened to Saul with growing interest. But few others paid heed, and many, recognizing him as the once flaming sword with which the adherents of the Messiah had been smitten, fled from him into the deep dives and crannies along the ancient Jerusalem wall. Some even screamed their curses at him and besought him with foul words to cease his blasphemies and get himself out of the midst of Jewry into the lands of the uncircumcised Gentiles.

"Get back to Tarsus!" a Pharisee shouted the bitter words one day. "Leave us to our laws and our tithing and sacrifices. Go you among the pagans and to them utter your blasphemies. Leave us to our God of Israel and His Messiah. Seek no longer to make them over for us to the fit of your evil pattern! Make your bed with the Gentiles!"

Make your bed with the Gentiles. . . . That night in the inn where he lodged Saul lay sleepless and pondered the days and the way ahead. He had this time been in Jerusalem two weeks. Luke had gone northward along the trail of the Jordan. In Galilee he planned to inquire of slave dealers and others who might be in position to help him in his search for his beloved.

In Jerusalem Luke had talked also with many persons about the carpenter of Nazareth, and he wanted to see others in the region where Jesus was reared and did much of his ministering. From them he hoped to learn more of the incidents in the Nazarene's life as related by witnesses who actually had seen certain of his marvelous deeds performed. "The story of this Galilean is an intriguing one," Luke had confessed to Saul the day he was departing. "I should like to collect material about him, and some day if the opportunity is afforded, I may write it down. And likewise the story of one Saul of Tarsus."

Wide-awake now on his mat, Saul weighed the two weeks in the capital of Israel. Simon in his gruff way had been kind but he had understood little of the great vision Saul had sought to reveal. James had understood even less, had shown no desire to understand. Only Joseph Barnabas, his friend of old, had caught a glimpse of what seemed to Saul so completely illumined, so utterly, infinitely grounded in truth.

Make your bed with the Gentiles. . . .

He lay long and thought, and he prayed to the Messiah to give him understanding, to show him the way, to make clear the road.

When he awakened refreshed, he sprang up, washed himself in cold water, offered his morning prayer, and after breakfasting lightly, went up to the Temple.

Saul cast himself down upon the cold stones and besought the God of Israel and His Messiah to direct him. Oblivious to the ministrations of the priests and the stir of the people and the cooing of the doves and the bleating and bellowing of the animals for the sacrifices, he lay in a trance, prostrate on the unyielding pavement of the Temple court.

The vision came. The Nazarene stood above him, smiled upon him.

"Get to your feet, Saul. Take your staff and gird up your robe, and get quickly out of Jerusalem, for they will not receive your testimony concerning me. Go you unto the Gentiles."

. . . I thank you, Lord of the world and all the stars, and Jesus Christ my Lord Messiah and Saviour, for the vision clear. . . .

In his pouch Saul folded a change of clothing. Amaziah provided him cheese, olives, pressed dates, two small loaves. To his rope girdle he fastened a gourd of water.

Barnabas walked with him along Mount Zion to the Praetorium, where they turned left and went along the way and out the gate on the road to Caesarea; there he would take ship for Tarsus and the region of Cilicia.

When they had embraced and given each other the kiss of farewell, Saul stood and watched Barnabas until he had disappeared over the rise in the dust-burdened road as he started back toward the city's wall. Then quickly Saul straightened the strap that held the pouch and tugged at his robe to let more air to his legs. Turning, he started trudging westward.

His staff he carried in his right hand, for today he was conscious of no pain in it. Unblinking, his eyes were on the road. And already in his mind Saul of Tarsus was beginning to see other roads crossing many lands, and the long sea lanes beyond.

King Herod Agrippa, tired of the banquets and gladiatorial games that Emperor Gaius and other notables of Rome had been giving in his honor since his elevation, had requested the Emperor to permit him to return to Palestine and assume the duties and prerogatives of his exalted office.

Agrippa also had renewed his request that the Tribune Longinus be assigned as his aide and Roman adviser at the new court he would establish in the former tetrarchies of Philip and Lysanias. Longinus, he had told Gaius, would be of invaluable aid to him and would likewise serve well the Empire in such a capacity.

The Emperor willingly had granted Agrippa permission to return to Palestine and take Longinus with him.

Three days before the royal party was to sail for the Palestinian port of Ptolemais, the tribune was summoned to the palace of Prefect Marco.

"You are being sent with Agrippa to Palestine as the king's aide," Marco revealed, when they were alone in the Prefect's inner office. "The Emperor has instructed me to outline to you your duties. In fact, he's left it to me to prescribe them.

"Longinus"—he leaned forward, his expression serious—"I know how you dislike returning to Palestine. Your father has related to me your unfortunate experience at Jerusalem. But in the crucifixion of that Jewish fanatic you were only doing your duty as a Roman soldier, and I trust that time will soon dim your remembrance of the incident. Furthermore, I promise to bring you back to Rome at the first opportunity, which shouldn't be too long from now."

"I don't relish going back, that's true, sir. If you found a way to return me to Rome it would make more bearable the thought of another tour of duty in that difficult province."

"I'll assure you I will, Tribune," Marco declared. "But while you're out there I'm not willing for a man of your abilities to be nothing more than serving boy to a ruler who at best seems to have little capacity for governing. So I've determined to employ you as much as possible in the interest of the Empire."

Quickly he outlined the duties Longinus would have in Palestine. First, he would keep both the Prefect and President Vitellius of Syria informed of Agrippa's conduct of the affairs of the small kingdom. From time to time he would visit Herod Antipas at Tiberias and report to the Prefect on the situation there, for trouble might develop between Agrippa and his brother-in-law and sister.

"Herod and his wife will likely be jealous of her brother, since Agrippa is king and Herod is still only a tetarch," Marco explained.

And Longinus would be expected also to visit Caesarea at intervals and report on the administering of the government in Judaea by Pontius Pilate's successor.

"As you have already realized, no doubt, there will be much traveling about Palestine and you'll be busy," the Prefect added. "But be careful to do nothing that will imperil your excellent standing with King Agrippa." He smiled wryly. "Isn't it fortunate that I put you in charge of Agrippa's imprisonment?"

"I'll be busy, sir, and it appears that I'll be out there a long time—years, I'm afraid, if I do all you have outlined." He shrugged, and smiled wryly.

"Oh, no, Longinus. I can see how I've given you the wrong impression. At most it should be only months, a year at the longest. The situation in Palestine just now is agitated, but it should settle down soon. But that is why you are needed out there at this time. When things have quieted—and they will now that Pilate has been removed—I'll bring you back to Rome, you can marry the daughter of Senator Flaccus and settle here"—he winked knowingly—"or you can marry her and take her with you."

When Longinus saw Lalage that night at her father's house he told her what the Prefect had said.

"And which do you wish to do?" she asked coyly.

"I don't want to do either," he replied, unsmiling.

She flushed, almost imperceptibly, but he saw it. And when she spoke, though she was still smiling, her tone was edged.

"Are you quite sure, Tribune, that you *can* do either?"

"You know I didn't mean it that way, Lalage," he told her, his countenance still serious. "You know what I want. I want to marry you and stay in Rome. I think you must have known that for a long time." He shrugged. "But how can I ask you to marry me and then go hopping all over the Empire with me? You know how I've been shunted from one province to another, the rough life I've had to live. How could I ask anybody who's been used to—to this"—he swept his arm about to embrace in its circle the marbled peristylium with its fountain and flowers— "to give it all up just to go with me? And now that I'm being sent back to Palestine—" He gestured with his hands out, shrugged.

"Have you ever thought of asking me if I'd be willing to go with you, even out to Palestine?"

"You might be willing, Lalage. But you don't know what it's like to live in the provinces. And I couldn't ask you to do it. It wouldn't work out. You're used to luxurious living. Life out there would be too depressing; you'd come home, and I couldn't blame you."

"You think I have no strength of character, Longinus, no moral stamina," she said, calmly. "Nor can I blame you for thinking so. I've failed already with two husbands."

"No, Lalage, I don't say that. Perhaps you failed in your appraisal of them before you married them." He grinned. "Maybe you'd be doing the same thing in accepting me." Then he was serious again. "No, Lalage, I don't think you have no strength of will, character, whatever you choose to call it. It's just that you've been brought up to enjoy this sort of life; you don't know any other. And I wouldn't be heartless enough to ask you to accept a new sort, the sort you'd have in a foreign land, a land whose customs, way of life, everything about it, would quickly become unbearable." He stood up, and now he smiled, and the grim look was gone. "But listen, Lalage, Prefect Marco promised me I wouldn't have to stay out there long. With Pilate banished the Jews will settle down and I can shortly come home. He said I'd then be assigned to duty in Rome. If I'm ordered out again, I'll contrive some way to quit the army. So, won't you wait—awhile longer?"

She stood up, caught his hand in her two. "Yes, Longinus, you know I will. But don't be gone long."

He pulled her close, kissed her closed eyelids, her warm lips. "I won't, my dear. I promise I won't."

She stood back a little way, looked into his face, and suddenly her expression betrayed apprehension.

"Longinus, when you go back to Palestine this time don't be afraid any more of that—that Galilean."

"It wasn't that I was afraid of him." But his expression once more was thoughtful. "It was just that I was—he seemed to be—" He broke off, smiled reassuringly. "But that's all in the past now."

## THE CROWN TREE 39

Tidings of the accession of Caligula to the imperial throne and his elevation of his friend Agrippa to be king of the former tetrarchies of Philip and Lysanias came quickly to Herod Antipas and Herodias at Tiberias. From time to time came stories also of the honors and lavish gifts the new Emperor was bestowing upon Agrippa.

But the young Emperor's generous treatment of her brother did not please the Tetrarchess. When after months of prodigal living in Rome Agrippa returned to Palestine with a Roman tribune as his personal aide and set about to establish a court more pretentious and extravagant than Herod's at Tiberias, Herodias became angered. She was infuriated when one of the court chamberlains, returning to Tiberias, reported to the Tetrarch that Agrippa's architects had completed plans for a marble palace that in every way would dwarf Herod's comparatively new white palace, and that his servants' liveries were more ornate and costly than the dress of the Tetrarch's courtiers.

Nor was her anger directed altogether against her brother and Emperor Caligula. She was equally, perhaps more, incensed against the Tetrarch. This day, the moment the chamberlain had left them, she leveled a long-nailed and resplendently ringed forefinger six inches in front of Herod's flaring nostrils and waggled it menacingly.

"I can't understand how you can be content to remain tetrarch of a puny little territory of fisherfolk and penurious tillers of the soil while Agrippa flaunts the banners of royalty and receives homage as a king! A king, mind you, not a mere tetrarch!"

She dropped to the slender chair with such force that Herod thought it might crumple beneath her. "Why don't you say something?"

The flicker of a smile lighted his round heavy face. "As is usually the case, my dear, you were talking; I was listening."

She jumped to her feet, furious. "Oh, you make me so angry! You stand there so calm, so unconcerned, you the son of the great Herod—the son, I tell you—willing to play second fiddle to one of his grandsons, son of one of the sons Herod murdered, your nephew!"

"May I remind you, my dear Tetrarchess, that this son my grandfather murdered was *your* father and that King Herod Agrippa is *your* brother?"

"How you infuriate me!" She stamped her foot. "You don't seem to care that your nephew, who until a few months ago was depending on you for his food, is now a king while you're only a tetrarch! You don't seem to care that his silly wife Cypros is queen and your wife is only tetrarchess! It's nothing to you that Agrippa has the ear of Caesar, that the Emperor has even assigned the Tribune Longinus to be Agrippa's aide, that he's a great man at the court in Rome, while you're—you're a nobody!"

Antipas shrugged, licked his fat lips. "But what can I do about it, Herodias? I'm not the Emperor, you know."

"Well I know it." Her tone was sarcastic. "But neither was Agrippa Emperor. He did know what to do. He went to visit him, as you could do. He flattered and cajoled him, as you could do. You well know how Caligula loves it. Go to Rome and make him a great feast. Give him presents. Tell him he's a great actor, an incomparable poet, the finest musician in all the Empire. Tell him he's a god greater than Jupiter."

"And perhaps arouse his anger against us. You know how fickle Caligula is, how quickly he'll renounce his friendship for one and bestow it on another."

"Exactly. So then you can inveigle him into casting aside my brother and bestowing his crown on you."

"But had you ever thought that Caligula might take the tetrarchy from us should a whim strike him?"

"He'd never do that. Nor do you think so. It's just that you're content with your present ease; you're satisfied with your soft couch and rich foods and strong wines and—"

"And beautiful Tetrarchess." He grinned.

She stamped her foot. "Oh, how furious you do make me!" Her eyes were flashing her anger. "You don't care about me. It's all right for my dear sister-in-law, who was once fortunate to get my castoff gowns, to wear a jeweled crown, while I remain a tetrarchess! Yes, that's all right with you!"

Antipas sought to reason with her. "Let Agrippa be king; let him parade his banners. One day he may utter some trifling word that angers Caligula and thereby lose his throne and his head. But let's remain as we are, Herodias, for our station could easily be far worse. There's little difference in our manner of living whether we be called tetrarch or king. And it will be safer if we do nothing to attract this mad Caligula's attention."

He reasoned and argued, but he did not convince Herodias. And in the end he agreed that they, with many personages of the court and servants to attend them, should go with a great array of costly presents to Rome.

Agents were sent out to procure the treasures of the tetrarchy and lands beyond it. Fine glass from the works at the Belus River near Tyre, bales of finest textiles dyed a brilliant purple from the plants in that same region, brass vessels gorgeously fashioned, perfumes of rarest delicacy, gifts of every type and fashion, were assembled at the white palace at Tiberias and packed in great cases. When all the preparations had been completed, the Tetrarch's party crossed to Ptolemais and set sail for Rome.

But already Fortunatus, one of Agrippa's freedmen, was aboard another ship sailing for the capital with a letter from the king to Emperor Caligula accusing Antipas of having conspired with the late Sejanus to overthrow the Emperor Tiberius. But even more serious was the charge that the Tetrarch was now in league with King Artabanus of Parthia in opposition to Caligula's authority in Palestine. Agrippa had been informed early of Herod's plans and had known what to do.

"I suspect that my beloved brother-in-law and sister will have a surprise when they are received by the Emperor," he said one day to Longinus when he heard that their ship had left Ptolemais.

## THE CROWN TREE 40

Fortune was with Agrippa's aptly named messenger, for although the vessel on which he was sailing was slower than the one that bore Herod and his wife, the two ships tied up in the harbor of Puteoli almost at the same time.

The Emperor Gaius received Herod and the Tetrarchess in his sumptuous sprawling summer palace at Baiae high on the hillside above the harbor. He was gracious and relaxed and betrayed little of his nervous, excitable, always suspicious nature. But before the interview had proceeded more than a few minutes, a servant fetched the letter brought by Fortunatus, and the Emperor broke the seal and began to read it.

Color flamed along his thin cheeks, mounted upward into his flaring ears, and then he smiled, and those about him knew that his smiling presaged nothing good for Tetrarch Herod. Often they had seen their half-mad Emperor smile that way, and frequently after such a smile a head had rolled or the arrows of the Emperor's archers had found their target.

"Information comes to me from Palestine, Tetrarch Herod, from one in whom I place complete trust, that you have been disloyal both to the Emperor Tiberius and to me. It is revealed that you conspired with the late Prefect Sejanus to overthrow the former Emperor Tiberius"—his voice was calm, even gentle, and his smile disarming—"and that you are now conspiring with Artabanus of Parthia to assemble arms sufficient for seventy thousand men with whom you propose at a convenient time to attempt to end the rule of Rome in Palestine." Now his face was flushing and his voice was abrupt as he glared at the Tetrarch. "What do you say to these charges, Herod Antipas?"

Herod's round face paled. He licked his thick lips, swallowed.

"There is no truth to them, your Majesty. The Tetrarch of Galilee and Peraea has never sought to overthrow Rome's rule. He has just now ended a long journey from his tetrarchy to pay homage to the Emperor, to bring him a few paltry gifts in token of his esteem, and to—"

"Answer me just this," Caligula interrupted, his voice high and tremulous. "Tell me if it's true or false. Do you have weapons for seventy thousand men in your armory?"

"That is true, your Majesty. But they were assembled with no thought of rebellion. I had given no thought to harming your Majesty." Antipas ran his red tongue over his lips. "On the contrary, it has always been my purpose—"

"What need would Israel have for seventy thousand men in arms?"

"But, your Majesty, I would be prepared in event enemies—"

"Be silent! I'll hear no more!" The Emperor's thin face was livid, his voice high, shrill. The smile was gone. He pointed a shaking finger at the ashen-faced Herod. "You deserve death as a traitor. You deserve even the death traitorous and rebellious Jews often get." A twisted smile raised the twitching corners of his sensual lips, and once more his voice was deadly calm. "I ought to send you to the cross!" He hissed the word. "But I'm going to spare you, though I'm stripping you of your tetrarchy and all your possessions and bestowing them upon my faithful friend and loyal servant Agrippa!"

Herod Antipas stood straight and speechless, nor did Herodias beside him utter a sound, though she clenched her white hands and her face was deathly pale. The Emperor, sensing their terror and sadistically enjoying all the more his own role, spoke again:

"It is my will, Herod Antipas, that you and your wife be banished forever from the tetrarchy over which you have been ruling, and I appoint the city of Lyons in Gaul as your place of residence as long as you live. I further command that you be started on your journey there immediately. Guards, take them away!"

They had reached the doorway when someone ventured to speak to the irate Caligula. When the two had whispered a moment, the Emperor ordered Herodias brought back.

"For the moment I had overlooked the fact that you are the sister of my beloved friend Agrippa," he said to the woman, his voice gentle again. "I understand that you have never been friendly with your brother, but nevertheless because of your relationship I'm restoring to you your own possessions, and although I won't countermand the sentence I've just pronounced upon your husband, I'll countermand yours. You are free, therefore, to return to Galilee or remain in Rome"—he smiled, pleased at his generosity—"even at the court of the Emperor, if you wish."

Now the eyes of the courtiers fawning on the dissolute young Gaius studied the pale countenance of the Tetrarchess of Galilee and Peraea. The Emperor too was watching her, impatiently now that she was hesitant in replying. "Speak out, Herodias," Gaius demanded. "I'm doing this only because you're Agrippa's sister. I'm sparing you from going into banishment with your husband."

Those about the Emperor turned again to stare at the Tetrarchess. Herod's guards had paused in the corridor outside, and through the wide doorway Herod himself could look squarely into his wife's face.

She lifted her eyes and confronted Gaius and in the same instant they met Herod's beyond the open door. She squared her shoulders.

"Sire, you have acted toward me in a most magnificent manner, for which I'm deeply grateful. You make me a most generous offer. But my love for my husband prevents my partaking of the favor of your gift of freedom for me. Nor is it right and just, Sire, that I who have been a partner in my husband's days of prosperity should forsake him in his hour of misfortune."

Her head high, she smiled wanly, and then she bowed to Gaius.

"Have it as you will." His tone was even and calm, but the corners of his mouth were twitching again, and slowly his crooked smile overspread his thin face. "You have chosen poverty and banishment. Therefore all your possessions—palaces, money, jewels, all but the barest necessities of raiment—I bestow upon Agrippa." Suddenly the smile was gone and his expression was wild, and he lashed out with his arms and stamped the mosaic of the floor. "Begone with her! I abhor the sight of her! Get her away! Away! Away!"

As the guards rushed out their prisoner, regal now after years of worthless living, the Emperor Gaius Caesar Germanicus sank heavily to his gold-cloth great chair, slumped forward, eyes on the floor, to rake with jerking soft fingers through his thinning hair.

Fortunatus sailed for Palestine on the first ship leaving Puteoli. He bore to Agrippa a message from the Emperor announcing that Herod Antipas and Herodias had been banished to Gaul and that Agrippa had been named to succeed to the rule of the tetrarchy of Galilee and Peraea and possession of all properties of the dispossessed former rulers. At once the exultant Agrippa began making plans to establish the throne of his enlarged tetrarchy in the white palace at Tiberias.

When Tribune Longinus heard of the fate that had overtaken Antipas and his wife he was not surprised. He recalled what Agrippa had said to him when the Tetrarch and Herodias had started for Rome; he had suspected that Agrippa had devised some cunning scheme to ruin his Idumean brother-in-law with the suspicious and fickle Caligula. But though Agrippa and Caligula had been the instruments of Herod's downfall, they had not been the cause, Longinus felt. Vividly now he remembered his conversation with Lalage in Rome that night after Caligula had banished Pontius Pilate. Judas of Kiriot, the faithless Judaean of the Galilean's Twelve who had betrayed his master, had hanged himself. Pilate had condemned Jesus to the cross and had been banished. Now a similar fate had overtaken the Tetrarch of Galilee who could have rescued the man of Nazareth but instead returned him to the Roman Procurator.

"Only one is left, and that is the man who killed him." The words were as sharply alive to him as though he had spoken them aloud. "I wonder when and how—"

The old horrors of the nightmares, the shapeless fears of his conscious moments, which he had never been able completely to dispel despite his labored efforts at dispassionate reasoning, were reaching out to possess him. Once again he felt the perspiration seeping from his forehead, his palms dampening.

. . . But these others were his enemies. I killed him, but it was only in obeying the orders of my superior. *I* was not his enemy; I even killed him to end his agony; it was actually a deed of charity. If he knows, if he is alive, he must surely understand that I am not his enemy. And even if I were, did he not pray to his god, to the one-God of the Jews, for his enemies? . . .

But his prayers, the sudden terrible thought struck him, did not save his enemies from the vengeful wrath of the one-God. And of those who had leading roles in the crucifixion, only he himself had escaped thus far this divine and fearful wrath.

. . . But *they* were his enemies. They had no sympathy for him, no feeling of compassion, no sorrow that the deed had been done. Pilate that day was troubled indeed, but he had not the courage to be just. Nor did Pilate ever suspect in the slightest that he might have been dealing with divinity in the form of a man. *He* prayed for them, but that did not protect them from the dire vengeance. Will his prayers save me? Am I not also his enemy? Will not the one-God so regard me? How can he know that even though I drove my spear into his tormented body, I had no hate for him, I did it only out of compassion? How can I approach this one-God to tell him, and having told him, escape perhaps the horrible fate that must await me? If only *he* would intercede, if only the Nazarene would explain to his father-God . . .

Abruptly Longinus stood up, and quickly he strode from his chamber and out upon the terrace bathed in bright sunlight. In the new warmth and radiance his apprehensions momentarily were thrust back and his fears for the time dispelled.

"Conjurings, out of my long associating with these superstitious Jews," he said, this time aloud. "Judas killed himself because of sore disappointment over his master's failure to become Israel's king and deliverer from the Romans; Tiberius had already lived too long; Pontius Pilate was a miserable incompetent; Herod Antipas and Herodias ran afoul of a demoniac who fancied himself being threatened. They all got what they deserved, and reason decreed that such fates should overtake them." He held out his palms to the warming sunshine. "Reason did not decree that the Galilean, an innocent man, should meet such an end, but"— he shrugged a shoulder—"many innocent men suffer and die, do they not?" He sat down on a stone bench, stretched his legs. "What have any imagined gods to do with it?" He looked from the terrace out upon the palace grounds, sloping away long and luxuriant in the glare of the sunlight. How solid and enduring is the earth, he suddenly thought, how fragile and evanescent the witcheries of disturbing dreams when you bring them forth into the light of day.

Longinus sat for a long moment and let the soothing warmth of the sun comfort and restore him as the images that had disturbed him fled away. Then he arose and went back into his chamber, for there were reports to be prepared for sending to the Legate at Antioch and others for the Prefect in Rome. And Agrippa was persistent in seeking his advice in getting the lavish court established at Tiberias.

Meanwhile, in Jerusalem, with the departure of Saul of Tarsus peace was once more settling on the worshiping throngs. No disputing voices were being heard in the Synagogue of the Libertines or at the Temple or in the cities of Judaea and Samaria or even as far away as Galilee.

The orthodox Israelites had been having difficulties enough with the now deposed Procurator Pilate, and in recent weeks stories had been coming to Jerusalem of the growing hostility of the Emperor toward the Jews and their one God. Messages from relatives living in Rome's Jewish quarter on the west bank of the Tiber at the foot of Janiculum Hill were revealing that the dissipated young Emperor had begun to consider himself a Roman deity rivaling even the great god Jupiter.

So orthodox Jews now had little disposition to molest the followers of the Nazarene as long as the members of that fellowship offered the required sacrifices and otherwise fulfilled the laws of Israel. The new High Priest Theophilus chose to ignore the fellowship, to close his eyes and ears to its activities. If he knew that his sister-in-law and her daughter Damaris his niece had been baptized into its membership, if he even suspected it, he gave no sign.

Wisely, too, the members of the fellowship had chosen not to provoke those hostile to them. They continued holding their meetings in secret, where often Joseph Barnabas saw the High Priest's niece. Sometimes in a secluded dark chamber down in Ophel they would come upon one another at a service led by James bar Zebedee or Simon or Joseph himself, or by James the brother of the Lord. Occasionally under one pretext or another they would meet in the rear chamber of Obed the tanner's workshop. At times, too, one would encounter the other at the Synagogue of the Libertines or in one of the courts of the Temple. On these occasions the girl would pass on to Joseph Barnabas reports that had come to her from the High Priest's palace. And Barnabas would relay them to Simon and other leaders of the Messiah's sect.

The fellowship was growing. Throughout Palestine, where small groups had taken root and flourished, but more particularly in Jerusalem in the very shadow of the Temple, men and women and even small children were testifying to their faith in the risen Messiah. Many of these adherents were Greeks, among them a handful from Antioch's expanding congregation; some were Jews from Alexandria and from as far away as Cyrenaica and more remote regions, some even were citizens of the great capital on the Tiber. But by far the greater number counted themselves sons and daughters of Israel. Those who had entered into the fellowship of Jesus had come through circumcision, if they were not already of the household of Israel, and taking upon themselves the burden of Israel's law. They first became Jews and then followers of the Messiah. The strange arguments of Saul quickly had been forgot.

So the followers of Jesus of Nazareth for the moment were dwelling and worshiping in peace. But it was a peace that threatened to degenerate into stagnation. The plant had been set out, had taken root, but it was not being properly watered. Soon it might even be stunted.

Rugged Simon was one of the first to appreciate the menace of complacency. True, the fellowship was adding members, even spreading out from Jerusalem, with here and there, particularly at Antioch, groups of the Messiah's adherents organized into congregations and holding services of worship. But growth was not as rapid as Simon felt it should be, and the situation was beginning to lie heavily on the fisherman's heart. Late one day as they sat in the courtyard of Mary's house he unburdened himself to Joseph Barnabas.

"I'm sore in heart, Joseph," he said, his round face solemn. "I've become a burden and disappointment to my Lord; I've failed him again."

"But why do you think so, Simon? Aren't you diligent day and night in ministering to those of the fellowship, and doesn't it prosper?"

"I've been diligent in work, but I haven't served the Lord in the ways and in the regions where he willed that I serve him." He shook his head. "Our numbers do increase, that's true, but not as rapidly as they should, and we ought to be spreading out far past the walls of Jerusalem."

The first of the apostles sat silent, staring at the fig tree beyond the spouting fountain. Then he lifted his eyes to gaze out across the huddled houses of Ophel, beginning to melt together now in the deepening shadows of twilight.

" 'Go you into all the world, and preach the good news to every creature.' That's what the Master commanded," he said, as if talking to himself. "Philip carried the good news into Samaria and even to the treasurer of Queen Candace of the Ethiopians, and he converted many souls. But I've done little to spread it beyond the confines of Judaea and Galilee." Simon seemed now oblivious of the presence of Barnabas. "No, I've failed him. I haven't heeded his command to tell his good story to the world."

"Just what did he command you to do, Simon?"

"Well I remember, Joseph. It was after he had arisen from Joseph of Arimathaea's new sepulcher. The eleven of us—Judas was dead—had gone back to Galilee and assembled on the mountainside where Jesus had said he would meet us. Suddenly he was there. It was all very strange; we could hardly believe it was the Master until he started speaking, and then we knew. No man, Joseph, ever spoke like the Lord Jesus. Such words, beautiful, melodious words, with such strength and power, such comfort to those hearing them. He said many things that day, and just before he left us he told us to go unto all nations, baptizing in the name of the Father and Son and Holy Spirit, and he promised that he himself would always be with us, even unto the end of the world."

"They are beautiful words, Simon my brother. Why don't you write them down, and other words he said to the Twelve, so that all those who want to learn about him will have the truth, even those of generations not yet born?"

"It should be done, Joseph, I agree. But you ask me, a poor fisherfellow who lives by boats and nets and smells continually of fish, and has never sat at the feet of the learned rabbis, to write a book!" He slapped his big leg with his palm and laughed. "Simon of Capernaum writing a book." But quickly his countenance sobered. "But it ought to be done, Joseph. Were someone learned in such things to write it, someone like Saul of Tarsus or Luke the physician, it would be a great gift to the world."

"You may not be skilled as a scribe, Rab Simon," Barnabas ventured to demur, "and you didn't sit at the feet of the rabbis, but you did sit at the feet of one wiser than all the rabbis and you must remember well his teachings, and his good works. Maybe you could tell them to someone like Luke who could write them down—"

"Maybe, brother. But let's talk about it another time. I'm tired and troubled in heart. I've been failing my Lord, disobeying his command. But I'm going to do better henceforth." He reached over, placed his big brown hand on Barnabas' shoulder. "As soon as I can get things arranged, Joseph, I'm going back down to Galilee. There I'll gain strength and resolution, and understanding, I trust, to do what he wants me to do. And I'll want you to go with me."

In the light of the moon now risen above the white rectangle of the Temple, Barnabas saw that Simon no longer was troubled.

Then the first of the apostles stood up, grasped the younger man's arm.

"Yes, that's what we'll do, Joseph. The Lord has given me another chance. I begin to see the way ahead. Now I can sleep." He smiled, and Barnabas knew the big fisherman was at peace. "I'm tired. The day's labors have been heavy. Let's go inside to our beds."

Two days later Simon and Joseph Barnabas went out through Dung Gate and climbed the hill toward Bethany. Below them and a day's journeying away lay Jericho in the plain above the Dead Sea. From Jericho up the trough of the Jordan it would be a week's hard walking to a mountainside in Galilee.

## THE CROWN TREE 42

They had hardly reached the lower shore of the Sea of Galilee and were still a long day's trudging from Tiberias when they began to encounter a steadily mounting procession moving toward Galilee's capital.

At the place where the way from Nazareth joined the Jerusalem road another stream of people, some riding beasts but most of them on foot, merged with the one pushing northward. Simon approached a sparse, stoop-shouldered Jew plodding wearily along, a gnarled staff in his right hand. The man had come a long way, for his robe was pulled high above knotty ankles and his face and matted beard were gray with dust.

"Peace be with you, brother." Simon bowed.

"With you be peace," the weary fellow answered.

"My friend here and I"—Simon pointed to Joseph Barnabas—"have been coming from Jerusalem and of late we have noticed many travelers going the same way. What draws them? Has Herod appointed a great festival at Tiberias?"

The thin fellow wiped the hem of his soiled sleeve across his sweat-smeared face.

"Old Herod Antipas will never appoint another festival in Galilee, or anywhere else likely," he responded, brusquely, and leaned forward to peer incredulously into Simon's face. "Stranger, haven't you heard? Didn't you know that Agrippa is sleeping in the bed of Antipas in Tiberias and ruling from his throne? Haven't they told you that Antipas and his covetous Herodias went to visit Caesar in Rome to cajole him into making Antipas a king instead of tetrarch"—he laughed, revealing a cavernous mouth from which most of the teeth were gone—"but that instead Caesar banished both of them and gave everything they had to Agrippa?"

"No, my brother, I hadn't heard it." He turned away from the fellow, caught Joseph's arm. "God is just, Joseph. Tiberius is dead, Pilate is dead or languishes in some far land, and now Herod is banished. The enemies of the Lord Messiah are getting their just deserts." He confronted the stranger again. "So the people are journeying to Tiberias to acclaim the new King Agrippa?"

"I wish that was the reason I'd walked all the way from beyond Nazareth." He shook his head solemnly. "You mean to tell me, stranger, that you've had no news of the decree of Caesar concerning his image?"

"Of a truth we've heard nothing. Does the decree promise dire things for Israel?"

"You can answer for yourself when I tell you that Caesar has ordered them to set up his image in the Temple at Jerusalem, and commands all Israel to bow down and worship him."

"No! God in Israel forbid it!"

"It's the truth, stranger. The Emperor's sent the Proconsul Petronius of Syria to erect the statue, some say in the Holy of Holies. That's why you see this throng going to Tiberias—to protest."

"Is Petronius there? Won't the Jews fight to keep him from setting up the image?"

"He's there, I heard it said. But I don't think we'll try to fight his soldiers; we'll try to reason with him, I hope. That's the report from Ptolemais, where Petronius landed. A multitude of Jews met him there and threw themselves in front of the Emperor's image and wouldn't let it be transported toward Jerusalem. When he threatened to set his troops on them, they told him they'd die before they'd allow that hated thing to be placed in the Temple. So he stopped the men trying to move the image, and he left Ptolemais and went straightway to Tiberias to see if he could find out what sort of arms Israel had with which to challenge him. There's where everybody's going—to confront Petronius." He wiped his face again with the soiled sleeve hem. "When you get there, stranger, you'll find countless thousands already there."

The fellow had not exaggerated, they discovered when they arrived at the Galilean capital. Jews by many thousands had pushed into Tiberias to throng its streets, overflow into every open square and fill it and swarm out into the fields long parched and deep in dust. The city was in tumult. Frenzied voices shouting defiance, gesticulating hands held high, proclaimed Israel's eternal refusal to bow knee to any save the God of Israel.

"No! No! We'll never do it! Never! Never!" shouted an old man who stood in the shadow of the columns before a great man's house near the palace of the deposed Antipas. "Every man's head in Israel will be laid on the headsman's block before one knee is bowed in worship of any man!" He confronted Simon and Barnabas, who had happened along at that moment. "Isn't that so, stranger?"

"Yes, though God forbid."

"God forbid? What do you mean?"

"That I hope it won't come to that. Is there no other way except to bare our necks to the pagans?"

"I'm afraid not, stranger. The Proconsul, they say, is a man of great stubbornness." He turned his head, spat into the dust. "And so is Caesar, the son of hell!"

The next day the two travelers from Jerusalem were able to

judge Petronius for themselves. He had sent messengers about the city to announce that he would give audience to the protesting Jews in a great field on the western outskirts of Tiberias. Simon and Joseph Barnabas had lodged at an inn on that side of the capital, and by daybreak they had managed to maneuver their way through the throngs already there to a position near the platform from which the great man was to address them.

Hardly was the dew dried on the dead grass—for the long drought and hot sun had left the cattle little on which to subsist—when there was a great commotion nearest the city gate.

"Make way! Make way!" They could hear the shouts, growing louder and louder, and presently the throng before them divided and along this lane suddenly opened Simon and Barnabas saw advancing toward them a company of Jews resplendently robed and with their beards carefully braided and heavily oiled.

"They must be the elders of the city," Barnabas remarked.

A fat Jew in a foul-smelling, greasy robe heard him.

"You're right," he said. "There's many a shekel in the pouches of those well-fed sons of Abraham." He chuckled and the tassels at the end of his cord belt danced. "That big one there"—he pointed—"with the fanned-out black beard and the big belly is Prince Aristobulus, brother of King Agrippa. He was raised at the court of the Caesars and has never done a day's honest work; you can tell by that rounded paunch." He tugged at his belt, hunched up the soiled robe. "As a usual thing I don't hold with those rich ones, and least of all that Herod crowd, but today I'm upholding their hands."

"What are they here for, friend? To make a plea to the Proconsul?"

"Yes," the fat one told Simon. "And may the God of Israel put burning words into their mouths!" He pointed again. "They're taking their places in front of the stand. It won't be long now until the Proconsul—" He stopped abruptly, for from the direction of the gate in the western wall came a trumpet blast, and presently a troop of Roman horsemen came galloping toward the multitude now packing closely about the platform.

Rapidly the massed throng divided once more, and the horse-men, their animals now slowed to a fast walk, moved through the opening ahead of a heavy chariot in which stood a tall and stiffly erect man in the uniform of a Roman officer. Behind the chariot rode another detachment of horsemen. At the platform the chariot stopped and the man descended. Quickly he mounted the platform, stood facing the thousands of searching, serious countenances, as abruptly the babble of excited voices ceased.

"Men of Israel"—the Proconsul's cold blue eyes surveyed the acres of people massed before him, their black eyes, grim and determined, focussed on his own unsmiling countenance—"weeks ago at the command of Emperor Gaius I came from Syria to Ptolemais to take the statue of His Imperial Majesty to Jerusalem to set it up in the Temple there in accordance with his command.

"You well know the reception I was given at Ptolemais. Many of you doubtless participated in that rebellion. When I issued the order to begin transporting the image, you swarmed about it and even threw yourselves on the ground in a solid phalanx before it so that it could not be moved. When I threatened to have you put to the sword by my soldiers, you bared your necks and declared you would die before you permitted Caesar's likeness to be erected in your Temple. I suspected that because of your stubbornness you had prepared to wage war against us, and so I came to Tiberias and examined into your capabilities. But instead of soldiers and arms I found only more protesting, louder supplications, more thousands vowing they would rather die than permit their god to be insulted."

The Proconsul paused, turned half around to speak to a tribune two paces to his rear and side.

"He seems to be thoroughly angry," Barnabas whispered to Simon.

"Yes, and I'm afraid we'll see much slaughter today. I pray the God of Israel—" He stopped, for Petronius, once more surveying the multitude silently regarding him with dark eyes plainly hostile and defiant, was about to resume his address.

"Men of Israel," he said, lifting his head and raising his voice to be heard on the rim of the crowd, "I am not a man hardened in heart. I would have no joy in seeing the soil of Israel running red with the blood of her sons. I recognize that they are a proud and stubborn people and that you are zealous for your god's maintaining his supreme station." He cleared his throat. "But I have been ordered by my Emperor to escort the image to Jerusalem and place it in your house of worship that it as a symbol of the Emperor might share the worship you give your god. He does not insist that you withhold worship from your god; the Emperor is content to share it. And only here in Israel is this worship being denied him."

Once more he was silent as he studied the people before him. Then he lifted his hand in quick gesture.

"I am a soldier of Rome. I've been commanded to set up the statue in your Temple. I have no recourse but to obey. Can a soldier do otherwise, men of Israel?"

His question gave the resplendently robed elders the opportunity they had been awaiting. Prince Aristobulus stepped forward a pace.

"O most worthy Proconsul," he began, his arms wide apart before him, palms up, in a natural but not servile gesture of pleading, "you have spoken the truth of the zeal of the Jews for the God of Israel and of our jealousy of any other gods, for we recognize none but Him. It is against our laws and our very nature, O great Proconsul, to bow the knee to any in the vast pantheon of the gods of Rome and Greece. It is expressly against our laws to permit within our holy places any likeness of any man or god. Gladly will we die before we permit such desecration and insult to our God, the only true God; gladly will we prostrate ourselves beneath—"

"Then what recourse have I, Prince Aristobulus, but to command my soldiers to fall on your people with their swords?" the Proconsul interrupted, his tone sharp with exasperation. "Aren't you defying the Emperor? Aren't you warring on Rome, even though you have no resources with which to wage war except sticks and stones and gnarled fists?" Petronius' face darkened in a heavy scowl. He twisted his head to catch the eye of the tribune behind him, who nodded solemnly. Then once more he faced the king's brother. "What do you say to that, Prince Aristobulus?"

Barnabas nudged Simon. "What can he answer the Roman, Rab Simon?"

Simon raised a restraining hand to clutch his companion's arm. "Hold your peace, Joseph, and pray God to put words on his lips."

Aristobulus carded with thick fingers his heavy beard, gave it a gentle tug, as if in deep thought. Then he thrust forth both hands in sudden gesture.

"It's a hard and stony road on which the orders of the Emperor Gaius have set your feet, O most noble Proconsul. You must travel it carefully and with a quick discernment if you are to avoid the shedding of blood the like of which has never been seen in this ancient and long-suffering land.

"You're a soldier of Rome, Proconsul, and a soldier must obey the commands of his superior. We Israelites recognize that. Yet if you do carry out the commands of Emperor Gaius you will have on your hands and soul forever the blood of countless Israelites who will die joyously rather than permit the desecration of the Temple and the insulting of the God of Israel."

He paused to give emphasis. Petronius and the soldiers behind him stood facing Aristobulus, erect, immobile, their eyes intent on this brother of the Jewish king whom they knew to be also a friend of Gaius. At the prince's back not a man of Israel offered to break the hush of the strained moment. Then Aristobulus resumed speaking:

"You must obey the Emperor's commands, O Proconsul. We must oppose their being carried out if we would be true to our God"—Aristobulus turned to the others in his delegation—"and God grant that we die before we prove untrue!"

"Yes! Yes!" A tall hawk-nosed Jew shouted his support.

"Indeed, God grant it!" Another man spoke up. And others chorused.

Aristobulus held forth his hands again to the Proconsul. "It is obvious then, O Proconsul, that there is but one course to be followed if the shedding of blood is to be avoided. The orders of the Emperor must be changed!"

"Yes! Yes!"

"He's right, O Proconsul! Hear him! Hear him!"

But Aristobulus turned, hand upraised, to quell the threatened tumult.

"I know the Emperor Gaius. My brother, King Agrippa, has long been his companion and devoted friend." Aristobulus was speaking again to Petronius. "Perhaps in the last year or so the Emperor has changed, O Proconsul, as rumors indicate. But he must still be a reasonable man. Why then would he wish the blood of countless good men of Israel? Can it be that he's unalterably determined to be worshiped as deity, as equal with our God of Israel? Can it be that he would see thousands slain for a whim, O Proconsul, a whim unworthy of the mighty Emperor of Rome?"

He lowered his voice, spoke calmly. "I don't believe he would. I feel that the Emperor, once he is apprised of the true situation, will rescind his orders. We beg of you, therefore, that you dispatch to the Emperor a letter conveying to him the insuperable aversion that we Israelites have to reception in the Temple of his image, or that of any other man or being. The message should likewise reveal how for many weeks now, both at Ptolemais and here, we have sworn to die before we would yield; how the farmers of Israel have left off the tillage of their ground rather than allow their sacred laws to be transgressed; how with the land unsown the Emperor will stand to suffer a great loss in revenue from the shrinkage of the taxes, and want will increase throughout the land." He paused, wearied with the efforts of his oratory, and then continued: "Make the Emperor see, O Proconsul, that if he persists, then the blood of a great host will be on his head alone." He bowed. "Thus do we of Israel offer to you our supplications." He stepped back into the front line of his delegation.

"Prince Aristobulus and men of Israel," Petronius, clearing his throat, replied in even, modulated voice, "for weeks I have listened to your speeches and paid heed to your supplications. I could have said a word and my men would have been on you smiting right and left with their swords. I have sought to reason with you, explaining that I am a soldier required to obey my superior, in this instance the supreme power of the Empire, the Emperor Gaius himself.

"But you have stiffened your necks and hardened your hearts against me, men of Israel. You have refused to give heed to my commands that you clear a way to Jerusalem so that my men may transport to the Temple the image of His Majesty." He lowered his voice, but the frown was gone from his countenance. "My soldiers are beside me. They have their weapons on them. I have only to utter the command. Men of Israel, shouldn't I do it?"

Not an Israelite uttered a sound. Simon and Barnabas looked toward Prince Aristobulus. Would he answer Petronius? What could he say?

They saw the king's brother turn his head, nod. Then there stepped out from the delegation a man whom they had not noticed before. He wore the uniform of a Roman tribune.

"It's the Roman Saul and I saw on the ship bringing us from Cyprus," Barnabas whispered. Simon caught the younger man's arm, for the tribune was about to address Petronius.

"I am Tribune Longinus, Proconsul Petronius," he said, saluting gravely, "under your command but attached to King Agrippa as Roman aide and adviser with instructions from Prefect Marco to keep Rome informed on conditions in the province. May I beg your Excellency's permission to speak?"

"You are the son of Senator Varro, are you not, Tribune Longinus?"

"I am, Excellency." Longinus bowed.

"Proceed, Tribune."

"I would not be presumptuous enough, sir, to offer you advice in this grave situation. But I have spent much time on duty in Palestine and out of personal experience I can support what Prince Aristobulus has told you. The Jews are a stubborn race;

they will die rather than permit what they consider the insulting of their one-God. In this situation the road to Jerusalem will be red with their blood before the statue of the Emperor is allowed to stand in their Temple."

"Then what course would you suggest that I take, Tribune? I welcome your advice." The Proconsul's expression was earnest, his tone sincere.

"I would suggest then, Excellency, that you follow the advice given you by Prince Aristobulus and send the Emperor a letter fully explaining the situation and asking his further orders. This will have the effect of delaying the disastrous shedding of blood that would certainly follow any attempt to move the image to Jerusalem. And I, sir, will be glad to bear your letter to Rome and hand it to the Emperor, who, I hope, still looks with favor on my father's family."

"I know of none who would be more favorably received than Senator Varro's son." The Proconsul evidently was impressed.

"But I would not go alone, sir, though I would represent you as an officer under your command. I would attempt to prevail upon King Agrippa to accompany me"—he smiled—"or, rather, I would accompany the King, who is as you know, sir, a great favorite of the Emperor, and the King could take with him other notables of the Jewish nation—"

"The suggestion has weight with me, Tribune," Petronius spoke up quickly, and Simon and Barnabas, watching intently, saw Jewish heads wagging agreement. Then the Proconsul faced the delegation headed by Prince Aristobulus, and the great host of Jews beyond it, a sea of grave, determined faces looking up in stony silence.

"Men of Israel, if I don't heed the command of the Emperor Gaius, I forfeit my own life," he declared. "Yet I tell you"— Petronius raised his voice—"that I do not think it just for me to have such regard for my own safety that I'd refuse to sacrifice it for the preservation of such a great number in Israel. Nor can I do anything other than applaud your determination to uphold your law, which has come down to you from your forefathers and which you consider worthy of preserving at the cost of your lives. Nor will I"—the Proconsul stepped forward a pace—"with the supreme assistance of your god sustaining me, suffer your Temple at Jerusalem to fall into contempt." Petronius paused, and the great multitude, eyes boring into his countenance, waited for his words.

"This then will I do, Prince Aristobulus and Tribune Longinus. I will write a letter to the Emperor advising him of the situation, the strength of your resolution, and urging him to countermand his orders concerning the statue." He paused again, and when he spoke his voice was grim. "I promise you nothing, men of Israel, beyond what I have spoken. My letter may greatly irritate the Emperor and he may turn with rage on me. But I'll risk that danger rather than see this multitude perish." He swept his arm in a wide arc before him. "So, men of Israel, get to your homes and see to the cultivation of your ground, which has greatly suffered through lack of cultivation and the great drought that burns it. My soldiers will not molest you, nor will I transport the image of Emperor Gaius to your Temple; instead, I'll send this dispatch to Rome covering the things I've told you and seeking to serve your best interests." He wiped his perspiring forehead, streaked now with the dust lifted from the trampling throng. "And were I in any manner worthy to raise my voice to your god, men of Israel, I would pray him to send on this tortured land his cooling, saving showers."

Petronius wheeled about, spoke to the tribune. The two, with the other Romans following, started down the steps. Before they had walked halfway to the waiting chariot great drops of rain peppered down. Looking up, they saw heavy clouds had gathered. The multitude, too, felt the raindrops and saw the clouds. A great shout went up, and men lifted their arms toward the fast darkening sky. As Petronius stepped into the chariot the clouds opened and the rain roared down on the famished earth.

Before the now abandoned platform Longinus saw the Jews prostrating themselves, some flat on their faces in thanksgiving, some on their knees laving their hands in pools already forming.

Simon Peter, kneeling not far away, raised his eyes toward the heavens, so that the rain ran down his dust-covered face and dripped in little brown drops from the end of his beard. "The God of Israel shows forth His pleasure when He looks into the warm heart and hears the good words of even a pagan son of Rome," he observed. "Praised be the God of Israel!"

"Praised be the God of Israel!" Joseph Barnabas, on his knees in the pouring rain, echoed the rugged fisherman's words.

## THE CROWN TREE 43

Hardly had Simon and Joseph Barnabas departed on the journey to Galilee when the calamitous news came to Jerusalem of the Emperor's command that his statue be set up in the Temple. Already the statue had arrived in the harbor of Ptolemais, the report declared, and the Proconsul Petronius was there with his troops to escort it to Jerusalem. In hours the city was aroused. On Mount Zion and in Ophel alike men spat when they spoke the mad young despot's name.

The new High Priest Theophilus immediately called together the members of the Sanhedrin in emergency session to consider what should be done. Never perhaps had the highest court of Israel been confronted with a graver crisis. Never before had pagan Rome in all its years of dealing with this subjugated small nation so grossly insulted Israel and Israel's God.

Along the semicircle of stone benches heads bobbed and beards wagged—combed-out thin wispish short beards, luxuriant thick beards, oiled and carefully braided, beards square-cut or pointed, some twin-spiked—as the Sanhedrin considered Israel's peril.

"The Emperor's a madman, completely insane!" A fat Pharisee thrust forth his thick white hands, the fingers heavy with rings. "Caligula would make himself equal with the God of Israel!"

"You're right, my brother," the High Priest agreed. "The Emperor is mad. Only an insane man would so challenge our God. But that makes Israel's peril all the greater, for we are dealing not only with a degraded man, a servant of Satan, but also with a mad ruler of mighty Rome. How can Israel stand against such an enemy and at the same time remain true to God? That, brothers, is our problem."

Solutions were offered, weighed. But not one Sanhedrinist was rash enough to suggest that Israel, even though she fought to the last man, could block the transporting of the Emperor's image from Ptolemais to Jerusalem and into the sacred precincts of the Temple itself. What then could be done?

"We have but one course, as I see it." One of the members had arisen, was straightening his habiliments. "We can never defeat Rome by force of arms. What arms do we have? A few spears and perhaps a bow here and there, and pruning hooks. Our young men would be slain and laid out in windrows behind the advancing conquerors, and our women, our children, ourselves would be driven as chaff from the threshing floor. Israel would be a land of universal weeping." His frown was dark on his round, perspiring face.

"But, brother, you said there was one recourse." The countenance of his neighbor two seats away was troubled. "What is it?"

"We must devise some plan that will cause the Emperor to relent. Only Caligula's withdrawal of his command can save Israel."

"But how do you propose to bring about a change in his nefarious plans?" Theophilus asked.

"There's one man"—he thrust forth his arm, forefinger pointing rigidly—"who has the ear of the despicable Caligula, and he's a Jew, though a profligate one of whom we are not proud."

"The new king, Agrippa?"

"Yes. Agrippa has spent many years in Rome, including much time at Caligula's court. Let us go at once to Tiberias, where Agrippa's lately installed himself in the white palace of the dethroned Herod Antipas, and seek his aid. Let us urge him to sail immediately for Rome and beseech the Emperor to rescind his orders to Proconsul Petronius."

Bearded solemn heads nodded agreement. Quickly it was determined to dispatch the High Priest Theophilus and other members of Israel's highest court to Tiberias to have audience with Agrippa and importune him to sail for Rome to appeal to his friend the Emperor. Speed would be of utmost importance, they agreed; they should go at once to Tiberias and urge the king to set out for Rome at his earliest convenience.

That evening old Annas met in secret with his son the High Priest. He had another reason for approving the proposed visit to King Agrippa, but he had not wished to divulge it at the meeting of the Sanhedrin. A lifetime of conniving had taught Annas that he could accomplish more by revealing his schemes to only a select few.

"The visit to King Agrippa will provide us an excellent opportunity, Theophilus, to strike a potent blow against these blaspheming worshipers of the crucified Nazarene," the old man said to his son. "That fellowship is growing, too, and unless something is done quickly to stamp it out, it may shortly challenge our true worship of the God of Israel." He leaned over, tapped the High Priest's knee.

"When you go to Tiberias, seek an opportunity to have an audience alone with Agrippa," he instructed the younger man, still an obedient son even though the chief man in Israel's priestly hierarchy. "Tell him then of the growth of this blasphemous fellowship and warn him that it is seeking already to overthrow him as a puppet of Rome. Fire his blood against them, Theophilus; inform him that I am bitterly opposed to this sect and that the heavier he wields his lash against these blasphemers the more perfectly he will please me and the more solidly he will entrench himself with the faithful and the influential of Israel." He smiled on his son, and licked his thick red lips. "You will know what to say, Theophilus; you're a son of Annas. Only be certain not to soften your words in counseling Agrippa to destroy utterly this blot upon Israel. And there is one man"—he leaned over until his face was close to his son's, and he lowered his voice, though no one else was in the chamber with them—"whom I particularly want to see removed from Israel. That one, you may have surmised, is the burly Galilean fisherman, Simon of Capernaum. Tell Agrippa I would be most happy to see the ax laid to his neck. And likewise to the necks of those other Galileans, the Zebedee brothers."

## THE CROWN TREE 44

As suddenly as it had begun the rain had ended and the suffering parched earth had drunk it ravenously. The air was fresh again and clean, and on a million newly washed stirring leaves—olive, apricot, oleander, grape, pomegranate—the sharp sunlight danced and quivered.

"It's a different world since the rain." Simon pointed eastward toward the little sea. "Even the sky and water are bluer. Many's the time, Joseph, I've seen it like this along the shore of Gennesaret." He chuckled. "Many's the time, too, we got a good wetting. But he never seemed to mind it. He was young, and strong as a bull yearling, and used to the outdoors. He always had a hankering after ships and the sea." Simon's eyes were still on the far-off water, gentled now and deeply blue. "I always had the notion that he liked fishing and ships better than fitting joints and swinging a hammer. I could tell you many a story about the Master and the sea, Joseph." Reluctantly, it seemed, Simon turned about, nodded his head toward the inn; they had been sitting on the rim of the cistern in the courtyard. "It's time we were seeing to getting something to eat. Most of those who came here to protest to the Proconsul have started for their homes by now, I'd say; it ought to be easier to find food. And after this morning's pushing and shoving, I'm well-nigh famished."

But the public room was still jammed with pilgrims. Some sat at the crude tables and ate from pouches they had brought; others had purchased food of the innkeeper and wine from his skins. Many walked from table to table, talking and laughing, their mouths filled with food and wine which from time to time in their enthusiasm they sprayed out on suddenly encountered friends.

Simon went up to the innkeeper. "We have consumed all the food from our pouches, friend," he said. "Could we purchase wine, and a loaf, some cheese and olives, and maybe a few pressed figs or dates?"

The fellow nodded. When they had agreed on the price, the innkeeper put the food before them, with the wine. They sought a table and stools. But all were occupied.

"Let's go outside and sit on the cistern," Simon suggested. "The air out there will be sweeter, too."

At the door they almost collided with a tall man, dusty from travel. He stepped back quickly, bowed. "I'm sorry, friends. I almost knocked the wine cups—" He stopped abruptly, his mouth still open. "Aren't you Simon, the first of our Lord Messiah's apostles?"

"Yes, brother, I am. And I'm sure I've seen you somewhere."

"Luke of Antioch. I was at Jerusalem with Saul—"

"Luke the physician! Peace be with you, brother. I knew I'd seen your countenance." He turned to point out the man beside him. "You must likewise remember Saul's friend and fellow pupil, Joseph Barnabas."

"Of course! Joseph, I'm glad likewise to see you again."

"We've procured food, Luke. Come eat with us. We're going to sit in the courtyard. There's no room left inside."

"But let me go in and purchase food and wine. Then I'll come out and sit with you. There's much I wish to hear from your lips, Simon."

In a few minutes he joined them at the cistern.

"Luke, a moment ago you spoke of *our* Lord Messiah. Why did you say *our* Lord Messiah?"

"Because I'm a member of his fellowship now." The physician's eyes revealed exultation. "I'm one of you, Simon."

"Then you have been circumcised and have been added to the synagogue at Antioch?"

"No, I haven't been circumcised, nor do I belong to any synagogue. I'm not a Jew, you know; I'm Greek."

"Yes"—suddenly the fisherman's eyes were questioning, disturbed—"but how then do you call yourself a member of *our* fellowship?"

"I've been in Tarsus with Saul," Luke answered frankly. "He accepted me into our fellowship."

The expression on Simon's grizzled round face betrayed his troubled mind. "But how had Saul authority to accept into the fellowship one who is not of Israel before he has taken on his body the sign of Israel and on his soul the burden of Israel's law?"

"Saul assured me that the fellowship of our Lord Jesus is composed of those who love him and have salvation through faith in him. Isn't that what Jesus himself taught, Simon?"

"Saul so contends. I had always thought that we entered into the fellowship through the body of Israel and that Gentiles to accept our Lord Jesus and become members of his congregation must first enter into the fellowship of Israel. Saul insists circumcision isn't necessary; he contends that upholding the law of Moses likewise is not necessary to attain salvation. To many of us in Israel his words were strange and touched on blasphemy." Plainly Simon was troubled, and then he smiled. "But nevertheless, Luke, I'm happy that you love our Lord Messiah, even though I can't say whether you are of his fellowship."

"But, Simon, isn't that for each man to say in his own heart—whether or not he is one in the fellowship of Jesus?"

"Perhaps, my brother. Since Saul came to us out of Syria's desert I've been troubled by his words. It's a problem whose answer I can't give. But I'm confident that Saul will yet be a strong and convincing voice on the side of the Master, and I trust you will be likewise." His assertion inspired a question. "By the way, Luke, have you been able to collect material for the book Saul wants you to write concerning the Master?"

"Some, Simon. On the way back to Antioch I talked with a number of persons who'd known him; they told me of many wondrous things he did. One day I hope I can put them down. The things Jesus did and said would fill many books, I'm convinced."

"Yes, many books, and they would not tell all the story." Once more Simon was looking out toward the little sea.

"I'd like also to record the story of Saul's change. Wouldn't it likewise be a story worth the telling?"

"It would," Simon agreed. "But it's my opinion that Saul's story, the principal part, hasn't been lived yet."

Simon and Barnabas recalled that when Luke was in Jerusalem he was searching for his lost beloved; they inquired if he had since been successful in his search.

"No," he replied sadly. "I've traveled much and sought diligently, but I've had no trace of her."

"You must not despair, brother," Simon counseled. "Pray to the Master and have faith. One day you will find her."

The next day, and the next, Luke walked the streets of Galilee's capital hopefully for tidings of his lost Aspasia. He talked with countless persons—in the market places, at the seashore where vessels landed passengers from various ports around the coast of the little sea, at the booths of the collectors of customs—but from no one did he hear a word of Aspasia. Fearfully he visited evil dives down by the wharves and dark loathsome places along narrow alleyways; in hope and in fear he accosted slave traders and procurers for brothels. But always he came back to the lodging place, where he shared a chamber with Simon and Joseph Barnabas, knowing no more than he had known when early in the morning he had departed.

After a while Luke concluded that Aspasia, if alive, was in some other region of the Empire.

"I'll return to Antioch and from Seleucia take a ship westward, perhaps to Ephesus or Corinth or Athens or even Rome," he confided dejectedly to his two companions one evening. "It must be that she's in some other part of the world."

"Then we'll go with you as far as Capernaum," Simon told

him. "We will be company for one another along the way." He caught the physician's arm, held it affectionately in his grasp. "But remember, brother, never abandon hope. And never cease to pray to our God of Israel to lead you to your beloved."

Early on the morrow they started northward along the shore of the sea. The shadows of the hills to the west were long on the water when they reached Capernaum. "Lodge with me tonight, Luke," Simon urged the physician. "It's late to be traveling. Get a good night's rest and begin your journey refreshed and in the cool of the morning."

The weary Luke accepted readily. But as the three men rested on Simon's housetop after the evening meal, the first of the apostles offered another suggestion.

"Rather than continue your journey to Antioch, Luke, why don't you accompany Joseph and me as we return to Jerusalem? We'll spend a very short season in Galilee, and then we'll travel back along the way westward of the Jordan through the cities of Samaria, and renewed in spirit we'll soon be back at the house of Mary of Cyprus. It might be that in the regions we traverse you'll come on tidings of your beloved. And if you think it best, you can leave us at Joppa and take ship to Antioch or the cities in the west."

"Through Samaria, Rab Simon? Should the first of the apostles journey through the cities of the idolators?"

"Many Jews would wonder, Joseph," Simon responded. "But didn't the Master journey time after time in that region?" His questioning was gentle. "If he counted himself not above visiting the Samaritans, my brother, should we?" He looked out toward the blue waters, now purpling in the fast coming twilight. "I'd like to retrace a journey the Twelve once made with him. I'd like to have you two drink at the well of our father Jacob at Sychar, where the Master talked with the woman of evil reputation and told her how she might drink of the living water."

"Of the living water? What did he mean?" Joseph Barnabas asked quickly. "Those are strange words."

"The Master often used strange but beautiful words, potent,

moving words, to express his meaning. By drinking of the living water he meant partaking of the salvation he so freely offered."

Luke's eyes lighted. "It was a beautiful way of making clear his teaching, wasn't it?"

Simon reached over, grasped the physician's shoulder. "Nobody else could say a thing just like the Master, Luke. He had a marvelous way with words. Go with us; you'll hear many stories of him from other lips."

"I could go with you as far as Joppa and catch a ship there to Seleucia or strike westward across the Great Sea." The physician pondered a moment. "I'll do it, Simon; I'll go with you."

## THE CROWN TREE 45

Before the sun had lifted out of the little sea they started. It was the morning of the third day after their arrival at Capernaum. They walked steadily southward. At Magdala, where the pear-shaped sea swelled farthest west at its greatest width, the three left the shore line and trudged southwestwardly until they came to Cana. Before they had left the village behind, Simon recounted the story of the wedding feast and how on that joyous night early in the young Galilean's ministry he had transformed the water into wine. Simon paused, pointed.

"It was in that house over there. See? The one behind the low wall. How the sight of that house brings back memories!" He swept his arm in a half-circle, and though his eyes were smiling, a tear slipped down his cheek into the stubble of his whiskers. "How all this region roundabout, these hamlets and hills and the sea across yonder—O Master, how they bring you back!"

For a moment his eyes lingered on the narrow streets of little Cana. Then he grasped his staff with a renewed firmness.

"Come," he commanded, "we'd better be on our way if we want to reach Nazareth before night. We'll lodge at the house of a friend I know well; and we'll walk about Nazareth. I want you to see *his* village; I want to show you the house in which he lived, and the carpenter shop behind it where he worked." Simon hitched up his robe, tightened his rope girdle. "Seeing his country, Luke, will help you when you write your story about him."

They spent the night in the small cluster of white-walled houses that clung tenaciously to the steep hillside, and when morning came they walked the narrow streets and even climbed to the summit of the slope from which the carpenter youth Jesus had often viewed the hills and valleys and a corner of the distant small sea. After they had eaten their midday meal they started southward through the plain of Esdraelon, climbed the rolling hills and came down again at Sychar, where they paused to drink from Jacob's well.

"This is a beautiful valley," Joseph Barnabas declared, as they sat down after they had drunk of the cool water. "It's sheltered by Mount Ebal on the north and Mount Gerizim to the south. And look how the vineyards and orchards run up the slopes and the gardens fill the level places. It's a paradise, isn't it?"

"It is, yes," Luke agreed. "It's a choice spot."

"I think it's one of the choicest spots in all Palestine," Simon commented. "But maybe that's because of the memories I have of this place."

"Now tell us about him and the woman, Rab Simon." Joseph's eyes revealed his eagerness.

The fisherman sat silent a long moment, his eyes fixed vacantly on the tomb of the great Joseph four hundred yards north of the well. Then he turned, his bearded face relaxed into a smile.

"The Master sat right there on the curbing of the well. It was near midday, and we were tired from much walking, and thirsty and hungry, too. But there was no vessel handy with which to dip from the well; nor did we have any food.

" 'Go into the city and buy food,' the Master said; 'I'll wait here until you return.'

" 'But, Master,' one of our group said, 'you're thirsty. Let's first find a vessel and let you drink.'

" 'No,' he answered, 'you need not. While you're gone someone is likely to come to the well and will give me water.'

"That's what happened. While we were buying bread and meat, this woman came to the well. He asked her for a drink and she dipped up water for him. Then he began talking with her and that's when he told her that if she sought of him a drink he would give her living water."

"Was she still here when you and the others returned with the food?"

"Yes, and we were surprised to find him, a Jew and a descendant of David, talking with a woman of Samaria. Yet I suppose we weren't entirely surprised either, because we knew how he was. He was never unwilling to talk with anybody, however low-born or evil the person might be.

"Soon the woman left, and we offered him the food and wine. But he didn't seem to be hungry, although before we went into the city he'd said that he was nigh famished. Somebody remarked to him that he didn't seem to be hungry any more. I'll never forget what he said, or how he looked. He appeared rested again, and his eyes had lost their tired look.

" 'I have meat of which you know nothing,' he said.

"Thomas didn't understand; he didn't have much imagination, that Thomas. You had to talk pretty plainly to him. Many times he didn't understand the Master, because the Master liked to make up little stories to emphasize the truths he was trying to teach; he liked to dress up his thoughts in striking words. The Master was a great teacher. That's why I can remember so well the things he used to tell us."

"But what did Thomas ask him, Simon?" Luke inquired.

"I'll never forget it. The Master was sitting right there." Simon pointed. "We were grouped about him.

" 'Did somebody bring you something to eat while we were gone, Master?' Thomas asked. Jesus smiled.

" 'No,' he said. 'That's not the sort of meat I meant. The meat that sustains and strengthens me is doing the will of Him who sent me, and accomplishing His work.'

"Then he went on to teach us a lesson. I remember that it was in the dead of winter and already much of the grain had been sowed. The Master used the time of year to make his point. That was how he taught; he used things about him that were easy of understanding.

" 'You say that there are four months until harvest time,' he spoke up quickly, his eyes bright. 'But I say to you, lift up your eyes and look on the fields, for they are already ripe for harvesting.' "

"The fields he spoke of meant the world, and the grain ripe for the harvesting was the people. Isn't that what he meant, Simon?"

"That's right, Luke; that was his way of saying something important he wanted us to know."

"A much more striking and effective way of saying it, too," Luke added. "His words fairly sang, didn't they?"

"Yes, and they likewise had marvelous meaning."

"The Messiah was always thinking of people, wasn't he, Rab Simon?" Joseph Barnabas had been listening absorbed.

"That's true. Always they were uppermost in his thoughts—God his Father and the people his brothers."

"I wish I could have seen him and heard him. Jesus in every way must have been a very great man, wasn't he, Simon?"

"Yes, Luke. The Master was the strongest, the gentlest, the most understanding, the quickest to forgive." Simon's gentle eyes suddenly took fire. "He *is* the greatest one God ever sent to walk this earth!"

## THE CROWN TREE 46

From Sychar the three journeyed westward along the narrow valley between the two mountains until they came out on the undulating plain of Sharon from which now and then they had a glimpse far in the west of the blue waters of the Great Sea. Along the rolling Sharon they traveled straight south, and soon had left Samaria behind and were once again in Judaea. When they reached Lydda and entered its gate, they lodged at the house of one of Simon's friends, for many followers of the Lord Messiah lived at Lydda.

This man told Simon of the sad plight of Aeneas, a neighbor and brother in the Lord Messiah.

"He's a paralytic," their host explained. "For eight years he has kept to his bed. He's of little service to those of his household or to himself, and he is greatly discouraged. Aeneas seems no longer even to hope. But if the first of the apostles were to go to him and lay his hands on him, and lift his voice to our Lord Messiah in behalf of him—" He broke off, his expression intent. "Simon, our brother so greatly needs your help! Tomorrow, after you've rested from your travels, won't you take him greetings in our beloved Lord, and pray for him?"

Simon promised that he would go. After they had eaten the simple evening meal and sought their couches, he lay long awake. It was about this time of year—and years ago—he recalled, when they had journeyed with Jesus through Samaria. Now it was all coming back so clearly; Jesus seemed nearer, more warmly present and alive and wondrously strong in the strength of the Father as Simon thought back on those days. Many were the nights when the fisherman and his companions had slept with the Master, huddled together in their robes beside the little sea or high on the slopes of Mount Hermon or in the courtyard of some Galilean farmer's modest home. And tonight Jesus lay once more beside him; he had no doubt of it, he knew it, he felt the Master's presence.

"O Master"—he said it as he had said it a thousand other times—"abide always close to me, guide my steps, show me the way, hold my faltering footsteps upon it. If it be Thy will, O my Master, accomplish through me great things for my brothers."

In the blackness of the night Simon saw clearly the shining face of the Nazarene as he had sat that day on the curbing of old Jacob's well and talked to them of the harvest ripe for the reaping. The Master's eyes were eager and warmly approving. A moment later Simon fell away into dreamless slumber.

He awaked early, refreshed. He washed himself in water fresh from the well, and combed his beard and earlocks. Then from his pack he took a fresh loincloth and girded himself, a clean cotton tunic, which he put on; over this inner garment he drew a striped cotton kuftan, and then his simlah, or cloak, unbelted and with wide sleeves, a garment similar to the one worn by Jesus on the day of his trial and won with a throw of the dice by a Roman soldier at the foot of the cross.

When they had eaten a light breakfast Simon went with his host and his two companions to the house of the paralytic.

Aeneas was lying on his mat close to an inner wall of his chamber. The curtains were drawn, and as the four entered they could hardly make out the form of the cripple.

"I've brought a man mighty in the works of the Lord Messiah, Aeneas," Simon's host said; "it's Simon of Galilee."

"The first of the apostles!" The man's voice was weak, thin. "Brother, if I could I'd arise to welcome you to my humble house. But for eight years I've lain here, paying for the sins of my youth. Yet were our Lord Messiah here to forgive and heal—" He had raised his head, but now he fell back inert on the bedding.

"Aeneas, my brother"—the fisherman leaned low to take the hand of the paralyzed man—"don't say that our Lord is not here. He is always present and close at hand to those who truly call on him."

"But my sinning is a curtain that separates me from our Lord Messiah." The man twisted on the mat, and in the gloom they could see his grotesque jerking.

"There's no need of any such partitioning, Aeneas. Draw aside the curtain and let into your soul the love and pardoning and strength of our God of Israel." He motioned to Joseph Barnabas. "Draw back the curtains that keep from this chamber the healing light of the sun."

A moment later the room was flooded with light.

"See how quickly the sun brightens the chamber and warms it,

Aeneas," said Simon, looking down on the man, whose drawn and contorted limbs he could now see clearly. "Just as quickly will the God of Israel, through His beloved Son our Lord, forgive your sins and heal your infirmities—if you call on Him out of a contrite heart."

The man on the mat made no reply, but he closed his eyes. "O God, have mercy on me, have mercy, have mercy." His voice was hardly more than a murmur. "In the name of Thy Son our Lord Messiah who died for us, have mercy, O God."

Simon stood above Aeneas, and then without another word he went to the window, stood a moment looking out eastward toward the Judaean hills. "Thy will be done, O my Master. Thy will be done through Thy sinful, faltering, but greatly loving servant and brother, O my blessed Lord Jesus." Silent now and unmoving, he gazed at the towering, rounded hills. Then he strode back to the man on the mat. Barnabas, seeing the look on his face, inquired:

"Rab Simon, would you like for us to leave you alone with him?"

"No, Joseph. I want you and Luke to witness the might of God." He faced the paralytic.

"Aeneas, by faith you are made whole." He reached down, caught the man's thin hand. "In the name of Jesus Christ, arise!" He lifted gently; and slowly, with spasmodic thrusts of his emaciated limbs, the man pulled himself to his feet and, swaying, clutched the hand of the first of the apostles.

"Hold fast, Aeneas; relax not in your faith, brother." Simon withdrew the hand that had been steadying the paralytic. "Now bend down and fold your bed; until you seek your rest tonight you'll have no further need of it."

Stiffly Aeneas bent over and worked with awkward hands. But soon he had folded the bedding into a compact square, and holding it in his arms, he stood erect once more.

"Take it and place it on the stack in the corner there," Simon commanded. "Walk, Aeneas. In the name of Jesus, walk! Walk!"

Already Aeneas, a new light in his eyes, a new vibrancy evident in the whole of his withered frame, was shuffling toward the corner of the chamber where the other bedding had been stacked.

Simon closed his eyes. "Hold him fast in his faith, O God; sustain him, strengthen him. O my Master, do strengthen the faith of Thy stumbling, erring servant, who this day has been so greatly honored as an instrument in Thy hand."

Before the sun had dropped low toward the Great Sea, Aeneas was seen by his amazed neighbors walking in the market place of Lydda and talking in a loud and joyous voice of what that morning had befallen him, and quickly the story spread abroad throughout the region of Sharon.

When the tidings reached Joppa, where there was already a growing congregation of the Messiah, the brethren sent two men to Lydda to bring the fisherman, for a sister in the fellowship, by the name of Dorcas, a woman who had spent her years in doing deeds of charity, had died and her disconsolate friends longed for the comforting presence among them of Simon the Rock.

He consented to go with them, and early on the morrow, with Luke and Barnabas on either side, he started for Joppa. Arrived in the port city, they went at once to the home of Dorcas. There they found a great assembly of friends, weeping and bemoaning the loss of the good woman, speaking of the almsdeeds she had done, reciting the many cheering words she had spoken to the discouraged and torn in heart.

"Where have you laid her?" Simon asked.

"In the upper room, Rab Simon," one answered. "Already she's been washed and laid out."

"Take us to her."

The upper chamber was filled with women, many of them widows, weeping as they looked down on the still, white face, others through their tears examining garments Dorcas had been making when she was stricken.

"See, Rab Simon"—a graying woman, her gaunt cheeks streaked with tears, held up one of them—"here is the tunic she was making for the crippled orphan boy who lives with his blind uncle in a hovel down at the wharf." She picked up a larger garment of cotton, with alternating stripes of red, yellow, green,

white, and blue. "And this kuftan was for the old uncle; she'd
nearly finished it." Carefully folding the piece, she returned it
to the stack of garments, pointed: "All these she was making
for others, and countless garments she has already made and
given to the cold and naked. Dorcas was always working without
stint for others, Rab Simon, and now we will see her no more!"
She slumped down on a stool, began to sway gently from side to
side, and the tears ran freely from her red and welling eyes.

"Offer not, sister, to limit the power of God and of Jesus
Christ His Son, our Lord Messiah."

"What do Rab Simon's strange words mean?" a woman whispered to another. "Aren't they a rebuke of Miriam? Nevertheless,
when we have laid Dorcas away in the tomb isn't it true that
we'll see her no more, on this earth?"

"Maybe Simon didn't understand that Miriam was speaking
of this world alone."

"No, I don't think so. He was speaking of something else." A
look of incredulity lightened by a thin hope began to overspread
her troubled countenance. "Could it be that Simon is of a mind
that the God of Israel might restore Dorcas to life—even now,
on this earth?"

Others too were whispering, and soon the whisperings had
grown to a murmuring as the eyes of the women centered on
Simon standing at the bier looking into the white face of the
dead woman. But he seemed not to notice it.

Then he turned about and raised his hand. Instantly all voices
were stilled.

"I must have quiet and solitude in which to seek the will of
God for our sister," he said, his strong and solemn but kindly
eyes embracing the group. "Will you depart now and remain
outside the chamber until I have need of you?" The question
was a polite command. "My brothers"—he nodded to Barnabas
and the physician—"stand inside the door and when they are
gone out see that no one enters."

In a moment the chamber was empty save for the three and the
still form on the bier.

"As you guard the door, brothers, pray with me that I may be shown the will of God our Father and His Son our beloved Master and brother."

Simon knelt beside the bier, his face buried in the coverlet, his great beard crushed out, his gnarled hands clasped together in front of his bowed head.

"O God of Israel, O beloved Jesus our Lord Messiah," the younger man at the door prayed, though the prayer was in his heart and not on his lips, "show Rab Simon the way, give him light, accomplish in him Thy will, grant him power, O God, O Jesus." He closed his eyes. Nor did he open them until he heard a movement at the bier. Beside him Luke the physician was staring entranced at the first of the apostles.

Simon had risen to his feet. The light from the window was full on his face, and as he half turned they saw the expression on the fisherman's countenance. It was ecstatic; glory sat upon it, and power—the strength of a thousand chariot horses—yet softened with a true humility.

Now he turned again and his back was to them. Simon was looking into the face of Dorcas, eyes closed, rigid, and chalk-white in the broad band of light from the window. The two men saw him reach down and take one of her hands, folded across the other, and gently lift it. The arm came up, stiff and unyielding at the elbow and the wrist, as unbending as a limb torn from a dead olive tree.

Then Simon spoke. His voice was calm and natural, but commanding.

"Dorcas, arise."

The physician Luke, gripping the door handle, tense, saw the woman's wrist give, and the arm sagged at the elbow. . . . Then he thought he saw the eyelids flutter. . . . Yes, of a certainty. . . . And the face was relaxing, and into the dead pallor a faint color was creeping and spreading.

Dorcas opened her eyes.

With gentle awkwardness the first of the apostles grasped the limbering arm and pulled, and the woman sat up.

"Who—who are you?" She was opening and closing her eyes as though the sudden light had brought stabbings of pain.

"An unworthy poor fisherman, my sister, whom God through His beloved Son our Messiah this day has honored far beyond his just deserts." He turned toward the men at the door. "Open it, brothers."

In the same instant Simon was striding toward it, and as Joseph unfastened it and swung it back on its hinges, Simon stood in the doorway.

"Now you may enter the chamber," he said, his voice calm. "But be orderly, and disturb her not unduly, for she is yet weary; she has come back from a far journey. Go in now and minister to her needs."

The three men stepped through the doorway into the passage outside the bedchamber.

But the women paid no heed to his admonition, for through the doorway the nearer ones saw Dorcas sitting upright on the bier and smiling.

"She's alive!" one screamed. And then another, and another. "Dorcas has returned to life! O God in Israel! Dorcas is alive!"

Now they were screaming and laughing and weeping as they pushed through the doorway and surged about the beloved sister.

Simon shook his head, but a great joyous smile lighted his bearded plain face. He grasped Joseph Barnabas by the arm.

"Come, brothers," he said to the two, "let's be gone, and quickly!"

Luke the physician turned his head to look through the doorway. "She was dead; I know it; I saw her cold and rigid." His expression revealed amazement, wonder, almost incredulity. "Now I can believe Saul's story, for now I have seen." He shook his head slowly, solemnly. "Mighty indeed are the acts even of the Galilean's apostles."

But the other two had not heard his murmured words, for already they were walking away along the passage.

News of the restoration to life of the good woman Dorcas spread quickly through the ancient port city. Hardly had Simon and his two companions returned to their host's house before people began to push into the courtyard.

They called for the fisherman. Some implored the master of the house to fetch him, others demanded loudly that he be brought out. Some were afflicted—diseased, lame, blind. They besought aid of the big Galilean who by some strange power had been able to breathe life back into the stiffened cold body of a dead woman. Others were only curious; they wanted to lay eyes on this worker of wonders. Many among them had witnessed the amazing deeds of one Simon the Magician, who months ago in Samaria after witnessing the healing works of Simon Peter and John ben Zebedee had sought to purchase from them authority to bestow the Holy Spirit, only to be soundly rebuked by them. But never had these people seen the Magician raise to life one who had died.

Many were Jews, but among them were Gentiles of various races and lands, for Joppa had drawn to itself people from the wide fringes of the Great Sea.

When Simon came out to them, several cast themselves at his feet to worship him. These he rebuked sternly.

"Get to your feet, brother," he commanded an emaciated tall fellow with a club foot. "I am only a frail, erring man like yourself. I have no power to heal or restore to life. I am only the instrument in the hands of God through which He accomplishes what He wills. God restored Dorcas." He reached down, caught the man's arm, helped him rise. But the fellow continued to cower before the fisherman.

"Then, sir, if you'd ask the God of Israel to straighten my foot—" He paused, looked Simon full in the face, his countenance mirroring hope and apprehension. "I'm but a poor man, sir, but I have a brother who with one other owns a fishing boat, and often they bring in heavy hauls. My brother would pay you well—"

He stopped speaking, for Simon was shaking his head sadly. "You don't understand. I have no powers to sell, nor even to give. I'm a poor man too, unlearned and sinful. If you would be restored, you must have faith in God and His power and love, and in His Messiah, our Lord Jesus Christ; not in me."

There were many who did profess their faith and join the fellowship of Jesus. But these were already of the synagogue at Joppa. And before night had fallen Simon had been sorely tried in body and spirit.

"Let us be gone from this house," he said to Barnabas and Luke, when they were washing for the evening meal after the throng had departed. "If we don't, an even greater multitude will seek us here tomorrow, for it is known where we're lodging. The people persist in not understanding our mission, and I'm not altogether certain myself what course I should take. I feel that it is God's will that we depart and go to an abode where I can have peace and solitude to pray for guidance."

"Perhaps to Jerusalem, Rab Simon?"

The fisherman did not immediately answer Joseph Barnabas. "No," he said, after he had reflected, "not yet to Jerusalem, for there's still work for me to do in this region. I feel that I am being led of God to do some good work. There's a man here in Joppa, one of our fellowship, in whose house we could find calm and a chance to think and pray and seek God's will for us. He lives near the city's wall, close beside the sea. We would be welcome there, too."

Early the next morning, before the sun had lighted the flat roofs of the old city, they slipped away to the house of Simon the tanner. This brother, honored to have in his humble abode the first of the apostles and his companions, lodged them in the upper chamber, reached by an outside stairway that led to the flat roof. From the roof one might see the sails of fishing boats far out on the Great Sea and sometimes even the flash of sunlight on the rising and falling oars swiftly propelling a Roman galley over the blue waters.

When Luke had talked a short while with his host, he excused himself. "I'm going down to the wharf to inquire if any vessels are leaving soon for Seleucia or the cities of the west," he explained.

But Simon remained on the rooftop. Up here, looking out toward the Great Sea and catching now and again the stir of a small breeze from off the waters of the harbor below, the apostle was reminded of his own house at Capernaum that faced eastward toward the little inland Sea of Galilee. He was reminded likewise of other days and other faces, but most of all he thought of his departed Master.

Today, the second day after his arrival at the tanner's, the fisherman was troubled. It was now toward the sixth hour and Simon was resting on the housetop while his host's wife completed preparations for the simple midday meal. Already the tantalizing odors from the oven were drifting up to him and whetting the edge of his hunger. He was still wearied, too, from the journeying southward and the exertions at Lydda and lately at the home of Dorcas. But he was more spent in spirit than in the flesh.

For Simon was unable to resolve the problem that had been brought to focus with the return of Saul of Tarsus, now further complicated by Saul's acceptance on his own authority of Luke into the fellowship of Jesus. Luke, too, had been demonstrating a devotion to the Messiah and the principles he lived and taught. Yet the physician was not of the house and bond of Israel; he was a Greek, a Gentile. Henceforth then what was to be the nature of the brotherhood of Jesus? Who would be admitted, and by what route should they enter?

Saul, fresh from his sojourn in the desert and testifying to his experience with the Master in that solitary place, had stood adamant for opening the doors of the house of the Messiah to all who in faith would enter, whether Jew or Gentile, circumcised or uncircumcised. And Saul was a Jew, a Pharisee of the Pharisees, a former student of the great Rabban Gamaliel, and proud of his Hebrew ancestry. Who had a greater right to speak for the Messiah than this man of Tarsus who through a soul-shaking personal encounter with Jesus had turned his back on the way he had been traveling and steadfastly had set his feet in the path of the Messiah's pointing?

But on the other hand who had more right to speak for the Messiah than his own brother? And James opposed Saul. Only through Israel, James held, was salvation to be attained. If a man would become a member of the brotherhood of the Messiah, let him first be circumcised and place himself under the law. Let him enter through the gate of the Chosen, for indeed is there any other gate admitting to salvation? That was the reasoning and that was the command of solemn-visaged, ascetic James, leader in Jerusalem of those who had taken upon their lips and hearts the name of the Galilean.

Simon the fisherman of Capernaum sat on the rooftop of Simon the tanner of Joppa and sought to find a proper course through the maze of his thoughts and doubts.

. . . O Master, show me the way. Place my unsure and stumbling feet on the path you would have me walk, for I have come to a place where the road divides and two ways lead off. What is that way that I should take? Come to me, as in the days in Galilee when I was heavy of heart, and point out to me so clearly that I will surely understand what road you would have me and my brothers of the fellowship take. Show us, O Master, lead us . . .

Sitting on a low stool, Simon leaned his head against the parapet, and the breeze lifting from the harbor fanned him. He will surely show me the course to take, the thought came to him, and with it assurance, for hasn't he always come to me in my moment of dire need? Simon closed his heavy eyes and let the breeze play through his beard. Yes, the Master will show me the right road. The Master always came to us when we were in distress. That frightening time on the sea when the storm arose and the waters threatened to engulf the fishing boat of the Zebedees, didn't he calm the storm and allay our fears?

Simon slumped against the parapet.

. . . I'm too tired to think clearly, hungry and tired and confused. But I love him and he loves me, and he will help. He'll show the way ahead for me and my brothers. The Master will point out the path—

He was looking upward and outward over the rooftops that went downward on a gentle slope to Joppa's harbor. At first it seemed only a small slit in the blue of the sky. Through the slit he saw emerging something of purest white, like a napkin freshly washed and hung up to dry and billowing outward with the wind. Swiftly it dropped earthward, and the slit behind it was gone and the heavens knit again into a single deep blue, and it grew and increased rapidly, and now it was become a great white sheet knotted at the four corners to enclose a heavy burden.

It swelled and bulged outward and quickly came to pause on a level with his eyes above the roof of Simon the tanner, and it twisted and writhed like a living thing, and looking into it he saw with amazement and a mounting repugnance that it held all manner of fourfooted beasts of the yard and the field and fold, and wild beasts, and slithering creeping things, and fowls of the air.

He would have turned his eyes away and fled down from the roof, but he was held there, his eyes drawn irresistibly to the great sheet and its horrible burden. And then the voice spoke:

"Rise, Peter; kill and eat."

But his whole being rebelled.

"Not so, Lord; for I have never eaten of anything that is common or unclean!"

"What God has cleansed, that call not thou unclean."

And once more the voice commanded him sternly to rise up and slay and eat of those things within the writhing great sheet. But the horror of the true son of Abraham possessed him, and he cried out against the abomination of eating flesh common and unclean.

"Rise, Peter; kill and eat." The voice was not to be quieted.

"Nay, Lord, I, an Israelite, a son of the covenant, have never eaten anything that is common or unclean."

"What God has cleansed, Peter, that call not thou unclean!"

Now there was a great convulsion of the huge sheet, and it twisted and contorted as the creatures imprisoned within it fought for release and squirmed and fell back one upon the other; and the sheet began to lift upward, as if some unseen giant hand had grasped the four corners and were bearing it away. Faster now and faster it moved upward and dwindled in size and retreated until it was but a small white patch high in the blue of the heavens, and then the slit opened in the sky and received it, and the slit closed again, and—

Simon sat bolt upright.

He was looking out across the Joppa roofs that dropped away to the harbor and the sky was serene and blue. A stray breeze stirred the unoiled hairs of his beard.

. . . The great sheet with its strange burden, was it a dream? Did it come to me out of weariness and hunger, or was it a vision sent from God? Was it an answer to my prayers, a light unto my feet making clear the way? Hadn't I besought of the Master a lamp in the night of my searching? . . .

He sat quiet and thinking, his eyes on the cloudless untroubled sky, his thoughts on the strange sheet with its great weight of live things, things forbidden of the good Jew to eat. "What God has cleansed, that call not thou unclean!" God speaking to him, the unlettered fisherman of Galilee. The God of Israel, yes; but not the God of Israel *alone*. The God of Israel and all the world and the stars illimitable.

. . . A vision, an answer to my prayers. "God cannot be limited, Simon, nor God's Son. Didn't Jesus tell you that *all* men are sons of God and didn't he call *all* men his brothers?" Can I call any man of faith unclean? Now, Saul, I begin to comprehend your words. And I understand you better too, O my beloved Master. "Go you into all the world and tell the good news to every creature." Yes, O Lord, but show me how. And cleave my tongue from my mouth if ever hereafter my words attempt to limit you, to possess you for Israel alone, even for my beloved Israel. . . .

He leaned back again and rested his head against the parapet, and he thought about the message of the vision. Hadn't God told him plainly that it was not for him to call unclean those not of Israel? Hadn't God told him that he had no right to limit to the sons of Israel those who in faith would give their hearts and hands to the Messiah and ask for admittance into the enlarging circle of the brotherhood? Hadn't the Master instructed him once again to go forth into the world, even the pagan world of the Gentiles, and proclaim the good news?

. . . But where, O God? Where would you have me go? . . .

He closed his eyes to shut out the rooftops and the blue sky and the soft white clouds, and listened for the voice. He closed his ears to the sounds about him, the distant boisterous voices and the singing of the men loading and unloading the ships at the wharves, the little voices of the tanner's wife and her pots and vessels as she bustled about in the courtyard below. He waited for the still small voice.

And up from the tiles of the roof it came to him, down from the silent still sky, out from the cool stone on which his head rested. He knew not from where it came, but he knew that he heard a voice, and that the words were clear and easy of understanding:

"Behold, three men seek you. Arise, therefore, and get you down, and go with them, doubting nothing; for I have sent them."

Simon got quickly to his feet. In that instant he saw Joseph Barnabas nearing the top of the stone stairway.

"Come, Rab Simon, the meal is ready, and the tanner is home and washed and awaits us."

"So do the three men, Joseph."

"The three men?"

"Yes, the three who have come for me."

"But we've seen no men seeking you, Rab Simon."

"They are down at the gate inquiring for me, Joseph."

Barnabas stood back, his forehead crinkled in perplexity, to allow the fisherman to descend. Then silent, he followed.

Around the corner of the house a man in the uniform of a Roman soldier and two others, by their dress evidently household servants, were talking with the tanner. Simon went directly to them.

"I'm the one you're seeking," he said. "Why have you come for me?"

"You are Simon of Capernaum?" the soldier inquired.

"Yes."

"We come from Caesarea. Cornelius the centurion, now stationed there, a just and upright man who venerates the God of the Jews and bears a good reputation throughout Israel, was instructed by your God through an angel to send for you and have you brought to his house that he might have words of counsel from you."

"I'll return with you," Simon answered. "But you are worn from the journey and you must rest with us until tomorrow, when we can start for Caesarea by the sun's rising."

"You remember Centurion Cornelius, don't you?" Barnabas asked Simon. "He's the one who rescued me from the stoning pit the day they killed Stephen."

"Yes, of course I remember him well. A good man, the centurion, one whom I regarded highly when he was stationed at Capernaum. And already I suspect why God has commanded me to return with these men. Even now, so soon, He begins to make clear the way we should take."

## THE CROWN TREE 48

Simon the tanner bathed thoroughly, rubbed his body with sweet oils and anointed his head and beard to cleanse himself of the stench of the hides, and before the sun had risen set out with Simon and Barnabas and the messengers from the Centurion Cornelius.

With them went Luke, for the physician had been unable to arrange for an early sailing from Joppa, since no vessels were leaving there soon for Seleucia or any of the western ports. So Simon had urged him to continue with them to Caesarea, where he thought Luke might find a vessel leaving earlier.

The day after their departure from the tanner's they reached Caesarea straight to the north, and the messengers led them at once to the house of the centurion.

Cornelius had called together a group of relatives and friends to await the arrival of his fisherman friend from Capernaum. But while they waited in the centurion's house, he himself went down to the gate to be the first to welcome this worker of wonders of whom already marvelous reports had reached Caesarea and the region roundabout. He was standing there when the visitors from Joppa rounded a sharp turn in the narrow street and approached the gateway. Immediately Cornelius ran toward Simon and fell on his face before the apostle.

"No! No! Centurion! Stand up!" Reaching down, he caught the Roman's arm, pulled. "I'm not one to be worshiped, Cornelius."

The soldier arose, brushed his tunic. "But, sir, the paralytic healed at Lydda, the dead woman at Joppa raised to life—"

"It was the work of God through our faith in His Son, Cornelius. It was not through any virtue in us." He turned to present his companions. "You must remember Joseph, Centurion, the one you rescued that day from the stoning pit at Jerusalem. And this one is Luke the physician from Antioch."

"Joseph Barnabas, I'm glad to see you again. Of course I remember that day. And, sir"—he faced Luke—"I'm happy to know you. I welcome all of you to my humble house."

Inside they found the kinsmen and friends of Cornelius. The group, he explained, was awaiting Simon's arrival. He presented his wife Pyrrha and she added her welcome. The eyes of the Caesareans were on him, Simon quickly realized, and he was afraid that some might offer, as Cornelius had done, to bow down and worship him. But in a few moments a servant entered, nodded to the centurion.

"The meal is ready," Cornelius announced. "Simon, you and your companions must be wearied and hungry. I would be happy if we might all sit down together, but if your ceremonial customs won't allow you Jews to break bread with us who are not of Israel, there's a table provided in another chamber where you and your friends—"

The fisherman shook his head and waved a hand in protest, and his round face broke into a smile that crinkled the small patches of beardless ruddy skin beneath his black eyes.

"We have no wish for a separate table, Centurion. It is indeed a law of the Jews not to break bread with one considered ritually unclean." He nodded toward Luke. "But the physician is not a Jew, and more than that, God has shown me in a manner no man could fail to comprehend that I should not call any man unclean. Now, my friend, let us eat and drink, for we are nigh on to being famished from our day's journeying."

Joseph Barnabas was plainly astonished and so were the tanner and even some of the friends of the centurion who were acquainted with the customs of the Jews. But none spoke. Nor did Barnabas question either the judgment or the piety of this bold and lovable first friend of the Lord Messiah. Without hesitating they went into the dining hall.

For the most part they ate in silence, and when they were filled, Simon addressed his host:

"Centurion, I came to you without questioning as soon as I was sent for, and I have not questioned you since our arrival. But now tell me, why did you send your men to fetch me here?"

"I do not doubt that you wonder, Simon. It's a strange story, one I myself don't understand. But it was about this hour, several days ago. I hadn't eaten; I was troubled. I tried to pray to your god; I know little about praying, Simon, and I never pray to our Roman gods. But I prayed to the god of the Jews as best I could."

Simon's black eyes were fixed on the soldier, as were those of the others in the chamber. He nodded to Cornelius to continue.

"I was troubled and perplexed, Simon. And then I'm sure I distinctly saw a man there before me. His clothes seemed luminous and his whole frame was resplendent. I was looking at him, amazed, when he spoke.

" 'Cornelius,' he said, 'your prayer is heard, and the good deeds you have done are remembered by God. Send therefore to Joppa and ask that Simon come to you. He is even now lodging at the house of one Simon a tanner who lives near the harbor. When he comes, he will instruct you.' "

"Then you sent the three men to fetch me?"

"Immediately I sent them, and you have done well in coming, for we are all gathered here before your god to hear all that he commands you to say to us."

The fisherman arose, rested a gnarled fist on the table; his black eyes swept the assembled company.

"May God be praised," he said, "for truly I perceive that He is no respecter of persons, but in every nation he that fears Him and strives to live righteously is acceptable unto Him." He leaned forward and his dark eyes seemed to catch fire and flame up, and his words took on a new intensity:

"The word which God sent unto the children of Israel through the preaching of peace by Jesus Christ, who is Lord of all, that word, I tell you, is also known unto you. It is the word that was published throughout all Judaea, after it had been preached by Jesus following the proclamation of John the Baptist."

He stabbed a forefinger before his face, raised his voice:

"That story, I say again, you know: how God anointed Jesus of Nazareth with the Holy Spirit and with power, how Jesus went about doing good, and healing all those oppressed of the devil, for God was with him." But now the fisherman lowered his voice, and his eyes once more circled the chamber. "This we know, this we can testify to, for we were witnesses to those things he did both throughout Israel and at Jerusalem, where they crucified him"—he paused, and fixed his searching bright eyes on the solemn countenance of the Centurion Cornelius—"whom God raised up the third day afterward, and showed him openly; not to all the people, but to witnesses chosen before of God, even including us, who ate and drank with him after he had risen from the dead." He stopped, his eyes still on the centurion's face. "You know, Centurion, that he arose. You remember how I met you as I came running from the tomb to bear the tremendous tidings to the others at the house of Mary of Cyprus. You know how in the days that followed he appeared unto many, even as far away as Galilee."

"It is true, Simon. I talked with those who guarded the tomb. I can testify that although no man moved the stone sealing the mouth, it had been rolled back and the tomb was empty. I know; I was in charge of the guard detail. And I heard how later he appeared to many of those who had known him."

"You have heard," declared Simon to the others. "And I say to you that he commanded us to preach these good tidings unto the people and to testify that it is Jesus Christ who was ordained of God to be the judge of the quick and the dead. He's the one of whom the prophets have foretold that through his name whosoever believes in him shall receive forgiveness of sins."

The first of the apostles waved his hand in all-embracing gesture.

" 'Go you into all nations and preach the good news to every creature,' he told us. But I did not comprehend the meaning of these words. I had sought to limit the good news to our people of Israel, those whom we call the Chosen People. As Saul of Tarsus, our brother in the Messiah, had tried to show me, I was seeking to bring men to the Master through admission to the household of Israel. Nor was I the only one." He was calm a moment, silent. And then he began again.

"But we erred, we failed, we fell far short of obeying the commands of our Lord Messiah. As Saul had declared and as we were warned in a vision while we tarried this week at the house of our brother Simon the tanner"—he nodded toward Simon—"we were wrong."

Then in dramatic fashion the fisherman told the story of the vision of the great sheet let down from heaven. He related his attempt to reason with God, to argue with Him, and told of the heavenly rebuke. He pointed out how the centurion's vision had supplemented his own to make clear the purpose of God.

"He speaks the truth! His is the true God!" shouted one of those of Cornelius' household. "His God shall be mine!"

"You're right, Lucius," another spoke out. "Let Israel's God be ours. Let us have no more to do with Jupiter and Venus and Mercury and all the other gods of the Romans, nor with Zeus and those of the Greeks."

"I am a Greek, and I agree." Luke added his testimony. "The Greek gods and the Roman gods are nothing. There is but one true God and He is the Father of our Lord Messiah, Jesus Christ, born of Israel but Saviour of all nations."

"The Lord God of Israel He is one!" exclaimed a Jew. "The physician has spoken aright. He knows the cure of sin as well as the cure of the ills of the body. Our God is not only the God of Israel but of all the world and the sun and stars, the God of every nation and tongue!"

And now the whole assembly was shouting and crying and talking, so that few could distinguish what any was saying, and some sat silent, swaying to and fro in the ecstasy of this incomparable moment.

"The Holy Spirit is upon us!" exclaimed one of the Jews. "God has sent His Comforter, even the Holy Spirit, to sanctify our coming together. Now we are one in the fellowship of the Lord Messiah!"

"Indeed, the Holy Spirit has now come down upon these not of the circumcision." It was Simon the tanner speaking. "The Spirit is poured out freely upon circumcised and uncircumcised alike, upon Jew and Gentile, so that they speak in tongues, magnifying the true and one God!"

"Simon of Capernaum, hear me!" Cornelius stood before the fisherman, and his voice was eager, appealing. "Cannot I too be a member of the Galilean's fellowship? He was my friend in

Galilee, and though my nation crucified him, I myself gladly acknowledge him as above all the men of earth, even the Emperor. I know he died and I know he arose. He has been calling me, Simon, and until this moment I have known no peace. But now that I take my stand with him, I am content!"

"And I likewise! I would be one of his band." It was the soldier who had come to Joppa to fetch Simon.

"I too!" shouted a servant.

Pyrrha, her eyes shining, walked over to stand beside her husband.

"And I. I want to stand with this risen Galilean," she said. "I take my place with Cornelius, Simon; I want his God to be mine."

Throughout the chamber the kinsmen and friends of the centurion were clamoring for admission into the brotherhood of Jesus. The first of the apostles held up his hand, called for silence. When the clamor had stilled, he spoke:

"Can any man forbid that these who have thus testified should receive baptism into the fellowship of our Lord Jesus, since you have witnessed that the Holy Ghost has come upon even them as He has come upon us of Israel?"

Not an Israelite offered to challenge Simon Peter the Rock, not a voice was raised in dissent. The perspiring bearded face of the fisherman was lighted with a great joy. He raised his eyes upward and closed them:

"I thank Thee, O God of all the world, and Thy Son our beloved Lord Jesus, for the vision at Joppa which has led Thy stumbling, unworthy servant to Caesarea and these our new brothers. Keep them, O God, forever in the hollow of Thy hand, and continue to show us Thy way for our feet to follow." For a moment he was silent, and then he opened his eyes.

"It is our wish, my brothers and sisters," he said, his round face joyous, "that you be baptized into the fellowship of our Lord Messiah in his blessed name."

That evening after the kinsmen and friends of Cornelius had gone and supper was finished, the centurion and his guests went up to the housetop, where Simon talked into the thickening twilight of experiences with the Master, beginning with his ministry in Galilee and continuing through the sad yet stirring moment of his ascension.

"It's a compelling story of immeasurable beauty," Luke commented. "I am all the more constrained to attempt to write it down."

"And I feel that I know Jesus better now than I knew him at Capernaum," Cornelius declared. "I am at peace, too; tonight I'll sleep untroubled." He was silent a moment. "I wish you would lead my friend Longinus to finding this joy. He is the man who crucified the Nazarene, Simon; and I'm sure he's had no peace since." He clutched the fisherman's knee in a new eagerness. "He's a man of influence, too; he would recruit others to our fellowship. My sister, for instance. Lalage already has heard Longinus and me talk of Jesus' crucifixion, and she has a slave girl, a Greek, whose beloved had become interested in the teachings of Jesus. Aspasia had talked to her about—"

"Aspasia!" The physician Luke, lying back against the parapet of the roof, sprang upright. "Centurion"—his voice was wavering between fear and exaltation—"do you know if her father was a merchant called Chionides, of the region of Thessalonica?"

"Yes, that was her father's name, I'm sure it was." For an instant Cornelius had hesitated. "Yes"—now he was certain—"I remember Lalage said Aspasia told her that her beloved was an Antiochene called Luke the physician!"

THE CROWN TREE  49

Two days after Simon with Barnabas and Luke left Tiberias for Capernaum on the journey that was to take them into Samaria and to Joppa and Caesarea, the High Priest Theophilus set out for Tiberias and an audience with King Herod Agrippa.

With him Theophilus took several of the craftiest members of
the Sanhedrin, apt pupils in diplomacy of that most cunning of
them all, old Annas. Having arrived in the capital of Galilee,
Theophilus at once sought and quickly obtained an audience
with King Agrippa, at which he and his fellow Sanhedrinists
formally presented their petition that he go to Rome and urge
Emperor Gaius to rescind his order to Proconsul Petronius concerning the placing of the Emperor's statue in the Temple.

Agrippa was anxious to please the Temple leaders, Israel's
most influential group, and thereby strengthen his hold on the
throne; he was also not averse to returning to Rome for a season
of gay living. But he did not wish to appear to have been too
easily prevailed upon.

"But haven't you heard the reports, O most noble High
Priest," the king inquired, "that the Emperor Gaius has come to
hold us Jews in contempt and has even ordered many to be
driven from Rome?"

"I have so heard, your Majesty," Theophilus answered. "But
he does not hold his good friend and fellow ruler Agrippa in contempt; on the contrary, what other man in all the Empire holds
the regard and affection of the Emperor that you command, O
Sire? It may be, it likely will be, O Agrippa, that you can by your
power over the Emperor even cause him to relent in his hatred
of us of Israel. It may be that you can not only cause him to
withdraw his order to Petronius but also lead him to relent in his
hostility toward our brothers of the Chosen Race living within
the walls of pagan Rome. As to that, O Sire"—the High Priest's
stern countenance was relaxed a bit now, Agrippa saw, and his
black eyes had brightened—"I have a plan that later I would
lay before you if you would grant me the honor of permitting
me another audience with your Majesty."

The king assured the delegation from Jerusalem that he was
in entire sympathy with their mission in coming to Tiberias; he
was inclined to make the journey to Rome, he added; he would
consider their petition carefully and on the morrow let them
have his decision.

Theophilus thanked Agrippa profusely, called him the defender and protector of Israel, and led his colleagues ceremoniously from the royal presence.

But that evening the High Priest returned alone to the king's palace and he and Agrippa closeted themselves in an inner chamber where none could eavesdrop.

"Today you suggested that you had a plan that might aid me in laying your petition before Emperor Gaius," Agrippa said, after they had talked a few minutes. "What is your plan, worthy High Priest?"

"It is a very simple one, your Majesty, but I am confident it will be effective. And if it is, it will work great good for Israel."

Quickly he outlined the scheme his father Annas had instructed him to present to the king.

"The Emperor is a young man given to whims and vagaries, to passionate affections and flaming hatreds, as I am led to understand him," Theophilus declared. "He is likewise a sadist who must derive pleasure through inflicting pain, and the present chief recipients of his torture are our people in Rome. We manifestly cannot change him, but I am convinced that we can cause him to level his wrath against some group other than our loyal brothers of the Chosen Race."

He leaned nearer the king, lowered his voice:

"There is a nefarious sect in Israel of whom you have doubtless heard, O Agrippa. It is a brotherhood, originally of Galileans almost entirely, that worships a man, even a dead man, a Nazarene whom the Romans crucified as a revolutionary who incited the people against the true worship of our God of Israel, traduced our laws and profaned our Temple and its worship, and even sought to overthrow the rule of Rome.

"This sect is growing rapidly and spreading throughout Palestine and to other parts of the Empire, even to Rome itself. Already it is challenging our true worship, our laws and traditions. Unless it is speedily stamped out, O Sire, it will grow into a viper in the nest of Israel that ultimately will destroy us."

"I have heard something of this sect," Agrippa revealed. "In fact, I have a Roman aide, a tribune, who was in charge of the detail that crucified the Nazarene of whom you speak. Though he never mentions it, I know that the Tribune Longinus was the officer who under Pontius Pilate executed the man." He smiled, as the plan of Theophilus began to reveal itself in his mind. "And you would like to transfer Caligula's current hatred of the Jews to a determination to stamp out this sect which in actuality, though it is made up in the main of Jews, I presume, is an enemy of our true religion?"

"You perceive the plan exactly, Sire," Theophilus said, his black eyes alight.

"But how can it be accomplished?"

"When you go to Rome to present our petition concerning the Emperor's statue, Sire, declare in your adroit manner that while Israel cannot bend the knee in worship to any man, it is loyal to the Emperor and exalts him as the ruler of the world. But add in your cleverest way that there is a certain band of people who are not only revolutionaries against Rome and seek the Emperor's overthrow but also worship as God a dead man, although they refuse to worship or honor the Emperor. In that way you may turn the ire of the Emperor upon them and remove it from the sore backs of our own loyal brothers."

"But what if Caligula should ask me why I haven't proceeded myself against this sect?"

"I had foreseen such a question, Sire. Therefore, before you go to Rome you must yourself begin the task of destroying these idolators, starting with certain leaders in Jerusalem."

"But I am not king in Judaea," Agrippa answered quickly. "My authority does not extend to Jerusalem."

"That is true, O Sire. Pilate's successor has the rule over us. But you are king in Galilee, and you have authority over Galileans even though they may be at Jerusalem. And the leaders of this iniquitous sect are Galileans, as was their chief." The High Priest's black eyes sparkled, and he leaned nearer. "You have ample precedent for proceeding against Galileans at Jerusalem, Sire. Do you recall that when this Nazarene seditionist was brought before Pilate in Jerusalem, he sent him to the Tetrarch Herod Antipas for trial, saying that Antipas as ruler of Galilee had authority over the man?"

"I believe I have heard the story, though I recall little of the crucified Nazarene's history. But tell me, O High Priest, were I to proceed against these Galilean leaders of this seditious and idolatrous sect, what would be the reaction of our orthodox, loyal people of Israel? Would they be offended, or would they approve?"

"Nothing else you could do, O Agrippa, would so elevate you in the esteem and affection of good Israelites everywhere."

Theophilus named Simon of Capernaum and the Zebedee brothers as the most obnoxious Galilean adherents of the idolatrous sect and declared their beheading by Agrippa's command would cause rejoicing in Israel and elevate the king in the affections of all Jewry. And when the High Priest a few minutes later left the king's palace, he and Agrippa were agreed on the course the king should take.

The next morning the Tribune Longinus was summoned to Agrippa's private chambers. Quickly the king told him of the visit the day before of the High Priest and certain members of the Jerusalem Sanhedrin and of his later conversation privately with Theophilus.

"So I have determined to go to Rome to petition Caligula to rescind his order," Agrippa declared. "And I want you to accompany me. But first I am going to Jerusalem to worship at the Temple, and to initiate a determined effort to stamp out an idolatrous band whose members insult Israel's God by worshiping a dead Galilean fanatic crucified some time ago at Jerusalem—" He paused, eyed the tribune. "I believe you were in charge of the detail that crucified him, Longinus?"

"Yes." Agrippa waited for him to recall the incident, but Longinus said nothing more. Then the king resumed his recital.

"The High Priest is a very clever fellow, Longinus, an apt son of Annas. He advanced the opinion that we might be able to divert Caligula's wrath from the Jews, whom he is just now

persecuting severely in Rome, by turning it upon these deluded
followers of that Nazarene. There are several leaders, fanatical
Galileans, whom he particularly wants destroyed. In apprehend-
ing them and having them executed, Longinus, I may require
your help. So I wish you to go there with me too."

"Sire, who are these people the High Priest wants killed?"

"They are persons of no consequence in Israel, Tribune. You
would not have heard of them. The principal one is a bold, brash
fellow called Simon, and there are two brothers, sons of a man
named Zebedee. The three are from the region of Capernaum;
they're fishermen."

Longinus nodded, but made no comment. Simon of Capernaum, friend of Cornelius, he remembered, however, and the
Zebedees, members of the original band of the Nazarene. . . . And
now Agrippa is asking me to ferret out these men, do them to
their deaths as I did their leader.

All that afternoon Longinus thought of the plot of the wily
High Priest and the opportunist King Agrippa and of his own
possible involvement. Once again he was being led into the shedding of innocent blood in pursuance of an evil design. This time
would he permit himself to be so led?

That night, after months free of dreams of the crucified Jew,
the face of the tall young man of Nazareth, harassed and sweating and blood-smeared, looked once again deep into his eyes,
and the questioning, pained voice spoke:

"Will you once again drive your spearhead into my heart?"

## THE CROWN TREE 50

Four days after Luke learned from Cornelius that Aspasia was
Lalage's slave, a vessel sailing for Cyprus and then Rome put
in at the port of Caesarea. Luke purchased passage and went
aboard. In his pouch he carried a letter to Lalage from her

brother in which Cornelius introduced the physician and urged her to grant Aspasia her freedom at once or permit Luke to purchase it.

"But don't reveal to Lalage or anyone else not of the fellowship that you are a member," he had warned Luke, "and under no circumstances let it be known that I have become a follower of the Lord Jesus. That would only infuriate Lalage, and word might even get to the Emperor."

The next day before the sun had risen Simon and Joseph Barnabas took the road that went southward along the Maritime Plain over the undulating surface of sandy low hillocks. The second day they crossed Sharon and the Shefelah and began to ascend into the hill country of Judaea. On the following afternoon the two entered Jerusalem.

"It's been a good journey, Joseph," Simon declared as they started toward Mary's house on Zion Hill. "Certainly it was a great day when the Centurion Cornelius entered our Lord's fellowship. And at Joppa I got a clearer understanding from the Master concerning what your comrade Saul was trying to teach; I begin to see that the fellowship of the Lord Jesus is not properly limited to those of Israel but should embrace every race and tongue."

"It was good, Rab Simon; and none would be happier about it than Saul. I wonder where he is now, and what he's doing."

But at Mary's house they were given distressing news. The persecution of the days of Saul of Tarsus had been renewed, this time by King Herod Agrippa with the connivance of the High Priest and the Temple hierarchy. Reports were going about Jerusalem that Agrippa, eager to show his zeal for the ancient faith of Israel and to court the favor of the priests, had promised the High Priest he would stamp out the fellowship.

While they were still discussing this frightening development, one of the housemaids, whom Mary had sent on an errand to a bazaar in the vicinity of Gate Gennath north of Mount Zion, came in weeping and almost exhausted from running.

"It's terrible news I bring, Mistress!" she exclaimed. "They've carried James bar Zebedee off to prison! They're saying he'll be killed!"

"What! Where have you heard this, Rhoda? Who gave you such tidings?"

"It was common talk at the bazaar, Mistress. They said that King Agrippa was determined to put an end to what he and the Temple priests call the heresy."

Mary's countenance had paled; her lips were drawn. She turned to her cousin. "I know you're tired, Joseph. But go nevertheless with Amaziah and see what you can discover concerning these terrible tidings. And guard well your tongue, my boy. No, Rab Simon"—she held up a protesting hand as the fisherman was arising as if to join the two—"you must remain here. It would be dangerous for you to venture forth."

When they returned they reported that James bar Zebedee indeed had been arrested by Agrippa's soldiers and Temple guardsmen, presumably on orders of the king, as he was leaving the Synagogue of the Libertines. They had dragged him off to Fortress Antonia, and as far as Joseph Barnabas had been able to discover, none of his friends had seen James after the heavy doors of the prison had closed on him.

But they had also learned something else. "Rab Simon," Barnabas reported, his haggard face solemn, "Agrippa has given orders to arrest you likewise as soon as you are found. We must conceal you; you mustn't let yourself be discovered."

"No, my brother, I'll not hide from Agrippa or the High Priest. I serve a King mightier than all the Caesars and priests of earth." Simon's round face showed no alarm. "If it's my King's will, He'll protect me from every enemy. I'll not be fearful, but will trust in my brother and Saviour the Lord Messiah."

And Simon continued to go his usual way.

For several days nothing was heard of James bar Zebedee. Then came the grievous tidings: James had been led forth from the prison and beheaded by the king's swordsman.

The elder of the Zebedees was the first to die of the eleven apostles of Jesus who survived Judas of Kiriot.

In the homes of many of the poor and lowly in Ophel, and here and there on Mount Zion where the more affluent of the fellowship dwelt, lamentations could be heard for the rugged fisherman of Bethsaida.

But the death of James bar Zebedee greatly pleased the High Priest and his adherents, and they communicated their pleasure and thanks to King Herod Agrippa and complimented the king for his zeal in seeking to preserve in its purity the worship of the God of Israel. They besought him to continue to purge from the vine of Israel those blasphemous twigs who worshiped the dead Galilean carpenter, and they reminded him that the worst of these fanatics, one Simon of Capernaum, had not been dealt with.

The king again issued orders for the arrest of Simon bar Jonah.

"Take him to the Fortress Antonia and place him in the custody of four squads of soldiers," he commanded. "Warn them to guard him under pain of death if he should escape them. When I'm ready I'll order him brought out before the people and beheaded."

Soon to Mary's house came the long feared but not unexpected dreadful news that the beloved bold Simon Peter, first of the Messiah's apostles, had been seized by Agrippa's soldiers and hustled away to the forbidding square tower north of the Temple.

Amaziah brought the report. He had heard it as he was crossing the bridge that spanned the Valley of the Cheesemongers to connect the Temple area with Mount Zion.

"The man told me he saw Simon when he was arrested," Amaziah said. "He declared the first of the apostles showed no fear, but readily admitted he was the man they sought. He even seemed happy to identify himself as a member of our fellowship."

Barnabas had been listening in fear and anger. Agrippa had killed James bar Zebedee; he would be even more determined, no doubt, to slay bold Simon bar Jonah. Prodded by Theophilus, he would bring Simon out and execute him before the people as a demonstration of his personal regard for the laws and customs of Israel and his determination to uphold them in traditional purity. Silently Barnabas prayed to the God of Israel to protect his beloved Rab Simon.

. . . Deliver him from Thy enemies, O God. How can we endure without the presence and leadership of our beloved Simon? . . .

When he had eaten a light supper, for today Barnabas had no appetite for food, he crossed the courtyard and went out through the gateway. Then he turned left and walked northward past the great houses on Zion Hill until he reached the high stone fence in front of the Palace of the Herods.

Here he paused and inquired of the porter at the outer gate for a man with whom he said he wished most urgently to speak. The porter for a moment appeared puzzled. Then his expression suddenly changed.

"Oh, yes," he said. "I place him now. But he isn't here; tonight he's on duty elsewhere." He revealed, however, where the man might be found. So Barnabas thanked him and departed. From the palace gate he walked on past the Praetorium, across the Pavement, alongside the low wall beyond which the flowers and shrubs of the garden were now in their glory.

But Barnabas did not pause to enjoy the flowers. For straight ahead and not far away in the lengthening shadows he could see the frowning battlements of Antonia.

In utter darkness in the lowermost dungeon of the Fortress Antonia, Simon bar Jonah lay silent and at peace.

When his guards had been changed an hour ago he had sought to talk with the two who had come on duty; he wished to tell them of his Lord Messiah and the joy awaiting them should they enter the Lord's service. But neither had been sympathetic or interested.

The one shackled to him on his right had laughed. He was a young man, Simon judged, perhaps in his early twenties, though the apostle had seen him only in the instant the weak light had fallen across him when the cell door had opened to admit the two. He was a Jew, perhaps a conscript serving his required enlistment.

"Hah! Old man, you speak to us of the joy you have in this fellowship of the so-called Messiah. You have the effrontery to offer me your kind of joy! Who would want it, I ask you? Isn't your Messiah dead, and tomorrow won't you—" He stopped speaking, and then he laughed again. "Old man, I don't want the sort of joy that awaits you!"

The other fellow had been sullen, uncommunicative. A Gentile, he probably had come from one of the regions northward from Syria.

"Cease your chatter, old one!" he commanded. "I don't want to hear anything about you or your gods. The only thing I wish now is that the three hours I spend each day on duty in this black hole of hell should pass quickly!" Simon could hear him trying to settle himself in a comfortable position.

So Simon had lain back and peered with eyes that saw nothing toward the stones of the ceiling lost in blackness. But there was no darkness in his heart, and with a clarity not born of earthly vision he saw the Master and felt his presence.

Simon recalled other days.

. . . The Passover here in Jerusalem, the last one with the Master, the supper in Mary's upper room. Poor Judas. God have mercy on his soul. He was the first of the Twelve to go. And the other day James bar Zebedee. What was the Jewish guard here beside me about to say a moment ago? Simon tomorrow? What does it matter?

. . . The courtyard of old Annas, and the little serving maid. "Were you not one of them with this Galilean?" O God, forgive me. But I never ceased to love you, Master.

. . . The crosses on the Hill of the Skull. The center cross, and I hiding back in the shadows. Forgive me, O God. And the tomb and the great stone and death, cruel and implacable. The empty tomb. And again the upper room, and you, beloved, again with us, again and forever, risen, ascendant. Here now, *here* beside me. It makes no difference, Master, what happens on the morrow. If you will it, take me; if it is your will that I labor longer in the fellowship, send thy angel, Master, to break off these shackles and lead me forth from this dungeon. . . .

He lay at peace in the blackness and thought of the gone days. Not a sound penetrated the great walls from outside the fortress. He did not know the hour, though as it was well into the third watch he reckoned it halfway toward the cockcrowing. The guard on his right stirred; his moving arm jerked at the iron cuff about Simon's wrist. He heard the youth snore gently. Nor did the other guard protest. He's asleep too, Simon thought, and in a moment both guards were snoring.

They are tired, fatigued from much duty during the day. But should they be asleep when the next shift comes at cockcrowing to replace them, they could forfeit their lives. Isn't that the law of the military? But before then I'll awaken them. So Simon thought as he lay calm and content with what the morrow might bring.

He lay still and thought of the stirring days in Galilee, by the little sea's shore and on its now quiet now angry waters, along the roads deep in dust, in milling throngs here in Jerusalem, out at

Bethany beside a tomb from which a dead man came walking at the gentle summons of the Master.

. . . I feel his presence beside me to strengthen me, to keep me steadfast. 'Go tell my disciples, and Cephas—' Cephas the Rock. I thank thee, Master, for having thus named me, for having thus shown faith in me. Give me courage for the morrow. If it brings the sword and the headsman's block, so be it. But if my work is not finished, then send an angel to loose these bonds and open these doors. Have not angels delivered the faithful in other days? Haven't they served in other times as the arm of the Lord? . . .

Simon straightened his long legs, shifted his weight, settled himself in the blackness of the dungeon. Beside him the two guards slept. His folded mantle lay under his head. His eyes were heavy now, and he closed them against the darkness and the unknown; he lay relaxed and at peace. No sound disturbed the dungeon save the heavy breathing of the guards shackled to him.

He must have dozed lightly and dreamed of the angel's coming. He must have heard a slight and unusual noise too, for he opened his eyes, and in the feeble light from the now opened door he saw a form bending over him. It grasped his shoulder, shook him gently.

"I—who—"

Simon, awake now, said no more, for the visitor, fingers across his lips, was commanding silence. Then he leaned down, whispered in Simon's ear.

"Get up quickly. Make no sound. Put on your sandals." He must have noticed the mantle then. He pointed. "Wrap it about you and follow me."

The fisherman slipped his sandals on, stood up. His arms were free of the cuffs. The chains, the cuffs sprung open, lay close to the silent, motionless guards.

The visitor went noiselessly through the doorway. Simon followed. At the end of a short corridor they climbed a flight of stone stairs and walked around a man slumped against the wall. The third of the quaternion of guards, Simon surmised. When they had climbed another flight of stairs that came out on a large rectangular areaway they encountered the fourth man, inert on the cold stones in the poor light from a flickering wall lamp.

Straight ahead was the great iron gate. They made for it. It was ajar, Simon discovered when he reached it, and they went through the opening and disappeared into the darkness.

The first of the apostles now knew where he was. They had come out on the south side of the fortress, toward the Temple. Rapidly they walked along the paved way beside Antonia. Simon's visitor, when they were even with the Gate Tedi, which gave access to the Temple from the fortress, pointed to the stone stairs that went down to the double cloisters.

"You know, of course, the way to the Gate Shalleketh and the bridge to Zion Hill?"

Simon nodded.

"At the house of Mary of Cyprus, Joseph Barnabas will be waiting."

Simon went down the steps, turned right. At the north Gate of Asuppim he turned left, walked the length of the cloisters that looked out on the Valley of the Cheesemongers. At the corner he went through the Gate Shalleketh and in the darkness stepped out on the bridge.

Ahead, on the ascending slope of Mount Zion a few lights showed here and there, and along the brow of the hill southward others lifted small yellow squares above the black valley.

## THE CROWN TREE 53

One of the houses in which the lamps burned, though the curtains had been drawn, was Mary's. Here many of the fellowship had gathered.

Since the news of Simon's arrest had got abroad they had been assembling at this house. Many had come from Ophel. These were the poor in purse and heart, now all the more desolate because their strong leader suddenly had been snatched from them. Some had come to the house from day to day, others had stayed. They lay on the stones of the courtyard, covering themselves from the dew with their bedraggled mantles, accepting gratefully the food distributed by Mary. Continuously they had prayed for the safe return of their beloved Simon of Galilee.

Tonight since sunset they had been praying with an earnestness seldom attained by even the most devout among them, for in late afternoon the terrifying report had come that early on the morrow Simon was to be beheaded. Prostrated on the stone floor of the house, lying face downward in the courtyard in an ecstasy of petitioning, they called upon the God of Israel and His beloved Son to send an angel to deliver Simon from the Roman dungeon. The midnight hour had come and gone but still they were praying.

It was nearing the cockcrow when Mary's little maid Rhoda, having slipped outside to sit on the stone bench and cool herself, heard a heavy belaboring on the street gate, and in the same instant a man's coarse voice demanding admittance.

"One of the brothers comes late," she said to herself as she ran to open the gate. "Maybe he brings news of Rab Simon."

She pulled back the heavy bar, opened the gate.

"God in Israel! No! It can't be!"

She slammed the gate shut again and fled screaming into the chamber crowded with fearful petitioners.

"Rab Simon's down at the gate! I saw him!" The girl's eyes were ablaze. "As God is my witness, it's the truth!"

Instantly the chamber was in an uproar as worshipers jumped to their feet.

"No! It can't be!" a brother shouted. "How could Simon steal out of the Tower's dungeon?"

"You're right, Jazreel." Another was shaking his head sadly. "When Simon comes from Antonia, he'll be led by soldiers. Rhoda, you didn't see him; you're overwrought with worry; you only thought you saw him."

"No! No! I tell you I saw him! He stood just outside the gate!"

"Maybe she saw his spirit," another ventured. "Maybe Agrippa has already slain him."

The knocking continued; but already Joseph Barnabas had dashed outside. He ran down to the gate, lifted the latch that had fallen into place when the girl had slammed the gate shut, opened it.

"Rab Simon! God be praised!"

"Joseph Barnabas, my brother!"

They embraced, kissed the kiss of greeting.

"Come inside, Rab Simon. Many are gathered here, where we've been praying for your deliverance."

Barnabas barred the gate and they went at once into the house, where Simon was greeted with screams of joy. But quickly he motioned to them to be quiet, and then he related how he had been delivered.

"Our prayers have availed," he concluded. "We prayed that God would send His angel to lead me forth, and here I am." Every eye was on him, and Simon sensed the drama of the situation. "I must have dreamed that the angel had come and was bending over me, shaking me. I opened my eyes, started to inquire who he was, but I saw his fingers on his lips—"

"Praise God! The Lord sent His angel—"

Simon motioned for silence to continue his recital.

" 'Get up, and make no sound,' he commanded. 'Dress yourself, and put on your sandals; take up your mantle and follow me.' When I rose up I discovered the shackles had been loosed. So we went out the cell and through the great gateway, which had opened to us, and I came straightway to you—"

"God be praised! He preserves His own. He sent down an angel—"

Once again the fisherman called for silence.

"When I learned that Agrippa was seeking me, I did not hide myself. I felt that if God desired me to be spared to work longer, He would preserve me. Now that He has snatched me from the hands of Agrippa I believe it is His purpose that I labor further toward establishing on the earth His kingdom—"

Suddenly Simon stopped speaking, for just now across the cool darkness of the Valley of the Cheesemongers came the sweet, clean notes of a trumpet.

"The cockcrow! The trumpeter atop Antonia. In another moment, with the bringing in of the new quaternion of guards, it will be discovered that I have disappeared. They may even awaken Agrippa, who'll be furious, and he may order an immediate search started. I perceive it is God's will that now I go into hiding." He held out his hands, as if in benediction. "Remain here and pray. If soldiers come searching and inquire where I have gone, you will not be able to say because you will not know. Meanwhile, call upon the God of Israel to dwell among you in the person of the Holy Spirit, and pray that His Son our Lord may shortly come and reign in righteousness. And may God be with you and in you. Amen."

Smiling, Simon tugged with gnarled hand at his begrimed beard; then he caught Barnabas by the arm. "Come, Joseph, once more I need you." In the courtyard he spoke again. "It occurred to me, Joseph, that you might have plans."

"Yes, Rab Simon. Wait here a moment." Soon he was back with two leather pouches. One he handed to Simon.

"You had great faith, Joseph. You had already prepared these. Food?"

"And changes of linen." He slung his pouch strap over his shoulder. "We mustn't lose any time. Beyond the walls, toward Emmaus, a place has been provided where you can rest in safety with one of our fellowship, and after the first fever of the search for you has subsided, you can continue on."

"*We* can continue on, Joseph."

"I was hoping you would wish it that way, Rab Simon. That's why I provided two pouches."

"But where to, Joseph, after we have rested awhile at the brother's house and the time's propitious?"

"There's one place the king would never think of seeking you. By the very boldness of it, it was suggested to me, nobody would look for you there."

They were going through the gateway now. As Simon hesitated, Joseph Barnabas pointed left.

"Caesarea," he said. "Centurion Cornelius."

## THE CROWN TREE 54

King Agrippa, zealous to show himself before the people of Jerusalem a devout son of Israel and defender of Israel's God, had decided to have a public testing of the faith and courage of the leader of the sect of the Nazarene. In the middle of the forenoon when all the city was astir, Simon would be led into the square before the Praetorium and in the presence of the multitude be given the opportunity of renouncing his allegiance to the crucified Jesus and cursing his name.

Should he do so, he would be freed from his chains. Should he refuse he would be dragged to a nearby block and forthwith beheaded. If Simon should renounce the Nazarene, Agrippa reasoned, he would condemn thereby his iniquitous, rebellious sect and it would wither away and shortly die; if he should refuse to recant and go to his death, then the king would be credited by the High Priest and the great of Israel with having destroyed the chief enemy of Israel's God and His law.

But before the king had arisen the report reached the palace that in the night the Galilean fisherman had escaped.

Agrippa was incensed. He gave orders that the city be searched, and soldiers were dispatched in squads to hunt for the fugitive. Careful search was made throughout the Ophel district; ruthlessly the soldiers and the Temple guardsmen broke down barred doors and forced open locked chests and tore away partitioning curtains and overturned rude furnishings. A detachment even visited Mary's house, but when she calmly assured the soldiers that Simon was not there and invited them to search, they left without further disturbing the household.

The failure to apprehend the escaped leader all the more angered the king. But when an aide reported that stories were being spread about that an angel of the Lord had struck off Simon's chains and led him from the dungeon, Agrippa raged. Such reports plainly said that in having Simon imprisoned the king had gone contrary to the will of God. Instead of being God's defender, in the eyes of the Jews the king was His enemy. Agrippa threatened to punish severely anyone heard repeating these stories.

But in the hovels in Ophel, along the slope of Mount Moriah, even here and there in great houses on Mount Zion, the sensational story was whispered: an angel of the Lord had been sent to deliver the first of the apostles from the hand of King Agrippa.

So those of the fellowship in Jerusalem began to put off their sackcloth and ashes for James bar Zebedee and to rejoice in Simon's deliverance.

Nor was the fisherman found. Agrippa, foiled in his ambition to make a public spectacle of the apostle's faith, now began to give his attention to final preparations for the journey to Rome.

Meanwhile Simon and Joseph Barnabas remained hidden at the home of the brother near Emmaus. Each day this man kept his ears open for tidings concerning the king's search for the fisherman and that night relayed them to his concealed guests. Once a small detachment of troops stopped at his house and inquired if a stranger of Simon's description had been seen passing along the road. But no search had been made.

One night, however, their host had exciting news. King Agrippa had left Jerusalem to go to Caesarea where he would take ship. He traveled with a great company of men and women under the escort of many soldiers.

"Now is the time for us to depart for Caesarea," Barnabas observed. "Round about the city the roads will be filled with people going there to see the king, and nobody will pay attention to two dust-covered travelers."

The next morning they set out, and on the third day they went through the gate into the port city and walked by a devious route to the house of Cornelius, taking care that no one was noticing them.

The centurion was happy to see his brothers in the fellowship; he assured them that they would be safe there. When they had eaten supper, he led them to the housetop where they would be secure from prying eyes and alert ears. Quickly Simon related the story of his imprisonment and how he had been freed.

"Longinus told me that you had been arrested but had escaped," Cornelius revealed. "In fact, he seemed to think that you might have come here to hide from Agrippa."

Barnabas, listening intently, remained silent. The centurion continued: "I'm concerned for Longinus. He is troubled; his mind is in turmoil. He might well become a follower of Jesus; sometimes I think he is almost a believer in the Lord. On the other hand, he might turn into a violent enemy of the Messiah and those of his sect; he might reverse the course of your friend Saul of Tarsus." He paused a moment, meditating. "Were Longinus to become one of us, he would of a certainty lead my sister into our fellowship, and likely many others in Rome. The Tribune is a man of much influence." An expression of deep concern, almost pain, overspread the centurion's countenance. "Simon, I wish we could do something to help Longinus."

"I do too, Cornelius; I greatly desire to bring him into the fold. What is the Tribune's difficulty? Is it a matter of lacking faith?"

"Yes, that is his problem, and it has become a heavy burden that he cannot put down. Since the day he crucified Jesus, without surcease, I suspect, he has been bearing that burden, for as he observed Jesus on the cross, I am convinced he had the feeling that the Galilean was more than a mortal man. Longinus has felt through the succeeding years a terrible and growing guilt that he has never been able to rid himself of, and I am fearful that in his struggle to unburden himself he may come to hate Jesus and those who profess themselves to be his followers."

"But why cannot the Tribune find his peace in our Lord?" Simon inquired. "Is it the question of the resurrection?"

"Yes. You see, Longinus knows that Jesus died on the cross. He killed him. And as a modern-day, educated, and deeply thoughtful man, he cannot bring his mind to acceptance of the idea that a mortal man could die and be entombed and three days later walk forth alive from the tomb. I believe Longinus wants to believe it; I know he had a great respect for the courage and nobility of the dying Galilean." Cornelius shook his head resignedly. "I believe the Tribune holds belief in a great universal divine spirit similar in every respect—or identical to, in fact— the Jehovah of the Jews. But he cannot understand how such a divinity could put on and relinquish at will the body of a man, he told me. He said he felt that to hold such a view was to be no more than an unlearned, superstitious pagan. And yet, Simon, Longinus cannot divest himself of this horrible thought that the thrust of his spear may have sent to death a god-man."

"It must be that the Master is pursuing him, Cornelius, wrestling with him to bring him into the fold of the redeemed."

"I am convinced that is true, Simon. I wish there had been more time for us to talk yesterday; maybe I could have nourished a little more the seed of faith he must carry in his heart. But the vessel bearing the king's party sailed shortly after Agrippa's group arrived." His face lightened. "There's a chance that on the voyage the High Priest's niece, who knows Longinus and understands the burden he carries, may be able to help him come to see—"

"The High Priest's niece? You mean Damaris?" Barnabas sat up straight, his eyes ablaze.

"Yes, she was in the group that sailed for Rome with Agrippa. Longinus said the king thought that if several beautiful young women of rank in Jerusalem went along it would give his petition more weight with the Emperor. Agrippa didn't know, of course, that Damaris is of the sect he's attempting to destroy."

"But a follower of our Lord Messiah should not have gone with Agrippa, Centurion." Barnabas shook his head. "It was not fitting."

"There were other women in the king's company," Cornelius

hastened to assure him. "Nor could Damaris refuse to go, because if she had that very fact might have betrayed her—and others, too—as followers of Jesus."

But Barnabas, his forehead furrowed in thought, seemed not to have heard. "When does another vessel set sail for Rome, Centurion?"

"We're expecting one within a week. I'm going on it myself, if my replacement arrives in time. I've been ordered home for a meeting with the Prefect, and a centurion is being sent here from Gaza to serve while I'm away from my post."

Barnabas grasped Simon's arm, but his eyes were intently fixed on the centurion. "When that ship sails, I'll be on it too."

## THE CROWN TREE 55

When the vessel on which Luke the physician had sailed to Rome docked at a wharf near the ancient Sublicius Bridge, he quickly went ashore.

But he did not go immediately to the home of Senator Flaccus on Quirinal Hill. Instead, he crossed the bridge and turned left to walk along the road paralleling the western bank of the Tiber until he came to the Portuensian gate. Inside the gate he turned right and began to ascend the slope of the Janiculum.

At one of the houses he presented a letter given him at Caesarea by Joseph Barnabas; the house was the home of kinsmen of Barnabas and they greeted the physician warmly. Quickly he revealed why he had come to Rome, and when he had bathed and changed to fresh clothing and had eaten a light meal, he retraced his way along the river street, across the bridge, through the Roman Forum's bustling crowds, and up the slope of the Quirinal.

A servant answered his knock for admittance at the mansion of Senator Flaccus, and Luke asked to be received by the Senator's daughter; he explained he was bringing her a message from her brother, the Centurion Cornelius. The servant asked him to wait in the atrium; in a moment he returned to announce that his mistress Lalage would receive him in the peristylium.

She was awaiting him there, and he bowed.

"I am Luke, a physician of Antioch," he introduced himself. "I come from Caesarea with a message—"

"Luke of Antioch! By all the gods! You've come for Aspasia."

"Yes, and I bear a letter from your brother in Caesarea." He drew the letter from the fold of his toga, handed it to her. "But please, before you read it," he pleaded, "how is she?"

"Aspasia's quite well," she answered. She glanced quickly over the letter. "Cornelius asks me to give Aspasia her manumission or allow you to purchase her freedom." She paused. "We'll talk about that later. Meanwhile, you'd like to see her, wouldn't you?"

Lalage called a slave hovering nearby. "Go, fetch Aspasia," she commanded. Then she turned to Luke. "Step into my sitting room. I'll have Aspasia sent in to you, and you can talk with no one to distract."

Then she went into the atrium and sat beside a tall jardiniere of fresh flowers. A moment later the slave returned with Aspasia, pointed to Lalage's private sitting room. "In there," he said.

Aspasia went quickly across the peristylium.

From the atrium a second later Lalage heard the girl's muffled scream of joy. She shrugged a white shoulder, smiled ruefully.

"Would that Longinus had been treated with the physician's medicines," she observed.

But it was only a few days before she saw the tribune. First, though, she would see her brother. The ships that brought King Agrippa and his delegation and Cornelius and Joseph Barnabas arrived on the same day and almost at the same hour. Hardly had the king's group been welcomed at the Imperial Palace by Emperor Gaius when the other vessel docked at the wharf near Pons Aurelius.

At the eastern end of the bridge they separated. Cornelius walked westward and a little north past Capitoline Hill to his father's house, where he was joyously greeted by his parents and sister. Barnabas trudged southward until he came to the Triumphal Way and then turned west to climb the slope of Janiculum; soon with much rejoicing his kinsmen welcomed him, and happily Luke the physician was still lodged with them. Luke revealed that he had found Aspasia. Meanwhile Lalage was discussing with her brother his letter about the girl.

"It's easy for you to ask me to free her," she said. "She's not your slave. How could I get along without her? Why couldn't she remain with me but marry Luke? Father could give him employment."

"But Luke doesn't want his wife to be a slave. He's a high born Greek, an educated, cultured man. And lately he's become—" He stopped.

"Become what?"

"Become determined to have her as his wife."

"I don't think that's what you were going to say," she observed quizzically. "But anyway I'm going to think about it a while longer before I give Aspasia her manumission." Quickly she turned her attention to a more interesting subject.

"When have you seen Longinus? How is he? When will he likely be coming home?"

Cornelius showed surprise. "Haven't you seen him? He left Caesarea on a ship that sailed well ahead of ours. I thought he'd have been here before now."

"I haven't seen him." Her face clouded. "Maybe he's here, but didn't want to see me. Could it be that—"

"Of course not, Lalage. His ship was slower, that's all. Perhaps it called at more ports."

"Cornelius, is Longinus—and are you—still troubled by the remembrance of that Galilean fanatic Longinus crucified? Could that be the reason—"

"The Galilean troubles no one, Lalage," he said quickly. "But when Longinus comes, say nothing to him about it. I think that would be best." His smile brightened his face. "And he will certainly come here once he has arrived in Rome."

That night bearers of a sedan chair stopped at the door of Senator Flaccus and the Tribune Longinus Aemilius Varro stepped from it.

"I came as soon as I could slip away from Agrippa," he explained, after he had greeted the girl with unfeigned ardor. "But he's kept me busy every moment since we arrived shortly before midday." He told her why Agrippa had come to Rome, and she revealed that Cornelius already had informed her. The tribune was happy to learn that the centurion was in the capital.

"Maybe we'll both be assigned to duties at home," he ventured. "Then Cornelius could send for Pyrrha and the children, and I could"—he grinned, and his eyes were dancing—"settle down too. I suspect that Cornelius would be as glad as I would be to get away from Palestine." Quickly his face had sobered, and she thought he was about to refer to the man he had crucified, but in the same moment his manner changed. "I've come from Agrippa to invite you to the banquet he's giving day after tomorrow night for the Emperor, when he plans to address Israel's petition to Caligula. As you doubtless know, the gladiatorial games begin that morning and he thinks the night of the games' opening would be a propitious time for staging the banquet; Caligula should be in good humor after a day of bloodletting. So ever since we arrived Agrippa has had people scurrying about to buy the finest foods and wines, and he's inviting Rome's society. Naturally he wants Senator Flaccus' daughter there, as the dinner companion of his aide, of course."

Lalage was beaming. "I wonder how the king's guest list happens to have me paired with his Roman aide."

"A remarkable coincidence, wasn't it?" He winked.

Longinus told her that Agrippa was planning to attend the opening of the games as guest of the Emperor.

"He wants me to sit with him in the Emperor's box. That's almost a command. I no longer look forward with pleasure to seeing men butcher one another, but if you'll go with me the games will be more endurable."

She said she would.

The next afternoon Joseph Barnabas too had a visitor, a Roman soldier, one of the guardsmen assigned to duty at the Imperial Palace.

"I come from Centurion Cornelius, who this morning has talked with Tribune Longinus," he announced. "They agreed that you should be warned not to come to the Imperial Palace in an attempt to see a young Israelitish woman who came to Rome in the delegation brought by King Agrippa, the niece of the High Priest, I understand, and"—he smiled appreciatively—"perhaps your beloved."

"But why?" Barnabas asked, his concern evident. "Has anything happened to Damaris?"

"No, I assure you," the soldier declared. "But the Centurion instructed me to explain to you that should you go to the Palace and be seen talking with her, it might lead to questioning by certain ones who might report to the Emperor your presence there, and in some manner he might discover that you are a member of an Israelitish sect against which he is raging."

"But I'm not sure I understand—"

"The Emperor of late has been very hostile toward the Jews, and since the arrival of King Agrippa he seems to be all the more opposed to this sect which worships a crucified Galilean. He thinks these people are fomenting a rebellion against Rome; he hates them far worse than he does the orthodox Jews. The centurion declared that if Caligula found out that Agrippa, who seems to have inflamed him against this sect, had brought some of them to Rome in his delegation, even unwittingly, he'd likely be enraged to the point of madness. In fact, he thought Agrippa might lose his kingdom because of it, or even his head."

"Then Caligula, at Agrippa's instigation, will attempt to seek out and destroy those who belong to this sect of which you speak?"

"No doubt," the soldier declared, nodding. "The Centurion felt that you would be incurring much danger in appearing at the Imperial Palace. He suggested that something might go amiss were you to be seen in conversation with the girl. But he suggested also that should you be most anxious to see her and perhaps speak to her briefly and casually without arousing suspicion, you might go to the gladiatorial games tomorrow, since there you could mingle with the multitude and hardly be noticed."

"A Jew attending those barbarous, pagan exhibitions?"

"Centurion Cornelius said that perhaps you would not wish to attend. But he thought that your desire to see the young woman might overcome your aversion. Should you decide to go, he further suggested, you should enter the amphitheatre early and push forward as closely as possible to the Emperor's box, in which King Agrippa and his delegation will be sitting as Caligula's guests. In that way you might see and speak briefly with the young woman. But he warns you to be very careful, to do nothing that would excite suspicion." The man smiled glumly. "As I said, Caligula lately has shown great hostility to those of your fellowship."

"Tell Cornelius I'll go, and I'll be careful." Slowly Barnabas nodded his head. "I probably won't even attempt to speak with her, though I would like to see her, since it's been a long time since I've even been near her." But he seemed puzzled, and then he spoke frankly.

"But tell me, friend, why did Cornelius entrust this information to you—about the fellowship, I mean? Did he tell you that I—and he, too—were—" He stopped.

"Members of the fellowship of Jesus?" The man smiled understandingly. "Yes, he did. And also that Luke the Greek physician is of the sect. But have no fear, Joseph Barnabas. I am likewise a member. I am Sextus, your brother in the Lord Jesus."

"You, a member of the Palace Guard, are of our brotherhood? Praise God, Sextus, my Roman brother!" They embraced warmly, and Joseph kissed him on the cheek. "I thank God and

His Messiah our Lord Jesus Christ! You, a son of pagan Rome!"

"Yes, and not the only one, my brother. In Rome already there are many enrolled in his fellowship. The plant has taken root and flourishes! Day by day souls are added unto salvation!"

## THE CROWN TREE  57

Shouting, tumultuous throngs surged into the vast amphitheatre adjacent to the Imperial Palace as the gates were opened for the first day's events of the gladiatorial games honoring Caesar Augustus.

From the beginning contest, the multitude had been promised, the games would be an orgy of bloodletting. Scores of the ablest gladiators in the Empire had been conditioned and trained, many of them fierce young blond giants from the forests of Germania. Some would be matched with captured soldiers or revolutionaries from other provinces, others would find themselves, almost weaponless, facing ravenous wild beasts. And Caligula had hinted that there would be even more startling exhibitions.

No effort had been made to seat the spectators in accordance with rank. Equestrians, even senators, jostled against freedmen and slaves, patrician women found themselves being shoved forward by women from the Subura's taverns and brothels.

But suddenly those in the aisles stopped pushing and stood in their tracks while the already seated thousands sprang to their feet and joined in a thunderous shout of acclaim for the Emperor, who with his guests was entering the imperial box through an archway opening from a corridor of the palace. The grinning young monarch, immensely pleased at the reception, waved his hand above his head and shouted his promise that the day's games would not disappoint them.

And now the heralds, who had been caught off guard by Caligula's precipitate arrival, with a great blast of trumpeting paraded him down to the front row of the marble seats in the lavishly festooned box. Immediately behind the Emperor came King Agrippa and after the king those who had accompanied him from Jerusalem. The king's aide, the Tribune Longinus, escorting the beaming daughter of Senator Flaccus, walked in the rear of the group, and they took seats two rows behind and to the left of the Emperor.

Caligula seemed relaxed and affable; he was bowing to many persons in the area about the Emperor's box, and smiling and saluting with both hands, on the fingers of which jeweled rings glinted in the morning sunshine. Agrippa, too, appeared pleasant, and he settled down in his cushioned marble seat with evident pleasurable anticipation to await the beginning of the games.

The multitude, which had shrieked and shouted at the entrance of Caligula, was hushed now as the Emperor arose and advanced to the altar to offer the sacrifice and dedicate the games to the great Augustus. When quickly he had finished, he stepped back to his thronelike chair in the center of the first row of the resplendent box and lifted his right arm to signal the start of the contests.

Immediately great doors across the circle and on the level of the arena floor were flung open and to the accompaniment of martial trumpets and cadenced thundering drums a troop of tremendous gladiators, wearing heavy helmets and carrying great steel-studded bronze shields and a variety of fearsome weapons— two-edged broadswords, four-pronged and hooked forks, sharp-pointed javelins, strong-corded nets—marched with military stride, their brass-greaved legs flashing in the morning sunlight, straight toward the Emperor.

When the first line was ten paces from the wall of the arena in front of Caligula, at a sharp command the gladiators stopped, brought their heels smartly together, lifted aloft their weapons.

"Hail, Caesar! We who are about to die salute you!"

Caligula raised his right hand, a silly grin smearing his narrow face.

Another command was given, the gladiators whirled about to divide the company into fighting pairs, and the mortal combat was begun. Swords rang against shields and other swords, nets circled through the air to pinion the stabbing arms of desperate swordsmen, battle-axes clanged heavily against tremendous tough shields, men fell fighting to the already bloodied sand, curses and shrill screams, agonized, frantic, mocking, piteous, mingled with the roaring of the multitude.

Tribune Longinus raised his eyes from the arena floor to study the young man in the central seat of the imperial box. Caligula was watching with ghoulish delight, his dancing sharp eyes darting from one fighting pair to another, his shrill voice shouting approval of some particularly bloody thrusting.

King Agrippa, too, was following the contests with evident enjoyment. In Jerusalem the king might profess devotion to the beliefs and customs and traditions of Israel; in Rome Agrippa often was more Roman than the Romans.

But suddenly a man just beyond the rail of the imperial box and a row behind the tribune was shouting to the man beside him.

"Look, Cluvius, those little men are about to snare in their net that huge bearded fellow with the tremendous broadsword! Look how he's raging!"

Longinus eyed the arena. A dozen midgets were swarming about a big gladiator who had just killed a bronzed giant whose bloody body lay almost at the big man's feet. The little men must have run out while Longinus had been watching Caligula and Agrippa. The giant may have scorned them when they came running across the scarred sand to accost him, but now he was thoroughly furious and perhaps a little alarmed, for the midgets were proceeding methodically and with apparent determination to destroy him.

In a frenzy he began hacking at the little fighters, but while those in front of him managed to evade his wild sword thrusts, others ran in from behind and jabbed thin long small spears into the calves of his legs and his bulging thighs. When he would wheel to swing his great sword at these tormentors, those in front would slash at him with their spears and then dart back out of range of his flashing weapon.

But one midget failed in his timing. He was thrusting at the hairy giant's middle when the broadsword caught him squarely in the neck. Longinus saw the dwarf's head fall to the shoulder and roll off to lie on the chest, held only by a string of skin and muscle, and then as a stream of crimson shot upward, the body of the little man crumpled into the blood-wet sand.

In the instant that the big gladiator had relaxed after decapitating the dwarf, however, four other little men from behind had thrown a net over his head and shoulders and now threshing arms, and two had hurled at his legs a chain with a ball at each end. Before the giant could realize what was happening, his sword had slipped from his grasp, his legs were pulled from under him, and he was on his back in the sand and entangled in the net.

Now the midget men were on him, slashing and jabbing with their sharp little daggers as he fought to free himself of the net. Already his huge frame was bloody from scores of wounds and his bearded round face was a gory pulp. Suddenly one of the dwarfs jumped up on his stomach, as the others chopped at his face and thrusting arms, and set the point of his sword over the fallen gladiator's heart. The big fellow, despite his grievous wounds and the blood that blinded his eyes, must have understood, for he screamed out in pain and terror.

"Mercy! O Emperor, mercy! Grant me a chance on my feet to fight these vermin! One chance, O Gaius! One chance!"

The midgets instantly stood motionless, poised, awaiting the will of Caligula. And now every eye in the vast amphitheatre was on the Emperor. He leaned outward over the railing of the box.

"You big fool!" he shouted. "You had your chance. A moment ago you were on your feet. But now, by Jupiter my brother, look where you are, you buffoon!" He slapped the railing with the palm of his hand and the stones in his rings flashed as his raucous laughter cackled above the ensnared and bleeding giant to echo tier upon tier across the hushed arena. Then suddenly his laughter ceased and a leer spread over his sensual face. "You ask for mercy, you awkward lout, because you can't fight! You can't even protect yourself against a band of dwarfs!" Once more he beat upon the railing with his hand and screamed his silly laughter. And leaning far outward, he thrust forth his right hand and slowly turned it so that the extended thumb pointed downward. And over the vast amphitheatre a sea of hands signaled thumbs down.

The dwarfs, seeing it, sprang back to their gory task. The one standing on the gladiator's stomach, his feet spread to brace himself, clutched his sword securely with both hands and sprang upward to push with all his weight the gleaming thin weapon straight downward into the man's heart. One piercing scream and the gladiator was quiet.

Now the midgets were bowing toward the Emperor's box, the spectators were thundering their approval; and as the little men ran out through the gateway that opened into the quarters of the gladiators the musicians burst forth with a crescendo of stirring sound. Caligula and his royal guest raised arms aloft and waved them in approbation.

Longinus turned to the girl beside him. "Have a look into the heart of your mighty Rome," he said, his lip curling. "See how the great brother of Jupiter and these fawning thousands wallow in the agony and blood of that poor oaf."

"Careful, Longinus," she said into his ear. "Someone might overhear."

But he appeared not to have heard her. He was looking once more toward the sanded floor of the arena, as if drawn by a horrible fascination, for a group of black slaves, naked except for red and yellow and green loincloths, had thrust iron hooks into the mouth and neck of the dead gladiator. Then as four of the slaves swiftly dragged the body toward the gateway, others with rakes and brooms smoothed out the torn and bloodied spot and spread fresh sand on it.

"Very amusing, Cluvius," Longinus heard the man in the seat nearby observe.

"Yes, a comic prelude to the opening of the games," his companion agreed. "If that's a sample, the games should be highly entertaining."

Before midday much more blood had been spilled on the sands constantly being freshened. Bears and panthers, elephants, tigers, lions, leopards, vicious dogs, slashed and tore and trampled one another to tortured, lingering deaths; a company of condemned criminals, dressed in the skins of animals, contended with bare hands as long as they could against packs of ravenous dogs turned loose on them, but soon were torn to shreds and many were partially eaten by the starved beasts.

Nor was there respite during the noon hour, for Caligula ordered a sumptuous luncheon served all those in the Emperor's section, and he ate with apparent enjoyment as he watched the blood of animals and men gushing forth in their death agonies to stain anew the arena's floor. The afternoon's program was continued in an orgy of bloodletting in which captives from other lands, criminals charged with murder, arson, robbery, mutiny, sacrilege, and even lesser offenses, and in some instances freedmen and even members of the equestrian order seeking the adulation of the throngs, fought with each other and with animals.

Soon after they had eaten, however, Caligula and Agrippa with their guests and attendants arose to leave the games.

"I'm glad," Longinus said to Lalage as they stood up. "I've seen enough blood spilled." He smiled wryly. "Have you?"

"Yes, quite enough. I must get ready for tonight, too."

As the Emperor's party moved toward the arched entrance into the palace many of the more curious of Rome pushed nearer to have a better view of the Emperor and shout their fawning acclaim. Longinus and Lalage were walking several paces behind Agrippa's delegation from Jerusalem when near the palace entrance a young man stepped quickly from the throng and clasped the hand of a young Jewish woman moving along slowly a few paces behind Agrippa; in another moment he released her hand and was swallowed in the crowd.

"That girl has an admirer, but he must be bashful," Lalage said. "I wonder if—"

"Let's get down to the street as quickly as we can," Longinus said, ignoring her observation. "Maybe we can hire a sedan chair if we hurry."

## THE CROWN TREE 58

They sat for a while before the fountain in the peristylium, but Longinus was strangely silent, meditative. Lalage reached over and with nail-reddened forefinger gently traced the veins in the back of his bronzed hand resting inertly on his knee.

"You didn't enjoy the games? They bored you?"

"They didn't bore me, but I didn't enjoy them," he answered, looking up. "They angered me. I suppose, Lalage, you think I'm a poor sort of Roman?"

"No, Longinus. But a different sort. Perhaps it's because you have been so long away from Rome."

For a moment he said nothing, as though he hadn't heard her.

"No, I don't think that's the reason," he finally responded, his forehead wrinkling. "I was thinking of that big gladiator those midgets killed. Probably some good-natured stupid fellow from a village in Gaul or the deep forests of Germania, dragged here to Rome to make sport for a silly ruler and an amphitheatre swarming with bloodthirsty, fawning idlers." He looked the girl in the eyes and in his own she saw a mounting perplexity. "Why, Lalage? Here we sit in luxurious comfort while that poor oaf lies dead and forgotten on some scrap heap, a mass of torn and broken bloody flesh and bone. Why? Have you ever stopped to question why the world, the Roman world at any rate, is like that?"

"I suppose I have, at times. But I don't like to, Longinus. After all, it's that way"—she shrugged—"and can we change it— if we wanted to?"

"Of course, if enough of us wanted to—enough. But do we want to, Lalage, as long as we're all-powerful, as long as we can watch poor devils fight and be cut to pieces and eaten by wild beasts rather than have them watch us? But what if it were the other way around? What if we Romans were a weak nation being overrun by soldiers from Gaul and Germania? What if one day a detachment of these soldiers should come to this house, kill Senator Flaccus, and send you and Cornelius off into slavery?"

She shrugged again. "Perhaps I should thank the gods that they willed that Aspasia should be my slave rather than that I should be hers."

"The gods. Ha! A rather weak attempt to rationalize, my dear."

"Then you have little confidence in our Roman gods?"

"I have none, as you know. Does any literate Roman?"

"Only as they choose to use them, I think." Lalage smiled. But quickly she was serious. "I'm glad you're an Epicurean, Longinus, though not a frivolous, libidinous one like Caligula, of course, but a sort of serious one who realizes that tomorrow we die even though perhaps we haven't to the fullest enjoyed today. I'm glad you reject this gods and immortality business. I had begun to fear that your experience in Palestine and your exposure to oriental philosophies had—"

"But did I say I was an Epicurean? Did I say anything about rejecting the belief that life is immortal? Did I tell you—"

"Didn't you just say that you rejected the idea of the gods, Longinus? Didn't you say that all sensible Romans did?"

"I said I had no confidence in Roman gods, and I haven't. They're pale nobodies. But I said nothing about any belief or disbelief in an after existence or the existence of a supreme spirit that rules the universe, an all-wise, all-powerful being—"

"Then you have indeed been contaminated by those oriental superstitions—"

"Why say contaminated, Lalage, and why call such belief superstition?" Longinus seemed to waver between being amused and offended. "You call it oriental and yet my old Greek teacher believed in such a being, an omnipotent, omniscient one-god essentially like the Jehovah of the Jews, and he was an educated, cultured, modern westerner if I ever saw one."

"I wasn't thinking so much of the traditional religion of the Jews," she hastened to assure him. "I thought perhaps you were still afraid of that—" She broke off.

"Of that Jew I crucified," he finished her sentence. "No, Lalage, I no longer fear him, if I ever did. I no longer have nightmares in which the Galilean on the cross haunts me."

"I'm glad, Longinus. You remember I told you that after the shock of that frightful experience faded out with the passing of time you'd forget that fanatical revolutionary—"

"But he wasn't fanatical and he was no revolutionary, Lalage. Nor have I forgotten him. But I don't fear him."

"Why should you fear him, Longinus?" She tried to make her laugh merry. "The man's dead."

He searched out her eyes. "Are you sure he's dead, Lalage? I'm not. On the contrary, I don't think he is. In fact, I'm virtually certain he's just as much alive right now as he was when we nailed him to the crossbeam." A thin smile spread over his face. "Now you must think I'm a queer sort of Roman, perhaps one who's a little disordered"—he tapped his forehead—"up here."

"Of course I don't, Longinus. But you said yourself that you knew he was dead, that you drove your spear into his heart."

"I did, Lalage. I know he *was* dead. When they took him down from the cross he was as dead as any man has ever been, as dead as that big gladiator is right now. But, Lalage, the Jews believe—and many other peoples, too—that although the body dies, the spirit, the essence, lives on. But in the case of this Galilean, according to many witnesses, his body was resurrected; in other words, Lalage, they say he came to life, the third day after he died."

"But, Longinus, you've just heard that; you didn't see him; you have been listening to the stories of his fanatical followers, and they—"

"They aren't fanatics, Lalage," he interrupted, his tone positive. "In many cases they are calm, taciturn people, not given to seeing visions, as the Jews call it. And remember, I've talked myself with quite a number of these people who declared they saw and talked with him. You know I've been stationed with Agrippa at Tiberias, which is in the Galilee region where he lived most of his life and to which he returned, they told me themselves, *after* he was crucified at Jerusalem. On this last tour of duty out there, I've made an effort to talk with as many people as I could who claim to have seen him. They haven't appeared to me to be either lunatics or liars, Lalage; in most cases they were just plain Galileans going about their ordinary tasks. They thrilled at the mention of the Nazarene, but they had no appearance of being fanatics." He paused. "Ask Cornelius; he'll tell you the same thing. He's seen such people at Caesarea and in Jerusalem when he was there on army assignments; they're scattered throughout Palestine, Lalage, and the number of the man's followers is growing rather than diminishing."

"But I understand, Longinus, that King Agrippa is determined to uproot and destroy this sect and to divert Caligula's present hatred of the Jews generally into a ruthless effort to ferret out and kill all those found to be followers of the Galilean. I had hoped that with their disappearance you would lose all fear of that man; in fact, I'd hoped you would entirely forget him."

"I don't *fear* him, Lalage. How can one fear a man, or a god, who dying had no hate for those who were killing him? And ever since that day, though I have fought relentlessly against it, I have been forced more and more to the conclusion—" He paused, apparently searching for the words that would explain his feelings. "It's—it's as though—" He hesitated again. "Well, I'll tell you this, Lalage," he said precipitately, "it's my conviction that neither Agrippa nor Caligula will ever be able to destroy his brotherhood or his teachings."

"By Bona Dea, Longinus," she warned, "be careful where you say this. Should it come to the ears of Caligula, who has fawning spies everywhere, he would be enraged."

The tribune smiled. "I don't intend for Caligula to learn
what I think either of the Galilean or of Caligula. In either case
it would certainly mean for me the Emperor's archers or his
headsman." Now the smile was gone, and again his countenance
was serious. "Lalage, there's hardly been a day since that Galilean was crucified that he hasn't been in my thoughts; you must
know that I have never been able to evade him. And in all the
years since I saw him crucified, since *I* killed him, in all the
searching after knowledge about him and his teachings from
those who were his followers, in all the times he has confronted
me in dreams or nightmares or visitations or whatever they were,
I feel that I have come in some manner at least to know him,
Lalage, to *feel* him. Do my words sound preposterous?" His expression was concerned, pained. He shrugged. "Let me say this,
Lalage: it's my belief that a thousand years from now, when
Agrippa and Caligula have been long forgot, after this Empire
perhaps has passed away, this Galilean's name will be remembered and venerated and throughout the world there will be a
host of men and women bowing down and worshiping him. He
was grounded in truth, he was truth, he *is* truth, Lalage, and how
can one destroy truth? Can an archer's arrow, or a headsman's ax,
or even a cross?"

"Then, Longinus, you believe this Galilean carpenter was also
a divine being?"

A moment his eyes, unblinking, bored into hers. She saw that
her question, blunt, inescapable, had shaken him. "How can I?"
he answered her. "But how can I *not* believe it?"

## THE CROWN TREE 59

Throughout the great dining chamber the drone of many
voices ceased abruptly, for the Emperor was attempting to get to
his feet. A liveried servant standing behind offered to steady him,

but Caligula, suddenly angered, struck him with open hand across the mouth.

"You would have the guests of King Agrippa think their Emperor was dizzy from too much wine, like some ordinary mortal," he screamed at the fellow, who stood stiff and frightened, his face ashen. Caligula swayed against the table, braced himself with left hand clutching the tapestried couch. "I could have you beheaded or shot with arrows for that," he declared, glaring at the servant. Then he turned to face the diners. "I could have you all shot with arrows, or beheaded by my swordsmen, or crucified!" he shouted. Then he threw back his small, half-bald head, thrust forth his bulging stomach, steadied himself on his thin legs. "But I'm not going to do it!" he shrieked, and the stilled chamber reverberated with his giggling. "So don't sit there with your mouths open and fear on your fat faces." He reached over, grasped his wineglass, long-stemmed and fashioned of finest glass from Phoenicia, turned to face the terrified servant. "Here, my good fellow," he said, thrusting the goblet into the man's hand, "I'll show you how a god can forgive. Drink from the glass of your Emperor." The servant's hand shook as he lifted the wine to his lips, hesitated. "Drink! Drink!" Caligula screamed. His leering face twisted into a smile. "Every drop of it."

The servant gulped down the wine. The Emperor took the glass from his hand, set it on the table. "Now fill it again," he commanded, his voice calm, and the man hastened to obey.

Caligula, his hand steady again, fingered the fragile stem. "Here, my good man, have another glass!" he exclaimed, and hurled the shimmering liquid in the fellow's face. Cackling gleefully, so that his sagging stomach shook and his ludicrous head bobbed on the long axis of his neck, the Emperor Gaius Caesar Germanicus, master of the world, slumped again to his couch.

King Agrippa, seated at Caligula's left, quickly was on his feet. He raised high his goblet.

"I propose a toast"—he signaled to the guests to rise, and there was a great stir and rustling of silks and finest linens and satins— "to our beloved lord and protector and friend, the mighty master of the earth, actor incomparable, framer of poetic phrases of deathless beauty, brother of the great Jupiter, that paragon of all virtues, our matchless Gaius, Emperor of Rome, lord of the earth and the stars!"

He lifted the glass to his lips, and the banqueters drank the toast with him, as throughout the great hall arose their thunderous acclaim.

When they had sat down again, Caligula pushed to his feet. His head thrust forward, cormorant-like on his long neck, its skin loose and reddened, he surveyed the diners, and then, his ill-natured countenance softened by a smile that mirrored good will, he faced King Agrippa.

"I have long known, O my beloved Agrippa, what respect and devotion you have for me and have appreciated the great kindness you have shown me, even though it meant hazards to yourself, which you underwent under Emperor Tiberius because of it. Nor have you ever failed to demonstrate your good will toward me, even though it might stretch the limits of your ability." He swept his hand above the board before him. "This great feast tonight is an example. Has there ever been a feast in Rome to equal it? Not in the hundred years since the great Lucullus has ever a board groaned with such a weight of delicacies to tease the surfeited appetite. Foods fetched from every province of the Empire: sea nettles from beyond Neapolis"—he pointed to the golden plate nearby—"fattened fieldfares, their craws bursting with wheat, oysters from the beds of Tarentum, purple shellfish, Phrygian grouse"—his hand swept along the burdened table—"sows' udders, peacocks of Samos, Ionian cranes, tunnyfish, starlings' tongues, boars' heads, fish, ducks, goose livers, pastries, eels —" He paused. "By the gods, there's no end to the variety of Agrippa's bounty." Now he turned again to face the king. "It would be a base thing were I not conquered by your affections, my dear friend. I am desirous, therefore, to make amends to you for everything in which I have failed you heretofore, for all that I have bestowed upon you is but little." Smiling, he placed his hand on Agrippa's shoulder. "But now anything you wish is yours if you but ask me, as far as my ability to obtain it for you may reach. "Speak up, Agrippa! Name your wish!"

"Now's the time"—Longinus, seated with Lalage near the corner of the great U-shaped table where they could look into the faces of the king and the Emperor, whispered into the ear of his companion—"for Agrippa to present that petition about the Emperor's statue."

Agrippa arose, smilingly faced the monarch beside him; his guests, holding their breath, strained to hear his first word.

The king must have sensed the tenseness; for a long moment he stood silent.

Would he ask for lands beyond the Jordan or northward far into Syria? Or gold, or the tribute from conquered lands, or a great palace in Rome in which to live while sojourning in the Empire's capital city?

Then he spoke:

"For your gracious words and noble generosity, O my lord the Emperor of the world, I thank you with all humility. Such is but the mark and measure of the great Gaius, ruler of Rome and the uttermost colonies and kingdoms. But in the days of the late Emperor Tiberius it was not out of any expectation of gain that Agrippa paid his respects to him who unknown to us would shortly sit in the seat of Tiberius. Nor did he arrange tonight's humble occasion in honor of the Emperor with any thought in mind that it would bring advantage to himself or cause the Emperor to bestow upon him any gift of any size or description. For already the gifts are great beyond deserving, and beyond the hopes of even a craving man, and though they be less than you now wish to grant, they are far greater than the worth of him who received them." With a low bow to the Emperor, King Agrippa took his seat on the tapestried couch.

Lalage leaned over, whispered to the tribune: "Do you suppose Agrippa's not going to make his request concerning the statue?"

"The king is clever," Longinus answered. "He understands the Emperor."

"My friend Agrippa is modest and his heart knows no greed," Caligula responded. "It is most unusual and refreshing"—the Emperor paused, smiling, to allow the diners opportunity to appreciate his witticism—"to come upon one of such modest tastes and inclinations as my beloved Agrippa." He bowed ceremoniously to the king. "But I insist that he accept some token of my gratitude and esteem."

King Agrippa arose again, bowed to Gaius. The great chamber still was hushed.

"O my lord the Emperor, since you have expressed your wish and determination to honor your humble subject in such manner, I will ask of you nothing for my personal gain or happiness, since what you have already bestowed has made me excel therein; but I will ask of you something that will make you known gloriously for your piety and will render Deity sympathetic to your designs, and for your subject Agrippa will be a great honor because it will show those concerned about it that Agrippa has never failed to obtain from the Emperor those things that he has sought of him."

The king paused, smiling, his countenance indicating no doubt that the Emperor would grant his request.

"Say on, Agrippa," Caligula demanded, a note of impatience beginning to show in his voice. "By Jupiter my brother, I'll grant your petition."

"It then is this, O my lord: that you will insist no longer on having your statue set up in the Temple in Jerusalem, which you have ordered done by your Proconsul Publius Petronius." Agrippa bowed low to Caligula, resumed his seat.

For a long pause the Emperor said nothing, and the stillness of the great chamber was frightening. Tribune Longinus realized how dangerous was the chance Agrippa had taken. Caligula was obstinate, and excitable. He had set his heart on being worshiped in the great Temple of the Jews alongside their strange and jealous god. Would he forego such honor even at the request of Agrippa? Or would he fly into a fit of uncontrollable anger?

Caligula sat silent a moment, his eyes staring unseeing. Then he clapped his hands together and a servant was beside him. "Fetch me a secretary, with materials for writing," he commanded, his voice strangely calm.

"I wish a letter written to Proconsul Publius Petronius at Antioch in Syria," he said, when the man appeared. And immediately he began dictating. He commended the Proconsul for his energy and promptness in escorting the statue to Jerusalem and setting it in the Temple in event he should have complied already with the Emperor's commands to do so. "If therefore you have already erected my statue, let it stand. But if you have not yet erected it, do not trouble yourself further about it, but dismiss your army, go back, and take care of those affairs which I sent you about in the first place, for I have now no occasion for wishing that the statue be erected." He looked toward Agrippa. "This I have granted as a favor to King Agrippa, a man whom I honor so very greatly that I am not able to contradict what he would have, or what he desired me to do for him."

Now he spoke to the king. "My friend, you have your wish." He turned to the secretary. "That's all. See that the letter goes on the first vessel sailing for Syria."

The secretary bowed, started toward the door. But before he had gone more than a few steps a messenger entered hastily. When he saw the secretary, he thrust a packet into his hand. "A message for the Emperor," he whispered, "just arrived from the Proconsul Publius Petronius in Syria. They say it's urgent and must be—"

"Fetch it here quickly!" Caligula had heard. "Open it!" he commanded. "And wait. It may require an immediate reply. Read it! And speak out!"

The letter began by reporting that the Proconsul had led the troops to Ptolemais. There the Jews had converged and vowed they would die before they would permit the Emperor's statue to be transported to their holy city and set up in the Temple dedicated to their one-god. It went on to recite the story of his visit then to Tiberias, the dire threats he had made against the stubborn Jews, and their repeated vows to die rather than allow their Temple to be profaned by placing in it the statue of the Emperor—

"Profaned! By the gods my brothers, they would call their pile of white stones profaned by the setting up within it of the likeness of the brother of Jupiter! By all the gods great and small—" Caligula sat forward, his hands clenched on the table, and his hollow cheeks began to flame and his deepset eyes to take fire. He pounded his fist with such vehemence that the golden plate stirred. "Go on!" he shouted. "Read his damnable insolence to the end!"

It was soon forthcoming. Petronius related how the chief men of the Jews, even Prince Aristobulus, brother of King Agrippa and friend of the Emperor, had come out on the plain before Tiberias and sworn that the Jews would never relent in their determination to die rather than allow the statue to be placed within the Temple, would bare their necks—

"Aristobulus, my friend! Friend of my youth, brother"—the Emperor's burning eyes sought the paling countenance of King Agrippa—"of my friend who honors me here tonight! Go on! Read, man!"

The letter soon concluded with the announcement by Petronius that he had yielded to the Jews, had ordered his army back into Syria, and was awaiting there further instructions from the Emperor, with the all too blunt recommendation that Gaius countermand his orders concerning the statue and permit the Jews to continue unmolested in the observance of their laws of religion, unless the Emperor was of a mind to lose both the country of the Israelites and the men dwelling within it.

"The Proconsul of Syria would disobey the orders of the Emperor then; he would countermand them!" Caligula smote the heel of his fist on the table. "By Jupiter my brother and all the gods, Publius Petronius, we will see if your insolence is allowed to go unchallenged and unpunished!" His blotched face was livid now, and his hand shook as he waggled a finger at the secretary. "Tear up the letter I just wrote him! Write this instead!"

The secretary hastened to comply.

"Seeing that you esteem the petitions made to you by the Jews of greater value than my commands, and have grown insolent enough to be subservient to their pleasure, I charge you to become your own judge, and consider what you should do now that you are under my displeasure"—Caligula stopped, and the great chamber was deathly still as the diners realized they had just heard the Proconsul of Syria sentenced to a suicide's death—"for I will make you an example to the present and to all future ages" —his voice was shrill, and once more he pointed with shaking forefinger at the man writing—"that henceforth none may dare to contradict the commands of his Emperor!" He settled back on the couch, spent by the passion of his suddenly flamed anger. "Send that letter, and see to it that it goes on the first vessel sailing for Syria."

The secretary bowed, walked quickly to the doorway at the Emperor's back, disappeared through it. Once again not a sound broke the unnatural hush of the great hall. Even the servants pressed back against the walls, fearful of making a sound that might draw the attention of the bitterly angry Emperor.

But now King Agrippa, white-faced and solemn, arose and faced his honor guest.

"O my lord the Emperor, monarch of all the lands and all the seas, allow not your just anger to wax hot against my people of Israel, for they did not urge the Proconsul of Syria to disobey the commands of our Emperor. They besought him only that he would join them in petitioning your Majesty's sufferance in the matter of establishing his statue in their sacred Temple. The people of Israel, though they worship no man but only the God of Israel, gladly acknowledge your Majesty as their lord and earthly ruler." He paused to give emphasis to what he was about to say. "We beg of you, O Sire, to distinguish between the true sons of Israel who worship only Israel's God and that blasphemous sect, Jews likewise, we are distressed to concede, who while refusing to ascribe to our great Gaius the attributes of deity happily prostrate themselves in the worship of a dead revolutionary, a Galilean fanatical carpenter crucified in just penalty for his blasphemy against our God, with whom he called himself equal, and sedition against Rome and her Emperor. We implore you, O Sire, to understand that these fanatics, who bow the knee to this dead Galilean and call him God but refuse all honor to our mighty Gaius, ruler of the world—"

"Enough! Stop!" The Emperor, now in his fury completely sobered it appeared, was on his feet. "You mean to say, King Agrippa, that you have permitted to grow up in your kingdom such a reprehensible band of seditionists as you have just described? You admit that you have not proceeded against them to uproot and destroy utterly them and their contemptible worship?" His eyes were alight with anger and foam was beginning to fleck his lips. Agrippa, plainly frightened, hastened to answer.

"Indeed, O my lord and Emperor, I have proceeded with determination to destroy those of this despicable brotherhood whom my soldiers have been able to ferret out, and I shall continue to destroy them as fast as they are discovered. Already the headsman's block runs red with their blood, and much other blood shall flow until—"

"Then there yet remain in your kingdom a considerable number who refuse me, the brother of Jupiter, the worship I deserve and demand but prostrate themselves before a dead carpenter, crucified on a Roman cross?"

"I suspect, Sire, there yet remain a number of these seditionists, and I shall be eager to assist the Emperor to the utmost of my power in having them discovered and immediately executed. One of these men, a burly fisherman of Galilee, we had arrested and he was confined in the Tower of Antonia, but in some manner made his escape. This fellow we shall capture on our return to Israel and have beheaded forthwith, along with all others of the sect we can ferret out." He hesitated, looked momentarily at the golden plate before him, then raised his eyes again to the furious flaming eyes of Caligula. "But, Sire, there are members of this nefarious brotherhood, reports have come to me, even here in Rome within the very shadow of your Majesty's palace, men who refuse you worship yet fall down before this crucified Nazarene."

Now Caligula did not scream out his denunciations, though his eyes blinked their fury. He seemed even calm, and when he spoke his voice was low and restrained.

"When he is calm and smiling, it bodes no good—"

Lalage's hand on his arm silenced Longinus' whispering; he had not taken his eyes from the monarch's face. Now Caligula was speaking again:

"I do not hold you accountable, my dear Agrippa, for the fact that some of these fanatical seditionists are yet alive, though I charge you to exhaust every means you have in discovering them and eradicating them. Nor was it unknown to me that such persons are thought to be residing in our capital, but I swear by my brother Jupiter and all the gods great and small"—his face was beginning to redden again and his eyes were taking fire—"to find them out, even though they live in the sewers of the Tiber's banks, and destroy them utterly!"

The Emperor started to resume his seat on his couch, but then he straightened again, lifted his sagging stomach, and looked straight into the still sobered countenance of his host as a sinister leer overspread his own.

"Stories have come to me, my dear Agrippa," he said, smiling crookedly, "that this seditious fellowship of late has been able to penetrate even into the households of the great in your kingdom of Israel." He waggled his lean forefinger almost in Longinus' face. "It may be, King Agrippa"—now his voice was rising sharply—"that you have fetched, even though unwittingly, some of these carpenter-worshipers with you to Rome. It may be"—he was almost screaming—"that some of them even sit here with us tonight!" He paused, and a deadly stillness blanketed the dining chamber, so that the frightened diners could hear the Emperor's labored breathing. Then his sickly smile softened his scowling. "Speak, Agrippa," he said, his voice calm once more.

"O Sire, your Majesty need have no concern for the loyalty of these who have come from Palestine to join with me in our humble petitioning," the king responded. "They are of the finest blood in Israel; they represent the great Sanhedrin and the Temple leadership, even the High Priest and those who uphold his hands." His face relaxed somewhat and with a quick gesture he pointed to a young woman seated across from him at one of the wings flanking the host's table. "We have brought such ones even as the beautiful niece of the present High Priest and the grand-daughter of the pious and learned noble Annas, former High Priest. All these persons are true Israelites, O mighty Gaius, and with singleness of heart they worship the God of Israel, give allegiance to our beloved Emperor, and curse all who would blaspheme the Name."

"The girl's face is white; she's frightened," Lalage observed.

"What decent woman wouldn't be—if she's beautiful—finding herself pointed out to that lecherous Caligula?"

"But I thought that perhaps—"

But Lalage said no more, for the Emperor, his voice rising again, was not satisfied with Agrippa's pronouncement. The Jews were a crafty people, he told their king; they were jealous of their Roman overlords and resented the interference of Rome in their affairs; they might well be concealing allegiances inimical to Rome and the Emperor.

"It is my command, therefore, O King Agrippa," he concluded, more calmly, "that you examine these Jews you have fetched to Rome and see if there be any among them who while refusing me worship bow their knees to the dead Galilean."

"It is a reasonable command, O my beloved Gaius," Agrippa replied, his face ashen, "and I shall do so and report to the Emperor as soon as he arises on the morrow."

"No!" screamed Caligula, "now! This moment! We shall not leave this chamber, Agrippa, until they have been examined! Guards, let no one leave!" He paused, and in lowered tones spoke again to the king: "Proceed, Agrippa. Call the name of each Jew present and ascertain if he will curse or adore the name of this Galilean. But first, I shall examine you, Agrippa, that none may be overlooked, and then you shall examine the others."

"Proceed, then, O mighty Gaius," answered Agrippa solemnly. "I have nothing, O Sire, to conceal."

"I have but this one question to ask you, O my beloved King Agrippa: Do you worship as a god that Galilean, executed during the reign of the late Emperor Tiberius, whom some depraved ones bow down to as deity?"

"O beloved Gaius, I do not worship this man! On the contrary, I have sought diligently to stamp out the nefarious sect that bows knee to him, and to erase his very name from the memory of Israel!"

"Very well, my dear friend. I knew what answer you would make. Now examine these whom you have brought from Palestine."

Agrippa bowed. Then he looked along the board, called the name of one of the delegation. The man, a squat Jew with a heavily oiled beard, arose and the king put to him the question he himself had been asked by the Emperor.

"I am of the line of the great King David. I worship none save the God of Israel." He bowed and sat down.

Agrippa called another name, and the Jew, tall and sparse, stood up. The king asked the question.

"I worship only God," he said. "I spit upon the name of this Galilean blasphemer!" He sat down.

Agrippa one by one called each man's name and each in turn, with some vehemence, denied allegiance to the crucified Jesus of Nazareth. When the last man had sat down, King Agrippa turned to the Emperor.

"You have heard, O Sire. Are you now content?"

"The women. You haven't examined the women."

"The women, O Sire?" Agrippa managed a thin smile. "In our land of Israel the men speak for all. I hadn't thought—"

"But this is Rome, my friend!" Caligula said it sharply. "Let those women speak for themselves and tell us what they believe concerning this Galilean!"

One by one as he had examined the men the king now questioned the women. But he did not call the name of Damaris.

"You have heard, O mighty Gaius," he said, and resumed his seat.

"But you did not question the young woman of whom a moment ago you spoke," Caligula observed.

"She is the niece of the High Priest and the granddaughter of the former High Priest Annas," Agrippa responded. "They are the most determined enemies of the Galilean's followers. And too, O Sire, she is unmarried. In Israel a woman unmarried is—"

"Examine her!" shouted the Emperor. "None will be overlooked. I have little faith in any Jew, even your High Priest himself!"

Agrippa nodded to the girl, and she arose. Lalage, watching her, saw her sway, but she quickly braced herself against the table and faced the king.

"Speak, O niece of the great High Priest of Israel and granddaughter of our noble Annas; tell our mighty Gaius, ruler of the earth and the heavens: Do you bow down to that dead Galilean, one Jesus of the village of Nazareth, a blasphemer and revolutionary against the good order of Israel and the Roman Empire?"

Damaris hesitated an instant and her black eyes sought the king's.

"I worship no dead Galilean and no revolutionary against Israel or Rome and no blasphemer against our God," she answered, her head erect, her countenance now calm, relaxed. "But I am a follower, though an unworthy one, of the Lord Jesus Christ, who lived in Nazareth, was crucified under the authority of Rome, but who arose from the tomb and ascended to live at the right hand of God the Father. Him, O King Agrippa, I worship in pride and with great love!" Smiling, she sat down.

Not a sound disturbed the frightful silence of the cavernous chamber. Then Agrippa, surprise and fright plain upon his bearded face, licked his red lips, swallowed. "I swear, O mighty Caligula, beloved ruler of the universe, I knew not—"

"Blasphemy! Blasphemy!"

"Death to this blasphemer! She disgraces the High Priest! She disgraces all Israel!"

"Blasphemer! She deserves stoning! O mighty Emperor, she speaks not for Israel!"

Along the table the bearded sons of Israel now were screaming their denunciations. But Caligula, his pimpled, splotched face inflamed almost to bursting, seemed not to be hearing the babbling of the angry and desperately frightened Jews. His eyes, fiery bright, were held an instant on the serene face of the Israelitish girl. Then he turned to look along the table beyond Agrippa.

"Silence, you Jews!" His voice was shrill, angry. The solemn, silent diners thought the young madman was about to fall into a fit of screaming, uncontrollable rage. Instantly the Jewish guests ceased their denunciations, and once more the great chamber was deathly quiet. Caligula, all eyes now on him, leaned out across the table, pointed a shaking forefinger at the girl. Then his eyes shifted toward the section where the officers of the Praetorian Guard sat.

"Tribune Chaerea!" the Emperor screamed out. "Take that woman into the courtyard and behead her! Now! Choose a detail and proceed immediately with the execution!"

"By Bona Dea, Longinus, the poor—"

Longinus squeezed her hand on the couch beside him, and glancing up into his face, she saw that he was pale and now his hand shook. She looked toward the guardsmen and saw that the tall Tribune Chaerea had arisen. In an instant he summoned several of his men and they stepped into the open way between the tables and began advancing toward Damaris, who seemed strangely unconcerned, Lalage saw. She was about to whisper something to Longinus when King Agrippa, his countenance plainly revealing his alarm, arose and faced the Emperor.

"O Sire, have mercy!" he pleaded. "Give this girl an opportunity to recant her shameful confession. Her uncle is High Priest in Israel. The effect in our land of beheading the niece of the High Priest—O Sire, think of the effect upon Rome's subjugated little Israel—" He broke off, for the Emperor, his whole thought centered apparently on the advancing guardsmen, appeared not to have heard him.

But then Caligula spoke. "Hold!" he shouted to Chaerea. "Return to your seats, for the moment."

Instantly the guardsmen turned about, and the Emperor faced the king his host beside him.

"This woman will never recant," he said, a heavy scowl darkening his pimpled red face. "Nor do I care what effect her execution will have in your dreary land, Agrippa." He had heard the king's plea. "For half a denarius I would put to the sword all the Jews in Palestine and Publius Petronius with them!" He stood up, surveyed the king's silent, frightened guests, turned to stare with fearsome frowning upon the line of Jewish petitioners beyond Agrippa. "The Jewish race is an abomination upon the earth, a stench in the nostrils of Rome. Look at me, you Jews!" he thundered, and the silent Israelites raised their heads from their plates. "You shall worship me yet! My statue will stand in your white pile of stones at Jerusalem, in the very center of your Holy of Holies, by my brother Jupiter and all the gods, I swear it!" Now he looked down upon the king beside him. "Agrippa, you have failed me, my friend, though I am sure you meant me no ill. You remain my friend and confidant. But my order concerning the statue must be obeyed, though I will not force upon you the task of seeing that it is obeyed." His eyes surveyed the diners.

"Tribune Longinus"—he had spotted the king's aide—"this task I place upon you, with full authority to carry it out if it means the death of every Jew in Palestine!" Longinus had arisen. "By all the gods, it is an omen! You are a happy choice. I have been told that it was you who crucified that Galilean revolutionary." He lifted a long forefinger, waved it like a serpent's tongue in the tribune's direction. "Tell me, Tribune, what sort of fellow was he? Was he entirely mad? Did he recant his fanatical teachings before he died?"

"On the contrary, O our beloved Emperor," Longinus replied evenly, his eyes level with the Emperor's, "Jesus of Nazareth was perhaps the sanest man I have ever encountered, and without a doubt the most courageous."

Caligula's mouth dropped open. For a long moment he stared unbelieving at the tribune. "By Jupiter my brother," he said, when he had recovered his voice, "can it be that you, an officer

in the army of Rome, a son of Senator Varro, would defend this
rebel carpenter of Galilee, this inciter to riot, this—this—" He
paused, his face flaming anew.

"He was not a rebel, O mighty Gaius," Longinus answered, his
voice calm, "nor was he one who incited to riot. He was falsely
accused, unfairly tried by Pontius Pilate, whom you rightfully
deposed, and was illegally condemned. I saw him tried, I led him
out to the Hill of the Skull, it was the thrust of my lance in his
side that killed him. He died, I know, and yet I know also, O
mighty Emperor, that the Lord Jesus arose from the tomb and
yet lives!"

The hall was hushed and every amazed eye was upon Longinus.
Caligula was smiling now, as he surveyed the tall and erect
tribune from head to foot.

"The Lord Jesus, you say, Tribune. The *Lord* Jesus. Then you
acknowledge this crucified Galilean to be your lord and yourself
his subject?"

The Emperor's smile was pleasant and his manner amiable, and
his voice was smooth and agreeable. The hushed throng about the
tables knew what that meant. Fearful, they awaited the reply
of Senator Varro's son.

"Since the day I crucified him, O great Caesar," Longinus replied, his tone calm and modulated, "I have sought to escape
him. But he has continued day and night to pursue me. Not in
anger or seeking vengeance, O my lord the Emperor, but in love
and understanding he has sought to bind me to himself." His
eyes, calm now and unafraid, swept the head table, rested an
instant on King Agrippa and various ones of the delegation from
Jerusalem, then across to Damaris, farther on to Senator Varro
and to Senator Flaccus seated beside his father, and paused a moment upon the Centurion Cornelius, and then he glanced down
smiling into the frightened eyes of Lalage. Quickly his eyes were
again upon Caligula. "You are my earthly lord and Emperor and
to you I continue to pledge my loyalty as a true son of Rome," he
declared. "But the Lord Jesus, I gladly proclaim, is my spiritual
lord and master, O Gaius, and to him I bow my knee in worship

and devotion." He raised his eyes toward the vaulted high ceiling. "O my Lord Jesus, I can flee from you no longer." Then in utter serenity he faced the Emperor.

"He's insane, O mighty Gaius, brother of the gods!" Senator Varro was on his feet, his face white, his lips trembling. "Long years in those hot lands in the company of those superstitious, insufferable Jews have addled his brain. Pay him no heed, O beloved Gaius; hold not against him his ranting—"

"Silence! Take your seat, Varro!" Caligula hunched forward, thrust forth his long arm, forefinger pointing, toward the uniformed son of Senator Flaccus.

"And you, Centurion Cornelius, you have just returned from that damnable province. Are you likewise infected with this evil disease out of Palestine? Speak! Do you too worship this crucified troublemaker?"

Cornelius got quickly to his feet, faced the Emperor with countenance untroubled. "I am a son of Rome, O mighty Gaius. Like Longinus, I have long served in her army, and to her Emperors, both Tiberius and yourself, O great Gaius, I have been loyal and faithful, and I shall continue so. But in the world of the spirit I am likewise a subject of our beloved Lord Jesus. I stand with Longinus my brother in the fellowship of the Nazarene, and I praise God that this night Longinus has taken his stand with us."

In the awesome silence of the great chamber the Emperor's host arose, white of countenance and trembling, and endeavored to speak quieting words.

"What Senator Varro has just said, O my dear friend of the many years, must be true, not only of Longinus but also of the Centurion Cornelius. They have both been under great strain. They have labored with loyalty and devotion for the advancement of Rome and Rome's mightiest of Emperors. Nothing else can explain this strange departure from sanity. Yet I must intercede for them, O most illustrious Gaius, particularly for Longinus, who has served me faithfully, who even saved my life in the days when I was a prisoner of your predecessor. I pray you, O

Gaius, friend of my younger days, listen to me now and close your ears to their desperate words. Allow me time, O my dear friend and lord, to talk with Longinus, to reason with him, to plead—"

"Quiet! Cease your petitioning!" Caligula waved a soft white hand, but his voice was natural once more and restrained. "I hold none of this against you, Agrippa, my dear friend," he said. "And I understand that this tribune has served you well in the days of your confinement and since. But my ears are deaf to your pleas tonight, even though on other occasions your eloquent words have won me. I cannot grant this boon you ask. These men are Roman soldiers. They are sworn to uphold Rome and Rome's Emperor." His voice was rising. "Of Romans I require that they bow to me their knees as one in the pantheon of gods. Am I not equal in majesty with my brother Jupiter? Yet these Romans"— he pointed toward them and his voice was shrill and angry—"not only refuse me worship but joyfully bow down to a crucified rebellious evil Galilean, an enemy of their land and their Emperor, a disturber of the peace—" He grabbed his wineglass and hurled it to the marble floor. "No! No! Agrippa, say not another word! I warn you, push me no further or I lose my patience!" Foam was flecking his thin lips, blood-red and trembling in his mounting rage. "Tribune Chaerea, summon your detail and drag these two traitors and the woman forth to the courtyard and with your swords cut them to pieces!"

Immediately the grim-faced Chaerea arose and with solemn nods designated the detail from his seated guardsmen; when it was completed the soldiers formed a hollow square in the opening before the tables and in cadenced step behind the tribune started toward Longinus.

"No! No! By all the gods, no, O Gaius!" screamed Lalage, as Longinus arose. "You must not, O beloved Gaius, you cannot do this! They have done you no injury." Her tone now was desperately pleading. She clutched at the tribune's hand, sought to pull him down again to the couch. "You do not understand, O Sire. They love Rome and you; they acknowledge you as their lord and Emperor. This other man, this Nazarene, is only their spiritual leader; he seeks not to overthrow Rome's government or her mighty Emperor; he's only—"

"*I* do not understand, says the daughter of Senator Flaccus; *I*, the brother of Jupiter, the ruler of the world, am an imbecilic fool, eh? But the beautiful daughter of the Senator is all-wise; *she* is the paragon of wisdom as well as beauty; *she* knows more than her Emperor; she's—"

"No, O beloved Gaius," the girl interrupted the brother of Jupiter, "beside my Emperor I am utterly ignorant. But I have heard both Longinus and Cornelius talk of this Galilean, of his courage, his compassion, his godlike attributes—"

"Then you too believe him to be a god, you likewise have become infected with this Palestinian malady?" Caligula interrupted, his scowl darkening. He reached for the new goblet a servant had brought and filled, and his hand shook as he fingered the fragile stem. "You too put him in a realm above your Emperor? You also bow your knee to him?" His voice now was shrill, angry. "Speak, daughter of Flaccus!"

"I never saw him, O mighty Gaius." Her tone now was as calm as his was agitated. "I only know him through Longinus and Cornelius and—certain others. For a long time I too scorned him and sought to induce my beloved"—her glance lifted quickly to rest momentarily on the strangely relaxed countenance of Longinus—"and my brother to forget him, to cast from their minds all thought of him. But I failed, and here of late, since they have returned this last time from Palestine, I have had the Nazarene much in my thoughts. He must have been the personification of all virtues, O Sire"—her tone had changed again to one of reasoning, pleading—"a completely good man who ruled, and still rules, in the realm of the spirit world—if there is such a world, O Gaius—where you rule the material world, where you command—"

"Silence! Cease your prattling! I will have no more of this foolish talk of two realms and two rulers!" Caligula's mottled face was livid. "Choose, daughter of Flaccus! Choose between us! Curse this dead carpenter and your traitorous tribune and brother, or take them and reject me, your Emperor, brother of Jupiter and ruler of the world and the stars!" He stabbed a shaking finger toward Lalage. "Choose, I command you!"

The girl looked up into the face of Longinus, and a smile trembled on her lips as the tense, hushed diners watched breathlessly. Then she arose and took the tribune's arm.

"I stand, O Sire, with Longinus—and his God!"

They expected it and feared it, but the Emperor did not fly into an uncontrollable rage. For a long moment he studied her flushed face, and a relaxing, pleasant expression overcame the scowling; then he spoke and his voice once more was unhurried, almost conversational:

"It is a shameful thing to destroy beauty, and what is more delectable than a perfectly formed woman, fit indeed for the Emperor's bed, her beauty enhanced by anger and fear? It is an even greater shame and misfortune when such a woman deliberately destroys herself." Still calm, Caligula turned his head slightly to face the Tribune Chaerea who with the others of the detail had paused respectfully in the center of the square between the tables during the colloquy of the girl and the Emperor. "Tribune Chaerea, proceed to carry out my command. Seize also the daughter of Senator Flaccus and in the courtyard with the other three hack her to pieces with your swords!"

Unhurriedly he lifted the goblet and drank. When he had drained the glass he set it down gently and looked along the board at the frigidly impassive countenances of the diners until his gaze was fixed on the tear-drenched face of Senator Flaccus. The Senator was attempting to rise from his couch, but Senator Varro beside him, his eyes red and streaming, restrained him, whispered in his ear.

Caligula's sudden amused cackling shattered the hush that had been broken only by the measured tread of the soldiers and their four prisoners advancing toward the opening in the square of tables. Then, as he reached for the goblet again and lifted it, he centered his attention on the retreating detail. When Chaerea neared the door, the Emperor suddenly stood up, shouted:

"Hold, Tribune Chaerea! Halt your prisoners! Face them about."

Instantly his command was obeyed. Caligula for a long moment studied the doomed four, and his narrow, sensual face reddened and the color mounted upward to his flaring ears.

"I've changed my mind," he said. "A quick death in the courtyard is not sufficient punishment for traitors against Rome and the Emperor. Nor would such a death, seen perhaps by only a few persons, have the proper effect. You should be required to die slowly, in agony long drawn out, before a great multitude. Such a death for each of you, witnessed by countless Romans, should serve to deter others from the commission of crimes of comparable enormity." He paused now, and the soft, disarming smile played on his ugly pustuled face. "I have decided, therefore, to decree your deaths as the final act of tomorrow's closing gladiatorial games." For an instant he was silent as the four stared imperturbably at him. "You have supported sedition against your nation and your ruler," he began again, his voice rising. "You have rejected your Emperor, refused him the worship he is due, and chosen to worship a man, a ranting fanatical seditionist, a homeless poor carpenter of Galilee long dead and rotted. You have chosen him and rejected me, you have scorned my protection and sought his. Tomorrow then, when you are being mangled and torn"—he pointed to Lalage—"and your luscious flesh eaten by ravenous dogs as the multitude screams its delight, call upon this dead carpenter to deliver you! By Jupiter my brother and all the gods"—he raised aloft his arm, fist clenched—"let your crucified Galilean save you, O you fools, and run me through with Chaerea's sword"—he pointed to the tribune's gleaming long weapon —"if he can!" He waved his long arm imperiously. "Take them to the Palace dungeons! Now!"

Chaerea turned precipitately and the small procession moved toward the door. Behind him the tribune heard the wild cackling silly laughter of the madman Emperor, and glancing backward, he was not surprised to see the mighty Gaius, brother of Jupiter and ruler of the world, jigging beside the still laden board, his punished sagging paunch swaying and bobbing. Then of a sudden Caligula stopped dancing, his raucous cackling softened into inane giggling, and he sank to his couch to drop his head face downward on the table against one of the golden plates. His right arm flung out caught the tall wineglass and sent it spinning and rolling to crash tinkling on the marbled mosaic. Quickly the darkly red smear of the wine spread along the white cover to run down and pour in a thin round stream on the pieces of the shattered goblet.

From where he was, the thought came suddenly to the Tribune Chaerea, the wine looked like a man's blood.

## THE CROWN TREE 60

In the blackness of his bedchamber in the home of his kinsmen on Janiculum Hill Joseph Barnabas lay wide-eyed and sleepless. He could not rid his mind of a foreboding that ill would come of his beloved's attending the great banquet given by the opportunist Agrippa for the licentious and pagan Emperor Gaius.

"It's no place for a good daughter of Israel to be," he said to Luke, who lay on a mat beside him, "breaking bread with pagans and evildoers whose hands are foul with their misdeeds."

"But she came to Rome for the purpose of serving Israel's God and the people of Israel, did she not, Joseph?" Luke asked him. "And if in so doing she must dine with pagans and sinners, will then the God of Israel condemn her? I think not. Nor would Saul of Tarsus disapprove of her course, in my opinion. And Saul is a Hebrew of Hebrews, is he not?"

But Luke likewise was troubled. He had been several times to the mansion of Senator Flaccus on Quirinal Hill and had seen Aspasia, but though Lalage had been pleasant she had remained adamant in her refusal to grant Aspasia manumission.

Joseph Barnabas had exhorted him to continue to pray to the

God of Israel and His Messiah and to maintain a steadfast faith in the love of God, and to rest in the assurance of His protection.

"I pray long, Joseph, as best I know how, for I am young in the faith, a veritable stripling among my elders," he had answered, "and I reach out and grasp for faith and seek to hold it fast, but I am weak. If I but had the faith of Saul or rugged Simon, if I but had them here—" He had broken off abruptly. "That gives me a thought, Joseph," he said after a moment, "and it is this: we must each strengthen the other's faith and strive to trust our Lord Messiah."

So they had talked long past midnight and had hardly dozed, it seemed, when two hours before dawn they were awakened by a gentle rapping on the door. Barnabas answered it.

The early visitor was Sextus. Barnabas took him into the bedchamber, lighted a candle, introduced Luke.

"I have heard Centurion Cornelius speak of you—and well—my brother," Sextus said.

"And I likewise have heard from Barnabas here a good report of you, Brother Sextus. What news do you have of Cornelius? When have you seen him?"

In the feeble flickering of the candle they saw his expression change.

"It's about Cornelius"—he said, apparently striving to maintain an even tone—"and the others—Longinus and his beloved, Senator Flaccus' daughter Lalage, and the Jewish young woman from Jerusalem who—"

"Damaris?" Joseph's countenance was paling. "Has any evil overtaken her? I knew she shouldn't have gone to the King's banquet. I—speak, Sextus!"

"I am sent by the Tribune Chaerea, commander of the Palace guards. But first, let me assure you that no harm has befallen the four—yet. And if our plans are successful, no injury will come to them. Chaerea sent me to tell you what arrangement is being made for rescuing them and what you can do to help carry out—"

"To rescue them? Then they're in bonds?"

"Yes, in the dungeons beneath the Palace."

Quickly he related what had happened earlier at the king's banquet for Gaius. Barnabas and Luke, aghast, shocked, sat silent.

"Now this is what Chaerea and the others plan," he said, when he had finished his recital. "But first, let me warn you"—he looked at one and then the other, his forehead crinkling—"not to say anything about this to anyone—not one word, remember —concerning anything I tell you. Is this understood?"

Each nodded solemnly.

"Tomorrow the Emperor is to be assassinated!"

"The Emperor of Rome! Assassinated!"

"Yes. Certain ones in the Praetorian Guard have been planning it for a long time. We had schemed to kill him on the opening day of the games, but our plans miscarried and we had to postpone it. But after what happened last night, we can't delay any longer. Longinus and Cornelius and the two young women know of the plot; Chaerea has told them. They will help us, of course, all they can."

Then he related in detail Chaerea's plans. The attempt on the Emperor's life would be made in one of the corridors of the Palace as Caligula was going from the games in midafternoon for refreshment or to rest briefly, as was his custom. As soon as he had been put to the sword the prisoners would be released and it would be the task of Luke and Barnabas to rush the women from the Palace and hide them in the house on Janiculum Hill.

"Should anything go amiss afterwards and friends of Caligula get control of the government they'd never think of looking for Lalage in a Jewish home," Sextus added.

"But Damaris?" Barnabas showed his concern. "Wouldn't they expect to find her on Janiculum Hill?"

"Perhaps, if they thought to seek her out. But they would be more likely to seek vengeance against the Romans. At any rate, we can't now change Chaerea's plans. The only thing to do is follow instructions—and pray to our Lord Jesus to give success to our scheming."

Then he gave them Chaerea's instructions:

"Go early tomorrow to the gladiatorial games and get seats as close as you can to the Emperor's box. Watch him carefully, though take pains to excite no suspicion, and when he and his party leave for the customary afternoon recess, try to slip out behind him in the rear of his guests and follow them into the corridor between the amphitheatre and the Palace."

He glanced about, intuitively lowered his voice.

"It is in one of the Palace corridors that he will be killed," he went on. "We will set upon him with our swords and slay him before his German guards can be rallied. Some of our group will be assigned stations along the passageways, because Chaerea will have charge of the guards. The tribune will approach him in routine fashion and ask him to assign a password for the next day, which is the Emperor's habit. Caligula will likely utter some obscene word, for that is his usual practice. Chaerea will then spring on him with his sword and those stationed nearby will join Chaerea."

"But how will the killing of the Emperor serve the four prisoners? When the slaying of the Emperor has been discovered, as it must be almost immediately, won't the Emperor's friends be incensed and turn on the four and kill them?"

"If our plan miscarries, Luke, yes. But we'll have to get them out of the cells before the German guards arrive. That has been arranged. The doors will be unlocked. And that's where you must help. The moment the women are freed, you'll lead them quickly from the Palace and bring them here, where all of you must remain in hiding until you are notified that it is safe to come out again."

Carefully he revealed to them what passages to follow in reaching the dungeon cells and from there how to find their way quickly along other corridors to a doorway opening upon a narrow and little traveled side street.

"But, Sextus, what will you do if the Emperor decides not to go out for a recess or chooses to put them into the arena earlier than he now plans?"

"If that happens and he calls for them, then we'll rush into

the imperial box and attempt to kill him. And if we fail—" He
smiled grimly. "But we won't fail." He stood up. "Soon it will be
dawn. I must leave. Remember your instructions." He paused.
"And pray, brothers."

Barnabas followed him to the doorway, let him out into the
darkness.

## THE CROWN TREE 61

Once again a roaring, gesticulating multitude poured through
the gates into the great amphitheatre in front of the Imperial
Palace. This was the final day of the games. And the Emperor
had promised, so the word had swept through Rome, that today's
events would surpass all previous ones in originality, lavishness,
and bloodletting.

What difference did it make to this howling horde if the
wastrel young Emperor had impoverished the Empire's treasury,
what did these pleasure-mad Romans care if he had robbed the
Senate of its privileges and powers and slain many of its members, what mattered it to them if he ruled without reason or
mercy, deciding issues of paramount importance on a moment's
caprice? Hadn't Caligula given them gladiatorial contests unsur-
passed in Rome's history? Hadn't he provided more animals,
more men, more novelties of agonized death-dealing, more blood,
than any former monarch?

So today they packed the tiers rising above tiers around the
vast marble circle. And in the throng, seated where they could
almost touch the railing of the imperial box, were Joseph Barnabas and Luke the physician. They watched as the Emperor
came into the lavishly festooned section, accompanied by his
guests, aides, and servants, and a detachment of tall blond mus-
cular youths, his personal guards from the forests of Germania,
and with an ostentatious sweep of his arm acknowledged the
screaming adulation of the multitude.

Caligula seemed in excellent spirits. He bowed and saluted and waved his white hands as he arose to offer the sacrifice to the late Caesar Augustus. With him at the altar were priests and a group of white-robed young women.

"The Vestal Virgins," Luke whispered to Barnabas.

And when near the end of the ceremony one of the priests stumbled while removing a vessel of warm blood from the slit throats of two lambs and a young ox and bespattered the resplendent toga of a pompous senator, the Emperor even laughed uproariously.

"On another day, Vatinius," the two heard a patrician behind them remark, "the Emperor might have held that priest's awkwardness not only an affront to Senator Asprenas but also to Augustus."

"Maybe Caligula holds the memory of Augustus as lightly as he does the good will of the Senator," the man beside him suggested. "I wonder if that blood spilled on old Asprenas is an omen?"

In another moment the great doors on the arena level were thrown open and once more the sanded floor was filled with heavily armed men marching toward the Emperor's box. Quickly they saluted him, divided into pairs, and in the next instant the blood-mad thousands were roaring and screeching their pleasure as swords rang against swords and from gaping great wounds red blood spurted and poured out on the darkening sands as men from many nations, sinking to the now fouled arena's floor to twist and convulse and cry out their agony unheard, died friendless and alone in the midst of the great throng.

Barnabas sat sickened to his depths as he thought of what the afternoon might bring. . . . Save them, O God, protect her from this monster, this unfeeling pagan fiend. . . .

The Emperor did not leave the box for the luncheon intermission. Again an elaborate meal was served him and his guests.

"That's good," whispered Luke. "He'll be more likely to wish a recess. And then—" But he said no more, smiled grimly. "Don't cease praying, Joseph."

Caligula ate quickly, and when he gave the signal for the games to be resumed, the master of ceremonies stepped forward, raised his arms for silence. Immediately the trumpeters blew a long blast.

The official announced that the nature of the games was being changed for the afternoon's program. Instead of mass killing, a refinement in the art of dispatching condemned criminals would be offered. The first event would be a presentation of the ancient story of Orpheus and Eurydice, with two slaves who had killed their overseer taking the roles of the mythological sweet singer and his wife and a Thracian who had broken his chains and fled from a Roman galley acting the part of Pluto, ruler of Hades.

"Good! Marvelous!" The Emperor clapped his hands and his small head bobbed. "We're going to have a drama!" Joyfully he slapped the fat cheek of a senator on his right. "I'm a great one for plays!" And the thousands in the stands, seeing Caligula's delight, thundered their approval.

Quickly Moorish slaves brought out large wooden sections which they set upright to represent the walls of Pluto's subterranean palace. In its center they placed an ornate couch, as other slaves brought small trees which had been fastened to supports; these they arranged to simulate a dense grove.

Their preparations completed, the slaves went out and in an instant returned with three sedan chairs, their curtains drawn. Two they carried into the palace of Pluto and the third into the grove. Then the empty chairs, their recent occupants not yet revealed, were removed from the arena, the doors were closed, and the trumpeter blared a fanfare.

Barnabas, venturing a look over his shoulder, saw the Emperor, his face propped in his hands, his elbows on the railing, staring straight ahead.

. . . Can he be thinking of still another refinement in killing? O God, protect them! Save her, O our Lord Messiah! . . .

Orpheus was the first to appear. He came walking from the clump of greenery bearing a lyre. He was a blond youth, perhaps from Germania, Luke surmised, close-shaven and bathed and oiled, and he wore a white toga thrown over his left shoulder that circled his waist to fall to his knees. He began to strum the strings lightly, and immediately musicians in the bands, joining in, swelled the volume until the music was heard to the topmost tiers.

But another figure had appeared; a few paces away Pluto had stepped to the center of the improvised palace chamber. He raised his hands straight above his head, turned his gaze upward as if seeking to see beyond the dark realms of his lower kingdom or perhaps to appeal for help to his pagan gods, and then, lowering his arms and beating with his fists his great hairy chest, he bellowed like a frightened bull.

"Hardly a dignified way to portray a Roman god, eh, Vatinius?" one of the men behind Luke and Barnabas whispered.

His companion laughed. "Maybe he knows Eurydice is on her way to visit him." He clapped a hand on the other's knee. "But I know little of the habits of the gods."

At that moment Eurydice came out from the smaller chamber and bowed to the god of the underworld. This slave appeared also to be a youth, either so young that he was almost beardless or closely shaven and with his face rubbed with creams and powdered. His wig of golden brown hair fanned out to his shoulders and was garlanded above his ears with a ringlet of flowers. But more startling was the stola of soft blue silk, it appeared to be, held at the waist by a wide girdle of crimson, perhaps velvet. Over the stola Eurydice wore a cloak of shimmering goldcloth.

Pluto advanced to meet Eurydice, while from the grove Orpheus, still strumming his lyre, moved slowly toward Pluto's palace.

The god of the underworld bowed low to the wife of Orpheus, ceremoniously removed from about her shoulders the golden cloak, laid it carefully across the back of the elaborately adorned couch. Then he took her hands in his and slowly pulled her to him in a crushing embrace.

"Great! Tremendous! Marvelously done!" The Emperor had stood up, was clapping his hands together, his head bobbing this way and that.

Now the god of the underworld and Eurydice were seated on the couch and it appeared that Pluto was about to make violent love to the wife of the lyre player.

"Caligula will be shouting again in a moment," the man behind them observed, as Barnabas listened, "because he thinks there'll be something obscene. He wallows in filth."

The man had hardly stopped speaking when the Emperor was applauding furiously once more, for Pluto with little gentleness had pushed Eurydice's white shoulders, now stripped of the stola, back on the silken couch and the wife of the singer Orpheus was scratching and pummeling and kicking realistically to free herself from the unwanted ardent advances of the lower world lover.

But suddenly Pluto loosened his hold on Eurydice and sat up, listening intently, and then quickly arose to his feet, for the charms of the woman could in no way match the sweet strains from the lyre. The god of the lower world opened the door, bowed to Orpheus. The lyre player, bowing, entered and ceremoniously greeted his wife, who had put her stola in order and had arisen. Now Orpheus and Pluto gesticulated a moment, and Pluto bowed to Orpheus and then to Eurydice. Orpheus started toward the door, still strumming the strings, and Pluto motioned to her to follow her husband.

"Do you know this story, Joseph?" Luke asked.

Barnabas shook his head.

"When there's time, I'll tell it to you," Luke answered. "It's amazing how faithfully these doomed men are following the mythological story." He turned to look again toward the arena.

Orpheus and Eurydice had reached the edge of the grove. He was still strumming the lyre and the bands were playing a swelling accompaniment. Nor had the blond slave, true to the ancient myth, looked back.

The roaring began in the arena's entranceway beneath the tier of benches off right. Quickly it was drowned in a screaming frenzy as thousands around the marble bowl leaped to their feet.

Then Luke and Barnabas saw the lions.

They came running out to the center of the arena from the

gateway that had just closed behind them, and for an instant they seemed startled by the uproar of the spectators. Great lanky beasts, they were half-starved and ravenous, and as two of the males, their manes almost touching the sanded floor, broke from the pack and came running toward the Emperor's box, those seated in the first rows screamed. But the Moorish slaves, armed with long poles tipped with sharp spikes, quickly turned them back.

It was then that the lions first saw the lyre player and the slave following him in the woman's costume. Roaring, they made for the grove.

Orpheus stopped, looked back. One of the lions, attracted no doubt by the vivid blue of the stola, crouched and sprang. The lyre player, like Orpheus of mythology, saw his Eurydice disappear. But not into thin air, as the fable had it, but under the snarling, fighting, hunger-maddened beasts crazed at the smell and taste of warm blood and quivering flesh.

Nor did Orpheus have long to look, for the lions, their whiskered muzzles gory, were upon him now, slashing, tearing, snarling—

Barnabas closed his eyes, but he could not stop his ears against the blood-yell of the holiday throng. Quickly through the mob's roaring he sensed a change in tone and now the multitude was laughing. He ventured to look again.

The lions had been longer discovering the naked Pluto. As they had dashed around the simulated palace chamber to spring on the two in the grove, he had slipped into the smaller room. But now the crowd was roaring in merriment, for a huge lion, nuzzling about the wooden sections, had found the slave and was about to spring on him when Pluto bolted into the larger chamber. At that instant the section of improvised wall on one side fell and three other lions sighted the big slave. As they made for him, he dived beneath the couch.

"Wonderful! The funniest thing I've ever seen!" It was one of the Romans behind them. "A great show, eh, Vatinius! An amazing act!"

Pluto's respite was but for seconds. In an instant the snarling, maddened, hungry beasts had thrust the couch aside and the lunge of one had rolled the naked slave on his back. Barnabas saw a great paw lifted, catlike; it slashed downward and across white flesh; the man screamed and the white turned crimson. But not for long, for the lions were fighting and snarling above him, and ripping and tearing.

Joseph Barnabas fought against nausea. Eyes closed, he clutched his stomach, tried to shut his ears to the crowd's approving roar. And after long minutes, it seemed, the multitude was calm again. The play was ended. He dared to look out once again on the arena.

All the walls of Pluto's palace were down, scattered and broken. The couch was on its side and the tapestry ripped and bloody. In the grove of Orpheus the little trees were overturned. The blue stola, splotched now with crimson, lay trampled and torn in the sand. Nowhere did he see the lyre. The white toga, more red now than white, was tangled in one of the thrown-down trees.

The lions milled about the destroyed sets, dragging their tails in the sand, licking their wet muzzles with red tongues, growling in low gutturals, yawning.

But one lion was still crouched, his head down, his forepaws clutching, over near the spot where the couch had sat. Barnabas could see his powerful jaws working. And he heard a bone crunched.

. . . God in Israel, O Jesus our Lord Messiah, protect her. . . .

He looked around quickly. The Emperor had arisen, and members of his Palace staff and military guard were closing about him. Many in the great amphitheatre thought the games ended, and already some were pushing toward the exits. The master of ceremonies, seeing it, signaled for a flourish of trumpets, and waved his arms wildly for silence.

"The games are not finished! Citizens of Rome, the liveliest spectacle of all is soon to begin! Be seated!"

Some on the fringes slipped through the gates, but most of those who were starting out, assured that another act would be presented, sat down. Order restored, the master of ceremonies continued:

"Citizens of Rome! Soon you will see four traitors to our Empire and our beloved great Emperor, desperate criminals who would deliver us into the hands of our enemies, suffer the punishment their heinous crimes deserve. A foreign woman, beautiful but depraved, and three Romans, a tribune and a centurion and his sister, sons and daughter of two of Rome's wealthiest and heretofore most highly esteemed senators, have been found to be members of a seditious and vile sect of revolutionaries recently originated in Palestine as worshipers of a fanatical Galilean who sought to usurp the throne of the Caesars. These culprits will shortly be brought before you and executed in a manner calculated to provide them slow and agonized death and give you novel and exciting entertainment!"

An approving shout greeted the announcement. But the official held up his hands again.

"Our beloved Emperor is fatigued, and must retire for a few moments. But he will shortly return and immediately after he is seated you shall have this final act I have promised you. Now, I suggest that you relax. But don't depart, citizens!"

Caligula was leaving the box; he was nearing the doorway opening into the passageway that led into the palace. His servants and soldiers formed a solid wall about him.

Luke too had been watching. His eyes sought Joseph's. "Pray, my brother. Pray our Lord Messiah."

The Emperor was almost to the entrance. In another minute he would be in the passageway. Throughout the ascending circles of stone seats men were standing up, stretching, stamping their numbed feet, gesticulating and chattering.

In the mounting confusion and unnoticed, they hoped, Joseph Barnabas and Luke the physician stepped into the aisle and pushed quickly toward the doorway through which Caligula that instant was disappearing.

They were inside the passage now. No one had tried to stop them. Up ahead, perhaps thirty paces, the Emperor was walking with his servants and guards. Beside Caligula was the senator on whom the awkward priest had spilled the blood from the sacrificed animals. Happily, none of the guards had turned to look back.

Sextus had revealed that the Emperor likely would continue along the passageway to a place where a corridor ran off obliquely toward the left. A short way down this corridor he would come to a door that opened into his private room, where he might pause, or he might walk on along the corridor to his apartments in the Palace.

But Sextus had cautioned them not to go past the first passageway that entered from the right, but to turn into it and follow it to a stone stairway. Descending it, they would come into a lobby on which the amphitheatre cells faced.

"Wait there," he had said, "until someone comes to release the women. Then take them quickly along the way I've just pointed out!"

The first passageway leading to the right. Yes, that's what Sextus had said. Caligula will go past it, and we'll turn off there—

"God in Israel!" Barnabas smothered his startled exclamation. The Emperor had paused there, was turning to go along the corridor to the right. He and Luke stopped, pressed against the wall.

Caligula was talking and motioning with his hand. "Go on into the Palace," they heard him say. "Senator Asprenas and I wish to go down to the cells to have a look at some of the gladiators."

"But, O mighty Gaius," an officer of the guards ventured, "no guards are stationed along that way. Should not we—"

"Go!" the Emperor screamed. "Who's here to molest me in my own Palace? Must I fear men or gods?"

The officer bowed, moved quickly away with his squad; Caligula and the blood-smeared senator turned into the corridor. Barnabas and Luke, fearful that the unforeseen whim of Caligula to visit the gladiators, perhaps to taunt Longinus, Cornelius, and the girls, had ruined Chaerea's long-planned conspiracy, resumed their stealthy pursuit of the Emperor. They were turning into the corridor—

"Quiet! Make no sound!" Two soldiers stepped out of the shadows of a recessed place in the wall, raised their swords. "What business do you have here? Why are you following the Emperor?"

"We aren't familiar with these passageways," Barnabas spoke out, though he kept his voice low. "Isn't this the tradesmen's entrance into the Palace kitchens?"

Quickly one soldier ran his hands along the arrested men's upper bodies and around their girdles. "No weapons. But they're lying; they're not tradesmen. Nor Romans either. This one's a Jew. And you're—"

"A Greek," Luke answered, "from Antioch."

The Emperor, pausing before descending the stairs, had heard the commotion. "What's the trouble, guardsmen?" he asked. "Who are those men?"

"Tradesmen, they said, Your Majesty, seeking the entrance into the Palace kitchens."

"Tradesmen? This is no way to the kitchens. Did they have weapons? Perhaps they were seeking to kill me."

"No, Sire, they had no weapons. I think they're simple fellows who unwittingly got into the wrong passageway."

The Emperor motioned to the guards to bring the men nearer.

"Where're you from, fellow?" He nodded in the direction of Luke.

"Antioch, O Sire. I'm a Greek physician."

"Then you're not a simple tradesman who's lost his way in the Palace." Caligula turned his attention then to Barnabas. "And you're no Greek. A Jew, by the gods. Where are you from, man? Palestine, perhaps?"

"Yes, O Sire, I am. But we were on no mission to harm you. We—"

"Silence!" His shrill command rang along the narrow corridor, bounded from wall to wall. "I have no friendship for any Jew or any who would associate with one, save King Agrippa"—suddenly his silly cackling echoed down the passageway—"and he isn't much Jew. Since last night I consider the whole race and nation of them an abomination." He looked straight at Luke and Barnabas. "You two were looking for an entrance to the Palace kitchens, eh?" His glance now was toward the soldier holding the arm of Barnabas, and quickly the grin was gone and he was scowling. "Guards, escort them to another entrance—the cell next to the arena—and throw them in there with the two traitorous soldiers and the two women who are soon to be eaten by a pack of ravenous dogs. You two *tradesmen*"—he paused, grinned leeringly—"can help them defend themselves—if you have the courage." The guards stood facing Caligula, clutching their prisoners, waiting for further instructions. "Go!" he stormed. "Move along with them!"

"Come!" Roughly they hustled the captive pair along the corridor and down the stairs, leaving Caligula and Senator Asprenas doubled with laughter at the Emperor's cleverness in disposing of the Palace trespassers.

At the foot of the stairway the corridor turned right, so that in a moment the four men were beyond the sight of Caligula and the senator. In that instant the guards released their holds on the prisoners.

"You can relax now," one of them said. "We're Chaerea's men."

"God be praised!" Barnabas lowered his voice, for the guardsman had signaled to warn that the Emperor might overhear. "But why did you give us such a fright?" he whispered.

"We were stationed in that recess to lead you to the cells where Longinus and the others are locked up, so you would be in position to get the women away quickly. But that devil came this way instead of going to his apartments. We had to get you past him, because he was between you and the women, you see. We could have cut him down there—Senator Asprenas is also one of the conspirators—but that might have spoiled Chaerea's plan." Meanwhile they had moved toward the cells, beyond the Emperor's hearing. "All the guards in this part of the Palace are our men," he went on, nodding in the direction of the arena cells. "Tertius, you go on with these men," he said to his companion, "and I'll slip back and keep an eye on Caligula. Something's delayed him. It may be that already Chaerea's—" But he said no more, disappeared up the stairs.

They went with Tertius, who spoke briefly with several guards outside the cells. Immediately they unlocked the heavy doors, and Barnabas had a brief reunion with Damaris. Meanwhile Longinus and Cornelius had been released and were standing in the corridor before their cells.

Tertius had hardly finished his assignment, however, when the other soldier appeared from around the turn in the passageway.

"Are you ready, Tertius?" He was plainly nervous. "The Emperor's coming out. As I thought, he had turned into another passageway to have a look at some dancing boys recently brought from Cyrenaica. Chaerea's down at the other end of the corridor. Remember, you two men must get the women past him to reach the passage that leads to the door opening on the street." He motioned. "You'd better get them here—near the stairway—so you can move fast."

Barnabas ran back, signaled the young women, and Longinus and Cornelius came with them. They stopped at the foot of the stairway just out of sight of the upper corridor. Tertius started up the stairs; Barnabas mounted several steps to venture a glimpse.

The Emperor, walking a pace ahead of Senator Asprenas, had reached the wider corridor and had turned toward the descending stairs when he evidently heard Chaerea's footsteps as the tribune advanced toward him along the passageway. He turned abruptly to face Chaerea. The tribune, sword in hand in apparent readiness to salute, approached and bowed.

"O mighty Gaius," he began, stepping nearer, "I beg of you the password so that I may make it known to the Palace guards."

In the meantime Luke and the four just released had eased noiselessly up the stone steps. The other guard had pushed into a shaded recessed place along the corridor some steps ahead. Now Caligula's back was to all of them, and they could not hear what he was saying in reply to Tribune Chaerea. They supposed, however, that he had given the tribune an obscene password, for his narrow head was bobbing and they could hear his witless giggling.

But the group at the stairs was looking full in the tribune's face and they saw that he was agitated; his countenance was flushed, and he stepped forward boldly and grabbed the Emperor's arm.

"You evil, foul-mouthed pig! That's the last obscenity you will give me!" Chaerea's words, ringing along the passageway, were sharp with contempt. "You're the misbegotten of a noble father, a disgrace to the Roman nation, a stench in the nostrils of mankind. But no longer will you trample on our rights, evil Gaius!"

"Silence! You will die in slow torture for this!" Caligula's blotched narrow face was purpling, as he snatched free of the tribune's hand. "Asprenas, give the alarm! When my German guards fall on you, traitor, you'll beg and plead for death!" He struck at Chaerea with a soft white hand, but the tribune dodged the blow, and stepping back, laughed in the Emperor's furious face.

"Asprenas is one of us, you bloated fool." He said it calmly, smiling. "He helped us plan your death. Your Germans won't come to your aid. The Palace is filled with men of the Praetorian, each sworn to kill you, each craving the honor that I'm about to have of ending your worthless existence!"

Caligula whirled about to face Senator Asprenas, now safely out of range of a sword's swing. Turning, he caught sight of the group at the top of the stairs.

"By all the gods! Longinus! Cornelius! Those women! How,

by Jupiter—" His manner changed suddenly; he smiled with disarming friendliness, held out his hands toward them. "I restore
you to your honored stations, men. Serve me this once, protect me
from this traitorous madman, and you may command of me what
you will."

Longinus and Cornelius folded their arms across their chests,
smiling grimly, held their places. The cornered despot looked
then toward Asprenas, but the Senator stood immobile, impassive. The Emperor must have understood. Desperate, he swung
about to confront Chaerea.

But already the heavy sword was descending. Caligula saw it,
twisted his ungainly frame, but not quickly enough. The blade
struck between the neck and the shoulder. They heard bones
shattered, and blood spurted through the cleft in the tunic to
deepen its purple.

But the wounded Emperor did not fall. Nor did he make any
sharp outcry. Groaning hoarsely, he lurched along the corridor
toward the group at the stairs. His left arm was swinging, useless;
from the shattered shoulder blood ran down his tunic to drench
his sandals and spread a thickening gory smear on the stones of
the floor.

" 'Let your crucified Galilean save you, if he can, you fools,
and run me through with Chaerea's sword!' That's what he said
last night!"

They whirled to face Longinus. The tribune was staring,
white-faced and grim, at the broken, bleeding Caligula. He lifted
an arm, pointed. "So quickly, O Nazarene, so quickly!"

But the vigilant Tertius had been looking along the passageway beyond the bloody drama in the foreground.

"One of the German guards!" he shouted. "He's seen; he's
going for the others!" Looking, they saw a soldier running back
along the corridor to disappear at the turning. "Hurry, men! Get
the women out before the Germans come with their swords
swinging!"

Longinus grasped Lalage's hand, squeezed it in his. "Yes, go!"
he said. "Guard them, men! And may the Galilean protect you!"

Already they were racing toward the stricken Emperor, now leaning against the wall and breathing heavily. But just as they got past him they saw emerging on a run from the connecting main corridor a group of Praetorian guardsmen. As the four pressed themselves against the stones of the wall, the soldiers darted past them, their weapons clanking. At the main passage Joseph Barnabas looked back. Soldiers surrounded Caligula, hacking, jabbing. Through their weaving legs he could see the Emperor, sprawled face down on the bloody paving.

The passageway was deserted, and now they were running along it. But just as they turned off into a small tunneled bypass leading out to the street, they heard the Germans coming, and the next moment the blond giants surged past the narrow opening.

"O Galilean, protect Longinus!"

Damaris heard Lalage, but she said nothing.

Now the sounds of the soldiers from Germania racing too late to the Emperor's aid were dimming. But the four fleeing did not pause. In the half-light of the close passageway they pushed along as fast as they could over the uneven stones. They were now at a place where the tunnel veered slightly, and as they went around the bend they saw it—a rectangle of thin light hardly fifty paces ahead.

"The outline of the door to the street!" Joseph Barnabas exclaimed. "Thank God, it must be!"

## THE CROWN TREE 63

Rumors were sweeping through Rome like blasts from off the heated sands of Arabia's desert. From Castra Praetoria on the northeast to the great Emporium at the bending of the Tiber on the southwest, from the Appian Way gates over Palatine Hill and the Roman Forum to the Field of Mars, countless differing and startlingly dramatic reports were being circulated.

Most Romans were talking in whispers, for few knew for a certainty what had befallen the Emperor Gaius in the passage-way between the amphitheatre and his Palace apartments. Some declared they heard he had escaped and shortly would fall on his enemies with a furious vengeance; among these certain ones even insisted that it had all been a ruse that the fiendish Caligula had devised in order to discover who were his true friends and who were fawning professed friends who really wished him slain. Many others, of course, were confident that Caligula was dead.

But most Romans, especially members of the Senate and others of equestrian rank fortunate enough thus far to have escaped his fury, were content to hold their peace and await developments. That would be less interesting, no doubt, but much safer.

At the house of Barnabas' relatives on Janiculum Hill the four visitors likewise were saying little. Nor since their hurried arrival after their terrifying experience at the Imperial Palace had they ventured outside. They little doubted that Caligula had been slain; the German guards could hardly have reached him in time to rescue him from the swords of the Praetorian conspirators. But in the fight that must have followed between Chaerea's men and the Germans the supporters of Caligula might have been victorious, and now they might be wreaking a fierce vengeance on those who had sought the Emperor's death.

But each had his thoughts, particularly Lalage and the physician. What had happened to Longinus and Cornelius, and her parents? Had her beloved and her brother been slain by the Germans, overtaken in the narrow passageway with the Praetorians and the bloody body of the dead Caligula? And had a mob of infuriated adherents of the slain Emperor—or still alive Emperor —wrecked her parents' home and killed them?

Luke, too, was concerned over his new brothers in the Lord Messiah, but his great fear was that evil had befallen Aspasia. Can it be, he asked himself over and over again, that I have journeyed so long and far and after so many vicissitudes come so near to possessing my beloved only to lose her forever?

But soon their answers came. Cornelius in civilian dress appeared at the house on Janiculum Hill. He brought sensational tidings.

"Longinus is safe," he revealed. "He would have come himself, but he has been busy day and night helping Claudius and Agrippa with the task of getting the new administration organized and operating—"

"The new administration? You mean Caligula's old dolt of an uncle?"

"Yes, he's the new Emperor, Lalage. But Claudius isn't the fool we've been thinking he was; I suspect he played the stupid fellow while his madman nephew was on the throne in order to save his neck, and now he's the Caesar himself."

Quickly he related what had happened after they fled from the Palace and during the several days that followed. All but a handful of the conspirators had escaped, though Senator Asprenas, who had not laid a hand on Caligula, had been cut to pieces by the Germans when they discovered him near the dead body of the Emperor, his toga bloody from the spilled blood of the sacrifices which they had taken to be the blood of the slain Caligula.

And soon after the assassination the Praetorians had come upon Claudius hiding in a closet of the Palace, had dragged him out, some thought to execute him but actually to proclaim him Emperor. For a time the Senate, fearful of what course the stuttering, shuffling old pedant might take toward its members, hesitated to approve the action of the Praetorian Guard. But when they saw that the army was determined and realized that it was all-powerful, they wisely confirmed the Guard's choice. In the negotiations between the Guard and the Senate on one hand and Claudius on the other, King Agrippa had taken a leading part; the opportunist Israelitish ruler had been able from the beginning, it appeared, to foresee the course he should take.

"And it has paid him handsomely," Cornelius went on. "Claudius not only confirmed him as Israel's king but added considerable territory to his realm. Now Agrippa will be ruler of a kingdom as large as the one ruled by old Herod the Great."

"But what of Longinus? And you? What's happening to you two?"

"I'm going back to the post at Caesarea. I don't know about Longinus, except that he wants to marry you." He grinned, turned to confront the physician. "And you, Luke?"

"I want to marry Aspasia." He was looking toward Lalage.

"I'm reluctant to give her up, Luke," she said, smiling, "but she is no longer my slave."

"Thank Israel's God and our Lord Messiah! And I thank you, my new sister in the fellowship."

"I came to tell you also that it's quite safe now, Lalage, for you to go home, and these with you. And another thing—Luke," he added, beaming, "I have tidings for you from Emperor Claudius. Longinus, working through King Agrippa, has obtained from the new Emperor a decree restoring to the heirs of the merchant Chionides the properties seized from him by the Roman government in the days of Sejanus and freeing from slavery Aspasia's brother Galenus. Galenus, Longinus revealed, is still in charge of the glassworks and textile plants on the coast of Phoenicia formerly owned by his father."

"May God and our Messiah reward you and Longinus my brothers and you my sister." Luke's eyes were incredulous. "Truly immeasurable is the goodness of God and the protection of His Son our Messiah!"

## THE CROWN TREE 64

That night Longinus came to the mansion on Quirinal Hill. He and Lalage sat before the fountain in the peristylium, relaxed, the tension and cold numbing fear of the recent days momentarily forgot.

"I shall miss Aspasia terribly," she said, after a long moment of silence.

"Then she's gone? You've manumitted her?"

"Yes. She and Luke are to be married as quickly as arrangements can be made."

"Lalage, why shouldn't we?" He sat up, his eyes bright now, his voice suddenly eager. "Has it not already been too long that we've been separated? Shouldn't I see our fathers tomorrow and ask them to make the arrangements?"

"Yes, Longinus, a long time I have wanted it. Yes, my beloved." In the light of the wall lamps her face was radiant. "And we shall build our own house and live the rest of our days happily and unmolested—here in Rome?"

Quickly a cloud darkened his countenance.

"No," he said, "not in Rome—for a while, at least." Then he looked long into her eyes, and his were serious. "Lalage, forgive me, but—I want to go back to Palestine. And I want you to go with me."

"But haven't you always said you despised the sight of Palestine and those chattering, quarrelsome Jews?"

"Yes, I have often said it, and I meant it, too. But in recent months I have begun to see things differently, Lalage, and since the other night at Agrippa's banquet—well, haven't you, too?"

"Yes," she answered, and this time her smile had no hint of derision nor her voice of sarcasm, "since I stood with you and Cornelius I have had a different feeling too about that Galilean. It's of him you're thinking, isn't it?"

"Yes. I still know so little about him, Lalage. But contemplating him and what he taught, though it's so imperfectly that I know him, fills me with a—a peace, Lalage, that I'd not had until at the banquet I stood up to face Caligula's wrath." He paused. "I want to learn more of this one who stood with me then and seems surely to be my friend and protector even though I killed him. And then, having come to know him better, I'd like to come back to Rome and tell our people about him."

Lalage's countenance was troubled.

"But should you come to Rome as an advocate of the Galilean, Longinus, would not Claudius, or any other who might be Emperor, have you killed as a traitor to the Empire?"

"Perhaps not, beloved, for soon, I truly believe, the followers of the Galilean will have great strength throughout the Empire. If not"—he shrugged his shoulders, gestured with his hands—"I shall still be determined to attempt it." He looked the girl full in the eyes. "I cannot escape this Jesus, Lalage; always has he pursued me, to bind me to himself. And now I no longer wish to escape him. I wish rather to be of his fellowship."

## THE CROWN TREE 65

The Tribune Longinus sat back comfortably on the portside foredeck and once again watched the distant shoreline of Italy crawling past. Almost straight ahead the high full moon dropped a shimmering silver track along which the vessel was moving steadily, for a freshening wind had filled the sails and given respite to the weary slaves chained below at their long oars.

It was past midnight now and quiet. Not a strident voice shouting a command nor even a murmured whispering disturbed the calm of the bright night. Longinus had left his bride and come on deck ostensibly to catch a cooling breath of the heavy salt air but actually to think and to attempt to bring order to his thoughts.

In their cubicle near the one he had just left, Luke and his wife perhaps now had retired for the night and in other places in the vessel's sleeping area Joseph Barnabas and Damaris had sought their mats. They planned to be married in traditional Jewish ceremony once they had reached Jerusalem.

Three pairs—three men, three women, and how strangely related—traveling from Rome to Jerusalem aboard the same vessel. Two of them Romans, son and daughter of rich senators, privileged citizens of the master race; two Greeks, the woman until a few days ago the slave of the Roman woman, but before her enslavement the fabulously wealthy daughter of a cultured family, and the man a sophisticated, traveled physician; two Jews, the woman the niece of Israel's High Priest, the man a Cypriote and friend—Longinus recalled when first he saw the two—of a strange, intense small Jew with a quick tongue and agile brain, by the name of Saul of Tarsus and proud of his Roman citizenship.

Three couples, two of them subject peoples of the other's nation and each of the three differing from the others in customs, traditions, loyalties, even gods, but now all six equal, brothers and sisters in the fellowship of the strange but impelling Galilean man-God, God-man.

Longinus sat looking at the suspended shining moon and meditated. This young Nazarene whose path had crossed his own on one unforgettable and unending day at Jerusalem, this amazing Jew whose utter love for his fellows held true and undimmed through desertion, derision, scourging, and crucifixion even to his dying breath, this incomprehensible Galilean who in his unutterable agonies of the flesh and the spirit could not be driven to curse his tormentors, this incomprehensible man—

"Who was he? O *his* God, who was—who is—this Galilean?" Looking up to the resplendent flattened disk of the moon, the tribune spoke aloud from out of the depths of his perplexity. "Where, O his God, from whom can I get the answer? Who can tell me, for certain, who this Jesus was, what he was, who and what he is?"

Undeniably, of a certainty, he was a man. Longinus knew that, he needed no witness to tell him that the Nazarene was a man, a physical being like countless others of Israel. He had observed him from before the dawning of that spring day in Jerusalem until the late afternoon; he had seen him suffer under the blows of the metal-tipped lashes, he had almost felt himself the man's agony as the heavy hammers of the soldiers drove the spikes through his ravaged flesh to impale him; he had seen the sweat and the blood pour from his tortured body to drip off his pinioned purpling feet; he had seen his head fall forward upon his heaving chest as his laboring gallant heart had surrendered.

And during the season he was stationed at Ptolemais and in the more recent period he was with Agrippa at Tiberias, Longinus had visited Nazareth and talked with many persons about the strange young carpenter. Numerous ones remembered him well and several of the older residents had even spoken of Joseph his father.

Jesus was a good boy and a hard worker, they all agreed, a strong tough-sinewed lad who could handle his end of any beam; he was perhaps a little more serious than most of the boys with whom he had played and worked, and faithful and devoted in his attendance upon the synagogue and his study of the writings of the prophets; in fact, some said, that had been his downfall, for he had studied and prayed and meditated until his brain had become a little addled. They had ventured the opinion that had he spent more time with his carpenter's tools and less with the holy writings and his solitary trampings in the woods and fields he would not have ended his days on a Roman cross in Jerusalem.

Already in Nazareth and the region round about, the tribune had discovered, there were those who readily testified that their young carpenter was of a truth the Messiah of Israel, the long-awaited man sent of God to deliver His people. But there were others, and many, who when the question was asked them smiled tolerantly, shrugged, and tapped forefinger to forehead.

The sheen of the moon lay upon the vineyard-carpeted hills of Italy, and the ship sped freely before the stiffening breeze in the course of the moon's shining. Once again Longinus lifted his eyes to study the lustrous ball.

Of a surety he was a man, but was he—is he—more?

In Galilee Longinus had talked also with men who declared they had seen him alive and walking and talking after he had died on the cross. And Cornelius doubted it not. Nor Barnabas, nor Luke.

As they had been preparing to leave Rome and on board ship Longinus had talked with Barnabas and Luke about this Galilean whose cause the tribune so dramatically had embraced. Their belief that Jesus was more than a man, even a good and

noble and surpassing man, had never faltered. To them the
Nazarene was man but also God, equal in majesty with the God
of Israel and the Holy Spirit sent to comfort men His brothers
following the Son's ascension.

Sitting in the ship's bow looking across the shimmering waters
of the Great Sea, Longinus thought again of his old Greek tutor
and that beloved philosopher's conception of the supreme being,
the one-God, as a synthesis of the true, the beautiful, and the
good.

But how can a man comprehend this synthesis? How can he
understand even its parts? Can a man see, hear, feel, smell, taste
truth or beauty or goodness? How can a man embrace that which
he has not seen or felt or heard or in any other way made comprehensible? How, O *his* God, can an earth-bound mortal see
God? Is it not because men must see and touch and bow down to
something tangible that they build idols of stone and bronze and
gold? Mustn't they have something material, something that per-
sonifies—

Longinus sat up straight, his eyes fixed on the dancing silver
of the moon's path but not seeing it.

Is not that the key unlocking the mystery of Jesus? When he
lived in Palestine was he not a man but also a man who personi-
fied God, who showed men his brothers what God was like, and
was he not likewise, and is he not, God who intercedes with God
for men His erring sons? Is Jesus not then a bridge linking his
old tutor's omniscient, omnipotent One and His lost and earth-
bound mortals? Is it not over this Jesus-bridge that the incomprehensible, ineffable One can descend to succor and save His earth-
lings? Is it not by way of this bridge that man can travel upward
to this One whom Jesus with such warmth of affection called his
Father?

How then does one come to comprehend this Jesus now that
he has gone in the flesh? For one long terrible day I was near
him, observed him, even pitied him. But, Longinus reflected, I
in no way comprehended him. I saw only a harried, beaten, tortured, strangely courageous Jew.

In his recent talking with Barnabas and Luke he had ventured the problem of comprehending Jesus.

"When we reach Jerusalem, spend a while with me at Mary's house," Barnabas had suggested. "There you will likely find Simon and John ben Zebedee and perhaps others of his Twelve who knew him best. Simon especially"—he paused and his alert eyes momentarily studied the tribune's face—"could tell you much, Tribune. None knew him better and none loves him more. Simon will be your best teacher."

"And Saul likewise," Luke added. "He talked with the Nazarene that day on the desert near Damascus, and in faith and much love he continues even now to live in intimate communion with him. If you could find Saul, he could teach you great things concerning Jesus."

Longinus had agreed to visit with them at Mary's house on Zion Hill and talk with Simon and the other apostles, and perhaps some day he might even seek out Saul of Tarsus.

"That will be good, for from them I should learn much," Longinus said aloud as he stood up, for Lalage would be wondering what had kept him so long away from her. "But no one, I'm convinced, can reveal him to me completely; I must after much effort and in faith and great love come in my own way to know him."

Longinus stepped to the rail and a long moment stood looking across the restless bright water toward the slopes of Italy, silver-green under the moon, and far beyond over ships and seas and many lands to a severe and forbidding rounded knob outside the wall of Jerusalem. But this time he could discern no crosses and contorted white bodies and bursting sweat and blood slowly dripping. He saw only high on the hill and tall and growing taller a smiling bronzed young man, arms outthrust to the earth's edges, who appeared to be neither a Jew nor a Gentile, Roman nor Greek, blond German nor black Ethiopian, but rather a noble composite of all his brothers. And as in imagination he looked, the tall one nodded and, still smiling, beckoned.

Hardly had Simon slipped back into Jerusalem from Caesarea with King Agrippa's departure for Rome when a warm controversy began to develop within the ranks of the fellowship. Reports had come ahead of Simon that on his former journey into Samaria and the coastal country round about Joppa the first of the apostles had been flouting the laws of Israel by eating with ritually unclean persons. Within the fellowship a new cleavage was beginning to appear, with one of the factions insisting on a strict adherence to all the laws of the Jews and the other contending that the Messiah had brought a new law less rigorous than the traditional laws of the Israelites.

The first faction insisted that the fellowship of Jesus was an organization, a way of life, within Judaism. Its adherents argued, just as they had maintained all the while, that before one could become a member he must first join himself to Israel and Israel's laws. One of the first requisites was circumcision. Certainly, these people declared, a man could not rightly be baptized until he had been circumcised. Yet reports coming out of the region of Joppa said plainly that the first of the apostles on his preaching mission into that area not only had sat down to meat with unclean persons but had baptized and received into fellowship uncircumcised Gentiles, even a Roman centurion and his household at Caesarea.

These soon came to be known as the party of the circumcision. They were orthodox Israelites who though they worshiped the Lord Jesus saw him first as a Jew, a greatly enlarged and more glorious King David, a Son of the God of Israel approachable only through the Chosen. They looked to the past and their eyes were able to encompass but a small circle.

At a meeting one evening in a crowded hidden chamber in Ophel a spokesman of this faction accosted Simon, challenged him. Whereupon Simon recited the story of the vision on Simon the tanner's rooftop and of what it signified, and of the subsequent conversion of Centurion Cornelius and his household.

"If then God gave to them the same gift He gave to us when we believed in the Lord Jesus Christ, I ask you who was I that I could withstand God?"

His dramatic recital for the moment appeared to have won them, so that those of that faction either approved or remained silent.

"Then God has granted also to the Gentiles repentance unto life," one man declared, his countenance radiant.

"Indeed it is so, praise the God of Israel!"

In the midst of this disputing came news to Jerusalem of the enlarging and strengthening of the fellowship in Antioch, which had been established in the days of the great dispersion that had followed the stoning of Stephen. Certain of Stephen's followers in the Synagague of the Libertines, whose membership included many Greeks and others not of the Chosen, were unwilling to see the fellowship of the Messiah held within the narrow limits of Judaism. They contended that Jesus, the Son of the God of all the world, had come to earth to save all men and not simply to be the Messiah of the Jews. When their preaching was frowned upon and it seemed apparent to them that Israel was intent upon appropriating the Lord Jesus to herself, these persons left Jerusalem and scattered abroad. Some even went northward as far as Antioch and beyond. Some crossed to Cyprus. Others ventured even to Cyrene and other regions far from Jerusalem. And wherever they went they carried the seeds of the great good news of Jesus the Saviour.

Now to Jerusalem came the report that out of the preaching to certain Greeks at Antioch by men who had sailed eastward from Cyprus and others who had crossed the Great Sea from distant Cyrene had grown a large and accomplishing fellowship. But what were these men preaching? Was there not danger that they might be offering the people of Antioch a doctrine not altogether of the nature of the truth that had been given these of the Jerusalem fellowship? Antioch was a wicked and idolatrous great city. Could it be that these teachers were in any manner compromising with evil by permitting their followers to be lax in the observance of the laws of Israel? And does not the Jerusalem fellowship have overlordship? Is it not responsible for the scattering of the seeds of the Messiah and for seeing to it that no tares are permitted to contaminate the true seed?

It was so agreed. The task and the responsibility, then, required their sending a faithful and true son of the Jerusalem brotherhood to Antioch to investigate the brethren in that city of great sinning, to remonstrate with those found in error and to encourage those discovered to be propagating the true faith of the Messiah.

But who should be sent? Who most effectively could fulfill the task? For days in meeting after meeting the members of the Jerusalem fellowship considered the problem and in much praying to the God of Israel and His Messiah they sought earnestly for an answer.

And then one day in the midst of their discussion the door to an inner chamber of a brother's humble house near Dung Gate was opened quietly and Joseph Barnabas entered. He was welcomed with great joy and when he related the dramatic story of the rescue of his beloved their sister Damaris and the three Romans and of the courageous acceptance of the Lord Jesus by the tribune and the centurion's sister, they warmly and with happy hearts offered thanks to their God and His Messiah.

Suddenly, as they were talking again with Barnabas, one of the elders jumped to his feet, and pointing toward the returned brother, exclaimed:

"Praise God! Is it not clear, brothers, that the God of Israel has preserved Joseph Barnabas that he might be the one to go on the mission to Antioch? Is he not a Cypriote who will understand and be understood by those of Cyprus at Antioch even though he's an Israelite who sat at the feet of Gamaliel and is learned in the law and the prophets?"

"Indeed, Joseph is the one!" another declared, and about the chamber brother after brother agreed.

"But already the arrangements have been made for me to marry Damaris, your sister in the fellowship," he protested, after they had told him of the plan to send one of their number to the great Syrian city on the Orontes; "too many months it has been delayed."

"Delay the start of the journey then until you have been married," the first brother declared as he stroked his beard, smiling, "and take your wife to Antioch with you."

And throughout the chamber solemnly heads nodded agreement.

## THE CROWN TREE 67

Once again the Tribune Longinus Aemilius Varro was quartered in Jerusalem's austere Tower of Antonia. But this time he and his wife occupied the commanding officer's apartment high in the tower's south side and overlooking the Temple.

The commander whom Longinus was succeeding had left for Joppa to sail for Rome and a new assignment. The transfer of command had been routine; the replacement of the commander had been related in no way to the change in Emperors, for the retiring officer weeks before Caligula's assassination had applied to the Prefect for another assignment.

Longinus had not sought the post at Jerusalem. Before leaving Rome, in fact, he had petitioned the Prefect to permit him to resign from the army, although he had said nothing of his plans to travel in search of further knowledge of the crucified Nazarene of whom he was now a professed follower. The Prefect had assured him he would give prompt consideration to his request for retirement, but had ordered him in the meantime to proceed to Jerusalem and serve as commander of the forces there until a new commanding officer could be selected and sent out to Palestine.

The tribune and Lalage had been in Jerusalem two weeks.

They had left Cornelius at Joppa, where he would take a vessel going northward along the shore to Caesarea; they had heard nothing of the centurion since their departure from the port city. In Jerusalem they had seen few persons they had known. Longinus had been busy with his army duties; once he had gone to Mary's house on Zion Hill, where he had seen Barnabas, but Simon and John ben Zebedee, he discovered, had gone down into Galilee. Luke and Aspasia had taken lodging at an inn near the Joppa Gate. And several times Lalage and her beloved former slave had spent the greater part of a day wandering along the Street of the Workers in Metal and among other shops in this exotic eastern world's crossroads. The two women also had paid a visit to Damaris, and the Jewish girl had told them excitedly of plans for her approaching marriage to Barnabas. Then only recently Longinus and the physician and their wives had been guests at the lavish wedding feast at Mary's house, to which Barnabas in traditional Jewish ceremony and pageantry had brought his bride.

This afternoon in his inner office in the Antonia's headquarters on the first level, Tribune Longinus was relaxing from a strenuous morning's routine when a rap on his door aroused him.

"The Tribune Cornelius from Caesarea to see you, sir," his orderly announced, when he had answered the rapping. In the same instant the door was pushed wide and Cornelius stood in the doorway, beaming and resplendent in a new uniform.

"Cornelius! *Tribune* Cornelius! Congratulations, my friend." He clapped his hand on his brother-in-law's shoulder. "Centurion, I didn't know—"

"Centurion?" Cornelius feigned a heavy scowl. "Tribune, mind your army manners! I'll have you know, sir—" He burst out laughing.

"A thousand pardons, *Tribune!*" Longinus, too, was laughing. "Cornelius, what good fortune for us brings you to Jerusalem?"

"You'd never guess, Longinus. I bear some lively tidings—all good. But first, how is my beautiful sister, your dutiful—I hope— wife?"

"Wonderful, more beautiful, still dutiful," Longinus laughed. "She's up in our apartments now, likely having her afternoon beauty nap. She will be surprised and delighted to see you, Cornelius; we'll go up in a minute. But tell me, what news do you bring from Caesarea?" He motioned to a seat. "Sit down, Cornelius; I can't wait to hear it."

"Well then, first"—Cornelius leaned back comfortably—"a day or two after I arrived at Caesarea I had a message from the Proconsul Petronius ordering me—"

"Petronius! You mean he isn't—"

"No, he isn't dead." Cornelius manifestly was enjoying the tribune's amazement. "Caligula's the dead one. But I was just as surprised as you are, Longinus. You see, the ship that brought to Antioch and the Proconsul the news of the assassination of Caligula arrived, fortunately for Petronius, before the one bearing the Emperor's letter ordering the Proconsul to kill himself. That vessel had left Ostia many days earlier, as you will recall, but it ran into heavy seas that took it far off its course and almost destroyed it; it sailed into Seleucia twenty-seven days after the news had arrived there that Caligula was dead."

"By all the gods!" But suddenly Longinus was serious. "I must try to stop using that expression, though for both of us it has never been anything more than a habit of speech. But now it's no longer even a proper byword. I should be praising the all-wise and all-good one-God."

"Yes, I suspect He had a hand in it," Cornelius agreed. He was silent a moment.

"But the other news, Cornelius? What other tidings do you bring?"

"I came to Jerusalem to fetch the proclamation of Emperor Claudius, which arrived just the day before I left Caesarea, re-establishing the right of the Jews to enjoy unhindered their ancient customs, including that of the worship of the God of Israel. This proclamation is being published throughout the world. I was instructed to post it in one of the courts of the Temple. The Emperor has ordered the proclamation displayed in all the cities, colonies, and municipal places over which Rome holds dominion, and for a period of thirty days."

"Does it name also those of the fellowship of the Galilean?"

"No. Agrippa, I understand, is determinedly set against them; he still courts the favor of the Temple group."

Longinus' face clouded. "I'd hoped he would relent. But likely he'll move his capital to Caesarea; perhaps you'll be able to soften him. At least you'll be in position to watch him, Cornelius." Then his expression changed. "Any other tidings, Tribune?"

"Yes." He grinned broadly. "The vessel that brought my promotion fetched also your discharge from the army. I have brought it"—he pointed to the leather pouch he had dropped beside his seat—"and the minute you have it put in your hand you'll be a private citizen of Rome, privileged to do as you choose."

"Wonderful!" Longinus jumped to his feet, beaming. "The Prefect came through with my discharge earlier than I'd expected he would." Then in the instant his elation was gone. "But I can't leave my post, Cornelius, until they send my successor."

"The new commander of Antonia is already in Jerusalem, Tribune. He brings with him his commission; everything is in order. He'll take over the moment you want him to do so."

"The new commander? But, Cornelius, who—where—"

"At your service, Tribune." Cornelius stood up, saluted smartly. "Your successor, the Tribune Cornelius."

Longinus, beaming, clapped his hand on his friend's shoulder. "I'm glad, Cornelius. In this post you'll be able to turn a hand often in behalf of those in the Galilean's fellowship, and I'm convinced they'll be needing it, because Agrippa, goaded by the High Priest and his supporters, is likely to become more hardfisted against all those who venture to be counted on the side of the Galilean."

That evening Longinus had two other guests, Joseph Barnabas and the physician Luke. They were delighted to discover that their brother Cornelius had just arrived at Antonia from Caesarea.

Barnabas revealed that he had been appointed to go to Antioch to carry salutations from the Jerusalem fellowship and to examine into the teaching of the leaders. Luke and Aspasia, he added, were leaving Jerusalem with him, but Aspasia planned to remain awhile at Tyre with her brother Galenus, now released from slavery, and heir with her to their father's great properties. Later she would sail from Tyre and join Luke at Antioch.

"We're planning to leave shortly, Tribune. But we could delay our departure for a few days if by so doing you could go with us."

"On the voyage out from Rome," Luke hastened to support Barnabas, "you said you wanted to learn more of the Galilean and his teachings. We suggested that you talk with Simon and others of the Twelve and likewise with our brother Saul of Tarsus. But the apostles have gone down to Galilee. You and I could talk with them there, for I also wish to learn from Simon certain things about the Lord and more also concerning the mighty acts of his apostles. From there we could go on with Barnabas to Antioch and you could accompany me to Tarsus, where you could talk with Saul. And from Tarsus if you wished you and your wife could take ship for Rome. In the capital, Tribune"—the physician's pleading was insistent—"you could accomplish great things for the Galilean's fellowship."

Barnabas didn't give the tribune opportunity to reply.

"You told us you were hoping to be retired soon from the Roman army," he hastened to interject. "If you think it won't be long before you can relinquish your station here, we'd be happy to delay—"

"I am no longer commander of Antonia, men." Longinus, smiling, pointed to Cornelius. "He is the new commanding officer in Jerusalem."

Before they left him to return to the house of Mary of Cyprus, Longinus had agreed that as soon as he and Lalage could complete arrangements the two would set out with them on the journey northward.

Lalage picked up her cloak, laid it lightly across her arm. "Ready, Longinus?"

The tribune squeezed shut the bulging leather pouch, fastened it, lifted the strap over his shoulder.

"Ready. I'm coming."

"You're getting an early start." Cornelius from the corridor had heard. "The pack animals are already on the way, in fact; and down at the square in front of the gate they're awaiting you with the horses saddled. I thought I'd walk there with you and see you past the city wall."

"I'm glad, Cornelius." Lalage caught her brother's arm. "But I wish you were going all the way with us."

"I do too, Tribune," added Longinus. "And it's good of you to provide the horses, and the donkeys for the baggage. Now that I'm no longer a Roman soldier—"

"It will be no extra cost to the government," Cornelius hastened to assure them. "I had to send them to Caesarea anyway to fetch supplies coming in from Rome." They were walking along the corridor now toward the stairs descending to the ground floor. "Did you get all your plans for the trip arranged?"

"As far as we could, I suppose. From Caesarea Barnabas and Luke and I, and Barnabas' servant Amaziah, are going across into Galilee to seek out Simon and others of the Galilean's original band and spend a short season with them. While we're in Galilee, Lalage and Barnabas' wife will be guests of Aspasia and her brother Galenus at his place at Tyre. Then when we come back from Galilee we'll take a vessel sailing for Seleucia."

"And then?"

"Barnabas and his wife and Amaziah will continue to Antioch to visit the members of the fellowship there; then they'll return to Jerusalem to report to the group here."

"And you and the physician and your wives?"

"We expect to sail to Tarsus to find Saul. Luke is very much interested in writing a book about the activities of the Galilean's apostles, as well as about Jesus himself, and he thinks Saul can be of much help by relating his own experiences." They started down the stairs. "And I'd like to talk with Saul too concerning the Galilean. Saul is a Jew, of course, but he is also a Roman citizen, and I have the feeling that he better understands and appreciates the Nazarene as a man apart from strictly racial and national limitations and loyalties. What do you think, Cornelius?"

"I agree, though I know little of Saul. But he is bound to be an intelligent fellow, a clear thinker, and although he's a loyal Jew, he must likewise be a man of the world who can see this Galilean on a level above the Jews—in fact, almost as the Greeks or even we Romans would see him, wouldn't you say?"

"I've hardly seen him, but from what I've heard about Saul, I'd say yes. When he was here in Jerusalem some called him the apostle to the Gentiles, didn't they? At any rate, I'm anxious to learn his views concerning the Nazarene. And Luke is hoping to prevail on Saul to journey westward with us into Macedonia and perhaps even to Rome."

They crossed the large entrance hall of Antonia and walked beneath the great main portal. On the terrace before the fortress they stood a moment looking out across the Pavement toward the Praetorium. Fleetingly Longinus turned his gaze a little to the right, where the crest of a gaunt ugly knob lifted above the rooftop of a squat stone house facing Antonia across the square. But he said nothing, and the three descended the marble steps to the Pavement. At the bottom Longinus turned, looked upward along the massive granite blocks of Rome's towering citadel.

"Farewell, Antonia," he said, half smiling, half serious. "It will be a long time before I set eyes on you again—perhaps never."

"I hope so," Lalage concurred. "And I wish you were going to Rome with us, Cornelius. How long do you suppose you'll be out here?"

"Not so long, likely. Maybe you two can get in a word with old Claudius." Then he was serious. "Are you concerned about returning to Rome now that you are of his fellowship?"

"No, Cornelius." Longinus, too, was in earnest. "It may be that we are going deliberately into danger"—he shrugged his shoulders, gestured with palms outthrust—"but what of it? For the first time in years, since that day here on the Pavement and out there"—with his head he motioned toward the Hill of the Skull —"I'm at peace. I want to learn more about him and his way and do what I can to strengthen and enlarge his fellowship."

They were walking now along the low stone fence beside the garden of the Praetorium, once again flaming and fragrant with its great variety of spring flowers.

"And it will grow in numbers and influence, too, Cornelius; I'm sure of it." His countenance and his tone emphasized his earnestness. "Already it has grown. Look, here in Jerusalem, up in Antioch, even in Rome. Day by day our fellowship grows— *our* fellowship, Tribune—Jews, Romans, Greeks, Syrians, peoples of every race and color"—he pointed—"like those flowers. And from these roots in time it will grow into a far spreading great tree, alive and green and still growing, like this tree here"—he half turned to point to a tree growing just inside the garden— "this sturdy rhamnus thorn which—"

Longinus stopped. Mouth open, he was staring in utter astonishment at the tree.

"Cornelius, *his crown!* You remember I picked it up right here and stuck the broken end into the dirt beyond the wall. It took root and grew! A symbol! Truly, a symbol!"

He saw that Lalage did not understand and quickly he explained.

"Strange, too, that I had not noticed it before. Maybe that is likewise a symbol. Unless you have him in your heart you don't see him; is it not so?" He pointed again. "See, under the tree, those tiny shoots coming out from its roots? Aren't they the symbol of other brotherhoods springing up in many places and yet to spring up?"

Longinus turned away from the tree and they started toward Mariamne Tower and the way beyond that led into the square before the gate where the others were awaiting them. When he spoke again it was as though he were talking to himself.

"Like the thorn tree his fellowship will grow and spread until one day it will encompass the earth, and though many will come with ax and sword and torch to destroy it, they will fail, for the tree will stand and give refreshment to those who rest beneath it."

## THE END

THE END

Rome
● Ostia

● Puteoli

Capri ●

MACEDONIA

Thessalonica ●

Rhegium ●

SICILY          IONIAN SEA          Athens ●

Syracuse ●

AE●

Cyrene ●

CYRENAICA